They were the most brilliant of England's Crown Jewels...

two twelve-pointed diamond stars given by Philip II of Spain to Mary Tudor on their wedding night. Centuries later, they adorned a tiara designed by Prince Albert for his beloved Queen Victoria.

Now they have been stolen—but by whom? Agents of the Maharajah of Kashgar? The Rothschilds? Bertie, the debt-ridden Prince of Wales? A coachman called Smith? *Or the Queen herself?*

"Will delight the same audience that enjoys the 'Flashman' series and Georgette Heyer's novels....The ending is a secret within a secret." —*Publishers Weekly*

And Emily Kimbrough says: "OH! WHERE ARE BLOODY MARY'S EARRINGS? is so good I can only use superlatives. It's the best of mysteries and that's only part of its delight."

"Intricate...sparkles with fun."
—*The New York Times Book Review*

W9-BVL-141

OH! WHERE ARE BLOODY MARY'S EARRINGS? was originally published by Harper & Row, Publishers, Inc.

Oh!
Where Are
Bloody Mary's
Earrings?

by
ROBERT PLAYER

PUBLISHED BY POCKET BOOKS NEW YORK

OH! WHERE ARE BLOODY MARY'S EARRINGS?

Harper & Row edition published 1973

POCKET BOOK edition published May, 1974

L

This POCKET BOOK edition includes every word contained
in the original, higher-priced edition. It is printed from
brand-new plates made from completely reset, clear, easy-to-
read type. POCKET BOOK editions are published by POCKET
BOOKS, a division of Simon & Schuster, Inc., 630 Fifth
Avenue, New York, N.Y. 10020. Trademarks registered
in the United States and other countries.

Standard Book Number: 671-78363-7.
Library of Congress Catalog Card Number: 72-9100.
This POCKET BOOK edition is published by arrangement
with Harper & Row, Publishers. Copyright, ©, 1972, by Robert
Player. All rights reserved. This book, or portions thereof,
may not be reproduced by any means without permission of
the original publisher: Harper & Row, Publishers, Inc.,
10 East 53 Street, New York, N.Y. 10022.
Cover illustration by Shannon Stirnweis.
Printed in the U.S.A.

Contents

This story is a figment of the author's imagination. A few of the characters are entirely fictitious; the others have been so long in their humble graves or marble tombs as to be now beyond all harm.

TUDOR
PROLOGUE

It began long ago, over four hundred years ago. All Spain lay brown and parched under a July sun. Only in the north, in the round blue harbor of La Coruña, could an Atlantic breeze ripple the water, gently lifting the pennons, gonfalons and banners of the big galleon.

They called her *El Espíritu Santo—The Holy Ghost*. She rode like a feather upon the waters and yet somehow seemed neither very holy nor very ghostly. Rather did she seem like some huge scarlet flamingo. Her hull and her high carved fo'c'sle were streaked with scarlet; her pennons were also mainly scarlet; the three hundred sailors swarming in her rigging wore scarlet livery; flying above all was the great standard of Spain, itself an affair of gold and black and scarlet, of lions rampant, of castles and Hapsburg eagles—all quartered together.

The Holy Ghost—beheld in awe and wonder from the crowded quays—had been built, painted and furnished to take the future King of Spain to his marriage with the Queen of England. Outside the harbor the Lord Howard was waiting with a hundred and fifty English sail, to escort *The Holy Ghost* to Southampton—as was hoped. As was hoped, for all up the English coast, at Plymouth and Brixham and Lyme, landing places had been prepared should the Spanish King feel sick.

Deep in the galleon's hold was the baggage of all the grandees of Navarre, Aragon and Castile, of a horde of young hidalgos. There were marvelous chests and coffers; there were leather bags crammed with jewels, crammed

13

with the pearls and gold of the Spanish Main; there were daggers, collars and corsages, goblets, buckles and caskets; there were also chalices and tabernacles and rosaries and pectoral crosses—all gifts to such priests as had adhered to Mary Tudor and the Faith. There were odds and ends to be thrown away on English whores. Also down there, among the creaking timbers, was a gift to the Queen—Spanish bullion that would need ninety-seven big wagons to drag it from Southampton to the Tower of London.

There was something more. It was rumored that the King's own cabin, with two noble swordsmen outside the door, contained the greatest treasure on board. That cabin, high in the stern, ran the whole width of the galleon so that Philip, for hours on end when the melancholy sat upon him, could watch from magic casements the foam of the ship's wash trailing far astern.

At one end of the cabin was Philip's bed with its coverlets of cloth of gold, and with the arms of Spain upon the tester. At the other end was the silver altar. It was upon this altar, just before the ship sailed, that the Cardinal of Toledo had placed the Body and Blood of Philip's Savior. It was before this altar that the confessor, a Hieronymite monk, said mass each morning as the sun came up over the calm sea.

Alongside the jeweled pyx was a plain casket of ivory. When the men's hammocks were slung below decks, then Ivan Pétya, the King's Russian valet, would tell all the secrets of that royal cabin. Pétya had been trained in Kiev, in the service of a prince of Muscovy. He had found his way by devious routes—he was a devious man—first to Byzantium, then to Venice and so to Madrid. He knew everything there was to know about intrigue and corruption and sex—and politics. He was now a double agent, "practicing," as the phrase went, against both England and Spain, against both Philip and Mary. He would tell his friends below decks, while they hung upon his lips, all there was to know about the King's Ganymedes and mistresses—and indeed rather more than all. And then he would tell them about Mary Tudor—not about her lovers, but that she had none, that she was plain and barren and frigid, that only through a miracle could she ever bear her king a child. And then he would tell them about the ivory casket upon the altar, and how it held the finest gems in all the world—those holy and miraculous diamond earrings which the Queen of England, to her infinite discomfort, would be forced to wear through her first marital night.

That was Pétya's story. A month ago, in actual fact, Philip had sent the Marquis de las Nevas to England, that he might lay before Mary the finest diamond in Spain—a table diamond—together with a necklace of brilliants and much else besides. These gifts, however, as the Marquis made clear, were no more than a consolation for Philip's defects as a correspondent. Philip wrote with difficulty, and to his future wife, ten years older than himself, he had been hardly able to write at all. He could never bring himself to the point. The Marquis de las Nevas had therefore hinted that the greatest gift of all, the gift which would redeem all, the King would bring himself to England—the gift of the Holy Earrings.

Cut from the finest stones from the New World, these earrings, these flashing twelve-pointed stars, two inches across, were doubly unique, both materially and spiritually. Materially because, in spite of the fabulous nature of each separate diamond, they were quite perfectly matched. No man could tell the left earring from the right. Spiritually they were unique because, it was devoutly believed, each earring, beneath its central diamond, concealed a tiny fragment of the Virgin Mary's robe—the robe she wore at Bethlehem. Each night at his *prie-dieu,* Philip could therefore clutch the earrings to his lips in an ecstatic kiss. Mary Tudor, it was true, was now nearly forty, but that hardly mattered; Philip had decreed that, not only at their wedding feast, but in their moment of marital consummation, she would wear the Holy Earrings. The wearer of such miraculous jewels could hardly remain barren. There would be a miracle and assuredly the Queen would bear Philip a son—a son who would one day bring England back to the Faith; a daughter was unthinkable.

On July 11, 1554, *The Holy Ghost* slipped slowly out of La Coruña harbor, the sound of the *Veni Creator* being carried across the water from ship to shore and shore to ship. On the sixth day they sighted Ushant and three days later passed the Needles. The King had not been sick—a good omen. God was with them. As the galleon moved gently up Southampton Water against the wind, these Mediterranean people, who had never seen a tide, cried out that there had been a miracle, a belief that lingered long in remote Spanish valleys.

As *The Holy Ghost* dropped anchor, the carved and gilded barge of England was rowed out to meet her. The oars flashed in the sun but already there were dark rain clouds over Hampshire. Beneath the silken canopy there sat, very stiffly, Arundel, Derby and Shrewsbury, also Renard, the Imperial Ambassador of Spain. The oarsmen and the lackeys wore the green and white of the Tudor livery. In the scarlet of the Hapsburgs, the Spanish lined the taffrail. They looked down upon these English—such strange creatures—with a little curiosity and much contempt. The Spaniards had been wondering for weeks what could have possessed His Catholic Majesty that he should have come to this outlandish island. The Spanish contempt was the greater because their curiosity was to remain unsatisfied. A Tudor Parliament had forbidden them to land. The King was to be allowed four hundred unarmed servants and—since nobody really wanted him poisoned—his own cook, his priest and nobility. Everyone else, week after week, must remain on board *The Holy Ghost*. This royal visit must on no account become a Spanish bridgehead.

The gray walls of Southampton looked out upon a scene of maritime activity such as they would never see again. The great galleon, its banners flying, dominated all. In serried ranks the Lord Howard's fleet showed line upon line of flags, one ship behind the other, until over The Solent they faded into the mist. *The Holy Ghost* lay isolated in her glory; around her on the waters, like buzzing flies around a lion, innumerable barges, wherries and rafts were carrying the baggage and bullion to quays and beaches where, beneath the flash of naked swords, they passed from Spanish hands to English.

The story of jealousy and hate had begun, but in the gilded Tudor barge, as it returned from the galleon, all was smiles. It was on the barge that Arundel invested Philip with the Garter. His banner would not hang in the Chapel at Windsor until he went there in the autumn, but it was on the barge that Philip placed his foot upon a golden faldstool that he might land on English soil a Knight of the Garter. A smile was frozen upon every face, and as these gentlemen stepped ashore there were even more smiles—smiles from all the Catholic peerage of England and Ireland.

The quay had become, quite suddenly, like a great parterre in the month of June. The English tailors and their French broiderers had excelled themselves. Of the English lords, Pembroke had ridden down from Wilton with a troop of gentlemen, some in black velvet and some in crimson, while Montague had jingled over from Beaulieu that morning, with a large retinue, to offer himself as the King's English equerry, and when Philip mounted, kissed his golden stirrup.

They all knelt on the cobbles to pray, using their gauntlets as little mats, while the Hieronymite monk sprinkled them with Holy Water. And then, with their feathered hats at their sides, they stood awkwardly in a great circle. Beyond the circle the grooms held the horses. Philip, for all his pietistic cruelty, had much worldly wisdom. Toward the English he displayed his charms—great charms—but to his own nobility he was more circumspect. With the excuse that poniards or poison might be hidden in their baggage he had been given a long list of every single thing that they had brought with them to England. Only Alba, the greatest of them all, was to be left alone by the spies and the guards. There was a good reason. Already, on the barge, an English officer had noticed that Alba clutched something beneath his saffron cloak. Thereafter he was watched. It was unnecessary. It was only the ivory casket that he carried for his sovereign. Those Holy Earrings, those fragments of Our

Blessed Lady's robe, could after all scarcely be entrusted
to porters or soldiers. They were, very nearly, a
sacrament.

But, apart from that, as Alba and Feria and Medina,
Celi-Pescara, Egmont and Hoorn, and even Ruy Gómez,
Philip's special friend, stood behind their King, he knew
to a button, to the last pearl, what each was wearing—
silver breastplate, jeweled aiguillettes, cloth of gold embroidered and powdered with devices, white satin slashed
with emeralds or trimmed with miniver, garters of pearls
. . . and all the rest.

Philip knew that these men were tall—chosen for their
height like so many guardsmen—and that he himself,
although neat, was short. Without a single jewel, therefore, he had clothed himself from head to foot in black. It
was a stroke of genius, in more ways than one. Nobody
except Pétya, the valet, need know that beneath that tight
doublet and trunks and elegant codpiece there was a fine
coat of mail. The folds of that black suit gave perfect
concealment; they also made every man on the quayside—
Spanish grandees and English lords—look bizarre and
even tawdry. For Philip, however, the black was a foil
both to his honey-colored skin and to that fair beard
which hid the Hapsburg jaw. He knew too that while
these other men's beards would be heavily perfumed, such
crudities were not for him. He had, of course, kissed
Arundel and Shrewsbury very warmly upon both cheeks,
but from now on he would kiss only the Queen, and for
her a perfumed beard was unnecessary; he would make
sure his breath was sweet.

The Queen was now lodged in the Bishop's Palace at
Winchester. She, pathetic creature, had long been pas-
sionately in love with Titian's portrait of Philip, praying
before it hour after hour as if it were some icon, her eyes
within inches of it, so short was her sight; praying always
that this man might give her a son. Every day, too, on
board the galleon, Philip had prayed before the Queen's
portrait, prayed that she might not have changed too
much sinch Holbein had painted her twenty years ago,

prayed that her mother's Spanish blood might give her a
little beauty.

For months this man and woman had wondered about
each other, and now at last between them there lay nothing but the gentle water meadows of the Itchen and the
great tower of Romsey. It would have been unseemly for
Philip to rush to his bride. For five days he lived in state
at Southampton, the road to Winchester, meanwhile,
being filled with wagons carrying baggage and gifts. During those five days the English summer had broken. On
the fifth day Philip saw something to which he was not
accustomed—a very green landscape beneath a very
heavy rain. The Spaniards were taken by surprise . . . but
the show had to go on.

The huge cavalcade, three thousand horsemen and
scores of coaches, set out from Southampton on a dark,
wet afternoon. The Spanish cloaks of velvet or satin, even
Philip's improvised cloak of felt, became soaked and satu-
rated within an hour. The English, under their oily sheep-
skins, laughed and enjoyed themselves greatly. The whole
sodden crowd stopped at the Hospital of St. Cross, just
outside Winchester, where Philip at last managed to
change his clothes. He entered the city upon a white
horse, his black suit now abandoned for a rich cream coat
embroidered with gold, and with a heron feather in his
hat.

The Deanery had been furbished and furnished for
him, but after once again changing his clothes, and the
rain having abated a little, he crossed the lawns to the
Bishop's Palace. At the door of the Long Gallery Philip
was seized with panic and with nausea. Excitement and
pleasure, it was true, had transformed Mary's sour face;
torchlight had also perhaps disguised her age. But, as
Philip whispered to Ruy Gómez, "Is she not very red and
white?" The nose was broad and, in spite of the dropsy
which was to start so many rumors of pregnancy, she was
very thin. She had but few teeth, bad sight and a perpetual headache. As she came forward to embrace him it was

with difficulty that he managed to kiss her on the lips in the English fashion.

And then, an endless business—many courtiers on both sides had to be presented, also Gardiner, Bishop of Winchester, and those other bishops who would aid him in the marriage ceremony. All this meant a plethora of ring kissing and benedictions, so that it was almost midnight before the King of Spain and the Queen of England could talk together by candlelight. They talked long rather than easily, she understanding his Spanish, he understanding her French—with a little Latin and Italian to help them out. She sang him a madrigal in Gaelic and he read her a sonnet from Petrarch. It was all marvelously false but, for all the disease and the dirt, the cruelty and the credulity of those days, these two had had a Renaissance education—and that at least was something.

After exhausting the language of endearment, they spoke of what was most in their minds—the fruit of their marriage. And so, after she had shown him her wedding ring—a plain hoop of gold "because maidens were so married in old times"—he told her of the diamond earrings. In the cathedral tomorrow, at the right moment, Alba would produce them and they would be laid upon the altar. He told her how the diamonds had been brought from the New World, and of how those fragments of the Virgin's robe had been brought to Madrid from a lonely monastery on Athos, and of how they would, for certitude, bring about her conception of a male child. Her eyes brimmed over with tears of joy. Not for one moment did she doubt the certainty of the miracle. Clearly, it was all a great dispensation from God whereby she might become an instrument for the redemption of her father's sins. She would not be barren. Not only was Philip here in Winchester but, by this single act, he had answered all her prayers. He would be the father of her son—which, as all Europe knew, was what he had come for.

"Ah, *mon cher Philippe,* our son is now assured. My belly will be forward by Michaelmas, my travail will be in Lent, our son will be born at Eastertide, and the people will rejoice at Maypole time. It is certain. The ways of

God himself are often very strange, but God's Mother at least will not desert us. . . . Oh, Blessed Virgin, Mother of the Lord Jesus, through the mediation of these most Holy Jewels and relics, grant us also a son."

He murmured the prayer after her and then they crossed themselves again and again.

"Oh, she will, Philippe, she will! Just think, a Catholic king for England and for half Christendom."

Philip's mouth hardened a little at this rush into *Realpolitik*. Half Christendom indeed! However, there was no point in discussing it now. First there must be a son. So he hurried on to tell her of his plans. He told her how he had arranged for the betrothal gift of the Holy Earrings to be entwined, as it were, into the ritual of the marriage sacrament. This might be unusual, but there was precedent for these things, especially among the Byzantine emperors. She would see when the time came, and with joy, exactly what he had planned. The earrings would be upon a golden salver so that Alba could give them to the Bishop; he, in his turn, would place them upon the altar to be blessed with the Bread and the Wine. Then, at the last moment, the Lady Margaret Clifford would fix them in the Queen's ears. After all, these glorious diamond stars were adornments of the flesh only in a very secondary way; primarily they were precious relics— a sacramental thing. Mary would wear them at the wedding feast but also through her first wedding night. That was necessary to secure a miracle, a son.

"Ah, yes, Philippe, that will be wonderful"—she was ready to agree to almost anything—"and after that we will lay them upon the altar of St. George's."

"St. George's—why St. George's?"

"The Holy Chapel of St. George at Windsor. You are now a Knight of the Garter, my lord, and it is now *your* chapel. When we go there together as Knights of that Holy Order, we will place your banner and your crested helm over your stall, and then to the sound of a great *Te Deum* we will lay the Holy Earrings upon the altar . . . in a golden reliquary."

"But you will wear them, Marie—at least sometimes. . . ."

"Tomorrow, Your Grace, and of course tomorrow night in our marriage bed . . . I will wear them then. I will wear them to conceive a son since I, too, am to be blessed among women. But after that, surely, the whole world must be allowed to kneel before them, to worship these holy and miraculous diamonds. Perhaps they will work miracles for other poor and barren women."

Philip's mouth had hardened for a second time. This pietistic emotion was all very well, but now his eyes were steely. His plans were being thwarted and that was a very novel experience. Half-a-million ducats' worth of diamonds locked up in an English chapel. Why, with a miracle to their credit, they might be worth twice that in the European market. He was deeply pious, but he saw no sense in the Queen's plan. She saw his displeasure; she tried to explain.

"You see, my lord, St. George's has more marvelous relics than any church in England. Even Westminster and Canterbury have not so many. It is like your church of St. James at Santiago da Compostella. The pilgrims come from all the world. Yes, St. George's is like that. Oh, Philippe, cannot you see how fitting it would be? Once our son has been born, a son born to redeem the world from heresy, then those Holy Earrings must surely be placed in some glorious reliquary to stand forever on the altar at Windsor . . . surely, Philippe, surely?"

The King of Spain remained silent. This was not the time to argue. He must talk to Renard, his excellent ambassador. He turned, therefore, from the subject of earrings to the far more painful business of making love. He gritted his teeth. It was too late to turn back: he was fully committed. It was weeks now since Mary Tudor, as was usual among the far-flung courts of Europe, had been married by proxy. She and Renard had together partaken of the Sacrament; they had placed rings on each other's fingers; they had been ceremonially unrobed in each other's presence, and then together chastely bedded—all in Philip's name. Indubitably, in God's sight, he was already married to this woman. So, very dutifully, he forced himself into making gestures of love—an art in which he was not without experience. A single candelabra was now burning. The log fire, on this summer evening, showed only a spark; the only sound was that of torrential rain beyond the thick walls. Very gently but awkwardly, because unwillingly, he took her in his arms.

The sun had risen into a stormy sky but for the moment it could still send a few shafts of light across the Hampshire hills—long shadows across wet grass. Philip had dressed early and now, with some kind of cloak over his white wedding suit, was pacing the terrace of the Deanery, his ambassador beside him.

"I am quite sure, Renard, that this miracle will happen. The Blessed Virgin, after all, could hardly desert the King of Spain—her own Catholic Majesty."

"Certainly not, Your Grace"—and Renard crossed himself—"but I can see that Your Grace is unhappy."

"Yes. The miracle will work, Renard. There is no doubt of that. Those little fragments of the Virgin's robe are vouched for by the most learned doctors of the Church, both in Byzantium and in Rome. They are an absolute assurance, especially just now, when the moon is waning, that the Queen's Majesty will not be barren."

"Then what troubles Your Grace?"

"The diamonds, Renard, the diamonds! We went too far. Any decent gold snuff box would have done for the fragments of robe . . . but half-a-million ducats of diamonds! Oh, Renard, what waste, what waste!"

"But, Your Grace, I do not understand. The diamonds are still there. . . ."

"No, Renard. They are lost to us—lost to Spain. Once the Queen is pregnant, once the diamonds have turned the trick, she will place them upon the altar of St. George's at Windsor—and forever, as a holy relic. We shall never see them again. What terrible waste!"

"But, Your Grace, it need never happen. The diamonds can be made to vanish. . . . She would never dare to tell you."

"Vanish—but how?"

"You know quite well, sir, that we have our ways and means. You know that this realm is riddled with our friends, our spies and our agents."

"Naturally, but this is the one case, Renard, where spies and agents are useless. You must know that the Queen, although ugly, is passionate. She is in love with me, but even more is she in love with her unborn son. That means that she is also very much in love with the Holy Earrings, her assurance of a miraculous pregnancy. She will dote upon them day and night."

"Listen to me, sire. The whole Court will move to Richmond in time for Advent. By then the Queen should be with child and the Holy Earrings no longer needed."

"But how will you know, Renard, that she is pregnant? It may not be obvious so soon . . . with these new farthingales."

"I am not so naïve as Your Majesty seems to think. I imagine that the Queen will proclaim her pregnancy from the housetops. All the church bells in England will be rung—and possibly those in Spain too. But in any case, as Your Grace must know, I have only to lift my little finger to get daily reports upon every movement of the Queen's bowels, upon every sneeze. The Queen will be pregnant well before Advent and the Court as always will move to Richmond. When the English Court travels, Your Grace, the noise and the confusion are indescribable—a score of wagons piled high with bundles, two or three hundred horsemen in the courtyard and as many squabbling women in the Queen's apartments. For the diamonds to vanish at such a moment will be the easiest thing in the world."

"But how, Renard, how? She will never let them out of her sight."

"She will, my lord, she will. Even the Queen of England sometimes sleeps and goes to her stool. . . . That will be enough."

"But again I ask how."

"The Lady Margaret Clifford, Your Grace, is reliable, and is also very close to Her Majesty. She will be the first of the Queen's attendants at the wedding this morning. . . ."

"I know that, Renard, but she is a very devout Catholic. Not only would she be loyal to her mistress but she would never, never defile the Holy Earrings. She would fear a curse."

"When will Your Grace learn that all the people here, in their own obtuse minds, are what you and I would call Catholics. The Princess Elizabeth herself, now gaoled at Woodstock, meticulously observes every feast and fast of the Church, and makes her confession. They are all Catholics . . . but, terrible as it may seem, they are English first and Catholics second."

"That, my dear Renard, is why the whole nation is in heresy; that is why we are here—to rescue them."

"They are not in heresy according to an Englishman, only in schism. The only issue—a very big 'only' I admit, my lord—is their allegiance to His Holiness. They actually call him a 'foreigner' as they call you a 'foreigner.' "

"Indeed!"

"Oh, dear me, yes. They even talk of 'reforming' *their* Church, if you please. Their stupidity is abysmal—even the flames of Smithfield cannot cure it—but it is, one must try to believe, stupidity rather than wickedness. It is all very terrible but I suppose that God may forgive them on the Last Day."

"I trust not. But what of it? You were speaking of the Lady Clifford and of the diamonds—my diamonds, Renard."

"The Lady Clifford, Your Grace, may be, as you say, a good Catholic, but for that very reason she is not beyond our powers. She is already our agent in small matters, and may be corrupted further."

"How so?"

"Doubly so. First, she nurses a resentment against the Queen. In childhood she had an illicit and lesbian passion for the Lady Jane Grey. She was at a window looking onto Tower Green when the Lady Jane was led out to die, and, well . . ."—Renard gave a significant shrug—"well, she remembers the day. That would be enough but there is something else. . . ."

"Yes, you said you had a double hold over her."

"Yes, indeed. We know, my lord, what the Queen does not know, that the Lady Clifford has a deformed toe on her left foot."

"My dear Renard . . . really!"

"It pleases Your Grace to laugh, but it is a curious fact that these English heretics are far more credulous than we Catholics. Naturally we are more sophisticated, more capable of using our reason, but sometimes I think these people have more faith."

"Perhaps you have been too long in England, Renard."

"Not at all, Your Grace. It is simply that the Lady Clifford has this deformed toe; indubitably, therefore, she is a witch—yes, a witch, my lord. Not only can we hold the terror of fire over her but, quite frankly, I would not like to be there if she were handed over to the London mob."

"You exaggerate, Renard."

"No, Your Grace. You may remember that the Lady Anne Boleyn had a sixth finger on her left hand. His late Majesty King Henry could, it is true, have had her burnt alive for incest, but, incest being the national vice, the sympathy of the common people would have been with the lady rather than the King. Once, however, it was known that she was a witch, the King was able to appear merciful by using the axe—or, strictly speaking, the sword —rather than the stake. He thus endeared himself to his subjects as being tenderhearted. Your new bride, Your Majesty, will recall the episode; she will not forget that her stepmother was a witch."

"The Princess Elizabeth, then, is not only a bastard but was born of a witch."

"Precisely so, Your Grace—something to note for future use."

"Maybe, but let us get on. What do you propose in this affair of my diamonds, Renard?"

"Only, sire, that the Lady Clifford will do whatever we want. I suggest that when the Court moves to Richmond, the Lady Clifford, choosing her moment—when the Queen is at her stool—will simply put the Holy Earrings in a cloth and drop them out the window—in the dark. I shall have an agent stationed there all through the night. Two minutes later she will make sure that the Queen actually sees her packing the ivory casket, now empty, of course. And then, my lord, when the earrings do not arrive at Richmond, it will be a certain Mary Finch—Keeper of the Queen's Jewels but otherwise a hunchbacked wench of no importance—who will be blamed and doubtless whipped, or even manacled. . . . That is neither here nor there."

"And after that, Renard. What then?"

"My agent will pass the earrings to the first link in a chain of loyal Catholics—real Catholics—until eventually they reach my house in the Strand, where, I need hardly say, Your Grace, they will be as safe as if they were in the Treasury at the Escorial."

"Have it your own way, Renard . . . as long as they never get into St. George's at Windsor to work miracles for barren peasant women—that is all that matters."

"Then Your Grace is satisfied with my efforts?"

The King did no more than shrug his shoulders. He looked up at the windows of the old Deanery. Someone had opened a casement, emptied a chamber pot and put out a mattress to rid it of lice. The King drew his cloak about his shoulders.

"Come, Renard, the world is awake. Let us brave this horrible rain. It is my wedding day—my second. Oh, Renard, Renard . . . never be a king!"

Renard had no desire to be a king, but he wondered—he had often wondered—whether it was even worthwhile being an ambassador. There were, of course, the glories of office and the joys of delicious intrigue. Most precious of all was to be at the spring of power, to be the recipient of royal but whispered confidences. He adored his office and all its trappings, and yet so often, so very often, he had measured the rewards against the burdens and found them paltry. One got blamed when one was blameless, and always, always, there was the chance of the dagger in the back, of the poison in the cup.

Above all, while Philip's governesses and tutors might

have taught him many languages and much music, they
had never told him the meaning of gratitude. Philip was
not, Renard felt, a master whom one could like. First in
Paris, and now in London, Renard had had to console
himself with large bribes and beautiful women. True,
there were also the shadier transactions which could not
be revealed even under the seal of the confessional—but
fortunately God was merciful and would understand.
Renard was loyal to the Church, to Spain and to his
office; it was only Philip whom he positively disliked.

So, as Philip gave that shrug of indifference and of
ingratitude, Renard suddenly glimpsed something bigger—
bigger for himself. He had served his master well and
owed him nothing. He owed Mary Tudor even less. Had
not Renard negotiated this match, this day's wedding, in
order to lead a whole nation out of heresy, into the bosom
of the Church and into the power of Spain? He had
scarcely been thanked. Half-a-million ducats' worth of
diamonds would really be a very small reward for his
work. Surely he deserved something. Those diamonds,
when on their way from the English Court to his house in
the Strand, could so very, very easily get lost, could they
not? Again and again he thrust the thought from him. But
again, later in the day, as he knelt in the cathedral, with
the organ reverberating round the vault and the boys'
voices rising to Heaven, the thought came back to him
with renewed vigor. That night he told his confessor of the
temptation racking his soul. Hardly had he been absolved
when the thought was again burning within him. He
deserved something, and God, surely, would not grudge
him this one thing. He had served God as well as Philip.
When the Holy Earrings had done their work, when Mary
Tudor had miraculously conceived a son, then neither she
nor Philip could have any further use for them. Their
palaces were stuffed with such things.

Only little Mary Finch—the hunchbacked Keeper of
the Queen's Jewels—was likely to suffer; she could be
recompensed and was, in any case, of no account. Again
and again Renard told himself that on one of his great
estates, far away in the hills above Cordoba, he would

build himself a wonderful house. He had always wanted it—a fairy château such as the King of France had been building by the Loire. It would be a dream come true. The diamonds would easily pay for it, and when it was finished it would be among the wonders of the world. God would approve this thing. He had served God well, and when the diamonds had been sold one by one in the Netherlands, those fragments of the Virgin's robe would be kept very secretly upon the altar of his own chapel. God could not mind that. Yes, Renard deserved this thing and, above all, it would be so very easy.

While Renard and his king were in the Deanery garden a horseman, forty miles away, was galloping over the bridge at Abingdon. He was almost at the end of his night's ride. Until long after midnight this man had been waiting in Winchester, waiting in the stables of The White Dog. At last, in the small hours, some lad had brought him a carefully sewn packet. The man knew what to do. By three o'clock he was past Newbury, where at a certain house there were dry clothes and a fresh horse. And now, in the clear, rain-washed dawn, he could look across miles of cornland to where the towers and spires of Magdalen, Merton and St. Mary's were catching the first sunlight. Clattering over the Oxford cobbles, assailed by the morning smell of cesspools, he could again feel the rain on his face. And then he was out of the town, into the mire of wet lanes.

In the old manor of Woodstock the Princess Elizabeth was at her table in the window, as restless as she was sullen. Earlier that year, from Palm Sunday until the end of May—long enough—she had been lodged in the Tower. And sometimes still in the night she would wake and feel her little neck; then often she would light her candle, open the amethyst locket so that she might look upon the miniature of her mother—whose name must never be mentioned. But now she was "free"—free to have a few of her own servants, free to move between Woodstock and Hatfield and Ashridge, free to be a prisoner. At that moment—and she could set her clock by it—two mounted men were patrolling the lane beyond the orchards. She could see their wet capes and their shining lances.

The Princess Elizabeth was twenty-one. Two months ago, when she had been rowed from the Tower to Richmond, and then taken on by road to Woodstock, the people of England had beheld her strange beauty for the first time: the high cheekbones, the aquiline nose, the ice-blue eyes, the auburn hair—as well as the great dignity with which she bore herself. The journey had been a triumphant progress. From the sides of the roads, which were gay with spring flowers, the people had showered gifts upon her. Her face had glowed with the glory of it.

She knew that it was all terribly dangerous. When flames from green logs had consumed poor Bishop Hooper the people had wept. For Mary's prisoner, as she passed through the little towns, they had stood in the gutter and sung old songs. Elizabeth knew very well that her own head was not secure upon her shoulders but thought it more likely that they would marry her off to some lecherous old prince in Savoy or Hungary; she would sooner die. All she asked was the fulfillment of her destiny—to govern. Very faintly, across the fields, she could now hear the bells of Woodstock. She knew that those bells, as those of every village in her sister's realm, were echoing the peals of Winchester.

It was Edward Courtenay, last sprig of the White Rose, who came first into the room. He laid a small sewn packet upon the table.

"May it please Your Highness—from Winchester. It has just come into the house under the baker's loaves."

Elizabeth cut the stitches and spread out the sheets with their crabbed Tudor handwriting.

"From the Lady Clifford . . . Is she reliable, Edward?"

"She is a double agent, Your Highness, of a curious kind. We have a check on her through the Spanish King's Russian valet, a man called Pétya, also our spy. But the Lady Clifford is very cautious; she serves both you and Spain."

"How so?"

"It seems strange but it is true, and as long as one knows it, then all is well. Her whole hatred is reserved for the Queen—she much loved the Lady Jane Grey. To the Queen she dissembles with skill, but she is to be trusted."

"All the same the silly woman has been wasting her time, while risking our messenger's life. This is hardly worth reading; it tells us only what we might have known."

The Princess read the sheets one by one and passed them to Courtenay, remarking upon them as she did so.

"Well, Edward, it would seem that Philip has arrived. . . . Of course: those bells would hardly be ringing had he been drowned at sea. He was not sick—more's the pity. He claimed a miracle as his ship sailed up The Solent—does His Grace think God is a Spaniard? And here the Lady Clifford tells us what we might have guessed, that Philip brought with him a vast retinue, but that no soldiers were allowed to land. . . ."

"That confirms what Your Highness knew, that Parliament is not too papistical."

"From the moment the King stepped ashore at Southampton it was smiles, smiles all the way, kisses and embraces for Arundel and Montague, and then the Garter. Well, well, what does this Lady Clifford expect? After all, the man is a Christian sovereign. Ah, ah! He was wearing mail under his shirt. Good, good! And between Southampton and Winchester he got soaked. God must be an Englishman after all, Edward!"

"The Lady Clifford, madam, may have a trivial mind, but obviously she learns much from Pétya, the King's valet. She misses nothing and she passes it on; on the whole she serves you well."

"True, and this must have been written very late last night. Listen, Edward: Philip and my sister were together until after midnight; he unlaced her bodice and fondled her breasts . . . old and withered, my lord, old and withered . . . or very soon will be."

"One would have thought, madam, that he could have

waited until tonight, but in any case she can hardly bear
him a child now. She is old beyond her years as well as
dropsical."

"If the babe does not leap in her belly by Advent, my
lord, then this poor prisoner at Woodstock will be in peril
of her life. I shall begin to matter, Edward, I shall begin
to matter."

"If the Queen were barren beyond all doubt, and Your
Highness were to become the heir apparent instead of
merely the heir presumptive, then frankly, Your Highness, I would not give a fig for your safety."

"We will make plans for that, Edward, sure enough.
But here, look, on the last sheet, is a different handwriting. A note from the crippled Finch, the girl who keeps the
jewels. Is she too our spy then?"

"Assuredly, madam. Finch has a sweet nature but she
is despised and ridiculed for her humped back, and may
have become bitter. Also, she is of Puritan stock and
cannot abide the Mass—that is enough."

'Well, listen to this. Philip has given the Queen's Majesty some diamond earrings—Finch calls them 'the Holy
Earrings'—and they are to be used at the wedding this
morning."

"Indeed, and what of it, madam? A pair of earrings is
neither here nor there."

"Maybe, but listen! These 'Holy Earrings,' it seems, are
not only priceless diamonds—that is nothing—but each
contains a tiny fragment of the Blessed Virgin's robe, the
robe of Bethlehem. What do you say to that, my lord?"

As Edward Courtenay paced the room he looked
grave. His whole tone had changed. He was frightened.

"I do not like it at all, Your Highness. I gather, from
what Finch tells you, these are not just earrings. They are
very holy relics. The King of Spain, madam, has been
very clever. I do not for one moment doubt the authentic-
ity of these relics. The Spanish pilgrim routes are marvelously organized and policed, and that, no doubt, was how
the sacred fragments came to Madrid. But, in addition to
that, the astrologers of Valladolid are the best in the
world. Philip and Mary will know each other's nakedness

this night. The moon is waning, while Venus, Saturn and
Mars are all in the ascendant. The timing is perfect.
These Holy Earrings—and who can doubt but that the
Queen will wear them in the hour that the marriage is
consummated—will give her the babe she wants. I do not
like it, madam. A miracle would seem to be almost ines-
capable. We must expect the worst: a Catholic prince
before Eastertide. Mary may yet be blessed among
women!"

Elizabeth would one day be famous for many things,
not least her outbursts of rage. As yet, however, this trait
was hardly known. The Lord Courtenay, therefore, was
more than startled to see, first, the color drain from her
cheeks, and then the papers and ink swept onto the floor.
She spat three times. She tore in two the necklace she was
wearing, scattering the pearls over the parquet. Only the
old nurse, eavesdropping in the next room, lacked surprise. She shrugged a shoulder. She had known for years
that these tantrums were not just childish rages—that they
were purely Tudor.

In the end the storm subsided. The Princess turned
upon Courtenay, white and trembling.

"How far back to Winchester?"

"Sixty miles, more or less, madam."

"The time?"

"Nearly noon."

"Can the horseman still be found?"

"At The Bear, madam."

"And this Pétya, the King's Russian valet, the Lady
Clifford and the crippled Finch—they are all in our pock-
ets? They will practice for us?"

Courtenay bowed assent.

"And Renard. Is Renard corruptible?"

"All Spaniards are corruptible, Your Highness, at a
price."

"Then it is all quite simple, Edward. The horseman
goes back to Winchester, and with plenty of money. You
will draft our instructions and he will see to it that they
reach the Lady Clifford. But you must hurry."

"I fail to understand Your Highness."

"Then you are a fool, Edward. There is only one thing that matters, man. The Queen must not wear those Holy Earrings this night and with this moon. She must be barren, Edward, barren—at all costs."

"That is clear enough, madam, but it will not be easy now. It is already the eleventh hour."

"Nothing which matters is easy. But somehow, between this day's wedding and this night's bedding, the Holy Earrings must vanish. Presumably there will be a banquet. Presumably the Queen will unrobe more than once before nightfall. A few moments will be enough—while she goes to her stool. The earrings can be dropped from the window."

Courtenay was silent.

"Can they not, Edward, can they not?"

"Winchester will be transformed into hell, Your Highness, when it is discovered. That is neither here nor there. But, may I ask, what would Your Highness do with these diamonds if you had them?"

"You are an idiot, Edward. Do you think I care what happens to them? Are not my own coffers stuffed with jewels and would I not give them all to be a queen with a son—a Tudor boy. All that matters is that Mary should be denied this miracle."

"I did not think that Your Highness wanted the diamonds for their value—that would be vulgar. I only wondered . . ."

"No, Edward, nor would I be such a fool as to put them on the altar at Windsor to work fertility miracles for other women. Might I not need them myself one day, and for that very purpose? No, you had not thought of that, had you? Meanwhile they shall be hidden away until they can be placed forever among the Crown Jewels of my Realm. And now, my good lord, you know what to do. For Jesus's sake, hurry!"

At last the bells of Winchester were dumb. William of Wykeham's great nave was empty and silent. The whole space of the stone-flagged floor was swept and deserted. Painted effigies and chantries of dead bishops echoed the richness of the roof. But for all the color and the carving it was the austerity that was overwhelming. The place was dark and empty. Then came the gleam of a distant taper. Two cowled monks were lighting candles before every shrine. Far away in Choir and Transept and Lady Chapel these little candles were almost lost in the gloom until, one by one, like stars at dusk, their number grew. Then, finally, came the tremendous blaze of light around the high altar. The cathedral was ready.

And now, every few minutes, the big western door creaked on its hinges. A few men would come in and close the heavy door behind them. First came English soldiers with drawn swords and daggers, stationing themselves at the foot of every pier. They were joined by a hundred torchbearers, the light from the torches making strange patterns upon the stone vault above their heads.

After that, in tens and scores, came men and women. Some flung down their cloaks to make a sodden pile just inside the door, while others spread them upon the paving to form kneeling places. If the candles, one by one, had been like the beginning of a starlit night, so the cathedral floor was now like a garden in April—it was, almost suddenly, crammed with flowers. As the grandees and the nobles arrived, their women knelt on the floor and crossed themselves; the men stood proudly, almost every one of them with a pole bearing a stiffened banner. Like armies arrayed, the English took up positions on one side of the nave, the Spaniards on the other, until the whole flickering torchlit nave was full of people and of heraldry, the people existing more as symbols of the living heraldry than the heraldry as symbols of men.

Peering down from the dark triforium gallery white faces now and again became visible. It was to this gallery that the small fry had been relegated: servants, secretaries, barbers and the like. Little Mary Finch, for instance, had been made to climb the winding newel, not because her rank was low (on the contrary she was the bastard of a Brandon), but because she was unsightly. And Ivan Pétya—ostensibly a nobody—had spent the last hour in that gallery, elbowing himself into a strategic position just above the Crossing; from there he could look down upon all the ritual and the ceremony.

It was immediately below Pétya that the two canopied thrones had been built. By midday Philip, with Alba at his side, was there with a mantle of cloth of gold, thrown back to show his collar of the Garter. As the bells stopped and the first *Te Deum* seemed to fill the vault, the Queen's procession moved down the cathedral. When William of Wykeham built this place he could not, even in his wildest dreams, have conceived of this moment. Mary Tudor wore white satin encrusted with jewels. She wore scarlet shoes. She wore a golden veil. The maids of honor and courtiers were innumerable. What was more unusual was the accompanying circus: prancing dwarfs, unkempt hermits, infant boys swinging censers until the incense hung in the air like the black clouds outside . . . and then the long line of priests, abbots, friars and nuns, so that the last in the line had to remain outside in the rain still chanting. Even at the height of the Middle Ages such a procession would have caused comment. It was excessive.

Gardiner held out his illuminated book. Alba placed upon it the ring, the plain hoop of gold. Philip, as was the custom, placed upon it a little pile of money. Then Alba, with a flourish, added the Holy Earrings. The Lady Clifford quickly and deftly fixed them to the Queen's ears. First a gasp and then a most curious shudder ran through the cathedral. What was this? What was going on? These diamonds had picked up the light from all the torches and candles so that even those at the back of the crowd had seen a prismatic flash of rainbow colors pass across the walls and across the choirboys' faces. In the night there had been many rumors about the miraculous nature of the earrings. There were some who now crossed themselves, a few who even prostrated themselves upon the pavement; most were merely curious.

Philip and Mary moved to the altar. Philip's heart was like ice. Mary was at the gates of paradise—the chosen of the Lord.

In the silence that followed upon the ringing of a

sacramental bell any man may commune with himself in secret. High in the gallery Ivan Pétya, the valet, thought his thoughts in Russian; he licked his lips and his eyes bulged at the glint of the diamonds. Behind him, little Mary Finch wept silently because she had been sent up here with the common servants on account of her crooked back and crooked legs. As the ceremony dragged on, her bitterness turned to hatred and then to cunning. The Queen must never be allowed to bear a child; there must be no miracle of the Holy Earrings. She leant forward and found herself shoulder to shoulder with Pétya. Their hands touched.

The Lady Clifford, kneeling one pace to the rear of the Queen, presented to the world nothing except a tight-lipped impassivity, hoping only, as she too took the chalice, that her thoughts might be hidden from her Saviour. Renard, the Imperial Ambassador, kneeling in his canopied stall, kept his dark eyes rigidly to the front. He gazed between the dark heads of Spanish choristers to the English boys across the Chancel. He saw nothing. He was dreaming of a fairy castle on the hills above Cordoba —and, as always, calculating and calculating.

As Philip raised his head from the Sacrament no shred of his sensual and sexual body stirred toward the woman at his side. He allowed his shifty eyes to slide sideways toward his wife's profile, to her ears, but this served only to concentrate his mind upon the coffers, the iron chest and the great cupboards in the Treasury of the Escorial, where surely the Holy Earrings must ultimately rest. As for Mary, she was carried away into a golden paradise; in the music of the organ and the choir she could hear only the harps of angels; she spared a thought, nevertheless, for the jeweled reliquary within which she would place the Holy Earrings upon the altar at Windsor.

The last long *Amen* had ceased to echo around the stone vaults of Winchester. All of Spain and England, seeking their banquet, had drifted across the wet grass, like fallen petals in the breeze. In the cathedral porch there still remained two figures, talking and talking. In some chaotic mixture of French and Spanish and Church Latin, little Mary Finch, Keeper of the Queen's Jewels, and Ivan Pétya, the King's valet, made themselves very clear to each other, each pouring greed and bitterness, cunning and hate, into the other's soul.

In the crumbling manor of Woodstock the Princess Elizabeth stood by her window. Almost unseeing she watched the rain pouring down upon the garden and orchards. Every few minutes she would glance at her clock, timing the events in Winchester, but thinking always with that clever, determined and courageous mind, that avaricious, cruel and acute mind, thinking always her own thoughts, thoughts of her own destiny, and of the destiny of the Crown Jewels of England.

VICTORIAN
EPISODE

1

The Bonnet Jubilee

A hot June day, one of the hottest of that broiling Jubilee summer of 1887. The press of traffic between Tower Hill and the Mansion House was tremendous. Wagons, drays, pantechnicons, omnibuses and cabs formed a solid block. The horses steamed. As the flies tormented them they shook their heads, jingling their harness. They struck sparks from the granite blocks with their great hooves. The sweating drivers and cabbies had long since passed from caustic cockney wit to resigned gloom. The tops of the hansoms bore their gay and tasseled linen covers, their summer clothing made by the cabbies' wives, while on the buses men had put up their umbrellas to ward off the blazing sun. The big bearded policeman at the corner of King William Street waved his white-gloved hand in vain. Nothing moved. This was a real traffic jam. The noise, the stink of dung and the heat were all terrible.

The little chocolate-colored brougham, picked out in scarlet, with the royal emblem on the panels and a Windsor gray between the shafts, was like an orchid in a cabbage patch. The coachman and the footman, buff-coated and with crepe bands on their arms, remained aloof above the hammercloth. To such remarks as "'Ow's the ole girl?" they merely turned up their noses or curled their lips. Inside the brougham, perspiring in his morning clothes, Sir Henry Ponsonby, Private Secretary to Her Majesty the Queen, pursed his mouth. His fine patent-leather boot, an inch of cloth top and pearl button showing below the striped trouser, tapped the floor in irritation. The City was no place for him, still less for Her Majesty's livery. He glanced uneasily at the plain white hat box on the opposite seat. He stopped pursing his mouth and closed it tightly in annoyance. He disliked these trips to the Jewel Tower. He disliked them very much. They were, thank God, few enough, not more than half a dozen since the death of the Prince Consort a quarter of a century ago. All the same there had been more than he liked. They were so melodramatic and unnerving, breaking the placid rhythm of family life and Palace routine. Besides, he reflected, while it was all very well to let the public see the Regalia itself, all those other jewels would be so much safer in the Strong Room at Windsor.

The glamour of his errand meant nothing to him. He had lived in high places too long. It was nothing to him that inside that plain hat box was yet another box: a casket of shagreen leather with golden clasps, three locks and a lining of cream velvet. It was nothing to him that embedded in that velvet was a galaxy of flashing stones—pearls, sapphires, emeralds and diamonds—stones that had come long ago from the treasure ships of the Spanish Main, to gleam around little white Tudor necks, on white bosoms, in shell-like ears, as gorgeous combs or to be sewn into wimples. It was nothing to him that, after three centuries, these stones had been brought together in one setting, that single tasteless piece of Victorian headgear known as the Tudor Tiara. It was nothing to him that in the Crystal Palace, all through the summer of 1851, the Tudor Tiara had been shown to the people, ostentatiously guarded by guardsmen—only in the end to be part of that priceless junk known as the Crown Jewels. He knew only that all this drama had made people think that the Tiara must be worth millions. In actual fact, Messrs. Garrard of Regent Street and Messrs. Ascher of Hatton Garden and Antwerp had fixed its value at about a million, but had admitted that if the Tiara were ever broken up the single stones might fetch quite surprising sums. Why the Tudor Tiara should be worth less than the sum total of the individual gems was a most peculiar fact—surely the opposite should be true?—so peculiar indeed that it was the one thing that had interested Sir Henry's precise mind. It puzzled him. Messrs. Garrard had never explained it to him. They were oddly reluctant to talk about it—even to the Queen.

But, so far as Sir Henry was concerned, that was all. He was not a romantic man. He knew just enough about art to enjoy the Prince Consort's Italian Primitives, and to realize that the Tudor Tiara, like most things from the Crystal Palace, was grotesque. That was all; he knew nothing about gems and did not want to. His life was wholly taken up with his family, with politics, with the papierasserie of a great Court and with the mechanism of government. For him, therefore, this was not only a very hot day, it was a wasted day. He was also annoyed that such responsibility should have been thrust upon him. He had quite enough on his hands at the moment with the Jubilee only a few days ahead, and this sort of jaunt was not what he was paid for. It was all most unfair and also, in his view, dangerous.

Sir Henry Ponsonby leaned forward a little in the carriage, not enough to be seen but enough to see. He looked distastefully at the traffic. Two naked urchins were frolicking under the spray of a water cart. They were quite nude. Someone should tell a policeman—the boys should be birched. What a mercy there were no ladies in the City. Sir Henry wrinkled his nose at the smell of the cart horses alongside and then, peering a little further, reassured himself as to his guard. Yes, his outrider was there, at a discreet distance such as would prevent him from being spotted as a detective but still allow him to keep the brougham well within sight. Inspector Hughes, mounted on his own roan mare, was tastefully disguised in broadchecked trousers tightly strapped under his boots, a black hacking jacket and a buff bowler—but with a holster under the jacket.

Sir Henry Ponsonby let his mind run on, wondering indeed why he should be there at all. Last year, when the Queen had opened Parliament herself (and would she never let the Prince of Wales—dear Bertie—do anything?), she had worn the little Coburg diadem—discreet and appropriate. He had hoped, when returning the diadem, that that might be his last ride to the Tower. But, oh no! He had not foreseen what a fuss she would make over this damned Jubilee. A plain thanksgiving service would have been ample. One moment she insisted upon being the stricken widow and the next upon being the Queen-Empress—it made life very difficult. That the Constable of the Tower, old Field Marshal Lord Wilson, should have given him such an excellent luncheon was scarcely a compensation. True, before he finally signed the receipt for the contents of the hat box, he had savored a most excellent brandy. It had been a very good brandy indeed. Its warming, delightful and soporific effect upon Sir Henry had been almost instantaneous—and was still with him. He was tired, he was worried and he was sticky—but he was also sleepy.

It was only his annoyance that was keeping him awake. He was making this trip for the second time in a week: six times in twenty-five years and now twice in a week. It was intolerable, but then, as he so often reflected, the life of Queen Victoria's Private Secretary was likely to be both intolerable and thankless. Nevertheless, like most men of position, he loved it all; that is one way in which men differ from women. Sir Henry put his hand in his trouser pocket; he felt very lovingly the single key on its thin gold chain, that little gold key which opened the red dispatch boxes. All down Whitehall there were at that moment Ministers of the Crown and Permanent Secretaries all handling with affection their little gold keys—symbols of power, position and prestige. Sir Henry was a man without vanity, and yet he found the little golden key a great comfort. It was something other men hadn't got. It made an intolerable life more bearable—even glorious.

The second trip to the Tower in one week. Four days ago he had fetched the Kohinoor. That the Queen, for the service in the Abbey, should wear an ordinary bonnet with the Kohinoor simply mounted as a brooch was reasonable—the suggestion of that reasonable woman, the

Princess Beatrice of Battenberg. True, bringing the Ko-hinoor to Windsor had been a nuisance, and getting it mounted, all in a week, had been a damned nuisance. Telegrams and messages had flown between Windsor and Regent Street. But the idea had been sound. But that the Queen should now, in a life of unending funereal gloom, suddenly decide to wear this atrocious Tiara not for the Jubilee itself but for a purely family dinner of a couple of hundred royals was really going to the other extreme. It was pretentious and self-indulgent. It was worse: it was out of character. The Abbey would have been different; and for that her children, one by one, had begged her to wear the Crown itself. They had been snubbed—was she not still in mourning? It was to be "the Bonnet Jubilee"— ladies in the Abbey to "wear bonnets and long dresses without mantles"—and yet, on the Jubilee eve, just for the family, there was to be this Tiara with its ghastly 1851 setting. It was perverse, stupid and unaccountable.

It was also one of those occasional throwbacks to Hano-verian vulgarity which Sir Henry loathed. True, the Hapsburg, the Greek, the Bourbon, Bonapartist and Ro-manov jewels would all be worn by somebody or other. The Waterloo Chamber would glitter with jewels. But the Queen knew, and had always known, that she could never compete with all that. That was one of the facts of his-tory, one of the facts about little England in a great Europe, one of the facts about, say, the Czar's Byzantine inheritance, or France's Bourbon loot. It was a fact with which, until now, the Queen had dealt in her own way. Like Napoleon, who wore his corporal's coat when sur-rounded by the gaudy Marshals of France, so the Queen, with a shabby black dress and a scrap of lace, had always made everyone in the room look third rate. This dumpy little middle-class Frau, thought Sir Henry, was the only woman in the world who had ever made dowdiness smart. That was her trump card and, so far as he was concerned, she had better go on playing it. It saved such a lot of trouble. Moreover, there was just the possibility that with the Tudor Tiara on her head the Queen might be making herself ridiculous, and, to be fair to Sir Henry Ponsonby, he did not really want that.

And what was all this nonsense he had heard from dear Lady Ely? She had come twittering to him, whispering in his ear, her eyes shut with excitement: Jays were making the Queen a new black satin dress, trimmed with miniver and covered with gold thread; also, presumably there would be a jeweled corsage, the Garter sash, at least one German and one Russian order, the Saxe-Meiningen pearls, the old Nemours lace veil "borrowed" years ago from the Empress Eugénie and never returned, the inevitable Albert locket, a tartan bow somewhere or other; and now, literally surmounting all, this absurd and irrelevant Tudor Tiara at that moment lying in its casket and in its cardboard hat box on the other seat of the carriage.

Still the traffic did not move. Sir Henry Ponsonby, usually an equable man, snorted with annoyance, both at the traffic and at the Queen. Why, he said to himself, the woman will be positively overdressed. Could it possibly mean, after twenty-five long years of gloom, that she was using the Jubilee to mark the end of mourning? Impossible . . . but if it was, God knows what might happen. He began to wonder. He had already been twice dragooned into some ghastly amateur theatricals. And apart from the usual gillies' ball at Balmoral, when she had danced Scottish reels till two in the morning—a deathly secret south of the Border—only last Christmas at Osborne she had danced a quadrille with Prince Alfred—with "Affie." She could never, naturally, approve of the *valse*—that was for the "fashionables" at Marlborough House—but (it all came back to him now) there had been other signs of life in recent months. The De Reskes, Jenny Lind, Grossmith, Irving and Ellen Terry had all performed in the Waterloo Chamber, and had been presented afterward as though they were ladies and gentlemen. Windsor was becoming almost gay.

Sir Henry shuddered. It might mean changing his habits. Later hours, more parties, more visitors to the Castle, a more frequent use of Buckingham Palace. It would all mean more work. He even began to see the Tudor Tiara

as a harbinger of change, and of change for the worse. Of
course, what the Queen wore was her own business. The
most he could do would be to have a word with the
Princess, or perhaps dear Lady Ely would speak to the
head dresser. Yes, the dresser, old Fräulein Skerret,
would be the one. Queen Victoria, after all, had always
preferred the advice of her servants—that long line of
nurses, governesses, footmen, gillies, dressers, and now
this sinister Indian servant, the Munshi—had always preferred their advice to that of her own children.

Sir Henry had begun to nod. He now gave a violent
movement. Through his Jaeger combinations and his trousers his perspiring buttocks had stuck to the tooled Spanish leather of the carriage seat. He winced as he freed
himself. The traffic had begun to crawl, but to the heat
and the stink was now added the noise of a thousand
iron-shod wheels on granite blocks. Sir Henry again closed
his eyes and reflected upon his wasted day. There were
masses of jewels at Windsor, and to insist upon a Crown
Jewel for a dinner party was unfair to everyone—to the
detectives, the police, the overworked footmen and, above
all, to him. . . . Five miles across London, from Paddington to the Tower and back again, on the hottest day of the
century, and then again next week to return the damned
thing, plus the Kohinoor. It was altogether too bad.

When he took office General Gray had warned him
about these idiotic trips, assuring him that they were
outside a Private Secretary's duties—a matter solely for
the Home Office. A Black Maria was clearly the proper
vehicle for the purpose. Sir Henry had written to Sir
Frederick Rogers, the Commissioner of Police; but he
could hardly have chosen a worse moment. The Queen
had been making it quite clear—recently and publicly—
that Sir Frederick hadn't been fulfilling his duties to her
utmost satisfaction. The Commissioner and the Home
Secretary were piqued, they were hurt, and short of a
direct command, disinclined to oblige the Palace. In
George IV's time the Crown of England had been conveyed through London in a coach, with a puffing
Beefeater walking on each side. The other day, when he

fetched the Kohinoor, Sir Henry had been given an escort of Horse Guards. He disapproved of this since it served only to advertise his whereabouts. For the Tudor Tiara, therefore, he had suggested the decent anonymity of a hansom cab. This had been instantly vetoed as being "quite impossible . . . and must never be referred to again"—hence the Palace brougham and the Windsor gray.

So here he was in the blazing sun, both sleepy and bad-tempered, in the middle of King William Street, with a coachman, a footman, an outrider and a hat box. Sir Henry pulled the silken cord and the footman opened the trap in the carriage roof.

"Sir."

"Fulleylove, this traffic is quite intolerable. Tell Macdonald, as soon as he can, to turn down one of these lanes to Lower Thames Street and then along the Embankment. It is simply terrible here."

"Yes, sir, most unpleasing. But you remember, sir, that it's Paddington we want, not the Palace."

"Of course, of course. Do as you're told, man, it will save time in the end."

"Sir." Sir Henry Ponsonby would have been surprised to see the coachman and the footman exchange a wink; royal servants do not usually wink in public.

Really, they could have come along the river all the way from Tower Hill. It might be a little further, but with the traffic at Ludgate Circus and Charing Cross getting worse every day, it was a great saving. Sure enough in a few minutes (and thanks of course entirely to him) they were passing Printing House Square and the end of Blackfriars Bridge. He remembered as if it were yesterday the opening of the bridge by the Queen. It had been her first emergence from the seclusion of grief and he had had to arrange the whole thing as if it were a second funeral. The bridge was soon behind them and they were clip-clopping along the Embankment, outpacing cabs and trams all the way. There was not a horse in the Royal Mews, Sir Henry said, who could hold her head so well or lift her feet so high as little Primelbund. He had specially asked for her. Inspector Hughes cantered bravely in the rear.

With a tiny breeze off the river the carriage seemed cooler. Sir Henry looked wistfully at the sailing barges and was reminded pleasurably of Cowes, rather less pleasurably of those infuriating journeys to Osborne. Of course he knew—he and Mary Ponsonby both knew—that they were fortunate. Had they not got Osborne Cottage as their home, just as they had the Norman Tower at Windsor? It was only at Balmoral that he "lived in"—that cold attic with the iron bedstead—and was parted from his family. But of course, even from Osborne he often had to travel to town, perhaps two or three times a week, and once (during the Greek crisis) it had been seven times. This always made him feel more like a messenger than a Private Secretary, so that he was sometimes resentful. He felt taken for granted. The year's round, for instance, had to go on at all costs. The dates were fixed and were sacred. The Queen's doctors had been dragooned into saying that her nerves would stand no change of routine. She had been exploiting this edict for a quarter of a century, refusing ever to return from, say, Osborne or Balmoral one day sooner than had been planned. The convenience of emperors, kings, czars, shahs, ministers of the Crown—not to mention the families of private secretaries—was neither here nor there. It did not exist. Windsor, Biarritz, Osborne, Balmoral, Osborne again for Christmas, and so back to Windsor—nobody mattered. There were only the most fleeting visits to town—Buckingham Palace, fully staffed, was virtually uninhabited. Sandringham she never visited—symbol of a world that she disliked. Sir Henry had become an intermediary for an absentee sovereign. It was too ridiculous!

And now, in the carriage, he was tired and he was nervous. He was no longer alert and he knew it. That Tower of London brandy, combined with the heat, was having its effect. He kept closing his eyes and then jerking them open again. He knew that even within the security of the brougham he must watch that million-pound hat box. . . . The path of duty might be hard but it was clear.

At a spanking pace the carriage passed under the grim black arch of Waterloo Bridge. He recalled nostalgically how, only a few years ago, the rusticated bastions of Somerset House used to rise straight out of the mud and the tide—a magnificent sight. He glanced up at the Adelphi, that shabby haunt of artists, and found himself thinking of it as building land—a large hotel so near to the Strand would surely be a fine investment for some innkeeper. London was becoming so cosmopolitan: only last week he had seen two Japanese at the Royal Academy.

He must have dozed a little for quite suddenly he realized that they were in Parliament Square. He was back at last on his home ground—the world he knew, the familiar world of Westminster and St. James's, of clubs, embassies and even palaces. There was a flurry of saluting policemen. He had been recognized—how nice! All round him there was a great hammering: only two days now before the Jubilee. The masts were up everywhere, ready for the banners—the heraldic banners of other empires and of royal houses, banners bearing the emblems of colonies and far-flung possessions. It was only the stands that had to be finished—all heavy planks and huge balks of timber—hundreds of navvies sweating in the sun. Sir Henry, in his dry way, thrilled a little; his blood ran faster at the sight of the busy scene, and even more at the thought of Empire.

They bowled along Birdcage Walk, one or two men raising their hats to the livery. How brightly the lake glittered in the sun as one saw it through the rich tapestry of foliage, and how trim were the lawns; the Office of Works should be congratulated; Sir Henry would draft a letter for the Queen's approval.

Between the trees he could just see the flagstaff on Marlborough House; it was without its banner. The Prince of Wales must be out of town—already at Windsor. Sir Henry's mouth set a little grimly. The Prince would want to talk—to talk about those perennial problems, debts and Eddy. All the world knew about the debts, but for the great British public, dear, unspeakable Eddy, Duke of Clarence, second in line to the throne, was little more than a mild joke—"Collar and Cuffs." What a pity, mused Sir Henry for the thousandth time, that little Georgie—not clever but good—had not been the elder boy. Primogeniture was all very well but Nature played her tricks. . . .

At the corner of Buckingham Palace Road the coachman had a little trouble with Primelbund: she knew better than anyone the whereabouts of the Royal Mews and was thinking only of cool hay. The coachman had to use his whip to make her turn right in front of the Palace en route for Paddington. A few moments later, however, and the brougham, with Inspector Hughes alongside, had Constitution Hill to itself. What a pity, mused Sir Henry, if the Queen ever threw open this fine avenue to the public. She was being pressed to do so, at least when the Court was out of town—which was almost always.

The police had opened the gates of the Wellington Arch and were holding up the Knightsbridge traffic; how much more thoughtful were these Westminster police than those in the City, so much more sense of what was fitting. In no time at all the brougham was in Hyde Park. The grass was more parched here, surprisingly so for early June, and there were too many bits of paper and orange peel about. Perhaps congratulations to the Office of Works should be left until the crocuses were out next spring, and then Princess Beatrice might like to write in her own hand—always a good thing.

Beyond the Marble Arch, all up the Edgware Road and along Praed Street, Sir Henry was once more in an alien world, a proletarian world which he neither understood nor liked. All these rough and probably dirty people jostling each other on the pavement . . . they were animals from a different jungle. Sir Henry could think of them only in terms of whether or not they might be "loyal." It was all most distasteful. He sat well back so as to shut it out, only, once again, to succumb to drowsiness. When the brougham finally stopped alongside the departure platforms at Paddington, Sir Henry Ponsonby was sound asleep.

Had he been awake he might have noticed a number of things. Although the Queen's Secretary did not quite qualify for a red carpet or a handshake from a GWR Director, everything was strictly according to protocol. A space had been railed off where the carriage could pull up, and where the Station Master, in frock coat and topper, and a stout Inspector of Police with a waxed mustache had long been waiting. They were flanked by four rather more ordinary bobbies, while a few yards away, trying to look nonchalant, was a plain-clothes detective with Dundreary whiskers, a meerschaum pipe and a straw boater. There were only a couple of onlookers—a youth in a ginger suit with a pair of carpet bags, and a golden-haired girl. It was the Inspector of Police who would carry the hat box to the train; porters do not carry Crown Jewels.

As the carriage stopped, the coachman leaped down on the off side in order, as the detective duly noted, to adjust Primelbund's bit quite unnecessarily. The footman had already jumped from the box and, running alongside the carriage, had opened the door, awakening Sir Henry with a light touch on the knee. He now stood deferentially, his left hand on the embossed silver knob, his right hand at his side clutching his cockaded hat. Inspector Hughes, having obeyed his instructions—"to escort Sir Henry Ponsonby's carriage as inconspicuously as possible from the Residence of the Constable of the Tower of London to the Paddington Station"—gave a valedictory salute and walked his steaming mare up the slope in search of water for her and whisky for himself. Inside the carriage Sir Henry pulled himself together with a jerk, realized where he was and stepped out. He looked in blank amazement at the footman.

"What's this, what's this? I thought Fulleylove was on duty. I was most clearly told that it would be Fulleylove."

"I was ordered to replace him, sir. I regret to say, Sir 'Enery, that Mr. Fulleylove 'as been attacked by the mumps—most unfortunate, sir."

"Dear me, dear me. Mumps indeed! I trust this won't mean an epidemic in the stables, and just at Jubilee time. Really. this is too bad of Fulleylove . . . usually such a reliable man. Dear me! How very vexing!"

"As you say, sir."

"And your name, my man? I don't think I've seen you before."

"Smith, sir."

"You're new to the service then?"

"Yes, sir. I was with Lord Iddsleigh, sir—first as groom and then as footman, until 'Is Lordship's sudden death, sir . . . on the staircase at No. 10 . . . dyin' in the Prime Minister's arms, I understand, sir. So I decided to better myself, sir."

Good heavens, thought Sir Henry, how the lower orders did exaggerate—sensation at all cost. Poor Iddsleigh, he felt sure, had been carried into the Cabinet Room some minutes prior to death, and had actually died on a sofa. Anyway, it was certainly not the footman's business.

"Well, Smith, I trust you will give the Household good service. If you do, you will have no cause to regret it. . . . But the first rule, my man—remember—is no gossip, no tittle-tattle."

"Sir."

The Station Master had been showing signs of impatience. He coughed and stepped forward.

"Excuse me, Sir Henry, but I have been holding the Windsor train for you. It should have left twenty minutes ago."

"Dear me, Mr. Station Master! I had not observed the clock. The press of traffic in the City was terrible. We were much delayed, and now . . ."

"Quite, sir. And now, since I shall have to lock you into your compartment, and since you *have* been delayed, I am wondering whether you might not care for, er, a wash . . . if you will pardon my mentioning it, sir."

"Thank you, Mr. Station Master, thank you. Yes, indeed . . . most timely, most necessary . . . especially as one gets older."

"Not at all, sir. Come to my office—rather pleasanter

than, er, the public urinals, if I may say so, sir. The Chief
Inspector will take your, er, hat box to the train and will
guard it until you rejoin him. There are four constables
here to escort him. You will find a tea basket in the
compartment, sir, and your coach has been routed right
through to Windsor—no need to change at the Slough
Station. . . . Everything in apple-pie order, sir . . . trust
the Great Western, sir."

"Thank you, thank you . . . all most convenient. Fulleylove—Smith, I mean—give the Inspector the hat box.
Handle it carefully, my man, and you, Inspector, pray do
not let it out of your sight."

"Certainly not, sir. The Metropolitan Force knows its
duty, Sir Henry."

Smith, as the detective again duly noted, now went
round to the far side of the carriage, since it was from
that door that the coachman had removed the hat box
after adjusting Primelbund's bit. The onlookers had now
drifted away. Sir Henry gave his last orders.

"Thank you, Fulleylove—er, I mean Smith. You and
Macdonald will return to the Royal Mews and will report
that your duty for the day has been completed. Now, Mr.
Station Master, pray lead the way to your office . . . most
timely, most timely."

The brougham went off at a smart pace but once in the
Edgware Road slackened to a trot. Hardly turning their
heads, for they knew only too well that they were being
admired, the coachman and the footman once again gave
each other a big wink—the second of the day. Then,
playing their role to the end, they looked stiffly and
silently ahead. Only a close observer would have noticed
that the two men, like so many who have lived under the
rule of silence, could talk to each other without moving
their lips. In the Buckingham Palace Road, fifty yards
from the Royal Mews, they abandoned the carriage. An
hour later, when Primelbund began to whinny for her
oats, it was found there by a policeman. For the two men,
as for Primelbund and for Sir Henry Ponsonby, it had
been a long hot day, longer than anyone knew.

Meanwhile, at Paddington, the vast space beneath

Brunel's iron roof was a splendid and magical sight. Shafts of June sunlight thrust down between the girders to illuminate clouds of steam—all steam, smoke and sun, orchestrated by the thud and whistle of big locomotives. The two glossy toppers, almost lost in the crowd, sometimes hidden by piles of trunks, mailbags or milk cans, bustled off to the Station Master's office. The stout Chief Inspector, holding the hat box as gingerly as a birdcage and as self-consciously as a sacrament, made his way to the Windsor train, now half an hour behind time. The four constables followed, well aware that they were part of a royal occasion. The detective, having no instructions about what to do if Sir Henry and the hat box were separated, was thrown into confusion. He remained in an agony of apprehension until the Right Honorable Sir Henry Ponsonby, K.C.B., P.C., G.C.B., having duly relieved himself, at last reappeared.

One other passenger—the jaunty youth in the ginger suit, with his two carpet bags—had followed the Chief Inspector, his hat box and his four bobbies onto the platform. He must surely have been aiming at the next train, and was now in luck with this one. Hard on his heels came the two toppers.

Sir Henry was now securely locked in his compartment. The hat box and the tea basket were beside him. It was cool here and he could gaze at the hat box more calmly than in the brougham. He had no great sense of history, but with his feet up he could now relax and could recall some of those Tudor sovereigns whose portraits he had seen a hundred times in the royal galleries. He thought of their jewel-encrusted garments, their necklaces, pendants and earrings, their buckles and belts, and how much of that jewelry was now with him in that railway carriage, all embedded in that one Tiara. He thought first, naturally enough, of the great Elizabeth, then of Henry and his wives, of "Bloody" Mary and even of some of their subjects—Bacon, Essex and Raleigh . . . and so on.

Sir Henry's troubles and his long, hot day were now over—or so he thought. In the Windsor train, after all, he was nearly home. Without dereliction of duty and with a clear conscience he could now finish his nap. History faded from his mind. By the time the train had rattled over the points, and before it had even begun to glide through Berkshire meadows, he was snoring heavily.

2

Bertie

The Windsor railroad station is accustomed to royalty and such other oddities as visit the Castle. It even has a bleak courtyard with a glass roof where, through the long years, most of the kings, queens and presidents of the world have—strictly according to protocol—been ushered into their carriages for the two-hundred-yard drive to the Castle. The station is still peopled by the ghosts of wedding guests and mourners, by the ghosts of coaches and hearses.

The Station Master, therefore, did not overrate Sir Henry Ponsonby. He knew he was only a secretary, if an exalted one. Sir Henry had to wait five minutes before being released from his compartment, and then had only his coachman to greet him. The Ponsonbys did not run to an outdoor footman.

"Good evening, Philpotts . . . a most fatiguing day."

"Good evening, sir. The heat in London must have been most trying, but you have escaped a good deal of coming and going at the Castle, sir . . . this Jubilee, I suppose. Allow me to carry the hat box, sir."

The two men, master and coachman, went out into the station yard. The little dark green carriage was waiting for them, but Black Beauty—usually a staid old beast—was rearing up on her hind legs and foaming at the mouth. Fortunately the youth in the ginger suit—so conspicuous at Paddington—had already come to the rescue and was having his work cut out to hold the horse's head. His two large carpet bags were beside him on the pavement.

"I'm doing my best for yer, guvnor! Thought as 'ow a train whistle might 'ave started 'er off like, but no—it was this 'ere bearin' rein. I'm blowed if it ain't drawn blood."

"Thank you, my man. My coachman can see to it now. I'm obliged to you."

Black Beauty was still trembling when Sir Henry got into the carriage. Philpotts had put the hat box on the pavement and in a few moments had calmed Black Beauty, patting her on the nose. Sir Henry leaned out of the window to tip the young man in the ginger suit. He gave him half-a-sovereign and instantly regretted it—a crown would have been ample. Then they were off, up the hill to the Castle, the hat box once more safely on the carriage seat.

As he clattered through Henry VIII's Gate and across the Lower Ward, Sir Henry sighed with relief. Very soon now he would be back in his own home, the Norman Tower, with Mary and the children. First, however, he must look in on his office in the Private Apartments to see such letters and telegrams as had come in during the day. He must also, and above all, put this Tudor Tiara in the strong room. He was not going to have it in his office all night—that would mean turning out his own little safe. And certainly he and Mary were not going to have this one-million-pound monstrosity in their own bedroom. The Castle strong room—somewhere down among the dungeons—was the proper place.

Back in his own office, Sir Henry Ponsonby put the hat box on his desk. He poured himself a hock and seltzer. He lit a Corona Corona. He gazed out the Gothic window. Really, you know, life in this place had its compensations—the Avenue and the Long Walk, the distant policies of the Great Park and of Ascot, the long afternoon shadows across the turf—all so much fresher and greener than in London. And then, through the other window, shimmering in the sun, the pinnacles of Eton College

Chapel and the great curves of the Thames—a perfect Cotman. And then, above all, there was the whole aura of Majesty—the feeling that one was near to Divinity, actually in the next room but one—the assurance that, after all, one was not quite as other men.

There were no letters of importance—they could all wait—and only one telegram, that the Emperor Frederick would be bringing a suite of thirty-five to the Jubilee instead of twenty. That was a routine matter, and Sir Henry turned gratefully to a folded note in the handwriting of the Princess Beatrice:

Mama and I trust that in spite of the heat your visit to the Tower of London was successful and that that precious Tiara is now safely at Windsor. Mama asks me to say that she would be pleased if you and Lady Ponsonby would dine tonight— quite informal. It seems hard after your exhausting day but, as you know, what must be must be.

The Maharajah and the Maharani of Kashgar arrived at the Castle this afternoon, their P and O liner being one day early. I suspect that he was annoyed because Mama was not with me on the doorstep when he arrived. And now I am afraid that Mama will insist upon trying out her Hindustani on him—oh dear! The Maharajah's aide-de-camp is a seedy and dubious-looking English colonel called Pinkerton; the Maharani's lady-in-waiting, a Miss Nummuggar, speaks only Urdu. How helpful.

Also dining will be the Denmarks, the Waleses with Eddy (again, oh dear!) and Georgie. The Salisburys will be with us if the P.M. can get away from the House in time. Not a very tactful moment to ask Ld and Ldy Randolph—not with the P.M. here—but as they are in attendance upon Bertie there was no help for it. My Henry is still laying foundation stones in Yorkshire. Mr. Arthur Balfour, as Minister in Attendance, will make the numbers right, plus, of course, the Dean and Mrs. Randall Davidson. Mama will see to it that Mr. Balfour is not put next to anyone clever—he must not have a chance to show off.

This afternoon—I knew you wouldn't mind—I sat in your

office for an hour. It was deliciously cool and the only place where I could smoke undetected. By the way, the Maharajah, having masses of jewels himself, is supposed to be an expert—has already been to Garrard's and Cartier's and doesn't think much of them! Mama thinks, therefore, that we might have the Tudor Tiara on show this evening and also for the luncheon guests tomorrow as they will not be at all the same people as those who will see the Tiara on Mama's head at the dinner. Also, if we show the Tiara tonight, presumably in the Great Corridor, it may help to break the ice when the Household and Family meet for coffee, specially as you, I gather, are expected to hold forth on its history. You don't know this yet; I am warning you. Papa's 1851 sketches for the design have been dug out of the Library to pin up on an easel alongside. I am warning you of this too as a slightly funereal note might be in order. By the way, I suppose the Tiara you brought from London today is the real thing.   Pss B.

Sir Henry Ponsonby gave this note a moment's thought. Then he read it again. Then, from sheer habit, he noticed the names of the dinner guests—one must have the right kind of small talk ready for them. Then he read the last phrase—"I suppose the Tiara you brought from London today is the real thing." He read it four times. Had he gone mad, or had the Princess . . . ? He liked the woman very much—she was the best of the bunch and the sanest—but really . . .

He took three sheets of the black-bordered Windsor notepaper and dashed off three letters of his own. The first was to his wife.

Darling. A terrible day—hot, tiring and irritating—all details later. To cap all we have to "dine" tonight. I was so looking forward to a quiet evening—perhaps coffee on the lawn and then a game of backgammon . . . but now! There is no help for it. She wants to show off this hideous Tiara, with me as cicerone. So, alas, my love, our salmon must go back on ice. I will be over about 7:00 to dress—no gongs or ribbons, thank heaven!   H.

And another note to General Sparling, the Master of
the Royal Mews at Buckingham Palace:

My dear Sparling. I was rather expecting to be served
today. on my visit to the Tower, by Fulleylove and Macdonald. I must admit I never really noticed the coachman, but the
footman—a callow youth called Smith—told me that he had
been ordered to replace Fulleylove, who had mumps. He had
been given his orders by Mr. Thomas, the head groom, but I
presume that you know all about this change in my arrangements. I am only surprised that I was not informed. Also, my
dear Sparling, a private secretary—if I may say so—should
not be fobbed off with a newcomer to the service; novices
should be tried out on the messengers' little berlins or the
servants' wagonettes. Much more alarming is this intelligence
about the mumps. Mumps indeed! This is really too bad. With
the Jubilee in two days' time an epidemic just now would be
disastrous. Every servant and carriage will be needed. The
disease, moreover—or so I have been told—is particularly
virulent and painful in the adult male. Kindly keep the Duke
of Norfolk informed as to the condition of your men, and let
me have a full report immediately. What a splendid horse you
have in little Primelbund.   Yrs Ponsonby.

And then one to the Queen:

Sir Henry Ponsonby, with humble duty, has received Your
Majesty's gracious command to dine tonight. which he and
Lady Ponsonby will be most pleased to obey. Sir Henry had a
successful visit to town. He took luncheon with Field Marshal
and Lady Wilson at the Tower—all very pleasant. The royal
parks were in all their summer glory. Your Majesty will be
relieved to know that the very beautiful Tudor Tiara—and
what a triumph of design—is now safely within the walls of
the Castle. Sir Henry suggests placing it on the onyx table in
the Corridor this evening, and also tomorrow morning for the
benefit of Your Majesty's luncheon guests. He forgot to
mention that at the Tower today Sir Henry inspected a
detachment of the Yeomen of the Guard—acting as Your
Majesty's representative. A splendid body of men. Sir Henry

trusts that Your Majesty's headache has quite vanished. He much looks forward to meeting the Maharajah and Maharani of Kashgar this evening.

After all these years the Queen's Private Secretary was still amazed at his royal mistress. Outside her very own curious experiences—a cloistered childhood and then, very suddenly, the big world—she was abysmally ignorant. She had read very little once the schoolroom days were over—the *Times,* specially printed for her on art paper, the *Berliner Tageblatt,* and an occasional dip into Marie Corelli were about her limit. She was often rude, selfish and thoughtless, and yet, somehow, Sir Henry seldom felt uncharitable toward her. The key to her character, as he had long since discovered, was her directness, her unalloyed simplicity—what was good was good and what was bad was bad; the good must be rewarded and the bad punished. Life was as simple as that. He realized that, given her impossible mother, those ghastly German forebears and her governesses, it was a miracle that she should be even presentable—after all, one might have been landed with another Queen Caroline! At least Victoria washed. He also knew that her simple shrewdness often came near to genius. Her dinner lists, for instance— Sir Henry knew exactly how she would arrange her table tonight. Arthur Balfour must be given no chance to dazzle anyone with his dazzling intellect, and indeed no two people who had anything in common must be next to each other—they might talk too much. Long ago there had been a disastrous evening when Uncle Cumberland and old Lord Lyndhurst had compared notes on the haunts of St. James's, and that other occasion when, from the soup to the savory, Macaulay and Carlyle had discussed the origins of Whiggery. Things were different now. The Queen had learned her lesson. Politics, religion and expectant motherhood were altogether banned, naturally, but the arrangement of the guests was also a very clever trick to make sure that table talk should remain small and general; on no account must the conversation ever rise above Her Majesty's head—that would never do, and so it never did.

Sir Henry Ponsonby came back to earth. A tinkle of his bell and the silent and liveried automaton was at his side, immaculate and pomaded, but with brandy on his breath.

"Ah, Wainwright. This note is for my wife. You must get it sent over to the Norman Tower immediately."

"Sir."

"This one is for General Sparling, the Master of the Mews at the Palace. If anyone is going back to town they must take it. Otherwise get it franked and taken down to the station."

"Sir."

"And this one is for Her Majesty; ask Her Royal Highness kindly to hand it to her."

"Sir."

"And then, Wainwright, I would like to see one of Her Majesty's dressers. I suppose there will be six on duty as usual—but preferably Fräulein Skerret."

"Sir. May I have permission to speak, sir?"

"Well, what is it?"

"Your own coachman, sir, Mr. Philpotts, is outside and would like to see you, sir."

As Wainwright silently vanished, Philpotts came in. As the two men passed each other it would have been improper for them to speak, but, somehow, Sir Henry sensed that either would have been glad to have murdered the other. Philpotts was now in gaiters, ratcatcher and white stock.

"What is it, Philpotts?"

"Black Beauty, sir. I'm worried about her."

"I don't wonder. Most unlike her to prance about like that. You must watch that bit and bearing rein, Philpotts."

"That, sir, with respect, was not the cause."

"But that ferrety youth, Philpotts—in the ginger suit—who was holding her head, he said the bit had drawn blood."

"Sir, that was not so. The bit and rein were perfectly adjusted. The blood was not from the mouth at all."

"Come, come, Philpotts, something had startled her."

"Yes, indeed, sir. She had been cut in the right foreleg, just above the hock, made with a sharp blade—perhaps a razor. We can ask the vet, sir, but there is no doubt about it. Two of the Castle grooms can vouch for it, sir."

"Very well, Philpotts, you were quite right to tell me. All very strange, very strange indeed. Of course it will have to be looked into, but that will do for now, Philpotts. Good night."

"Good night, sir."

Sir Henry Ponsonby, with a puzzled frown, finished his hock and seltzer. He was worried and, worse still, he did not know why he was worried. The feeling had been coming on all day; it had been started by the fumbling ineptitude of that foolish nonagenarian, Field Marshal Lord Wilson, the Constable of the Tower of London; it had been increased by the unaccountable absence of his favorite footman, Fulleylove, and now it had been capped by Philpotts.

With his cigar still in his mouth, the frown still on his face, Sir Henry placed the hat box on a chair, opened it and lifted out the shagreen leather case. This he placed on his desk. He then pulled from the pocket of his coat skirts a tiny box of gold filigree. It held three keys, one topped by a sapphire, one by an emerald and one by a pearl. Each of the three escutcheons on the case bore a corresponding stone. Sir Henry now removed the Tiara from its bed of cream velvet and placed it upon his blotting pad. The whole Tiara—there was no doubt about it—was quite repulsive. It summoned up all the ghastliest memories of the Crystal Palace. On the other hand, the gems were unrivaled—probably unrivaled in the whole world. Sir Henry, knowing nothing of jewels, was fascinated mainly by the sheer ugliness of the thing.

"Ach, mein Gott! It is too beautiful!"

Fräulein Skerret, the Queen's senior dresser, had come into the room. She was a privileged being who never knocked on doors. She wore a tight dress of black bombazine with tiny steel ornaments; also a curious little starched cap. She was said to be over ninety but was unchang-

ing and ageless. Trained in the Palace at Darmstadt, she
had come to the Queen at her accession. If Sir Henry
Ponsonby sometimes believed in the myth of royalty,
Fräulein Skerret believed in its divinity. For her, to her
dying day, there would be only one Prince—Albert—not
least in matters of art. She was now holding up her hands
in ecstasy at the marvelous Tiara which "he" had designed.

"Ach, mein Gott! It is too beautiful!"

"Ah, good evening, Skerret. This is the famous Tudor
Tiara, which Her Majesty will be wearing for the great
Jubilee Dinner in the Waterloo Chamber. It will have to
go in the strong room, but I thought you should see it and
measure it now—I see you have a tape on your reticule.
This Tiara, Skerret . . ." as if she didn't know ". . . has
been in the Tower of London for thirty-six years, and
although the separate gems are all some three or four
hundred years old it has never, so far as I know, been
worn by anyone. It may need altering to suit Her Majesty's present—er—coiffure, and there is also the problem
of the veil . . . we don't want a disaster like the one we
had at the last levee."

"Ach, no, sir. That was too frightful . . . everything
came away . . . everything, diadem, veil, coiffure, absolutely everything . . ."

"Quite, Skerret, quite . . . best forgotten. Meanwhile,
this Tudor Tiara is being shown to the guests this evening,
on the onyx table in the Corridor."

"Ach! It will look too marvelous. . . ."

"Quite. But I was wondering, Skerret, whether you
could, very quickly, get a suitable cushion covered with
black velvet. Her Majesty might not like to use one of the
Garter cushions, and in any case they are probably all
locked up in the Chapel."

"It shall be done, sir."

"Thank you. I am now going over to the Norman
Tower to dress. Examine and measure the Tiara, then
lock this door—here is my key—and return the key to me
before dinner through one of the footmen. Have the vel-

vet cushion put ready on the onyx table and I will see to the rest. Good night, Skerret."

Outside Sir Henry's office the long passage—red carpet, white paint, gilded mirrors, lacquered Marie Thérèse cabinets and Albertine gaseliers—all combined to frame in an almost endless perspective. Sir Henry had been ready to slip through a little side door leading by way of a newel to the courtyard and so to the Norman Tower. This was not to be. From the far end of that rich perspective a portly gentleman was hurrying toward him—a figure not unknown throughout Europe.

Edward, Prince of Wales—dear Bertie—wreathed in blue cigar smoke and with the Star of India at his throat, was dressed for dinner, except that he still had to discard his smoking jacket. The guttural, bronchial and Teutonic voice hailed Sir Henry down the length of the passage. There was no escape. The Prince was almost in the room.

"Hello, Ponsonby, you're the very man I wanted to see. Ah, ah, so you have Mama's gewgaw. Handsome object, I must say. Good evening, Skerret."

Skerret bobbed her curtsy and stood aside. The two men now had the Tiara between them.

"Hm, as I say, very handsome. Of course taste and fashion change. I was brought up, so to speak, on the Crystal Palace. I know nothing about art—never did— but I know what I like. Now frankly, Ponsonby, between ourselves, wouldn't you say that this was a bit gaudy for Mama?"

"I very much fear so, sir. I can't understand it—so unlike Her Majesty to make such a mistake. Perhaps the Tiara's close association with your father clouded her judgment. You know he designed it himself—we have his drawings. But what can we do, sir? The Princess Beatrice just won't interfere in matters of dress—she says she's been snubbed too often. A word from you, sir, to Lady Ely . . . or possibly Fräulein here could say a word to the Queen. . . ."

"No good, Ponsonby. Mama will have her own way. I know exactly what her idea is. With all these relations, all those Germans, Russians and Danes coming over for the Jubilee—not to mention the Orléans clan with their marvelous Bourbon jewels—Mama just wants to fly the flag—it's as simple as that."

"You know, I never thought of it like that, sir."

"Oh, dear me, yes. After all, whatever they may say about us Coburgs, the Tudors are English enough for anyone—I know they were actually Welsh, but that doesn't matter—and all these superb gems really are Tudor, I gather, and really are superb—eh, Ponsonby?"

"There's no doubt about that, sir. And I think you're right about the Queen—a gesture to show that even in jewelry the Old Country can hold her own. Well, she always seems to have her own reasons for what she does. And the jewels themselves, as you say, sir, really are Tudor—the equivalent in jewelry of, say, St. George's Chapel in architecture—the finest gems of the sixteenth century, at any rate outside Spain. . . . If only they weren't in such a ghastly setting; but that is the one thing that is impossible to mention."

"Quite. And the actual gems—you can identify them all, Ponsonby?"

Sir Henry took a very large envelope from his desk.

"Almost all. Here is the file, sir. Here you see engravings from Holbein's paintings, Nicholas Hillyarde's and Isaac Oliver's miniatures, as well as photographs of effigies and so on. It's a regular parlor game of 'spot the jewel.' This enormous pearl, for instance, in the very center of the Tiara, may be identified quite easily in the Hatfield portrait of Elizabeth, where it lies like a fine plover's egg in the middle of the royal bosom, only to crop up again in James II's scepter . . . quite a fascinating story. And then again, sir, these twelve-pointed stars—said to be worth all the other stones put together—are almost certainly Mary Tudor's wedding earrings, a gift from Philip of Spain."

"Really, poor old Bloody Mary, eh?"

"Yes, sir, and there are many other romantic tales

hidden in this Tiara. . . . But I understand that I am expected to dilate upon it all this evening after dinner."

"Poor old Ponsonby, eh?"

"Oh, I survive these things, sir."

"I am sure you do; I admire your resilience. However, we'll come back to the Tiara later. Skerret, you may leave us—give me Sir Henry's key."

Skerret duly bobbed, to vanish in search of black velvet and a cushion.

"Now, Ponsonby, a word with you. With all these Jubilee guests in the Castle I must help Mama as much as I can; I shall be kicking my heels here for a couple of days. Can you spare me an hour sometime?"

"So far as duty permits I am at your service, sir."

The reply was cool, but Sir Henry knew only too well what was coming, and the Prince knew that he knew. Sir Henry's mouth had tightened.

"Yes, Ponsonby, you're right . . . it's the old story. Parliament still thinks that Mama should pay my debts from her Civil List—Gladstone started that here. Mama thinks that Parliament should pay them from Revenue— Dizzy started that one. Dizzy, of course, was right, but he's dead. Now, as you know, ever since Papa died I have performed more and more of Mama's social duties, in town and abroad—what Gladdy called 'the visible attributes of Monarchy.' Clearly these are public duties and the public should pay for them, in other words Parliament. Now you, Ponsonby, know Parliament better than I do. Talking to ministers is your daily job. Anything you say will be much better received than if it came from me or from any of my friends, all of whom are supposed to connive at my extravagances. Cust, Hirsch, Esher or Dickie Fisher, let alone the Rothschilds—no member of the Cabinet would listen to them. So, it's up to you, Ponsonby, for Mama's sake as well as mine. I thought that perhaps you might have a word with the P.M. tonight."

"I might, sir, if I thought that it would be of the slightest use. But I must remind you that this is a liberal administration, almost radical—intent upon soaking the

classes for the sake of the masses. No, I am not hopeful;
but may I at least know, sir, whether your finances are
worse today than they were, say, a year ago."

"Well, there's still that old debt of £80,000 on Sandringham. It still stands."

"Dear me, dear me, I had hoped that that was paid off
long ago."

"It's no good saying 'dear me, dear me' like that. On
Sandringham my conscience is absolutely clear. It was a
capital expenditure on property reverting, in effect, to the
Crown. Whether or not Eddy ever marries and lives
there—or Georgie, since I can't see Eddy ever marrying—
the place will be an asset to the nation—the finest game
bag in England—and yet I'm supposed to actually restore
the capital. It's not only unfair, it's rotten finance."

"Maybe, sir; but whether the Treasury would ever take
that view is another matter. After all Sandringham is not
a palace—of which you have too many. It's your own
house and you bought it yourself, sir, in preference to
living in one of the houses on Crown Land, of which
several were available."

"Rubbish, my dear Ponsonby! How could a gentleman
nowadays live in a place like Bushey or Claremont—no
sport for his guests, and much too near London or Windsor. Anyway I wouldn't want to be on Mama's doorstep,
and I had as much right to buy Sandringham as Papa
had to buy Balmoral."

"Your father had some Coburg money, Your Highness.
In any case, I am merely stating the view of the Treasury.
A Select Committee of Parliament would probably be
even more critical. The time is not propitious. What else,
sir?"

"Oh, well, there's always Poole of course, but then I
suppose that Savile Row expects to wait for its money—
it's a tradition of English life. Anyway it's less than £10,-
000 and Poole can always borrow on what I owe him."

"Ten thousand, sir, for clothes!"

"You know nothing about it, Ponsonby. With my ample—er—girth I really can't wear a suit more than twice.
You don't understand. There are all the uniforms. Kilts

are expensive and Poole has just had to send his head
cutter to Berlin to check the details for my Death's Head
Hussar uniform. These colonelcies, Ponsonby, are
damned expensive . . . harness and accouterments as well
as just clothes . . . swords, hats, decorations and God
knows what else."

"And your wine merchant?"

"Really, Ponsonby, perhaps you would like to see the
butcher's bills. Oh, well, if you must know—about the
same as Poole. I had to lay down a cellar at Sandringham,
you know."

"But, Your Royal Highness, I can't possibly put debts
like these in front of either the P.M. or the Queen. Such
debts are far more shocking than the really big things
such as the Household. They would be horrified."

"What you must make them realize, Ponsonby, is that I
live as I do solely for the sake of the nation. As long as
Mama sticks to her shabby weeds, and won't be seen in
public, then I have to deputize for her—without her
income. I don't even get an allowance for entertaining
foreign sovereigns—a big item."

"Can't you raise money, sir? After all, there must be
assets—the Duchy of Cornwall, for instance."

"I can't touch it—all entailed for the next P. of W. But
of course you are right. Naturally I *can* raise money,
although not so easily as you might think. Don't you see,
my dear Ponsonby, that while my tradesmen can borrow
on my debts to them, I can't go around borrowing money
from my friends as other men can—and do. Nobody is
ever going to dun the Prince of Wales, but in return, don't
you see, there is a certain *noblesse oblige*. I can't behave
like a cad; therefore I can't exploit my rank. You must
know that."

"But isn't there one single extravagance of which Your
Royal Highness could divest yourself—at least as a
start?"

"It's all very difficult. There's the *Britannia* for in-
stance. They make me Commandant of the Royal Yacht
Squadron and won't pay me enough to keep a boat at
Cowes."

"You could consider a smaller yacht, sir, and sell the *Britannia*."

"I can't afford to keep her, but I can't sell her either. Boni de Castellane, with all those Jay Gould millions in his pocket, offered me £10,000 for her—just what I owe Poole—but now he's backed out, almost bankrupted himself on his pink marble palace in the Avenue de Bois—bloody fool! That was a blow. To be frank, Ponsonby, that was one of the things that brought me here today. That . . . and other things."

"Other things . . . gambling debts, sir?"

"Peccadilloes, my dear man, peccadilloes! People think I gamble and so I do, but always in strict moderation. Oh, I know that my Tattersall account is a running sore, but, like Poole, Tattersall's can borrow on it. As for the card debts—the Jockey Club and White's—they have never exceeded three figures in one evening."

"And in Paris . . . ?"

"Oh well, naturally the Faubourg St. Germain stakes are rather higher, but even so—my God—just compare it with Regency times when whole estates used to pass over the card table."

"Those times have gone, sir. Few remember them and none would tolerate them, least of all from a man in your position. They are as obsolete as dueling."

"A man in my position! Exactly. You've hit the nail on the head. My position! It's so damned unfair. I have to be all things to all men—never myself. Half the nation cheer themselves hoarse—here or in Ireland—if I back a winner, and the other half wink or shake their heads if I do so much as cross the Channel. And why on earth, Ponsonby, should it be all right to lose a fiver at whist and a mortal sin to lose it at baccarat? Tell me that. Besides, damn it all, I win as well as lose, don't I?"

"No one doubts that, sir. You are lucky on the turf and skillful at the card table. But don't forget that ever since the Reform Bill governments have been very sensitive about the Nonconformist conscience or—which is much the same thing—the middle-class vote. That is a fact of political life. But to go on to other things, sir. What about the cost of all these cozy establishments which you provide for your—er—friends? . . . if I may be allowed to ask."

"Don't be such a fool. Of course you may ask—we're both men of the world, aren't we? Besides, you know better than anyone that I adore Alix, but you also know that her heart is always in the nursery or in Copenhagen— when she isn't there herself. You also know, or you damn well should know by now, that I am a virile man. I am a man who cannot sleep alone. And that, my dear Ponsonby, is that—one of the physiological facts about His Royal Highness the Prince of Wales. After all, what do people expect? I'm a Hanoverian on both sides; I'm damned lucky not to be riddled with disease. Thank God I'm not even a hemophiliac like half my miserable cousins. But I *am* fond of women—and women are expensive."

"I must accept your own estimation of yourself, sir. I am concerned only with the financial consequences."

"Well, I have a streak of loyalty in me. I may get tired of people—even of a beautiful women—but I don't drop them."

"We all know that, Your Royal Highness."

"Well, then, I haven't the slightest objection to you knowing everything. Nellie Clifden—not so young now, bless her—still has chambers in Dover Street, and Hortense Schneider in the Rue Royale—with a modest settlement for both ladies. That for a start."

"And the Villa Olga at Dieppe, sir?"

"What?"

"The Villa Olga, sir. At Dieppe. Is it still there? Little Olga must be growing up. . . ."

"Good God, Ponsonby, you know about that. And neither Alix nor Mama suspect a thing."

"You are naïve, sir. In any case, it's my business to know if I am to be of any use to you."

"Well, you can forget it. Olga Alberta is the dearest child in the world. She is very, very beautiful, Ponsonby, with marvelous hair below her waist. In Dieppe the people are kind; they call me her 'godfather,' *le parrain royal de la petite*. But you can forget her; she and her mother are provided for forever, and the capital written off. She is my most precious secret."

"Very well, sir, but with the French Government putting twenty detectives in Dieppe every time you see the child, secrecy is relative."

"I don't care a damn. In two years Olga Alberta will be here—her first London season. She can never be presented at Court but when she dances in the great London houses she shall wear the finest diamonds in the world—I swear that."

There was a palpable silence between the two men. Both had dropped their eyes to the Tiara on the desk between them. It was Ponsonby who, rather sharply, changed the subject.

"Let us get back to business, Your Highness. There was a Miss Walters, if I remember rightly."

"Skittles? Oh, she's Hartingdon's friend now. No trouble there, Ponsonby. I must tell you a joke about her one day."

"And this Parisienne, Your Highness, known, I believe, as—er—La Goulue?"

"I do wish, Ponsonby, that a man with your responsibilities would stick to the facts instead of reading the newspapers. True, I paid for champagne all round that night at the Moulin Rouge—my own affair, I think. But I am not in the habit of sleeping with cabaret girls."

"I stand corrected, sir. And Miss Le Breton?"

"Miss Le Breton, Ponsonby, as you would know if you would only read the newspapers, is now married to a Mr. Langtry and has become a wealthy woman as well as being a good actress. People may stand on chairs in the park to look at her, or so I am told, but Langtry doesn't mind, and it costs me not a farthing . . . so really, my dear Ponsonby, she is quite irrelevant."

"I suppose you give her presents, sir. It all mounts up."

"Of course it mounts up. Knollys is selling capital all the time as well as borrowing on my expectations. Those expectations, I need hardly remind you, Ponsonby, are stupendous. I am the most gilt-edged thing in Europe. But I can never, never take advantage of it. I cannot exploit my rank. Prinny did, you know, both with Barings and with Coutts, and the prestige of the Crown dropped to rock bottom. That did far more harm than all his blowzy mistresses."

"Oh, I see all that clearly enough, sir. Have you yourself any solution to offer?"

"The obvious one and the correct one. Dizzy told Parliament years ago that my expenditure was bound to exceed my income by £20,000 a year. Dizzy was the only Prime Minister who realized what it meant—financially—to live in Society—the first man with less than a hundred thousand acres ever to hold the job. What he said is still true. The point is, Ponsonby, and Dizzy saw it—the point is that I do so much for Mama—twenty of her guests filling Marlborough House this week—that that £20,000 should come from her Civil List. In any case, what on earth does Mama do with all her money? If she handed over to me officially, if I were Regent, there would be no question . . ."

"No, Your Highness, but that has not happened and won't—not until pigs fly. Moreover, with this Cabinet I am, frankly, not at all sanguine about your affairs. It would be madness to speak to Salisbury at the moment—there's always that puritanical streak in the Cecils—and in any case the government is far too busy with Ireland and Egypt to pay attention to anyone's mistresses or gambling debts—even yours, sir."

"I must say, Ponsonby, I thought better of you."

"I am speaking for the Cabinet, not for myself, sir."

"Well, well, let's go through it all tomorrow morning. Knollys has it all down in black and white. After all, it's his job, not yours. But sooner or later Mama has got to be tackled and that, my dear man, brings it back to you. If I went to Mama myself she would only give me one of her jobations, as if I were still a naughty boy. It is for you to reason with her, Ponsonby; but do remember that she has a very warm spot in her heart for me—if only she can be made to forget what Papa would have said. You convince Mama and she will convince Salisbury."

"I'll do my best, sir, when this Jubilee is out of the way."

"Good, but don't wait too long. And for heaven's sake, Ponsonby, keep my wife out of this. Alix has no extravagances. In Paris last month two of her ladies each ordered a dozen dresses from Worth, and God knows how many hats. Alix ordered only three. Mama likes Alix well enough but is always looking for faults—she loathes the whole Danish connection of course—and Bismarck writes a poisoned letter every week or so. If Mama can blame Alix she will. . . ."

"The Princess of Wales's name shall not be mentioned, sir."

"All right then, but don't wait too long, Ponsonby. The Paris couturiers seem to have less faith in my credit than have the London tailors."

"Very well, Your Highness; but frankly I am not at all optimistic, not at all."

"Then what is your own suggestion—damn it?"

"Your Highness can always go to the Jews."

The two men were still standing with the Tudor Tiara between them. The Prince threw away his cigar end, savagely cut and lit another, and then walked across to the Gothic bay. He stood there, gazing at a landscape still basking in the sun. For fully five minutes there was silence except for the Prince's heavy breathing. At last he turned back to the desk.

"May I ring your bell, Ponsonby?"

In less than twenty seconds—he must have been almost by the door—Wainwright, salver at his side, was making his obeisance.

"Ah, Wainwright, please ask one of the princesses to tell Her Majesty that I would like to see her in her own room—I suppose she will be in the Gold Room—in about a quarter of an hour—better say seven o'clock."

"Sir."

"And to add my apologies for appearing before the Queen in a smoking jacket, but the matter is urgent."

"Sir." And Wainwright vanished.

"And now, Ponsonby, the Jews! What the hell do you mean, go to the Jews! Really, you know, I am most unwilling to remind you of our stations in life, but I do resent your remark. It has, to start with, a very nasty anti-Semitic twist. Secondly, as you well know, some of my best friends are Jewish—not to mention several of the Queen's most loyal subjects."

"Your Highness has completely misunderstood me."

"I hope so; but really, Ponsonby, it did rather sound as though you were advising a visit to the nearest pawnbroker."

"Oh, no, sir . . . really!"

"Or, alternatively, that some of my Jewish friends might be more amenable to a financial deal than my gentile ones."

"Allow me to explain, sir. Anti-Semitism was far from my mind. On the contrary I was thinking of the great qualities of Judaism. It pleases Your Highness to be humorous about pawnbrokers. May I remind you, sir, that a merchant banker is but a glorified pawnbroker. Your Highness will doubtless remember that the three golden balls which hang in our streets were the arms of the Medici family—worthy predecessors, sir, of the Rothschilds, and incidentally not Jews."

"Ah, so that's it, is it? Go on, Ponsonby, go on."

"Well, you will remember, sir, that eight years ago, when Lord Beaconsfield bought the Khedive's Suez Canal shares, he needed an enormous loan at three hours' notice. You will also remember that he got it—in two hours—from Baron Nathan Rothschild—his security, the British Empire."

"Yes, yes, Ponsonby, of course—one of Monty Corry's more romantic Dizzy stories. Unfortunately I am not the British Empire."

"The whole Rothschild tribe, to put it mildly, sir, is well disposed toward Your Highness."

"Maybe, Ponsonby, but, as I say, I am not the British Empire. I am an officer and a gentleman. It would be caddish—possibly even unconstitutional—to offer my rank, my person, let alone my prospects, as some kind of security . . . it would be pawning the Throne! If Mama died the whole thing might become a public scandal—half the new King's Civil List in pawn to the Rothschilds! And then, if I died, just think of poor Eddy's position. Pawning the Throne . . . and for Eddy of all people, or if he died, for good little Georgie. Yes, Ponsonby, pawning the Throne!"

"Not quite, sir. Some of your gentile friends might think like that—Esher, Beresford, Fisher—although others, such as Lord Randolph, might think it rather a clever wheeze. The Rothschilds, however, would think very differently. Their discretion would be absolute; money is in their blood. Remember, sir, that there is more money in the Vale of Aylesbury than anywhere else in the world outside the City of London. A few minutes' chat with the Baron Nathan in the library at Tring, and your troubles are over. A million-pound loan, with His Royal Highness the Prince of Wales as security . . . why, sir, it would be one more battle honor for the House of Rothschild, and also a secret that would be kept forever. I beg you, sir, I beg you. A million pounds—take it, Your Highness, and then hand it to Maurice Hirsh and watch him play with it on the Stock Exchange. I beg you, sir."

"No, Ponsonby, no. I will not and cannot offer myself as security. One day the Treasury might have to redeem me. Another generation of Rothschilds might foreclose. The scandal could be the end of the monarchy. Nobody believes it, you know, but unlike the other men I really own very little. Now if I was one of the great dukes—a rent roll from a hundred thousand Irish acres and half-a-dozen London squares—life would be simple. Or, Ponsonby, if I had great possessions in tangible form—a few Rembrandts or Raphaels or even, say, the Kohinoor—something Natty or Ferdy could put in their strong room in exchange for the check—I should at least feel like a gentleman. But I have nothing like that. Sandringham is not paid for, the pictures all belong to Mama, the Kohinoor and the Cullinan belong to the nation, and the Duchy of Cornwall is entailed. Now if only I had one single thing of my own—a single object worth, say, the odd million, something which I could just hand across the table to Natty, any evening over the brandy—that would be different, Ponsonby. That would be how I like things. Yes, yes, that would be quite different. . . ."

There was another long and rather terrible silence. The two men were not looking at each other. They both had their eyes fixed upon the bizarre object on the desk. Very gently the Prince of Wales put out his fat hand and turned the Tudor Tiara round and round, examining the jewels one by one.

"Very well, Ponsonby, until tomorrow then. But something must be done soon. I'm pretty desperate, you know. Now let us forget money. Let us look at this pretty object." He held the Tiara aloft.

"All Tudor gems, Your Highness, from many sources. Spain was particularly generous, as were our own great Catholic families. But of course the work of assembling the gems and of designing the setting was entirely your father's. The librarian, Herr Mütter, has all his meticulous drawings."

"He was a meticulous man, Ponsonby. My God, he was! And so this pretty thing is our own property— Mama's and then mine in due course. Our own personal property to do what we like with, eh, Ponsonby?"

"Strictly speaking, sir, I should want to refer that question to the Solicitor-General. Crown Jewels, surely, are held by the Crown on trust, not by the Sovereign personally."

"Nonsense, Ponsonby. They're ours. In George IV's time, for instance, in the Pavilion at Brighton, Lady Conyngham often wore the Great Sapphire—and it has never been seen again. One of her bastards, Mountcharles probably, must have pawned it, but no questions were ever asked."

"Those days have gone, sir. The Queen would never agree. . . ."

"Never mind the Queen. Remember, jewels don't become Crown Jewels merely by being put in the Tower for safety . . . there's a lot of rubbish in that place anyway."

"True, sir, but the matter is legally very complicated . . . and I have not yet dressed for dinner. Your Royal Highness will excuse me."

"I'll keep your key then. A quiet smoke here, with a go at your decanter, will soothe my nerves very nicely, ready for my chat with Mama. Now, be off with you."

Sir Henry Ponsonby walked across the little courtyard deep in thought. What a hopeless creature the Prince was. Popular of course, but not always with the right people . . . more at home in Paris or Dublin than in London. Sir Henry had heard the whole story of the debts many times and always with the same excuses. He would have to tackle the Queen sooner or later. Fortunately she really did have a warm place in her heart for Bertie—"Bertie is a dear, good boy"—and did not disapprove of his antics nearly as much as people supposed. After all, she had been brought up in the shadow of the Regency . . . men will be men, and it was not for a daughter of the House of Hanover to cast the first stone. "Society," as she often said, was "heartless" and "showy" but she never blamed it for being "wicked"; it was the function of Society to be wicked, just as it was the function of the Court to be moral. If her affection for Bertie was sometimes muffled, that was only when Albert's ghost, redolent with all the tight-lipped prudery of Stockmar or Uncle Leopold, had triumphed over her better and more worldly nature. Privately she might scold her son; publicly she kept a loyal silence, and within reason—or even beyond reason—would do anything for him.

Sir Henry Ponsonby was far more critical than the Queen. The Prince of Wales was a damned nuisance—a spanner in a well-oiled machine. Sir Henry disliked his personal habits. Why on earth, for instance, had the man dressed so early for dinner? It was this disgusting habit of drinking before dining—an American custom which Jennie Churchill had imported from the Jockey Club on Long Island. The Prince had probably already been boozing for an hour with the Denmarks and Randolphs—both sexes.

And these smoking jackets—they might be all right in Virginia or even at Marienbad, but now they were being worn every night at Marlborough House and even in the clubs. Horrible! And why the Star of India? The Maharajah would be officially honored tomorrow—the Princess had said so—and now Sir Henry would have to go to his bureau and get his own precious Order of the Bath. Then he would have to summon Mary to his dressing room to clip the ribbon behind his collar. Then the damned thing would have to lie flat on his chest, which meant a shirt front instead of the frilly one which was probably already laid out for him. Sir Henry snorted with annoyance, but could at least thank God that he did not yet have a smoking jacket and did not consume spirits just before breathing in the Queen's face. . . . There were limits!

The courtyard was now in shadow and quite cool. These long June nights . . . the children would hardly be in bed yet; there might just be time for a game with them while Suzanne was doing his wife's hair. He looked up at the Norman Tower—yes, he could see nanny's shadow on the blind. The story of his day's work, with all its worries, would keep until he and Mary were in bed, peaceful and secure. He looked back at the blaze of gaseliers, just lit in the passage outside his office, noticing how they picked out the pattern of Wyatville's lacelike plaster vaulting. Wainwright had not yet pulled the curtains and Sir Henry could see the massive head of Albert Edward, Prince of Wales, as he bent over the desk.

Up there in Sir Henry Ponsonby's office, the Prince was alone, with the door locked on the inside. He was fat, he was florid, he was immaculate. His eyes were bloodshot. The cigar was set at an angle as the lip curled. He had swallowed two brandies. He had taken a magnifying glass from the desk. He was examining the diamonds with great care—those diamonds which, long ago in the Choir at Winchester, had flashed with all the colors of the rainbow. The Prince bit hard on his cigar. He was swearing quietly in German. He glanced at the clock. It was time to see Mama.

3

Mama

She sat in the little Gold Room. Was she a mummified puppet or was she some kind of Buddha—rigid, almost immobile among her possessions? She had been walking on the South Terrace with Beatrice and with dear Lady Ely, and now, with two hours to go before dinner, was still wearing her curious hat, that little pouf with its hint of crepe. She still wore her mantle with its sparkles of jet.

Her stature was negligible. Only years later, when they saw her coffin, did Englishmen realize how little was their Queen. But now, at this moment, on June 19, 1887, she completely dominated this private temple in which, for this hour, she had enshrined herself. It was a small room, not so much furnished as redolent with the somber gold of the embossed walls and heavy picture frames, also somber with the browns and whites of sepia photographs and creamy statuary—and the yellow sunlight filtering through drawn blinds.

The Gold Room, in this golden light, might well be a shrine, but it was also the royal counterpart of a thousand parlors of a thousand British matrons. Nothing here for use or for beauty—every inch a memento, a gift, a souvenir, a relic, a votive offering. For more ordinary widows there would be the texts, the Berlin woolwork, the waxed flowers, the "present from Broadstairs" and the photos of nephews who had long since ceased to write. The Gold Room at Windsor was no more than an apotheosis of all such sanctums—the parlor of just one more selfish, bourgeous old woman. Two hundred photographs, each in its repoussé silver frame, some with sprigs of white heather, some with black bows—all these kings and emperors and czars, and over a hundred royal or serene highnesses. Here, however, in this room they were transmuted from their royal status into the long list which she carried in her heart—Vicky and Fritz in Potsdam, Nicky and Alicky far away in Petersburg, and Eugénie, so handy at Chislehurst . . . and then there were the rest: Liko and Drino and Tino and Sandro, Affie and Louischen and Lenchen and Ena, and Georgie and Eddy and May—four generations, all long-nosed and long-mouthed, and all at that moment, in their hot uniforms and hot corsets, moving in their hot wagons-lits, from ghastly palaces all over Europe, toward Windsor, or toward that no less ghastly palace at the end of the Mall, moving, all of them, toward this Buddha squatting in her shrine.

And there too, among the photographs, were all the other relics, christening mugs and mourning rings, the glass case for funeral cards, the locket, with his mother's hair, that Albert had given her in the woods at Rosenau, the children on their ponies at Laeken, the shells they had glued onto boxes, the miniature of Aunt Adelaide—so kind in '37—and the Barbary dagger from Hughenden, the one Monty Corry gave her in '81 when they opened Dizzy's tomb that she might put china roses on the coffin. Quite the largest photograph was of dear Lehzen, with its memories of the schoolroom at Kensington. There was Stockmar's gold turnip watch, and the last Valentine from Lord Melbourne—so amusing. And there, next to her chair, was Boehm's statuette of John Brown, and the picture of Grant, who, next to Brown, was the nicest of all the gillies. But it was the family that one came back to. The poor Empress of Germany and the Prince of Wales were at either end of the mantelpiece—busts of blood-red marble. And there, over the mantelpiece, was Landseer's "Last Shoot"—Albert by Loch Muick with a dead stag . . . idyllic days! But the altar of the shrine—also Albert— was in white Carrara marble, silhouetted against the drawn blind, the wreath of immortelles around his brow.

In this last hour before dinner, she was working, reading and signing. Reading and signing—it was her whole life now. There was a knock on the door. She put away her spectacles—spectacles were not allowed at Windsor. The corners of the mouth remained down, but the whites of the hooded eyes just showed as she looked up at her eldest son. He clicked his heels. He kissed her hand. She pecked his cheek.

"Good evening, Mama. How well you look."

"You know that I am never well. . . . My dearest boy, what a stranger you are."

He waited ten ticks of the clock before he was told that he might sit.

"Well, Bertie, I am bound to say that it is pleasant to have you at Windsor . . . for a change. I suppose you still recognize the old place."

"It is always delightful to be here, Mama; but you know how busy I have been in London and in Dublin. By the way, that was a successful affair . . . a few black flags hung out in Cork, but cheering crowds everywhere . . . or—er—almost everywhere."

"Yes, Bertie, strange as it may seem, I do read the newspapers. I also noted that your visit to the Viceregal Lodge coincided very happily with the Punchestown Races."

"Now, Mama, really . . ."

"And that Alix was not with you. She's a sweet child, Bertie, but all these months at the Amalienborg . . ."

"Three weeks, Mama . . ."

"Don't argue with me, Bertie. It was quite long enough to leave you open to temptation. And when Alix is in Denmark, as I suppose she must be sometimes, it would be kind of you to visit your poor old mother. I can't imagine what you do with yourself in London, or why you live in Norfolk—a most outlandish county."

"Not more outlandish than Aberdeenshire, Mama."

"Bertie!"

"You never will realize how much I do for you, Mama,

both in London and Norfolk. It was at Sandringham, only the other day, that Willy and the Blue Monkey . . ."

"Really, Bertie, you're impossible. The Blue Monkey— I suppose you are referring to the Portuguese ambassador, the Marquis de Soveral."

"Yes, we all call him 'the Blue Monkey.' Anyway, he and Willy initialed the Mozambique treaty in my library at Sandringham—a diplomatic coup for England. And now, tomorrow night, there will be twenty highnesses at Marlborough House. The suites will have to go to places like Claridge's, but even so, God knows where everyone will sleep. . . . And I don't get a penny for it, Mama."

"Now don't start all that, Bertie. We've been over it a hundred times. You're a very wealthy man and should be glad to show gratitude for your wonderful upbringing and for having had such a wonderful father."

"Yes, Mama, I am not ungrateful; but there are lots of calls upon my money. . . ."

"You've plenty of money, Bertie, if only you wouldn't squander it . . . all this entertaining Society—useless, selfish creatures. I see that you and Alix have had the Duchess of Manchester to dinner again. . . . I told you not to."

"We must choose our own guests. . . ."

"But you had her on a Sunday, Bertie. You've no sense of what is fitting."

"We were talking about money, Mama. That is why I have come to see you. I take on all the—er—pageantry, so to speak, all your London obligations and all the visits to foreign capitals, and never get a penny for it."

"Nonsense. You got several thousands for the Czar's funeral."

"Pooh, Mama. It hardly paid for the cravat pins I had to hand round. Anyway, if my efforts were recognized by Parliament, then you could easily suggest that I should be paid for them. As it is, you shut yourself up here or in the Isle of Wight—or vanish to Balmoral—while I do all the work and get nothing. It's most unfair."

"You just don't know what you're saying, Bertie. You are being cruel and unkind to a very lonely old woman. I have nothing to live for, and you know perfectly well that both Sir John Reid and Sir William Jenner have laid it down, once and for all, that my nerves cannot stand more than a few hours of London. God knows how I am going to get through Wednesday; I shall be an utter wreck. Besides, there is my grief."

"Very well, Mama. As always, when you take that line, there is nothing more to be said. But I have just been talking with Sir Henry and that is what I wanted to see you about."

"Sir Henry! Why on earth should you talk to him? You never asked me if you could. Sir Henry Ponsonby is my secretary, Sir Francis Knollys is yours. You should have asked permission."

"No, Mama. There is a certain point where your Civil List and my Parliamentary Grant are on common ground. Should not something, now and again, be transferred from one to the other? After all, you must have far more money than you need, while clearly I have not got enough. The solution is obvious."

"How often, Bertie, must I ask you not to talk nonsense?"

"Oh, well, that wasn't really quite what Sir Henry and I were chatting about."

"Now come, dear boy, what is it? You know I cannot bear uncertainty. It makes me ill. Say what you have to say, for heaven's sake."

"Well, Sir Henry and I were just running over some of my commitments, my expenditure and so on, and . . . er . . ."

"Oh, do get on, Bertie. You make me quite nervous—and don't fidget with your cuffs like that."

"No, Mama. Well, Sir Henry and I discussed the possibility of a loan."

"A loan—have you gone mad?"

"Not at all. The Hanoverian sovereigns almost lived on loans. The Hoares, Childs and Burdett-Coutts all made fortunes out of them."

"That was quite different. That was history, Bertie. Keep to the present."

"Well, as I told Sir Henry, I wasn't prepared to exploit my rank, to pawn my expectations, so to speak."

"I should think not, indeed."

"Well, we thought—Sir Henry and I, that is—we thought that perhaps in exchange for some real security, some intrinsic but valuable object that really belongs to us, not to the nation, that somebody—Sir Henry mentioned the Rothschilds—might fork out the cash."

"Might what?"

"Might lend the money, Mama."

"Oh, indeed; and where, pray, will you find such security? You've already sold half your stocks. You'll be borrowing the Crown itself next."

"No, Mama, but while Sir Henry and I were talking, we were looking all the time at this Tudor Tiara. He's brought it from the Tower this afternoon. It's in his room now."

"Bertie, you must have gone stark, staring mad—and Sir Henry too. I would expect it of you, but not of him—always such a nice man. Now, no more nonsense. It will soon be time for me to dress for dinner, and for you to remove that revolting American jacket. Do try to dress like a gentleman, Bertie."

"Yes, Mama; but about the Tudor Tiara—do tell me more."

"Very well, my boy. It's a wonderful story. That Tiara was one of the finest works of art in the Crystal Palace. Papa spent many hours upon the beautiful design. Presumably Sir Henry now has the original—not a mere replica."

"A replica, Mama! What on earth are you talking about? A replica, and in the Tower of London!"

"Oh, yes. There were two or three. Your Papa, Bertie, although nobody appreciated it, was a very fine Christian. He was not, thank God, a radical or a Liberal but he followed his Saviour in his belief that 'blessed are the poor'—provided of course that they are hardworking and respectable. He even built model dwellings alongside the Crystal Palace, well ventilated and with taps, just to show what might be done for the deserving masses. And so, when he created such a supreme work of art as this Tiara, he felt most strongly that the laboring people should see it—if only to bring a little beauty to those grimy streets where God had cast their lot. At least three replicas of the Tiara were made, one for Liverpool, one for Glasgow and one for somewhere else—I forget where."

"I never knew that, Mama."

"You never know *anything;* and don't interrupt. Yes, three replicas—not valuable, of course, but almost indistinguishable from the original. They were shown in the Industrial North in '51 and '52, and then one of them was shown in Manchester at the great Art Treasures Exhibition in '57. After that they were stored somewhere or other—probably at the Art College in South Kensington which Papa founded. But of course after '61 I was too crushed, too utterly bowed down, even to think of such earthly things."

"What an extraordinary story, Mama."

"Oh, yes, it has always been assumed that the real Tiara went to the Tower; but I believe that there may have been some sort of muddle at South Kensington—these Bohemian types, you know, so clever but so careless."

The Prince of Wales was now gazing at a picture near the ceiling. He was forty-six. He had spent most of those years learning how to get his own way. He had met defeat at the hands of his father. His mother was different; her affection, her selfishness and her arrogance could be exploited if one knew how. The stream of wrath could not be dammed; it might be diverted. It might, for instance, be diverted in the direction of Sir Henry Ponsonby. The Prince glanced at the clock. There was still time.

"Yes, a curious story, Mama, but of course Garrard's could tell us immediately whether the Tiara on Sir Henry's desk is the real article or not. If it is a replica I am surprised the people at the Tower have never said anything. . . . But there, perhaps it's not worth bothering about."

"Not worth bothering about! But, Bertie, the separate

stones may be worth millions. . . . Mary Tudor's earrings alone. Of course it's worth bothering about."

"Possibly, although Ponsonby says it's not yours anyway."

"Not mine! Not mine!" The royal pallor had flushed crimson. "Not mine! Sir Henry must have gone off his head. Of course it's mine. There is no question of it. It was my own Angel's work, my own Angel's idea. And nearly all the gems were our own, or else gifts—gifts to Papa personally. Of course it's mine! What on earth can Sir Henry mean? Disgraceful!"

The stream had been diverted. Bertie could now sit back and let it happen.

"I don't know what he was driving at, Mama. He said that the Tiara must belong to the nation, otherwise it wouldn't be in the Tower at all. He said that the Solicitor-General might object if we used it as security for a loan. I said that I was sure it was yours to do what you liked with. . . ."

The Queen's hand was hardly raised from the table—only the pudgy fingers. It was the command for silence.

"That will do. The matter must not be discussed. Sir Henry must be taught to mind his own business. Dear General Gray would never have behaved like this—not as long as my dear one was alive. And the Tiara too, with all its sad memories! It is too bad. Sir Henry should have kept quiet until I consulted him. The Tiara is ours, yours and mine, Bertie, to use as we like; the matter must never be referred to again. Speak to Sir Henry, Bertie, suavely, of course, but let him see that he has blundered. And now, Bertie, about this loan from the Rothschilds."

"Yes, Mama. I know that I am a very imperfect son, but I really do have great responsibilities. Alix and I do our very best to uphold the dignity of the Throne, you know, just as Papa would have wished."

"You are a dear, good boy, Bertie, if only people would try to understand your difficulties."

"I do my best, Mama, but it is all terribly expensive . . . all this keeping up appearances."

"Of course it is. Now about the Tiara. In view of Sir

Henry's unaccountable and indeed outrageous behavior, say no more to him about the loan. You understand that."

"Not a word, Mama. I quite agree."

"No, nor to your own Sir Francis Knollys. He also might have some absurd legalistic notions. I am sure he and Sir Henry talk us over. No, after the Jubilee I shall simply announce that I am keeping the Tiara at Windsor—that is all anybody need know. And then, Bertie, in due course, and with my permission, you may make use of it in a way which will have my approval."

"Oh, thank you, Mama. That will be simply wonderful!"

"Don't be foolish. It will be no more than good business. A great stroke for the House of Coburg. Papa would have approved and, what's more, so would Baron Stockmar. It will enable you to leave your affairs in apple-pie order for dear Eddy and for Georgie."

"That will be splendid, Mama. Parliament is always so mean to the younger generation. And Georgie is already so good and confiding. I wish I could say the same of Eddy. I am paying his debts, you know, as well as my own."

"Eddy is unspeakable. That is the cross you and Alix have to bear. Keep it secret at all costs—from the public, I mean—that is all that matters. It is Uncle Cumberland all over again. But still Eddy is your heir, and he and Georgie must both be provided for one day. But what were we talking about?"

"The Tudor Tiara, Mama. I shall take it to Natty or Ferdy at Tring, and then . . ."

"You will do no such thing. Baron Ferdinand would twist you round his little finger. I hope you don't think that *you* have any Jewish flair."

"Really, Mama, why should I?"

"Why shouldn't you—if you listen to gossip."

"Oh, you mean the old story about Grandma Coburg and the Jewish riding master at Rosenau . . . the year before Papa was born."

"That, Bertie, is the kind of cruel nonsense that people

in our position have to put up with—and in silence. Mind you, I'm not saying that Lieutenant von Hanstein wasn't very elegant and handsome—he was. But the Duchess Louise was a dear, sweet, faithful creature. It was all wicked lies. But who, may I ask, was so monstrous as to tell you this story?"

"Papa, Mama."

"Never. Never. He never spoke of it. When?"

"Oh, I was about fifteen, I think. Walking up Glen Gairn. We'd gone on ahead leaving the gillies and ponies behind. Papa tried to tell me how babies were born, as if I didn't know, and then he told me about his own birth, how everybody said horrible things about his mother so that she had to go and live in Paris. But tell me, Mama, have I any Jewish blood?"

"Certainly not, Bertie. What an idea! And that is why you must on no account deal with the Rothschilds yourself; they would get the better of you."

"Then what do you suggest, Mama?"

"Give the Tiara to Baron Hirsch."

"To Maurice . . . I didn't know that you had ever heard of him."

"Certainly I have. First, get Knollys or Esher to take the Tiara straight from here to Hirsch at Bath House. On no account, at any time, must you have it in your own possession. And none of this nonsense of house parties at Tring or Waddesdon, where you spend the night knocking on each other's bedroom doors. Hirsch must do the thing properly, negotiating with the House of Rothschild in their City offices, in a decent manner."

"You are very shrewd, Mama."

"I have had to be. Set Jew against Jew. The Rothschilds may be part of history but none of them is quite like Hirsch. Pure flair! It is difficult to invite him here—he's been blackballed at the Jockey Club—but he writes to me regularly."

"Writes to you—great heavens!"

"Don't exclaim like that, Bertie. Why shouldn't he write to me? He sends me a list every week, a list of your holdings on the Stock Exchange, and I check the prices in the *Times*. Hirsch has done very well for you, Bertie—copper, sugar and foreign railways."

"Oh, yes, Mama; but I had no idea you knew anything about such things."

"They interest me, and I have to keep an eye on everything. It was Hirsch, for instance, who, on my advice, told the French police to keep the moneylenders out of your hotel in Paris. You are a dear boy, Bertie, but you are not the man of the world you think you are. How could you be, brought up as you were?"

The Prince of Wales was silent. After nearly half a century Mama still left him dumb with amazement. Whenever he had one of these tête-à-tête talks with her she always began as his mother and ended up as the Queen. First he had thought he was in for a scolding, then she had turned right round and given him what he wanted—the Tiara—and in the process had assumed entire control of everything.

"And if the Tiara is only a replica, Mama?"

"It won't be—I know that—but if it is then the real thing will be safely locked up in a cellar in South Kensington, so that can soon be put right. But remember one thing, Bertie."

"Yes, Mama."

"Remember that the Tiara may not be worth a million—it sounds quite absurd to me—but remember that the twelve-pointed diamond stars, one on either side, are more than half its value."

"So Sir Henry tells me."

"Yes, they were Mary Tudor's wedding earrings—'Bloody Mary,' as they will call her. She was a most unsatisfactory woman. She had no babies and she was a Roman Catholic. However, she was firm with her bishops and her husband gave her some magnificent jewels. So remember, Bertie."

"Yes, Mama."

"And now I just have time to dress for dinner, while you have time to take off that jacket."

"Yes, Mama."

In the labyrinth of Windsor are many corridors. The

Great Corridor, or "the Corridor" as they call it, is a grander affair. Looking onto the quadrangle of the Upper Ward, it is often gloomy, but on this particular evening the tall mullion windows threw bars of sunlight across the carpet. The sunlight also gilded the rosettes of Wyatville's ceiling, causing them to sparkle like little suns in their dark coffering. The whole length of the Corridor was punctuated by white marble busts, each on its malachite pedestal—busts of those who had once strutted there—while in every embrasure was some object, curious, grotesque or sentimental. The total effect was majestic, rich and middle-class.

Across the Corridor, opposite these tall windows and these *objets d'art,* a long line of varnished doors, each in its crenelated frame, opened onto the whole suite of Private Apartments. Tomorrow the Queen would use the State Apartments, their grandeur more attuned to the Houses of Hanover and Coburg. Tonight, however, all was intimate and informal—or at least as informal as was ever possible. Except for the Maharajah and Maharani, everyone would know each other.

At nine o'clock two dinners would be served. At one of these, night after night, whenever guests could be fended off, the Queen would dine alone with the Princess Beatrice. This was known as the "Family Dinner." Its setting was the Green Drawing Room (with the smaller Winterhalters) and the Green Dining Room (with the smaller Landseers).

The second dinner—the "Household Dinner"—was much jollier. It was for the ladies and gentlemen in attendance, for secretaries and equerries, for physicians and clergy, for the suites of visiting sovereigns and for such guests—actors and actresses, for instance—as could hardly expect to dine with the Queen herself. There were two rules. The first: no laughter must be heard in the Green Dining Room next door—hence the suppressed giggles. The second: the two dinners must end at the same moment. As the Queen gobbled this was barely possible. When the major-domo tipped off the Household that the moment had come, the *bombe surprise* had to be left a

ruin upon the plates, the pineapples and nectarines untouched, while the gentlemen, having gulped down their
sweet sherry, sprinted to the distant water closet, only to
queue behind the Prime Minister or Mr. Balfour. Only
thereafter could the "Family" and the "Household" meet
democratically for coffee in the Corridor.

Tonight, her Jubilee so near, the Queen was in a hospi-
table and, indeed, expansive mood. There were twenty-
four covers at her table; there were to be ten courses
instead of the usual eight. She would be entertaining one
of her own tributary princes, a reminder to others that she
was Empress as well as Queen.

Half an hour to go before dinner, a quarter of an hour
before they would all assemble in the two drawing rooms.
Since everyone at Windsor must always be where they
were supposed to be, the Corridor and drawing rooms
were still completely deserted. The Caroline plate, the
Ming porcelain, the Nemours napery, the Albertine
epergnes, the Palatine candelabra, the Yorkist salt cellars,
the smilax and roses, the fruit from the glass houses, had
long since been set out with precision, but in all that vast
expanse of carpet, where the sun was now striking almost
horizontally through Venetian blinds, there was no human
soul. Not a soul except a single footman guarding the
Tiara, and he, since footmen have no souls, hardly
counted. An hour earlier and he would have worn tight
trousers and pomaded hair; now it was officially evening
and so his hair was powdered, his calves padded, his
stockings of silk.

He was alone. The silence was absolute. Then far away
at the end of the Corridor, there was the rustle of a satin
dress. This was unprecedented. It was barely half past
eight. It was against the rules. The soft step came nearer
until, ever so slightly, the man dared to slide his eyes
sideways. It was a black dress—black with a silver
thread. There was the brilliant white of the starched
widow's cap. The man stopped breathing. She lifted one
eyebrow—the Windsor signal of dismissal. He vanished.
Just ahead of her the Queen could see the onyx table. She
walked past her own Crimean medal—"Blessed Are the

Merciful" in diamonds; she walked past the assegai that had killed the Prince Imperial; she walked past General Gordon's Bible, eternally open at the 23rd Psalm. And then, at last, she was in front of the Tudor Tiara. Skerret had found the black velvet; Sir Henry had placed the thing to advantage. He had set up two gilded easels, one for the Holbein engravings, one for the Prince Consort's own drawings.

She looked at the Tiara very closely. It was thirty-six years since she had seen it in the Crystal Palace . . . how clearly she remembered it in its handsome glass case railed off and guarded by guardsmen. On that day, May 1, 1851, the Crystal Palace had been so packed with marvels, all, in a way, her precious Angel's doing, although for this one exhibit he was so particularly responsible. She had stood there, thirty-six years ago, on Albert's arm, with the sunshine pouring through the great glass roof. The old Duke of Wellington had been with them, and Sir Henry Cole and, for some reason, Mr. George Stephenson and, of course, Mr. Paxton, who had once been a common gardener's boy. And there, at her side, had been dear Vicky and poor, dear Alice, both in their sprigged muslin and their little pantalettes, with Bertie in a sailor suit (H.M.S. *Bellerophon*) and behind them little Arthur in his nurse's arms.

She had been so happy. Nobody ever understood how wonderful life had been . . . then. And now, more alone than ever in this vast, empty Corridor, she dabbed her old eyes. She put out her hand, her pudgy fingers, and touched the Tiara, caressing Mary Tudor's diamonds. She looked up to Heaven. . . . Albert was surely with her, watching her as he must always do. The tears were streaming down her furrowed cheeks. One might have heard her murmur—"Oh, Bertie, my dear, dearest son." She looked left and right—a carpeted desert of emptiness. She put both hands upon the Tiara. Ye Gods! What is Majesty going to do? In her long life she had faced many difficult moments, but none like this. The doors of all the drawing rooms and dining rooms were closed. There was nobody. She did what she had to do. Five minutes later, with a trembling hand but a firm step, she walked back to her little Gold Room.

A dowdy party with a little brilliance. . . . The Maharajah's coat of black watered silk—made by Poole—was buttoned to the throat; his turban was of dazzling white, making the untidy complexities of English shirt fronts and ties look foolish. The Maharani wore a sari of deep and mysterious black-green with little constellations of amethysts—like a starlit night seen in the dark waters of an Indian river, the current swirling as her body moved.

For all the other ladies, had they but known it, this was a fortunate year. The old crinoline had quite gone; there was now the sweeping tulip skirt, while neither the bustle nor the full sleeve had quite arrived. The bodice was cut to reveal so beautifully a good bust, the hair drawn up from the nape of the neck—lovely necks above lovely busts. Alas, however, this had been fully realized only by the Princess of Wales, her dress having been created by Worth, and by Lady Randolph Churchill, her dress created in a cottage at Blenheim. All the others, in deference to the Queen, wore untidy coiffures and perpetual mourning.

The presentations and hand kissings were smartly disposed of in the Green Drawing Room—or as smartly as possible. True, the Queen was disappointed to find that the Maharajah's equerry, so far from being a handsome oriental who might have said a word to the Munshi, her own dear Indian servant, was merely a rather dubious English officer called Pinkerton. True, the Maharajah had knelt on both knees, and when welcomed in Hindustani had replied, in an Etonian drawl, that he spoke no German. True, Lord Randolph had asked dear Eddy (known to the family as Eddy but to the world as the Duke of Clarence, or "Collar and Cuffs") when he would get his first command at sea. Eddy, who would never know port from starboard, only giggled. But at last all these strange creatures were got to table, a gold-and-scarlet footman behind each chair, and with the Munshi, in white-and-yellow satin, behind the Queen. The Queen knew perfectly well that at, say, Woburn or Hatfield, there would be two footmen behind each chair; Bertie and Alix could ape such aristocratic nonsense if they chose—she knew better.

Gloom and apprehension hung over both dinners. It had been rumored that there was to be a "treat." At its very worst this meant amateur theatricals, with the Munshi piqued at being put in the back row with the dressers, and the footmen piqued at his being there at all. At its dubious best a treat might be a brief lecture from a distinguished guest—a disastrous magic lantern was still remembered. This evening the lecture was to be by old Ponsonby himself. Nobody knew why.

If the Household Dinner was subdued, the Family Dinner was more so. Only those who enjoyed hearing the Queen squash all attempts to make small talk bigger got any fun. The Maharajah's comparison of the Irish Question with the Buddhist-Hindu problem was strangled at birth: "If only the people of India, Maharajah, would join the Church of England, like everybody else, life would be simpler." Bertie, in return for his riposte that since Mama was an Anglican at Windsor and a Presbyterian at Balmoral, she should be a Catholic in Dublin, was told not to talk such wicked nonsense. When Arthur Balfour quietly asked his uncle, the Prime Minister, about an appointment to the See of Durham, he was told down the length of the table that "Durham Cathedral always looks so well from the railway—one of the joys of our journey to Deeside." The real difficulty, however—what to do about the Duke of Clarence—had been neatly solved in advance; Eddy was placed between Lady Esher, who didn't matter, and the Maharani's lady in attendance, Miss Nummuggar, who spoke no English. Bertie, to his fury, had been placed between two ladies who, palpably, offered no temptation to flirtation.

People's thoughts, however, are more fascinating than their words—the thoughts of these twenty-four peculiar minds. His Royal Highness the Maharajah of Kashgar, on the Queen's right, was wondering whether there were any jewels in this ghastly place better than his own—and how

DINNER AT WINDSOR, JUNE 19, 1887

H.M. the Queen

H.R.H. the Maharajah of Kashgar	H.M. King Christian of Denmark
H.R.H. the Princess of Wales	H.R.H. the Maharani of Kashgar
The Very Rev. Randall Davidson	The Marquis of Salisbury
Lady Jane Ely	Lady Ponsonby
Colonel Pinkerton	H.R.H. the Prince of Wales
Lady Randolph Churchill	Mrs. Randall Davidson
Mr. Arthur Balfour	H.R.H. Prince George
Lady Esher	H.M. Queen Louise of Denmark
H.R.H. the Duke of Clarence (Eddy)	Lord Randolph Churchill
Miss Nummuggar	The Marchioness of Salisbury
Lord Esher	Sir Henry Ponsonby

H.R.H. the Princess Beatrice of Battenberg

to get hold of them. Her Royal Highness the Princess of Wales, next to him, wondered who would be the real hostess at Marlborough House on Thursday, and then began to dream about the magnolias in Copenhagen. . . . The Very Reverend Randall Davidson, Dean of Windsor, was wondering why he had not been asked to say grace; he had found a charming one in an old Book of Hours, and was now feeling hurt. Lady Jane Ely was wondering whether the Queen might not make a fool of herself by wearing this idiotic Tiara, and rather hoping she would—she had been so snappy lately. Colonel Pinkerton was wondering what he was going to get out of all this, and whether or not he could double-cross the Maharajah in the matter of jewels. Lady Randolph Churchill, apart from wondering, as always, how on earth she had ever landed herself with this gang, was jealous of the Maharani; Alix being, after all, no more than pretty, Jennie Churchill expected as of right to be the only beautiful woman at Windsor. Mr. Arthur Balfour, while looking clever, was wondering how to improve his forehand drive at tennis. Lady Esher, four months gone, was wondering whether the Queen would notice—the crinoline had had its advantages. Eddy, with his mouth open, was wondering how to pay his bills at Willis's—all those private rooms for entertaining naval cadets; if only he had something to borrow on. Miss Nummuggar was wondering whether this mixing of the sexes at dinner, which she had so dreaded, was after all so dangerous—the men were so ugly; and whether or not the Munshi might be an untouchable in disguise—which he was. Lord Esher was wondering whether he might not still be the Prince of Wales's executor when the Prince died—he would hardly make old bones—and if so whether he should not then burn all the papers. Her Royal Highness the Princess Beatrice was wondering why Mama was in one of her moods: it was not her bowels and so at the moment it must be Bertie; later, after red beef and ice cream washed down with iced water, it would be indigestion. Sir Henry Ponsonby was wondering for the tenth time what had

happened to Black Beauty that afternoon at the station.
The Marchioness of Salisbury was wondering whether to
accept Mr. Oscar Wilde's invitation to write for a Society
magazine. Lord Randolph Churchill was wondering why
they did not give medical certificates to prostitutes in
London as they did in Paris. Her Majesty Queen Louise
of Denmark was wondering whether dear Alix was really
past childbearing or whether it was all Bertie's fault, and
why dear Alix had never had her share of the Family
jewelry. His Royal Highness Prince George was not wondering anything very much—and never would. Mrs. Randall Davidson was wondering whether to have gas put
into the Deanery or whether the vacancy at Canterbury
might not come soon—cancer was so unpredictable. His
Royal Highness the Prince of Wales was wondering why he
should have to eat his mother's beef and mutton when he
might have been at home enjoying grilled oysters followed
by ortolans in brandy or quails *à la Greque,* or both.
Lady Ponsonby was wondering why on earth the Queen
should send Henry all the way to the Tower of London
for the Tudor Tiara, when all the time it was upstairs,
locked up in Albert's bedroom, the famous Blue Room.
The Marquis of Salisbury was wondering whether he
could ever get new blood into this awful family—all so
unmentionable, so difficult. Her Royal Highness the Maharani of Kashgar was wondering whether the Queen
knew that one could see the cleft at the top of the Princess
of Wales's bosom, and would be as shocked as she was.
His Majesty King Christian of Denmark was wondering
why his spies were so useless; he had learned more about
the Queen and Bismarck in three days at Windsor than
anyone had told him in a year; they must all be corrupt—
corrupted by the Queen's Prussian relations.

And her Majesty the Queen . . . the Queen was just
wondering and wondering; she hardly noticed what was
going on round her; crouched over her plate she might
now and again show the whites of her eyes, or even
speak, but she knew the whole business by heart, and had
for years and years. So she just went on wondering and
plotting . . . wondering, and thinking about dear, dear

Bertie and the Tiara, and Dizzy and John Brown and the dear Munshi . . . whom everybody seemed to dislike.

Only when coffee was served, only when the Household and the Family had assembled in the Corridor, could Windsor enjoy its brief democracy. In the Dining Room the Queen had taken a peach; she would not eat it, but the signal had been given. Everyone knew that no matter what remained on their plates or in their glasses they had just ten minutes. At the end of ten minutes they must be flattened against the walls of the Corridor while large baroque chairs were set for majesties and highnesses. A few more presentations might be made, a few more words said about the weather or the horses . . . and then it was time for coffee and for the "treat."

It was all very odd, set in all that delicate and spiky Gothic—twenty-four people from the Queen's dinner, thirty-eight from the Household, including six tall and sinister gentlemen from the Maharajah's suite, all in zebra-striped turbans, together with "the Maharani's Secretary," a twittering little eunuch in pince-nez. The scene was animated, bejeweled, bourgeois and ridiculous.

The Prince of Wales, who had had the courage to bring his brandy glass from the Dining Room, still stood in the doorway, looking with fascinated cynicism at all these orientals—his mother's subjects—who could so easily buy him out. He looked also upon these giggling, gossiping English ladies—rusty black, ill-fitting corsets and ill-used curling tongs—only to feel a vast yearning for a slaughter of birds at Sandringham, an afternoon at Newmarket, a breezy day at Cowes, or, best of all, a great ball at Marlborough House, with the carriages lining the Mall, a summer night heavy with the scent of banked orchids, the scarlet marquee on the lawn, gorgeous uniforms, ribbons and stars, rich Jews and beautiful women, all chic, opulent, subtly perfumed, wicked and delectable . . . and all turning and turning slowly in the Mandela Waltz. And even that, he said to himself, was nothing to what he might do one day. . . . One day he would take back Hampton Court as a palace: an English Versailles. He would need the diamonds and he would need the Rothschilds.

Why, here at Windsor the only smart women in the whole room were his own Alix and Lady Randolph; the only seductive one, the Maharani. Alix wore an astonishing confection—coffee-colored satin, no gems or bows—with a great swirling skirt below a tight bust, and a coiffure that was an André masterpiece. Could it really be that only a couple of hours ago he had told Ponsonby that she had no extravagances? Oh, well, Ponsonby probably hadn't believed him anyway, and it didn't matter now that Mama was giving him the Tiara.

He turned his bloodshot eyes from his own wife to Lady Randolph. He could only just believe that Jeanette Jerome had been the loveliest girl on Long Island. She had given Randolph two sons, but then Randolph was easily pleased; she was not the Prince's type, not at this stage of his life, not in this mood. Now the Maharani was quite a different matter. She was not only beautiful and serene; in her oriental way she was chic. If the toilette of the Princess of Wales could be outshone anywhere in England that night, it might well be by that particular sari. At dinner he had thought of the sari as being like stars reflected in a dark river; now he saw it as the starry sky itself, so that as the Maharani walked it was as if clouds were blowing across the constellations. Also it was very subtly and surprisingly made, so that just now and again one glimpsed an emerald corsage—no more than glimpsed. And yet, only a few moments ago—oh, God!—he had heard his mother call it "native costume"!

He sipped his brandy from his big balloon glass. Over the rim he could watch the Maharani almost unnoticed. She was not only beautiful and serene. She was dark, mysterious and indefinable. Oddly enough, in all his forty-six years he had never, not even in India, considered an oriental woman; not seriously, that is, not as a proposition for the bedroom. Such a thing, he now reflected, would surely have panache, piquancy, novelty, daring, cachet . . . or wouldn't it? Probably it just "wouldn't do." There was the Indian army to think of, there was Mama, the position

of the Viceroy and of the Empire. Oh, God, no, it would
never do! In any case the wives of a Maharajah (there
were three more at Claridge's in the guise of "aunts")
were surely closely guarded day and night. Perhaps they
sold their wives in Kashgar, sold them for diamonds, for
instance. What nonsense! He was hot with desire but
managed to shrug his shoulders, dismissing a dream to
turn his gaze upon the Prime Minister.

The Marquis of Salisbury had failed to bring his brandy from the Dining Room: "You won't need your glass,
Prime Minister; we're having coffee now." He was content, however, to dominate the whole scene with his great
domelike head—portentous insignia of the Cecils. His
head made him look wise when he was not even thinking.
His nephew, on the other hand, was exercising his vivid
charms upon the Princess of Wales. She was not wasted
upon him—Mr. Balfour had written a treatise upon beauty; it was only that he was wasted upon her.

Once again the Prince's eyes moved above the rim of
his glass—to the Tiara. He frowned. Ponsonby had set it
well upon its black cushion. The purple curtains had now
been pulled behind it, the gaseliers had been lit; and yet
somehow the Tiara seemed to lack a little of the luster it
had had in Ponsonby's office two hours ago. It didn't
matter . . . Garrard's would give a valuation and then the
Prince would be able to buy all the things he loved, able
to buy them for years to come—as long as Mama was
alive; after that the Rothschilds would be unnecessary.

Was it true, he wondered, that the Maharajah was
really a connoisseur of gems? All these Indian princes had
masses of gems but that didn't mean that they understood
them. The Maharajah, handsome devil, was now looking
very sulky but also smug. He was sulking because at
dinner he had three times—oh, so casually—mentioned
the Order of the Garter, and three times—oh, so diplomat-
ically—it had been explained to him that it was a reli-
gious order given only to Christian sovereigns . . . tomorrow he might like to see the Chapel. That was nonsense.
He knew perfectly well, everyone knew, that after the
Crimea the Garter had been given to the Sultan; he was

therefore enraged. The veins stood out upon his forehead, his eyes bulged. He had been insulted. He craved
revenge. The Prince of Wales was much amused.

Sulkiness and smugness, however, always possessed the
Maharajah when he was in England. They had possessed
him at Eton where he had been baited by snotty little
boys. His loathing of the West had been ingrained in him
at the age of twelve. He was, therefore, eaten up with
desire for revenge. He was smug because he knew that
the single ruby in his turban was worth more than that
absurd Tiara. Not that he was contemptuous of the Tiara;
he was merely realistic. The setting was an outrage; he
would melt it down to make rings for his retainers. But
the gems . . . ah, yes, the gems; some of them, the
diamond stars for instance, he would be glad to add to his
collection.

The Maharajah beckoned to his aide-de-camp, Colonel
Pinkerton. The Prince lowered his brandy glass. He was
no longer amused. He was alert. Only yesterday he had
had a note from the India Office—"Very Secret." While
not wishing to alarm the Queen, the Permanent Secretary
thought that His Royal Highness should know that Colonel Pinkerton had been cashiered in '84; he had almost
certainly robbed the mess at Darjeeling, and by the stan-
dards becoming to an officer and a gentleman should long
ago have blown out his brains. Pinkerton now leaped to
his master's side. The Maharajah whispered fiercely:

"Pinkerton."

"Your Highness."

"I would like that Tiara in my baggage—see to it."

"Your Highness, I understand perfectly."

The Maharajah now elbowed his way to the onyx
table. He looked more closely at the fountain of jewels
upon the velvet cushion, and then closer still until his
bulging eyes almost touched the diamonds. His expression
changed. He held up his hands in amazement. Surprise,
shock and puzzlement chased themselves across his satur-
nine face. He glanced behind him. They were busy chattering, had hardly noticed him. The Queen's sight was
appalling. The Prince's eyes seemed to be upon him—

only to be hurriedly withdrawn. Again he beckoned to his aide-de-camp.

"Pinkerton."

"Your Highness."

"I do not want the Tiara—trash!"

"Your Highness, I understand perfectly."

The Prince was now devoured by curiosity. What was all this whispering? He must know. The detectives must be warned that something was in the wind, Heaven knows what. There was a voice at his elbow, that of his difficult and unspeakable heir.

"P-papa."

"Eddy—how very nice of you to address me. I wasn't sure that we were on speaking terms."

"No, P-papa, p-please. That is how your father used to scold you . . . p-please, P-papa."

"Very well, Eddy; but when you do dine here with Grandmama—and we none of us enjoy it—do try to behave like a gentleman; try to say something to those next to you at dinner."

"That Indian woman spoke no English."

"There were others around you. But what is it?"

"This T-tiara, P-papa."

The Prince glanced sharply at his son.

"The Tiara—what has that got to do with you?"

"Whose is it?"

"Really, Eddy, what an extraordinary question! What put that into your head?"

"I only wondered. Well, P-papa, who d-does it b-belong to?"

"If you must know, it belongs to the Family, but why?"

"To G-grandmama, then to you, then m-me."

"What are you driving at, Eddy? Speak up for heaven's sake."

"I'm in a fix, P-papa."

"We all know that. It's entirely your own fault and you know that you have to be punished for it. Frankly, Eddy, we just don't know how to deal with you. A world tour might not be so bad, my boy. At least it would get you away from your ghastly friends into the more wholesome atmosphere of a naval wardroom."

"That's all you know about the Navy, P-papa. But this, T-tiara, P-papa, couldn't we make use of it somehow? We're b-both in the same b-boat. I need c-cash and you need c-cash. We could p-pawn it and split the takings . . . and live happy ever after. G-grandmama need never know."

"This is quite enough of your impertinence, Eddy. You forget yourself! You are breaking your mother's heart as it is . . . don't make things worse. That is enough!"

"Very well, P-papa, then I must l-look after myself."

The footmen were serving coffee. The Queen refused it; it was easier to control a situation when not encumbered by a cup and saucer. Everyone else was allowed exactly five minutes to gulp down the tepid liquid in the golden cups from Portugal. Normally the company would disperse to other rooms—to whist or backgammon or to turn idly the pages of albums until, terrified to yawn, they could no longer keep their eyes open. This, however, was not a normal evening. There was the "treat." It had to be gone through. The Queen liked "treats."

Her Majesty spoke to Lady Ely.

"Jane dear, will you please tell someone to ask Bandmaster Fane to silence his men, and to thank him. The excerpts from the Savoy operettas were most entertaining."

The Queen turned to Lady Cadogan.

"Sarah dear, will you please ask Princess Beatrice to tell someone to tell the major-domo that we want silence."

These messages having been duly passed up and down the ranks, and Coldstream Guards laid down their instruments in the middle of a bar, the major-domo tapped the floor with his staff . . . and there was silence.

"Now, Beatrice, say your piece, dear."

"Yes, Mama. Majesties, highnesses, may it please you; lords, ladies and gentlemen: you may know that tomorrow night, at a great family dinner party in the Waterloo Chamber, on the eve of her Jubilee, Her Majesty will wear this famous Tiara, created by my beloved papa, but never worn before. Here it is on the onyx table. Sir Henry Ponsonby has kindly undertaken to tell us its curious history."

Nobody was sure whether or not to clap; "Papa" having been mentioned, better not. The Prince of Wales, still aloof at the back of the crowd, emptied his glass. He was still watching the Maharajah—now a most extraordinary sight, walking to and fro in a frenzy, beating his breast and wringing his hands. He kept whispering to Pinkerton until a cough from the Queen told him that he was making himself conspicuous. The Prince made a sudden decision. Quietly, through the dining rooms, he slipped away. His absence might not be noticed for half an hour. . . . Ponsonby could be long-winded.

Sir Henry knew what was expected of him—or so he thought. He began solemnly with a few words about the Prince Consort. He explained how Albert, when he first came to England in 1840, had begun to catalogue the royal possessions, and had then gradually brought together the scattered jewels of the Tudor and Stuart epochs. He explained how, ten years later, for the Great Exhibition of 1851, the Prince had had the finest of the gems set in this marvelous Tiara, made to his own design. And here, on the easel, were the Prince's very own drawings, masterpieces of meticulous draftsmanship. There was, at this point, a dab of the royal handkerchief, also a suspicion of a wink from Arthur Balfour to Randolph Churchill.

Sir Henry now got down to business. He actually touched the great pearl, hanging, so to speak, on the forehead of the Tiara. Then he pointed to it on the Hatfield portrait of Elizabeth. "The reality is here on the Tiara; its simulation by Holbein's brush is something that you, Mr. Prime Minister, may see every day upon the wall of your home." The Marquis of Salisbury woke up in order to nod.

As for the jewels of Mary Queen of Scots, went on Sir Henry, they had been a great problem. When she came to England as a prisoner, this wanton creature left a vast quantity of French jewelry behind her at Holyrood, and all

this, in due course, came to us with the accession of her
son, James I. This big ruby, however—and here Sir
Henry placed his finger upon the apex of the Tiara—was
more romantic. It had been the lid of the locket within
which Mary of Scotland had kept the sacramental wafer
smuggled to her by the Pope; probably, therefore, it was
secreted in her bosom when the axe fell. It was found in
the Vatican Treasury in 1850 and, thanks to Cardinal
Wiseman, restored to the English Crown.

"And now," went on Sir Henry, "I turn to the *pièce de
résistance,* the *bonne bouche* of the Tiara, to those gems
which are said to be half its value. You will all have
noticed these two magnificent clusters of diamonds . . ."
heads were craned forward ". . . these twelve-pointed
stars, one on each side so as to flank the face of the
wearer. You will all remember that Mary Tudor, who
bears such an unfortunate sobriquet, also contracted an
unfortunate marriage. On the eve of that marriage—it
was in Winchester Cathedral—the bridegroom, destined
to be our foe at the time of the Armada, gave his bride
these superb diamonds in the form of earrings. They had
come to Europe in a Spanish treasure ship, one of those
Drake missed . . ." slight laughter ". . . and after Mary's
death disappeared completely. It was presumed that they
had found their way back to Spain. Anyway, three hundred years later, among the many gifts showered upon the
Duke of Wellington after the Peninsular War were the
diamond earrings. In 1851 the old Iron Duke gave them
to the Prince Consort that they might be the glory of the
Tiara. So you see a strange tale will complete itself tomorrow night when Your Majesty, beneath Lawrence's portrait of Wellington in the Waterloo Chamber, will wear
this Tiara in which Bloody Mary's Earrings are so mag-
nificently set. I now turn to . . ."

"Thank you, Sir Henry—most instructive. That will be
enough."

Sir Henry Ponsonby was startled. He had been interrupted. He had been cut off in full flood. Had he gone on
too long? Had he given offense? He still had much to say
about Anne of Cleves' emeralds, about the seed pearls

from Henry VIII's gloves, about Sir Francis Bacon's shoe
buckles, not to mention Lady Jane Gray's stomacher. He
was startled. He was also hurt.

"Thank you, Sir Henry; most instructive and—er—
romantic."

"I trust, ma'am, that I have not tried your patience."

"Not at all, Sir Henry; most instructive, if not very
edifying."

"No, ma'am?"

"No. Maybe I am prejudiced. I always say that I am a
Stuart. I have never held with these Tudors . . . a thoroughly bad lot."

"Really, ma'am . . . I don't see . . ."

"No, Sir Henry, there can be no two opinions. A bad
lot. Of course things are different now; but they knew
perfectly well they were doing wrong. And moreover, Sir
Henry, I have never liked this vulgar way of referring to
Mary Tudor. I know that she was a Roman Catholic—
that would never be allowed now—and that she burnt
people alive. That too would not be allowed today—
more's the pity. But, after all, she was a queen. . . .
Come, Beatrice dear, it is after eleven."

Everyone waited until the Queen and the Princess had
disappeared. The other royals followed smartly, knowing
exactly where they would find Bertie, baccarat and brandy. Then came the stampede of the Household to such
corners of the vast castle as they could each call their
own—to gossip and cocoa, or to French yellowbacks. The
Corridor, gaseliers still blazing, remained silent and almost deserted—deserted save for one figure. Tall, wil-
lowy, gangling, His Royal Highness the Duke of
Clarence—dear, unspeakable Eddy—stood by the onyx
table. The lower lip was pendulous. He blinked and muttered.

"I must l-look after myself, must I? I'm in a b-bloody
fix. They say I'm n-no use, that I m-must be p-punished.
I'll show them. I'm a man. I d-damn well will look after
myself. I will—so there!"

At the far end of the Corridor, very quietly, someone
had opened one of the folding doors—ever so slightly. A

head appeared; a black face beneath a white turban. It was the Maharajah. It vanished. Eddy had hardly recovered from the shock when there was a sound behind him. He whirled round. A door had opened—the door to one of the dining rooms. A head appeared; a black face beneath a yellow turban. It was the Munshi. The color drained from Eddy's face. His choker collar almost strangled him. His long cuffs shot out from the gold-laced sleeves. His hands twitched even more than usual. His face twitched. He took a step toward the onyx table and toward the Tiara, which, by some unwonted oversight, Sir Henry Ponsonby had left unguarded.

4

Beatrice

Back in his office, Sir Henry Ponsonby flopped into one armchair, his wife into another.

"Well, Mary, what do you make of that? I had only been talking for five minutes. It was damned rude."

"But, my darling, you've been treated like that for twenty years. What are you fussing about? It's nothing new."

"This is different. Something has upset her. . . ."

"It often does."

"Yes, Mary, she's upset every day of her life; but she always tells me what it is. She tells me before anyone, even before Beatrice. This time she hasn't said a word. What is it? It can't have been the few 'bloodys' that were bandied about—surely?"

"Of course not. That was her excuse. She's not squeamish. The public may think so, but you and I know better. After all, the older generation were the most foul-mouthed gang in Europe. Hasn't it ever struck you, Henry, that although advanced people are now talking so oddly about 'the Victorian Age,' the Queen is not particularly Victorian? No, no, it wasn't the 'bloodys.' As you say, she's upset. She has committed herself to this vulgar Tiara and now, for some reason, wants to get out of it, doesn't want it talked about."

"But she could just change her mind—wear one of her little diadems, and nobody would say a word. No, something has upset her. She hardly spoke to the Maharajah at dinner, except to snub him. And now I—I, of all people— am not in her confidence. I don't like it, Mary."

"Henry, my darling, you may be a model royal secretary, but what a good thing you never went into business."

"No doubt—but why?"

"Can't you see, dear, that the Tiara itself is the thing they are all worried about. Not only the Queen. Bertie has none of what the newspapers call his 'usual bonhomie.' Randolph told him a dirty story and he never even smiled. Beatrice is like a cat on hot bricks, and even poor Eddy seems aware of his surroundings."

"But why, why?"

"You're being a little obtuse, Henry. Don't you see there's a million pounds' worth of hideous jewels lying there on that hideous onyx table. Everything in the place is catalogued and labeled—Albert saw to that—but this is a new-found wonder, a windfall, and all they want to know is to whom it belongs—to the Queen, to Bertie, to Eddy? . . . Even the Denmarks would like it for Alix one day. The Maharajah I wouldn't trust an inch, and even dear Beatrice must be wondering."

"Beatrice . . . really, my love!"

"Why not? If the Tiara belongs to the Crown—the Crown, that is, as an institution—then in due course it goes to Bertie and after that to Eddy. If, on the other hand, it belongs to the Queen personally, under Albert's will, then she can pawn it, sell it, leave it to Beatrice—the comfort of her old age—or anything she damned well likes. It's rather like the palaces: they belong to the Crown, whereas Balmoral is her own private property— all the difference in the world. And when the private property is worth a million pounds and is also in highly portable form . . . well! Anyway, I suppose Bertie is the most interested person—the bankrupt heir. He at least must want to know whether the Tiara will ever be his or not . . . if so he could borrow on it now, you know."

"But, good God, Mary, what has made you think of all that?"

"It's only too obvious, isn't it?"

"But, Mary, Bertie came into this room as soon as I was back from the Tower this afternoon, and asked me that very question. Sometimes I think, my love, that you must be the cleverest woman in the world."

"No, Henry, I'm not clever but I'm always right. Mark my words: Bertie has seen you already; *she* will be after you in the morning."

"But again, why?"

"Why? Because Bertie is head over heels in debt and Parliament won't give him a bean. When Beatrice married last year she got only an extra ten thousand on the grounds that she was still going to live at Windsor, and so, naturally, her Henry blues it, popping over to visit various Battenbergs and so on. He's human; you can't expect him to spend the whole of his life with mother-in-law. I repeat, darling, there's a million pounds, or more, going begging, and they're all buzzing, to say the least, with curiosity."

"But why? Damn it all, they're rich. Oh, I know their incomes aren't what people imagine; but the State—Office of Works, Office of Woods and Forests, Commissioners for Crown Lands and so on—pays for everything. They don't *have* to have places like Balmoral and Sandringham . . . but they do . . . and then grumble."

"But, Henry, they just don't see it like that. What they do see is half a dozen of their subjects—the big dukes, Sutherland, Bedford, Devonshire and the rest—living more royally than themselves and . . ."

"But that is quite different, Mary. The dukes are landed

aristocrats, the royals are middle-class—like you and me. You have only to imagine a Cecil or a Cavendish on the throne to realize what a middle-class crowd the royals are . . ."

"Of course; but that's just what hurts. Don't you see, Henry, that poor Bertie goes over to Germany, lives in baroque palaces with his awful relatives, or takes a whole hotel at Marienbad, and then comes home to complain about his tailor's bill? They're all quite absurd, the whole lot of them; but one does see that a million pounds is not to be sneezed at. Hence the burning issue: is the Tiara theirs or not?"

"Of course it's not theirs, Mary; don't be silly."

"Well then, whose is it? It must belong to somebody."

"It's—it's—oh, well, I suppose it's part of the Crown Jewels."

"The Regalia?"

"Well, no, not exactly . . . but it has been kept in the Tower of London, hasn't it? . . . with all the other junk?"

"For less than forty years. Now, come, Henry my darling, you just don't know whose it is, do you? Now I do. I have all the time in the world. I spent the morning in the library with that nice Herr Mütter. Now look: Albert got some of the gems from foreign courts, others he cadged from old Catholic families—Arundels, Talbots, Throckmortons and the rest. The commissioners for the Great Exhibition paid for the setting as a kind of gesture to Albert and his Crystal Palace. They never claimed the Tiara and never can."

"Then that doesn't get us any further. Did you discover anything else from your nice Herr Mütter?"

"Of course. When the Great Exhibition closed Albert had the thing sent to the Tower—a clear implication that it was on trust for the nation . . . yes, an implication; but it was never legally consigned to anyone. The Constable of the Tower, considering the august source from which he received the Tiara, probably never checked either its ownership or its value. If it was really Albert's private property it almost certainly now belongs to the Queen, although his executors never said so; equally it could be argued that he meant it to belong to the nation. So, either way, my dear Henry, for any member of the family to sell it or even pawn it might be illegal and would certainly be scandalous; for the Queen, with all the Albertine associations, it would certainly be blasphemy . . . unless of course . . . unless . . ."

"Well . . . unless what, dear?"

"No. That's unthinkable."

"I said—unless what, dear?"

"Well, you see, Henry, several replicas were made—for the provincial galleries, I suppose—and the Queen kept one of these for herself, or so she said."

"Now what are you driving at, Mary?"

"Well, it's just possible, isn't it, that for her 'Angel's' sake she sent a replica to the Tower, and that the original, the real Tiara, is upstairs in Albert's bedroom, the Blue Room, in mothballs, so to speak, with all his clothes. It would be just like her."

"Good God! But the Tower would know."

"No. As I said, they might not check, and if they did would never dare to say anything."

"All right. But you must be wrong. If the real Tiara, Bloody Mary's Earrings and all, is in the Blue Room, what on earth was the point of my journey to London today? She's got the Tiara and she can wear it tomorrow night."

"My dear Henry, you really are rather simple sometimes. You know perfectly well, even if you haven't been there for years, that the Blue Room is untouchable . . . that the wreath still lies on the pillow, that the clean linen is laid out every morning, the nightdress placed on the bed every evening, that everything must remain exactly as it was on that night of '61. Nothing, nothing must ever be touched—least of all the Tiara, locked up in that huge wardrobe."

"Hm!"

"And pray, my love, what does that mean?"

"Nothing, my dear, nothing . . . only that our Bertie, for one, may have different ideas."

"Well, I hope *you* didn't put them into his head."

"Of course not, my love, of course not."

"If you did, and there was a scandal, he would say it was all your fault—that he only took advice."

"Oh, well, sooner or later the matter will have to be settled. I envisage months of correspondence with Garrard's and with the Solicitor-General. I wish the damned thing could have been left, forgotten, in its glass case in the Tower."

"Henry, my darling, you are not going to be allowed ever to forget it again. The hunt is up. Whatever the public may think, nobody, you know, has ever really thought of trying to steal the Crown and Scepter; it's just not practical. But this is different. The Tiara is fair game and far too many people know about it—the Royal Family, servants, policemen, Beefeaters, railwaymen, the Maharajah, Colonel Pinkerton, Lord Randolph, the Munshi, Miss Nummuggar, Eddy . . . not to mention the carriage footman called Smith and the young man in the ginger suit—the one with the carpet bags. . . ."

Sir Henry leaped from his chair. He stood looking right down on his wife. He was even trembling a little.

"Ye gods, Mary, what in heaven's name are you getting at?"

"Well, Henry, my experience of human nature tells me that when a strange character says that his name is Smith he is probably lying."

"Oh, don't be so ridiculous. The coachman, Macdonald, must have seen him and known him."

"You said that you never saw the coachman's face, that he never got down from the box. . . . I expect his name was Jones. And all that nonsense about Smith having been in service with Lord Iddsleigh—a man whose death has just been in every newspaper—all a little too obvious, don't you think?"

"My dear Mary, you may be very clever, but this is a bit much. And the boy in the ginger suit, what about him?"

"What indeed? Remember that your train was held thirty minutes for you at Paddington. The next one was not for three-quarters of an hour—I looked it up in Bradshaw while Suzanne was doing my hair for dinner. 'Ginger suit' boarded the train when you did. Why? He was much too late for that train, much too early for the next. Oh, my Henry, do try to think! And then at Windsor he must have nipped out of the train in a flash—run down the platform while you were waiting for the Station Master to let you out. 'Ginger suit' was already holding Black Beauty's head when you and Philpotts came out of the station . . . dear old Black Beauty, steady as a rock."

"But, my love, this may be all very ingenious but it's also great nonsense, and you know it. I never once lost sight of that hat box from the moment when I took it from the table in Field Marshal Wilson's library . . ."

"After a very good brandy . . ."

". . . until I carried it into this room myself."

"Didn't you, Henry, didn't you? . . . Just think, my love, and then think again."

"Oh, well, if you must . . . There was a call of nature, inevitably; but the thing was always in good hands. Anyway, what are we talking about? The Tudor Tiara, real or replica, is here in the Castle safe and sound—and that is all there is to it. Whether Bertie raises money on it or not is an entirely different matter."

"So it would seem."

"Really, my love, I simply don't understand you."

"Well, he can't raise money on a replica, can he? Anyway, we shall see. But now it's time for bed. Be off with you, back to the Corridor, and take that hideous thing to the strong room. I'll wait here, then we can walk home across the courtyard to get some air."

The Corridor was deserted, the Tiara unguarded. Sir Henry felt a twinge of guilt—he and Mary had talked too long. Only one of the big gaseliers was now burning. The curtains had been drawn back so that one could see the terrace bathed in moonlight. Sir Henry Ponsonby's steps echoed strangely in this emptiness. He took the Tiara in both hands, clutching it to his shirt front. He listened. Away in the darkness at the far end two people were talking, whispering. Sir Henry walked back to the great stair. His curiosity, at this point, got the better of him. Still clutching the Tiara, he climbed to an upper landing from where he could look down upon the door from the Corridor. In a few moments he heard steps upon the marble. It was the Maharajah of Kashgar and the Princess Beatrice. They stood leaning on the balustrade.

"Yes, it's gone now, Maharajah. I expect Sir Henry Ponsonby, Mama's Secretary, has taken it to the strong room. . . . But what you have been telling me is terribly serious—quite too shocking."

"Your Royal Highness must forgive me. I had to speak to someone. Naturally I did not wish to trouble the Queen. The Prince of Wales is now—er—otherwise engaged, I understand. So I ventured . . ."

"You were quite right, Maharajah. Mama must know nothing of this until after the Jubilee. She would be frantic. You see, Maharajah, apart from the value of the Tiara, it is intimately associated with my father, and for Mama that means . . ."

"Your Highness need say no more. I understand perfectly. But of course you will tell her one day."

"I hope not. These things upset her so. If our own detectives or the people at the Tower can solve the problem, then she need never know."

"Quite, quite. I do see that. But, Your Royal Highness, I would like Her Majesty to know that I have done her this small service. Perhaps in return . . . she is so generous, so kind . . . and that lovely blue ribbon . . . the Garter, I mean . . . a little something between fellow sovereigns . . . a memento of my visit to Windsor."

The Princess, so impeccably trained, bowed and changed the subject; the Maharajah was meant to know that he had made a mistake.

"I must not detain you, Maharajah. Mama is now with her dressers, but she likes me to be there, in the Blue Room, when she says her prayers. You are certain you are right about the Tiara?"

"Oh, yes, Highness. Otherwise I would not have spoken. I had no magnifying glass but of the big pearl I am almost certain. Of the diamond stars on each side, the famous earrings, I am absolutely certain. There can be no doubt at all. Wonderful workmanship but mere paste, mere paste—nothing more."

"I see. Then we must speak of it again tomorrow. Meanwhile, on your honor, Maharajah, not a word to anyone, I beg you. Good night, sire."

"Your Royal Highness, good night."

Eight o'clock on a June morning, the day before Queen Victoria's Jubilee. The State Apartments both at Buckingham Palace and at Windsor—not to mention the streets of London—had been prepared and garnished. The Office of Works had spared no effort. They had done their worst. Clearly it was to be a sweltering day. There was one oasis. The Ponsonbys' little breakfast room in the Norman Tower, with the Venetian blinds lowered, was cool and pleasant. Sir Henry had disposed of his porridge (every year he brought a sack of oatmeal back from Balmoral) and also of his kedgeree. He was now weighing in upon his bacon, egg and kidney. He had already turned from the outer to the inner page of the *Times* (as he always did) to check his own writing of the Court Circular. Its uninformative brevity was his daily pride.

Windsor Castle. 19th June 1887. Their Majesties the King and Queen of Denmark and Their Royal Highnesses the Maharajah and Maharani of Kashgar have arrived at the Castle. Her Majesty gave a small dinner party.

He nodded in self-satisfaction. His wife replenished his coffee cup. The parlormaid came in with the post. As he took his letters from the salver, throwing two across to his wife, he noticed that one of his was a folded sheet sealed with a wafer—clearly sent across from the Castle. It was not (thank God) from the Queen; that would have been conveyed by more exalted hands. This was a hurried and nearly illegible scrawl from the Princess.

Sir Hy. I am extremely worried, have hardly slept, and must see you without delay. I *do* realize how busy you are, but will be in your office when you come over to the Castle —about nine o'clock.   Pss B.

Sir Henry picked up the next letter, a black-edged royal envelope, postmarked in London at 12:20 A.M.

> The Royal Mews, Buckingham Palace Road, S. W.
> 19. 6. 1887

My dear Sir Henry.

Your disturbing letter has just reached me (11:05 P.M.) by the hand of a servant returning here from Windsor. I hasten to reply so that I may catch the midnight post. I can assure you, dear Sir Henry, that there is no epidemic of mumps, or of anything else, in the Royal Mews. One mare had glanders but has quite recovered. On the other hand I am utterly bewildered by the goings-on here—all most unwonted. A few days ago Fulleylove received a telegram from Newcastle summoning him to his mother's deathbed. I gave him leave. He returned this afternoon to say that his mother was in the very best of health. Sir Henry, what is the meaning of this hoax? Fulleylove is a trustworthy fellow—this was no dodge to avoid work. And now, on top of that, I have your information that you were treated to a downright falsehood by your footman this afternoon. We have no footman called Smith. I will keep you informed—also the Master of the Horse.

With my regards to dear Lady Ponsonby,
I am, Sir Henry,

> Yours most sincerely,
> Roderick Sparling

P.S. I open this letter to give you most terrible news. A constable has just called (11:40 P.M.). It was certainly Macdonald who took out the brougham this morning in order to meet you at Paddington at 10:25 A.M. and then convey you to the Tower. And now, Sir Henry, Macdonald's body, most savagely mutilated and with the throat slit from ear to ear,

and stripped of the livery, has been taken from the Paddington
Canal at Iron Wharf. It was found by a bargee. So, it would
seem that the footman of your carriage was an impostor and
that your coachman was murdered. Frankly, dear Sir Henry,
in view of the nature of your errand I am thankful that you
yourself escaped with your life. And now, with the Jubilee on
Wednesday, I must ward off the newspaper hounds at all
costs. You will, I know, agree that Her Majesty must know
nothing. Tomorrow morning I visit the mortuary—most distasteful—and the police station. I will try to reach Windsor
and attend you in the afternoon. Pray telegraph me if this is
not convenient. It is now upon the stroke of midnight but I
shall send this by runner to the Charing Cross Post Office so
that you may have it in the morning. You can imagine my
state of mind.   R.S.

Very, very calmly Sir Henry Ponsonby spread the Dundee
marmalade very, very evenly upon his toast. He then
turned to the leading article. Routine must be preserved.
If he was not calm he must appear so.

"The nation is sound at heart, Mary, or at any rate the
upper classes. I see they are paying as much as a guinea
for a seat on the processional route."

"How amazing! But your coffee is quite cold, dear.
What can have come over you? I only hope there will not
be any traffic in forged tickets."

"What a suspicious mind you have."

"The world is a very wicked place, Henry. I am suspicious because in my experience the worst always happens
. . . and those in high places are usually the most wicked
of all."

"Really, dear, you shouldn't say things like that."

"I speak from experience. Now, my love, you have a
busy day tomorrow—we all have to be in the Abbey by
eleven—and you were tired last night. Take it easy today—
have you much on?"

"Oh, dear me, no! Nothing at all! Only that the Princess Beatrice is so worried that she has hardly slept; I am
seeing her in a few minutes. After that I have to see the

Prince of Wales about another hundred thousand or so of his debts, which I suspect he has hidden from Knollys. Tonight there is the family dinner in the Waterloo Chamber, with a couple of hundred royals staying in the Castle. Tomorrow they have all to be got back to London again, in the right trains and carriages, and into their Abbey seats, and all according to protocol, and every one of them touchy. I have every reason to believe that the Tudor Tiara has been tampered with, and at Buckingham Palace they have a very nasty murder on their hands."

"I am not in the least surprised."

"Mary!"

"It's no good saying 'Mary' like that. If you will insist upon positively advertising the existence of a million pounds' worth of jewels in search of an owner, something of the kind was bound to happen. I am the very last person in the world to say 'I told you so'; but if I wasn't I should. I suppose it was Macdonald, the coachman, who was murdered."

"Mary!"

"It's very elementary, Henry, if only you would think. But you know you haven't asked me about *my* letters. . . . Now they're *really* exciting."

"Well, I'm glad there's some excitement in the house—it may prevent us from getting bored."

"Don't be sarcastic, Henry. It doesn't become you. Two letters, one from each sister on the same day—now that's exciting if you like. Sylvia's Dorothy is to have a little stranger before Christmas—I must ask Philpotts to drive me into town to buy some wool. And then Henrietta's Tom has got the Washington Embassy. A pity it's only America, but I suppose you pulled the wires for him and that later on he may get somewhere important like Vienna. Now you must admit that that is more exciting than your squalid murder or that silly Tiara. . . . But all the same you'd better be off to the office. There's salmon for lunch."

"That's something. And now, dear, as you say, off to the office . . . just like other men."

He kissed her. As he left the room she reached for the *Times*. She always liked to see who was dead.

In the red-carpeted passage outside his office the Princess was already pacing up and down, almost in tears.

"Be seated, ma'am, and tell me what it is all about."

"Sir Henry, I am worried to death. After your brilliant little lecture last night—and it was unpardonable of Mama to cut you short like that—the Maharajah asked if he could see me privately."

Sir Henry decided that honesty was the best policy—up to a point.

"Yes, ma'am, I saw you both on the great stair."

"Sir Henry, I don't trust the Maharajah an inch."

"Nor do I, ma'am."

"And Bertie says that that Colonel Pinkerton was a byword in India—an absolute bounder. But still, the Maharajah is an expert, and also, except that the silly man wants the Garter, disinterested. His knowledge of gems is recognized throughout the world—you know that."

"I do, but what is the trouble, Highness?"

"Bloody Mary's Earrings are missing—that's all."

"But, ma'am, they were part and parcel of the Tiara last night, since when it has been in the strong room."

"No, Sir Henry: according to the Maharajah those diamonds are nothing more than paste; very clever imitations, but almost worthless. He seems certain."

There was a long silence. Sir Henry produced a gold box and they each lit an Egyptian cigarette, surveying the gilded ceiling through wreaths of blue smoke.

"Your Royal Highness, you must not let this be one of *your* troubles. The Queen is your care and that, if I may say so, is enough for any woman. The Tiara is *my* responsibility."

"You are so kind; but all the same, where are the earrings? We must know."

"It needs careful thought, ma'am. Offhand I would say, first of all, that the story must be kept from the Queen, at any rate until tomorrow. If she was told now . . . well, I need hardly say what Windsor would be like."

"Precisely, Sir Henry."

"Secondly, but only between ourselves, I would say that the real diamonds may be in the Maharajah's baggage or, of course, Colonel Pinkerton's. The Tiara, or rather the box containing it, never left my sight between the Tower of London and this room, so I would think that it may have been tampered with in the Jewel Tower at almost any time in the last thirty-six years, or possibly en route to the Tower in 1851. After all, cleaners, packers, builders, guards, even one corrupt Beefeater . . . we just don't know, and never will."

"But, Sir Henry, we must know . . . for everyone's sake. All kinds of people may be suspected, not only underlings, but even people like—er—like ourselves . . . someone head over heels in debt for instance, or someone mentally deficient, or . . ."

"My dear Princess, say no more. These are terrible thoughts. Believe me, I too have had them. I too had very little sleep."

"They are thoughts we cannot ignore."

"Quite so, but the police, you may be sure, will consider every possibility, everyone—high or low. The first thing, however, is to clear the matter with the Tower of London. They may have some quite simple explanation. But we must get in touch immediately with Field Marshal Lord Wilson. He's in his dotage—served as an ensign at Waterloo—but we can only do our best—here and now."

Sir Henry tinkled his bell.

"Ah, Wainwright."

"Sir."

"Kindly find me someone reliable who can take a message to town on the next train."

"Sir."

Wainwright vanished.

While they were waiting, Sir Henry spoke to the Princess almost in a whisper.

"Tell me, ma'am, is there something else wrong—I mean apart from the Tiara?"

"Wrong . . . how?"

"Wrong with the Queen . . . and with the Prince of Wales. Curious silences, nerves. The Prince had none of his usual—er—vivacity last night. As for the Queen, I am no longer in her confidence. Why, Your Royal Highness, why?"

"I just don't know, Sir Henry. But you are right. Would it be too fanciful to imagine that this Tiara is upsetting everyone—as if it carried a curse?"

"Fanciful, yes. But it is a feeling shared by my wife."

"Really."

"Oh, dear me, yes. Mary, ma'am, is very matter-of-fact; she is also very astute. May I suggest a heart-to-heart talk . . . she would be honored."

"Oh, yes, indeed. I will arrange it. Now please write your note to Field Marshal Lord Wilson while I finish my cigarette."

Windsor Castle
20.6.1887

My dear Field Marshal.

May I first of all thank you and dear Lady Wilson for your warm hospitality yesterday. I can assure you that the *Châteauneuf du Pape* and the '07 cognac were worthy of the luncheon—need I say more? Her Majesty was much gratified to hear of the smart appearance of the Yeoman of the Guard.

My dear Wilson, I am most distressed, as I am sure you will be. It is *alleged*—I emphasize the word—that the Tudor Tiara has, at some unknown date, been tampered with, some of the more valuable gems, particularly Mary Tudor's earrings, being replaced with paste replicas. Frankly I do not see how this could have happened since I took receipt of the Tiara yesterday—I never lost sight of it. We have this big family dinner in the Waterloo Chamber tonight, so I cannot ask you to stay in the Castle, but if you and Lady Wilson can take afternoon tea with us in the Norman Tower we may be able to sort out this unpleasant business. I dare not send you a wire; the Tower does not, I think, have the Queen's cipher and a telegram *en clair* might be disastrous. The royal train, for the conveyance of the Emperor and Empress of Germany, the Czar and

Czarina, and others, with families and suites, will be leaving Platform No. 1 at Paddington Station at 3:00 P.M. If you and Lady Wilson care to make use of the rear coach, the enclosed card is your authority. My own carriage will await you at this end. I am, Field Marshal, with regards to dear Lady Wilson,

Yours most sincerely,

Henry Ponsonby

By the time Sir Henry had finished a second note a young stable groom—black suit, white stock, horseshoe pin, and billycock in hand—was at Sir Henry's side.

"Your name, my man?"

"Wicklow, sir."

"Very well, Wicklow. You should take the next train to Paddington, then the twopenny tube to Tower Hill—that's probably quicker than hailing a fly. At the Tower of London you must go to the Constable's residence and insist—you may say your orders are as from the Queen—*insist* upon giving this letter personally to the Constable. You will wait for a reply if asked to do so. You understand?"

"Sir."

"You may then take some refreshment, Wicklow, after which you must go to Garrard's, the jewelers' establishment in Regent Street. It is under the colonnade in the Quadrant."

"Sir."

"You will then deliver this second letter to Mr. Friedman, the manager, and again insist upon handing it to him personally."

"Sir."

"You will then return to Windsor and report. And on no account, Wicklow, must you gossip with any strangers on the way. You may go."

"Sir."

As the groom vanished, Sir Henry noted his name, and the time, upon his blotting pad.

The Princess Beatrice was now in tears.

"It's no good, Sir Henry. Those replicas must have been perfect if it took the Maharajah to spot them. Also

they were an elaborate arrangement of interlocking stars—
almost impossible to copy. How was it done?"

"Careful sketches, ma'am, or possibly photographs in
these days, all made in the Tower. What the underworld,
I believe, calls an 'inside job.'"

"Surely, Sir Henry, that's most unlikely. There were
also Papa's meticulous drawings, every gem exquisitely
delineated . . . anyone with access to the Castle library . . ."

"Such people are well known, ma'am."

"There are the genuine students, supervised by Herr
Mütter, and there are—er—people like ourselves. *We* can
wander in and out as we like."

This raised rather ghastly implications and it was several minutes before either of them spoke again.

"Your Royal Highness, it becomes clearer every moment that our secrecy must be absolute."

"Of course."

"No, ma'am, there is no 'of course' about it. We said
that the Queen must not know because it might cast a
shadow over the Jubilee. She must never know."

"Never!"

"Let us be frank. You know as well as I do, ma'am,
that Her Majesty puts her trust in the most extraordinary
people. There is dear old Skerret, for instance, well into
her nineties, who, for all we know, is told everything in
the privacy of the bathroom. Then there are these new-
fangled Indian attendants, as formerly there was John
Brown, and long ago Lehzen, whom your father had to
get rid of. But above all, of course, there is the problem of
the Prince of Wales."

"I don't understand you, Sir Henry. The 'problem' of
the Prince of Wales? Of course we must tell Bertie about
the Tiara . . . the Crown Jewels . . . his position . . .
his worldly advice . . . surely . . ."

"Please, please, Your Royal Highness, do not press me
on this. The Prince and I have already had a most
curious talk about the Tiara—most curious. He seems to
think that it is his. Beyond that I am pledged to secrecy. I
beg you to say nothing either to him or to Princess Alix. I
beg you."

"Oh, very well, if you say so; but . . ."

"Apart from my own position, ma'am, there is the dinner tonight—Germans, Danes, Russians, French, all looking daggers at each other. If they knew the Queen was wearing faked jewels, there is enough malice there to send the news round the world. . . . Prince William alone . . ."

"Oh, dear me, yes—those awful mustaches. But surely, Sir Henry, Bertie is different. He is one of us. He is, after all—well—heir to the throne."

"We have been frank about the Queen's servants, ma'am. Let us be frank about the Prince's friends. *He* may be discreet; his *friends* are not, not after a twelve-course dinner, followed by three or four brandies in the Holbein Room."

"They are men of the world."

"Oh, come, Princess, you are being naïve. Can you seriously imagine Lord Randolph, say, or Mrs. Keppel or the Blue Monkey or Rosebery or Mrs. Langtry, or even Dickie Fisher ever *not* telling a secret? It would be told in bed if nowhere else."

The Princess bit her lip. She had no illusions about Bertie, but, like Mama, she was fond of him. She lit another cigarette and once again watched the smoke curling up to the ceiling.

"Sir Henry, there is something else. I hardly know how to say it, it is so difficult . . . it is about poor Eddy."

"None of us, ma'am, can forget the Duke of Clarence. That is an abiding problem."

"In any other walk of life, Sir Henry, one wonders whether he would even be allowed out. . . ."

"Whereas in fact he is always out—from eight P.M. to eight A.M."

"Perhaps I shouldn't have mentioned it, but . . ."

"It had to be mentioned. His vices are unspeakable. So are his debts. So is his cunning."

"His cunning?"

"Oh, dear me, yes! He may sit there with his mouth open, but he can look after Prince Eddy all right. They devise punishments for him. Nothing could be more useless. Madam, I am the Sovereign's Secretary: do you imagine that the Duke of Clarence—second in line of ascent—is not in my mind every day? When I shaved this morning Eddy and the Tiara were dancing before my eyes. Always, however, there is another who must come first. . . . I am her devoted servant."

"Dear Sir Henry, of course. But then we have agreed to tell Mama nothing."

"We have, ma'am. But if she is not to know, then nobody must know. She must not be upset. More important still, she must not be subject to blackmail. She could become the center of a 'Bloody Mary's Earrings scandal' compared with which a flutter at baccarat or another Dilke case would be nothing. The monarchy itself might go under."

"What next then, Sir Henry?"

"Next, we establish our facts. I have just sent for Garrard's diamond expert to examine the Tiara; we do not accept the Maharajah's word alone. Second, may I hope that you will join us for tea this afternoon? Frankly, ma'am, Field Marshal Lord Wilson is now almost *non compos mentis;* but he *may* offer some simple solution. May I tell my wife you will be with us?"

"Oh, please do, Sir Henry. You are a great comfort. Now I must go: Mama will be fidgeting."

"There is just one thing more, Your Royal Highness. I must repay confidence with confidence, even if I shock you—as I am going to do."

"Please . . ."

"It will be a great shock. Yesterday a coachman called Macdonald was supposed to drive me from Paddington to the Tower and back again with the Tiara in the afternoon."

"I remember Macdonald—a very decent sort of man."

"Late last night, ma'am, his body, with the throat slit, was taken from the canal behind Paddington Station."

"Oh, no! How terrible! How very terrible . . . and what does it all mean? What is happening to us all?"

The Princess swayed as if she would faint, and Sir Henry took his brandy flask from his desk.

"It does indeed . . . although I cannot quite see how or why. I should add that the footman was a complete impostor—not an employee of the Household at all. He has vanished—the brougham abandoned in the Buckingham Palace Road."

"But what does it all mean, Sir Henry? What is the link with the Tiara and the diamonds?"

"Well, if it was an attempt on the Tiara it failed. The Tiara is here in the strong room, and I am still alive."

"The Tiara is here, yes; but with faked diamonds."

"True, but it was never out of my sight. The paste replicas must have been substituted for the real diamonds before the Tiara left the Tower or after it reached Windsor—both impossible. I admit, Your Royal Highness, that I am a very worried man. I don't know which way to turn. I need your help. But now, ma'am, Her Majesty will be waiting for you."

Sir Henry rose to open the door for her; she remained seated in the armchair by his desk.

"No, Sir Henry, Mama can wait. It is time for her to learn that there are others in the world. You have something else on your mind. You have just said you needed my help . . . well?"

"Yes, ma'am, there is one other thing. In your kind note, which I found on my desk when I got back from London, you said something which, frankly, shattered me."

"Perhaps I should not have said it . . . better to forget it."

"We can hardly do that now, ma'am. You said . . ." and he picked up the note ". . . you said, 'I suppose the Tiara you brought from London today is the real thing.' Now what, in heaven's name, did Your Royal Highness mean by that? I *must* know."

To his amazement the Princess buried her face in her hands and burst into tears. It was minutes before she could speak.

"Sir Henry, I don't think I can tell you what I meant.

And, for the first time, there is something I cannot tell Mama."

"But you must tell me, ma'am. Truly you must. I am your friend and it is your duty to tell me. Please . . ."

"Very well. You know all about the Tiara replicas, the ones that were made for exhibitions."

"I didn't, but I do now."

"Well, naturally everyone assumed that the real thing, complete with Bloody Mary's diamonds, went to the Tower of London, and that the replicas went to—oh, I don't know—Manchester, South Kensington and so on. Anyway, the family also knew that Mama had kept one for the Blue Room."

"That was—well—at least understandable."

"Sir Henry, have you ever been in the Blue Room?"

"In all these years at Windsor, no, ma'am, never. I have never been asked. Mary has been once."

"It's quite uncanny, you know. The Blue Room, not Frogmore, is the real mausoleum. Papa's valet is still in the service solely so that he may put out Papa's clothes, towels, boots and shoes, every day of the year. It is ghastly . . . the deathbed always ready to be slept in. Mama says her prayers there morning and night."

"I know, of course, that the room had been kept untouched, but all this . . ."

"That's not all, Sir Henry. In the big wardrobes, with their sliding doors, are Papa's possessions—albums, cameras, sketching gear, alpenstocks and so on, as well as decorations, uniforms and jewels. Also . . . also, Sir Henry, the *original* Tiara—the real thing."

"Good God . . . then the one from the Tower was only a replica."

"Oh, yes. You see, Papa having designed the Tiara, it must never, never be touched. It could not even be worn tonight, hence your visit to the Tower, to fetch the fake."

"I see, I see . . . or I am beginning to see. Please go on, ma'am."

"Well, there are only two keys to those wardrobes—golden keys—of which Mama has one. I have the other. Yesterday afternoon, when Mama was walking on the terrace, I acted on impulse; I went to the Blue Room—all the blinds down on that sunny afternoon—and I looked at the Tiara. I had not seen it for many, many years, but there it was, sure enough, in all its glittering glory. Even in that dimmed room it flashed."

"Well, well, Princess, that's certainly a curious story, but, knowing Her Majesty as we do, nothing to worry about . . . all part of the parcel of life at Windsor. And, of course, the whole mystery is solved; the Tiara from the Tower is a replica, the Maharajah was right, and the genuine article is upstairs in the Blue Room. Our troubles are over. . . ."

"No, Sir Henry, I have not finished. Listen. Last night, after my talk with the Maharajah, I decided to have one more look at the *real* Tiara—the Blue Room Tiara. I stayed with Mama, as usual, until she had said her prayers at Papa's pillow, then I used my golden key to open the wardrobe. I suppose I had some hazy idea of comparing the real Tiara with the fake. The original Tiara was well displayed in the wardrobe, under glass on a purple cushion, on the middle shelf. I had seen it, as I have explained, only that afternoon while you were in London. . . . Sir Henry, it had gone."

"Good God! What do you mean, 'gone'?"

"What I say—vanished! The purple cushion was empty. The Tiara had been there, in the darkness of the wardrobe, since Papa's death twenty-five years ago. Now it has gone."

"Wainwright."

"Sir."

"Do you know whether Mr. Bellow is in his office?"

"At this hour, Sir Henry, it is highly probable."

"Ask him to attend upon me."

"Sir."

Sir Henry now extracted a large volume in red-and-gilt morocco from a drawer—the Windsor Guest Book for 1887. He studied it until Mr. Bellow presented himself, immaculate in sponge trousers and fawn frockcoat. Mr. Archibald Bellow, having been superannuated from Bow

Street to the sinecure of house detective to Windsor Castle, now spent his days trying not to look like a detective.

"Ah, Bellow, good morning. I have just been studying the accommodation for the Maharajah of Kashgar's party. The Maharajah and Maharani, I see, have the Queen Adelaide Room. Then, let's see, there's Colonel Pinkerton, Miss Nummuggar, two valets, a lady's maid, the numerous gentlemen in attendance and a pansy calling himself the Maharani's secretary."

"That would be correct, sir, apart from small fry in the servants' quarters. Bar Colonel Pinkerton, sir, they are all Indians."

"Quite, Bellow, quite. I shall see that the servants and the eunuch are given tickets for the Abbey tomorrow—there are still some odd seats left in Henry VII's Chapel for underlings. That, Bellow, will leave the coast clear. All the bedrooms must be searched—thoroughly."

"Certainly, sir. And what may I ask is the nature of the documents you are looking for?"

"Not documents, Bellow. Diamonds."

Mr. Archibald Bellow's eyebrows shot up into his bald head. He had envisaged documents. He had done this job before, when the Foreign Office wanted an advance draft of a treaty . . . but diamonds . . . now that was something!

"Indeed, sir—a little unusual."

"Yes, Bellow, two diamond stars, twelve-pointed. You can take your time: nobody can return from London until the evening. But your search must be thorough and leave no trace. I shall expect to find a sealed report in this drawer when I return. Here is the key. I think that is all, Bellow."

"Thank you, sir. That is quite clear."

As a matter of duty and routine Sir Henry had now taken steps to deal with Field Marshal Lord Wilson, with Garrard's of Regent Street and with the Maharajah. He expected nothing to come of any of it, but it had had to be done. Now, at last, for the first time since breakfast, he

could sit back and think. When he had told the Princess
Beatrice that their troubles were over, that the problem
was solved—the Tower of London Tiara being a fake, the
Blue Room Tiara being the real thing—he had almost
meant it. Now that he was alone the doubts came crowd-
ing back into his mind.

Most important of all, the secret must be rigorously
kept. The Prince of Wales must get his loan and the
Queen must be protected. There was the awful possibility
that in one of her 1861 paroxysms of grief she had
defrauded the nation. Moreover, grief or not, Sir Henry
already knew that she had some very odd ideas about
property—to say the least. And when Knollys tried to fix
the Rothschild loan for the Prince the truth would
emerge. If the Prince was not actually suspected of trying
to pass off a fake Tiara on the Rothschilds, which would
be absurd, he would certainly be furious at having been
made to look a fool. He might even blame Sir Henry . . .
"You should have known better, Ponsonby, than to bring
back such rubbish from the Tower." He would also be
furious with Mama for hiding away the genuine article
through the years.

Another thing haunted Sir Henry and shocked him
deeply. A fake among the Crown Jewels—and that is how
Fleet Street would see it—would be a major scandal,
involving the Queen's personal conduct. It would also
mean a huge manhunt, while all the time three people,
the Queen, the Princess and Sir Henry, knew perfectly
well that somewhere in Windsor, in some bureau or chest
or even under the Queen's bed, was the real thing complete with Bloody Mary's Earrings, the very things for
which the police of all Europe would be hunting.

Of course, as Sir Henry told himself, there was the odd
chance that the Princess's story was not true. The Queen's
emotional obsession with death may have made her believe, as the years passed, that a replica Tiara in the Blue
Room wardrobe had indeed been her own Albert's treasure. At sixty-eight she was already muddled, especially
about the dead and the past.

Finally, if the Tower Tiara was a replica, what had

been the point of all those goings-on yesterday—the murdered coachman, the sham footman, the boy in the ginger suit, the injury to Black Beauty and so on? If there had been a gang at work—and to Sir Henry it was a big "if"—they too, like everyone else, must have thought that the Tiara from the Tower was the real thing. . . . Anyway, he told himself, thanks to his vigilance they had failed.

He tried to face the problem. His Royal Highness the Prince of Wales was going to raise a loan on a fake, while somewhere in Windsor an obstinate and impregnable old woman had hidden not less than a million pounds' worth of precious stones. That was the gist of it. In an agony of thought Sir Henry sank his head in his hands. Another complication occurred to him.

Problem piled itself upon problem. There seemed no end to it. What about these upstart South Africans, these Astors and Norths, at the very core of the Marlborough House set? . . . Millionaire diamond merchants, the whole lot of them. These men would do almost anything to get their hands upon the earrings. They would know what to do with them. It was not just that those glittering stars, in Jo'burg currency, were the price of a yacht or a palace; no, it was not just that. . . . Sir Henry might not know much about these things, but he had chatted with these men, specially with Oppenheimer, at Marlborough House dinners, and he did know that the mere release of such diamonds could turn the world market upside down. The South African Diamond Syndicate would pay the Prince a very handsome price indeed for the earrings, not to sell them but to prevent their being sold. . . . If they were genuine, they might even pay him to put them back in the Tower in perpetuity. Diamonds must remain rare. So these men, too, if it came to the point, would be glad to explode the bomb in the Prince' face, to tell the whole world that this famous cache was worthless. Meanwhile the real secret would still be, so to speak, under the Queen's bed.

From his open window Sir Henry looked down upon the East Terrace. What he now saw once again changed everything. What he saw might alter all their lives; it might launch the British Empire upon a terrible—but of course not enjoyable—scandal. The two gentlemen in attendance, Lord Randolph and Colonel Pinkerton, were away on the far side; Sir Henry could imagine their recherché chat. On the lawn beneath the window the Maharajah and the Prince of Wales were locked in talk—head to head. Sir Henry was stunned and furious. The Princess had pledged the Maharajah to secrecy. The Princess and Sir Henry should have known better. The man was clearly incapable of keeping a secret—especially if he could see a chance of the Garter at the end of it all. The Prince now knew that his Tiara was worthless, that the loan and all possibility of a loan was off. The Royal Family and the nation had been robbed—and in a big way. Sir Henry might be blamed. The Castle would be filled with police. At the Jubilee Dinner that night there would be only one thing to talk about, and they would wallow in it. After all the Queen had been rude enough to most of the clan at one time or another, and all spite and malice would be let loose. Grandmama had been swindled; it would be irresistible. Apart from that, any whippersnapper of a Balkan gentleman-in-waiting, or even some bankrupt princeling, could be selling the whole story in Fleet Street the next morning.

There was a knock upon his door—a loud and peremptory knock.

"Your Majesty."

It had never happened before. In all his long years of service Sir Henry Ponsonby had been summoned to the Queen's room some three times a day, perhaps several thousand times in all. She had once taken tea in the Norman Tower—for his Silver Wedding—and once at Osborne Cottage to see her godchild. She had never visited his office. He wondered whether she had ever before knocked on a door. She sniffed.

"Someone has been smoking here, Sir Henry, and in the morning too!"

"Yes, ma'am. I must admit that when the burden of

work is heavy I find a cigarette very soothing . . . in complete privacy of course."

"A cigarette . . . there are three stumps here."

"Yes, ma'am."

"If you can only work under narcotics, Sir Henry, you had better consult a specialist. After all, the work itself must be very light; or do you need more help?"

"Thank you, ma'am, no. But of course just lately there has been the Jubilee. But perhaps it was about the arrangements for tonight's dinner or the procession tomorrow that Your Majesty wished to see me."

"No, why should I? Those arrangements were made weeks ago, and are in good hands. My confidence in you is complete, Sir Henry. I wish I could say the same about the Home Secretary, but I suppose he understands processions. Sir Henry, I am most concerned about this Tiara. That is what I wish to talk about."

"Certainly, ma'am—the one which I brought from the Tower."

He could have bitten off his tongue—he was supposed to know of no other.

"What on earth do you mean, Sir Henry? Of course I mean the Tiara from the Tower—the Tudor Tiara. There is no other. Really! While you were giving us your dissertation last night, I was pondering upon it. The gems are magnificent, while the setting is of course in perfect taste."

"Indeed, yes, ma'am, we are all agreed about the setting."

"Yes, Sir Henry, but it was, you know, designed to be seen—in the Crystal Palace that is—seen rather than worn, a setting for the display of the Tudor gems. Looking at it again, after so many years, I think that for one my age, and in my sad state of widowhood, it is perhaps a little too magnificent . . . too large. I shall *not* wear it tonight, Sir Henry. The Darmstadt-Hesse Tiara might do very well for this family party, or perhaps better still, the little Coburg Diadem that I wore for the last opening of Parliament . . . but definitely *not* the Tudor Tiara."

"May I say very humbly, ma'am, being no judge in

these matters, that I entirely concur in Your Majesty's decision. I will see to it, ma'am, that the Tiara is safely returned to the Tower of London."

"No."

"I beg your pardon, ma'am?"

"I said 'no,' Sir Henry. It must *not* be returned to the Tower. It should never have been there at all. And that raises another matter—the ownership of the Tiara."

"Indeed, ma'am, are there any doubts?"

"One would have hoped not. But if there are, Sir Henry, they must be most firmly squashed. My dear husband brought those gems to England through his own personal efforts, thanks to our wide connections. Others were gifts from old English families. They would certainly not have wished such sacred relics to be exposed to the vulgar gaze."

"Quite, ma'am."

"The phrasing of my Dear One's will, although strictly private, makes the matter clear beyond all doubt. The Tudor Tiara, Sir Henry, is mine, mine personally and not part of the Regalia. Only in the fullness of time, and through *my* will, can it ever go to the Prince of Wales."

"Yes, ma'am. Would Your Majesty wish to have the whole matter confirmed by the Solicitor-General?"

"Certainly not. That is totally unnecessary. Have I not made myself clear? I shall not wear the Tiara tonight. I shall never wear it. It must never go back to the Tower of London—it is private property, not a Crown Jewel. It must today be placed in the Castle strong room. Its case—and I presume it has a case—must be under my seal."

"Yes, ma'am. You do not think that perhaps Field Marshal Lord Wilson may raise difficulties—the Tiara was in his charge."

"That is immaterial; he may be given a receipt."

"Yes, ma'am."

"Then it must be brought to my room within the hour so that I may affix the seal. After that nobody must ever see it as long as I am alive. It is sacred to the memory of a widow. It should never have passed from my care."

"The Commissioners for the Great Exhibition of 1851,

ma'am—you do not think that they may ask questions?"

"Mere officials, Sir Henry, administering the funds. I am astonished that you should even mention them."

"I apologize, ma'am."

"Very well. And now, Sir Henry, pray go to the strong room and do as I have said. After that I never want to hear of the matter again."

"Your Majesty will announce, presumably, that the Tiara is being preserved at Windsor instead of at the Tower—if only to allay curiosity."

"That's as may be. Now about tonight: I have decided to wear the little Coburg Diadem. It is modest and has family connections."

"But it is in the Tower, Your Majesty."

"I know. Fortunately it is barely noon. You will have ample time, Sir Henry, to slip back to London and fetch it. . . . You may even be able to return on the Royal Train if you hurry."

Very slightly, beneath his Jaeger combinations, Sir Henry began to sweat.

"Is that all, Your Majesty?"

"Thank you, Sir Henry, yes."

But it was not all. They were standing in the doorway looking down the long red-carpeted passage. There was a cry.

"Mama! Mama!"

At the far end, rushing toward them, was a towering figure in a Norfolk suit. He was flourishing a cigar. He was crimson with rage.

"Mama! Sir Henry!"

"Be calm, Bertie. In our position one must not get excited: it does not do. Now, what is the matter?"

"Mama, we've been swindled. Bloody Mary's Earrings are a bloody fake."

From the dumpy little woman at his side Sir Henry Ponsonby heard a sharp intake of breath.

"That, Bertie, is quite impossible. And what language! You must not talk nonsense, Bertie. How often have I to tell you that?"

"But, Mama, the Maharajah says that the rest of the Tiara is the real thing, quite genuine, but that the diamond earrings are only paste."

"Nonsense, Bertie. That is quite impossible. I happen to know that it is impossible. The Maharajah should mind his own business. Quite impossible . . . I know."

5

East of Bow Creek

It was Guy Fawkes night—a night without a moon. A thin fog hung with menace over the West End streets, hardly enough to halt the trams or buses, but enough to diffuse the gas lamps into huge stars, enough to make the horses' breath hang upon the cold air, and to make the theatergoers hurry home for fear of worse.

In the Haymarket only the cabbies' noses showed above their mufflers, while the cockaded footmen, for all their little bearskin capes, froze upon the box seats of the carriages, hundreds of them awaiting the fall of the curtain at half a dozen theaters. Across the Circus one could still see the blazing lights of restaurants, or the occasional rocket screaming across the sky, but as one went east the fog got worse. Around the Strand, in the little streets between Covent Garden and the River, it was a real fog; far away in Canning Town, so it was said, a man could not see his hand before his face—a good night for an escapade.

In Pall Mall, twenty yards from the Marlborough Club, a most conspicuously inconspicuous black carriage was picking up two late diners, gentlemen in red-lined capes and silk hats. A quarter of an hour later it was setting them down in a very shadowy corner of Wardour Street.

"Well, Serge, that covers our tracks, I think."

"Yes; and now the usual aliases, Your Highness?"

"Of course. You are Colonel Levi. . . . His Excellency the Baron Serge de Staal does not object, I presume."

"Not at all; and Your Highness?"

"Oh, as always, 'Major Chester.' And don't forget that last week you nearly let the cat out of the bag—and at that crowded coffee stall."

"Your Highness has been pleased to tell me so six times."

"Well, one must be careful. It was a miracle it didn't get into 'John Bull.' "

"Anyway, to be frank, sire—'Major,' I mean—it's not your alias we have to worry about, it's your figure."

"Don't be ridiculous, Serge. I'm not the only fat man in London. Besides, just look at me. These bushy eyebrows and this monocle, this touch of rouge, all so easily put on in the carriage. The perfect old buffer—what?"

"I must admit that . . . Major."

"And above all, Serge, everyone knows that after Goodwood no gentleman would wear a silk hat in town— that is the master stroke. Our disguise is complete."

"I wasn't really thinking—er—Major Chester, that you might be recognized in the street. . . . I was thinking of later, at supper or—er—possibly in bed."

"Leave that to me, Serge. I can look after myself. That dear, innocent little Trixie must be told to keep her mouth shut. And I'm sure she will, bless her heart!"

"So be it, if you are content, sire. But you are being naïve, are you not? After all, the Prince of Wales of all men—and you are the only person who just won't see it—to sleep with the Prince of Wales, that is the one secret on earth no woman will ever keep."

"Nonsense . . . and in any case, my dear Colonel Levi, a well-lined pocketbook can do much. But enough—we are here for pleasure."

They had walked briskly through the fog to Leicester Square. The flaring jets outside the Empire cast a curious, shadowless light upon the faces and billboards—a Beardsley monochrome in black and white. It was the second interval, and in the crowded foyer, thick with the blue smoke of a hundred cigars and heavy with the scent of women, they were obsequiously but inconspicuously welcomed. A couple of sovereigns and a couple of envelopes were handed to a commissionaire who, quite clearly, knew what was expected of him. Once, long ago, for the hell of it, they had mixed with the riff-raff of the Promenade. It had been risky to the point of danger. Tonight the Prince sat well back in the box, well screened by de Staal. It pleased them to believe that they were unnoticed.

"Well, Serge, the show is half over, but see how well I have timed it. Behold your own particular friend, little Connie Gilchrist. I confess she's a stunner. I have always said so. You have taste in these matters, my dear Serge . . . obviously."

Down in the stalls and in the circle, to the fury of their womenfolk, men were clapping holes in their gloves for Connie and her skipping rope—so ingenuous, so petite and yet so sophisticated.

"Yes, yes, Serge, I admire your taste. Very pretty indeed, a delicious morsel—but if you take my advice, never sleep with the Talk of the Town. It leads to trouble. You have to share her with other men, and then it gets around. Look at poor Skittles. And God knows what it may do to a man—look at Randolph, a wreck at forty."

"Chacun à son gout, sire."

"Oh, quite, quite. But now . . . here she is. My Trixie. Take the glasses, Serge. Back row of the chorus, second from the right . . . and next to her, her friend—called, believe it or not, Daffodil . . . most extraordinary."

"You forget that I have already met your friend Trixie, and that, for your sake, sire, I have done rather more than meet her . . . all very *très intime* . . . a most respectable girl; she had to be—er—handled."

"Thank you my dear chap, thank you. I am never ungrateful."

"I am always ready to serve you—er—Major Chester.

At least I can assure you that she will prove as bedworthy as she looks."

"I don't doubt it, I don't doubt it. Always look for them in the back row, Colonel Levi. They may put the old harridans there—they also have their piquancy, you know—but that is also where they train the novices— pretty little innocents from nowhere. Trixie is as pretty as a doll. And for me, you know, that is a great change."

"Yes, indeed, sire. And please remember that you owe a little to my Connie."

"How so?"

"Well, it took Connie as well as me to bring Trixie to the point."

"Why was that, Serge? Surely a 'Major' is enough of a ..."

"To be frank, sire, she does not like fat men, and, as I have said, she is respectable—positively virtuous."

"Hm!"

"However, Connie demeaned herself by actually speaking to a girl in the chorus. That did it. Trixie is ready for you tonight, sire, when the curtain falls. Our table is engaged at Rule's—the usual table."

"Miss Gilchrist will be duly rewarded, Serge. You know that. But now let us look at Trixie. Of course in the ordinary way give me a beautiful woman, *une grande dame* . . . but also, just now and again, a simple little *ingénue* . . . so easily pleased and no trouble afterward."

"Oh, well, Major Chester, as I say, *chacun à son gout*. I can only hope that it all works out as well as you expect. It has been an honor to serve you, sire."

The curtain had fallen, and as the Empire emptied itself into the fog, the two men mixed with the crowd. They strolled across the muddy square. How the Prince adored these escapades . . . even mud was a novelty! For half an hour they watched the play at Thurston's, that the girls might complete their toilettes. The envelopes had gone to the stage door; the assignations had been made. At midnight, on the corner of Charing Cross Road, Connie Gilchrist, sitting well back in her hansom, awaited her

Baron de Staal, alias Colonel Levi, knowing perfectly well that he was the Russian Ambassador. On the corner of Rupert Street, in another hansom, little Trixie, all dimples and curls, awaited her Major Chester, knowing perfectly well that he was the Prince of Wales. Ten minutes later, in Maiden Lane, amid the plush, the gold, the clatter and the rich smells of Rule's, all four were gathered around the grilled oysters and the champagne.

The pubs had closed long ago, but the bars around Fleet Street have their own hours. At one o'clock in the morning, fifty yards up Fetter Lane, the Saloon of The Flying Fish was noisy and noisome with the gentlemen of the Press—mainly editors hanging around for the Paris cables to come in, or for reporters to come back from the country—all very knowing men, passing bets on horses, on actresses, on the next election or the next hanging. There was the occasional pansy, neat and natty, to deal with opera or Society; but mostly these men were hirsute, red-faced, red-necked. Every man's breath smelt of beer, every man's eyes were bloodshot, every man had the night in front of him. The spilt booze, the spittle, the fag ends and the sawdust made a good slimy floor. This was a place of polished brasses, a ship's figurehead, stuffed animals and patriotic chinaware—Napoleon III, Garibaldi or the Iron Duke could see his own image again and again in the cut-glass mirrors. The porcelain beer handles went up and down; the swing door to the urinals went to and fro.

There was another door. Tonight (to the annoyance of the "regulars") it had PRIVATE chalked across it. Beyond it was the snuggery—a cozier version of the saloon: lots of little colored lamps, a horsehair sofa, varnished kegs, a blazing fire and, screening the entrance from Johnson Passage, a large stuffed bear. If the saloon was drowned in beer, the snuggery was drowned in rum. Mrs. Barker—known throughout Fleet Street as "Buffers"—had been bringing in the rum jugs all evening.

A cozy scene should be a cheerful scene; this, in spite of the five men well disguised in drink, was not so. They had reached only the quarrelsome stage, and dared go no further. They would need their nerves before dawn. So, when Buffers brought in the twentieth jug of rum she was told to bugger off. The men wanted the room to themselves.

Tom Shrimp—and if he had another name nobody knew it—lay flat on the horsehair sofa, his yellow ferrety nose pointing to the ceiling, his pink eyes shut.

"The Captain"—and they called him "Captain" since "no names" is a good rule—was stamping around, raising his fists and spitting in fury—waiting for someone who didn't come.

On one varnished keg sat Mr. Wainwright. Scrupulously "mistered" by everyone, Mr. Wainwright had a bare hint of blond whiskers, was dressed to the nines—adenoidal and scrofulous.

On another keg was "Smith"—a very useful name—a toff with an Inverness cape to hide his evening clothes. He had been dining out West (in Mount Street to be precise) but he knew better than to show his shirt front in The Flying Fish.

The fifth man, only the whites of his eyes showing, stood mute and sullen against the wall. He had been born somewhere in the bogs of Sligo but they called him "Cabby." Oddly enough he had once actually been a cabby, years ago before that long holiday on Dartmoor where Smith had made a buddy of him—one hot afternoon in the quarries.

The Captain had stopped stamping around. He stood in the middle of the room, swallowed his last rum of the night, and then swore rather better than a trooper.

"It's after one o'clock. Where the bleedin' 'ell is that bloody bitch? Where is she? Where's Daffodil—blast 'er eyes? She's your doxy, Shrimp. Where the 'ell is she? I'm askin' yer—for Gawd's sake."

"Oh, shut yer great mug, Cap'n. They'll 'ear yer in the saloon."

"Shut yer own blasted mug, Shrimp—with that squeak o' yers—yer li'l rat. Yes, me fine boyho, it's you we'll all swing for yet. Yes, yer rat—swaggerin' aroun' Paddington in yer smarty ginger suit. I watched yer. That bloody suit cried aloud to 'eaven. Yes, and those great gaudy carpet bags, as big as elephants. Yer might as well 'ave proclaimed us all from the 'ouse tops. Every blasted copper and porter will know yer again—yer young dolt."

"Damn yer bleedin' eyes, Cap'n. What's got yer? The trick bloody well worked, didn't it? We've got the Earrings, 'aven't we? Wot more do yer want—the Crown and Scepter? . . . Yer make me tired."

"We shall see, Shrimpo, we shall see. It's not all over yet—not by a long chalk it ain't."

"Well, four months gone, and not a clue 'ave they got."

"Nah . . . and we ain't got a cent neither. And any day we'll be due for the rope or twenty years 'ard . . . yes, you too, me lad. Oh, I'd like to see you, with yer fancy ways, in broad arrers . . . or standin' on the drop. Learn from yer betters, can't yer? 'Ere's our friend Smith, now . . . discretion itself, if I may make so bold, Mr. Smith. Ho, ho, yes, I liked yer li'l tale of poor Lord Iddsleigh dyin' in the Prime Minister's arms—pulled the wool very nicely over old Ponsonby's eyes—very nicely indeed, Smith. Then there was Cabby 'ere—never even showed 'is blinkin' face. Yer see, the trouble with Shrimp . . ."

"That's more than enough from you, Cap'n. I've told yer already, ain't I, to shut yer mug. Me Daff' is doin' the job fer yer now, ain't she? And I bloody well did it fer yer at Paddington—didn't I now? . . . Come clean, now, did I or didn't I?"

"Arl right, Shrimpo, arl right . . . I grant yer were a cog in me machine. That's wot yer were, kid—a cog, a bloody cog."

"Yer bloody swine. Cog! Cog! Gawd, and to think I did the 'ole job fer yer. These blokes 'ere, Smith an' Cabby, were just common murderers, neither better nor worse—throat slitters. But 'oo worked the wheeze that got that there Fulleylove roight up to Newcastle an' back? Yours truly. I 'ad more brains than arl you blokes rolled into one . . . puttin' one of those blinkin' great carpet bags—bottomless bags—first over one 'at box, in that split second when Smithy 'ere 'ad shoved it on the pavement for me, on the off side of that there brougham, and just when Sir 'Enery was busy with the Station Master, goin' off to piss . . . an' then pickin' up the other bag to show an identical 'at box for the bobby to take to the train. . . . It was all a bloody miracle, I'm tellin' yer."

"Oh, clever, I don't deny it, Shrimpo, but yours weren't the only brains—mine too, as yer very well know. . . ."

"Arl roight, Cap'n . . . and then didn't I create a 'contretemps,' as they calls it, when I nicked Sir 'Enery's nag at Windsor, so as to do that 'at-box trick in reverse, the diamonds—Bloody Mary's Earrings as they calls 'em—'aving been swapped round in the train from their real Tiara to our replica . . . did I or didn't I now?"

"Oh, arl roight, arl roight! 'Ave it yer own way. Christ, the conceit of the kid! But I'll 'and it to yer on one thing: yer a good jooler's boy, nippy with yer tools."

"Good jooler's boy be buggered! That weren't the 'alf of it. An' wot will you lousy bastards give a kid loike me when we settle—a nice pat on the back? Garn, Cap'n, you make me retch."

"Now you just bloody well be'ave yerself, Shrimpo, takin' arl the credit loik tha'. We're all gents, ain't we? We'll play fair with yer an' with yer Daffodil . . . but yer not the only bloody pebble on this 'ere beach—so don't be'ave as if yer was."

Shrimp lapsed into silence. He heaved himself off the horsehair sofa and staggered to the table. He swore at the empty rum jug. Then, standing under the gaselier, in the middle of the snuggery, he started on a fresh tack.

"Arl roight then, Cap'n, fair enough. But 'oo got that fake, that replica as they calls it, of that Tiara out of that there Royal College of Art? Wasn't it me—with a bit of 'elp from Smithy 'ere . . . wasn't it now? Tell me that."

"Not so fast, Shrimpo, my boy . . ." It was Smith talking now. ". . . Not so fast. Arl you blasted well did was to keep a lookout, toimin' the bloody bobby on his beat. Not, moind yer—and I'll grant yer this—that a bloind man couldn't have nicked that college. There was me—conquerin' 'ero of a thousand cracked safes—an' all

I 'ad to do was to walk into the place with me jemmy and dark lantern. A little kid could 'ave done it—easy. An' all there was, lads, was a big wooden cupbid with—wot d'ye think—'1851 EXHIBITION REJECTS' painted on it in big white letters. Kind of 'em, weren't it? An' yer could 'ave opened the thing with a penknife—easy! I ask yer! It was dead easy; but it was yer pal Smithy, Cap'n, wot took arl the bloody risks. If that bobby 'ad come along, Shrimpo would 'ave been down the Exhibition Road loik a streak o' lightnin' . . . yer can bet yer bloody boots on that."

The Captain had sat down at last—exhausted with stamping and fuming around the room. He and Shrimp were now side by side on the horsehair sofa. Neither the scrofulous Mr. Wainwright nor Cabby had yet said a word. But again the Captain turned to Shrimp.

"Since yer being taught a thing or two, my lad—an' arl fer yer own good—yer moight note the 'ighly gentlemanly conduct of our friend Mr. Wainwright 'ere—footman extraordinary, as we all knows, to 'Er Bleedin' Majesty Queen Victoria . . . eh, Mr. Wainwright?"

"Oh, not at all, Captain, not at all; only too willing to oblige, I assure you. And very simple too, I might add, given of course a few brains and a little education— Harrow and Trinity, gentlemen, Harrow and Trinity—of a rather higher order than might be comprehensible to our young friend here. Very simple. A message to be left in Sir Henry's dressing room when it was beknown to me that he was not in residence—and I might add that my scarlet coat is the entrée to every corner of the Castle—a swift glance in Sir Henry's closet, and then . . . why, then, gentlemen, an identical hat box from Lock's, the toffs' hatters in St. James's Street. Petty cash due to yours humbly, two golden sovereigns for a high-class billycock . . . as I would have you remember, Captain, at your convenience . . . the billycock being necessary for the sake of the box. Two golden sovereigns plus fares from Windsor, et cetera; say two pounds, ten shillings."

"Mean bastard. An' 'e'll want 'is share of the bloody swag just fer goin' to St. James's and back . . . Christ!"

There were now three knocks on the side door into
Johnson Passage; an interval of ten seconds, then two
knocks; an interval of ten seconds and then one knock.
Like a flash Cabby had bolted the door into the saloon,
while the Captain, half hidden behind the stuffed bear,
unlocked the Johnson Passage door, letting a whiff of cold
fog into the snuggery.

"Oh, Daffodil, we were thinkin' as 'ow yer'd never
come. Where the 'ell 'ave yer been?"

"A stiff rum, fer Gaw'd sake . . . 'Ello, Shrimp."

"'Ello, duckie."

There was no rum left, but the Captain had a brandy
flask in the skirts of his coat. She had a mighty big swig
and then the five men closed round her, mouths set, eyes
staring, their lives and cash all at stake.

"Well, Daffodil, wot's the news? Wot's the news, girlie
. . . quick."

"'Ere, not so fast, boys. First things first. I don't know
as 'ow ye've told me wot I'm gettin' out of this little spree.
Come clean now, Cap'n, or me and my li'l pal Trixie can
double-cross yer yet—the 'ole lot o' yer. I'm a 'uman
bein' in me own bloody roight, yer know, not just Shrimpo's skirt."

"'Ell's bells, Daff, we're all gents 'ere, ain't we? *and* all
witnesses to each other. But honest, Daff, this is the big
game, yer know. Yer'll be arl roight, Daff . . . a lidy fer
loife . . . dresses, jools, carridges, the blinkin' lot. It's as
big as that, Daff. But fer Jesus' sake, now, tell us the
news. We're burstin'."

"Well then, blast yer, she's done it. It's on fer this very
noight."

"Done it? Who's done it? What's on? Fer 'eaven's sake,
Daffodil."

"Trixie, my li'l chorus mate—she's done it. This very
noight, 'ere an' now, she toikes 'Is 'Ighness, Gawd save
'im, to my cozy little plice in Brunswick Square . . . oh
yes, the clean sheets are on the bed, boys, and—wot d'ye
think?—a foin new chamber pot with the Prince of
Wales's feathers on it! What ho! What ho!"

"Oh, Gawd Almighty! Struth! Oh, Christ!" The Captain gave her two smacking kisses and walloped her bottom.

"Oh, yes, they're all at Rule's now—a tête-à-tête supper as they calls it—the four of 'em."

"Four of 'em—oh, Gawd, that buggers it up!"

"Now don't worry, Cap'n. They'll be splittin' up later. There's the Rosshan Ambassador and little Connie Gilchrist. . . ."

"Wot! *The* Connie?"

"Why not? She'll take 'Is Blinkin' Excellency off to Chelsea. And that, boyhos, will leave our Trixie all alone with 'Is 'Ighness. They're as thick as thieves over the bubbly . . . an' our Jo' waitin' for 'em with 'is 'ansom."

"Oh boy, oh boy!"

"Oh boy my foot! You look after Trixie. It's Trix 'oo's sellin' 'er blasted virtue for yer—'er virginity, and not a bloody cent 'as she 'ad, not as yet."

"She will, Daff, she will; keep yer 'air on! Just you wait. Oh Gawd, we'll all be rich forever an' ever, amen."

"Orl roight then, but moind—a moighty big share goes to our Trixie, or you'll swing—an' I mean it—the 'ole bloody crowd of yer . . . see!"

"Only Cabby and Smith are for the gallows, Daff—*not me*."

"Don't talk such balls, Shrimp—showin' yer ignorance. When I says the 'ole lot of yer, I means wot I says. Slittin' the coachman's throat is nothing. But—an' get this into yer thick 'eads—tonight's work is 'igh treason, assaultin' the heir to the throne. It means the rope."

"We know, we know. We can take care of ourselves. You jest tell us yer story . . . and fer Jesus' sake get on with it."

"Well, I'm only sayin' be fair to Trix. She's a decent kid, livin' with 'er Mum, 'an yer jest don't know wot she's doin' fer yer."

"Come on, Daff—yer story fer the love of Moike!"

"Hm! Well, this is 'er first supper with 'im—and at Rule's. But of course, what ho, it's not jest supper! This is a noight of noights. Tonoight is bed!"

"Where, Daff—fer Gawd's sake . . . an' when?"

"I've told yer, ain't I? An' don't get so darned worked up. Yer'll need yer nerve before termorrer. It's fixed, I'm tellin' yer. When they're through at Rule's an' she's got 'im jest that little bit fuddled, then she'll take 'im off to my place in Brunswick Square—by the Foundling—or that's wot 'e'll think. But—an' this is it, Cap'n—it's our Jo' who'll be droivin' the 'ansom."

"Yes, yes, Daff, good ol' Jo'—but do get on . . . wot then? I can 'ardly 'old meself."

"Well, Cap'n, just by Brunswick Square are some stables, a mews koind of a place, with a dead end. The Colonnade they calls it. It 'as a couple of oil lamps. Yer can bloody well smash those—but quietly, moind. Jo' will turn 'is 'ansom into the Colonnade an' then you bastards will be waitin' with the four-wheeler. I don't 'ave to tell old skunks loike you wot ter do. But, fer Gawd's sake, remember this is not a bit o' common kidnapin'—it's 'igh treason. . . ."

"Yes, yes, Daff. Don't 'arp on it so, don't 'arp on it. Arl the same, ol' girl, well done. We won't forget yer, nor yer li'l chorus mate neither."

"Then get busy, lads, get busy. They may be another hour at Rule's—she says 'e guzzles—but yer can't tell fer sure. If he's randy he may be wantin' bed more than supper . . . an' yer must be waitin' fer 'im in the Colonnade . . . got it?"

"We've got it, Daff, we've got it."

"Roight! An' the room in Canning Court is arl ready fer yer . . . and no more rum tonight . . . got that too?"

"Ay, ay, Daff. Come on, boys. We've been on our bloody arses long enough. Shrimpo, get on the box with Cabby . . . the rest can pile inside. . . ."

Maiden Lane at two o'clock in the morning. The fog was really thick now, everywhere, but Jo' as he whipped up his hansom was not worried; he and his mare knew every inch of this great city. He was even laughing into his muffler at the very thought of his passenger; this was the night of his life.

The Prince of Wales was slightly fuddled, a little drowsy and very happy. He remembered now, when he was a boy, the Prime Minister had taken him for a ride in a hansom to see the sights. Papa had demurred but, as Dizzy said, the hansom is the gondola of London; one can see everything from it. He could almost hear the old Jew, so cocky at having coined a phrase. And now, yes, one could see everything—dimly through the fog. Already men were washing down the streets and flushing the sewers. A few early wagons were arriving at Covent Garden. They saw the occasional mail van and once he and Trixie heard the fire engines, bells clanging and harness jingling. In Drury Lane a few prostitutes were still showing their wares—their white flesh—at the windows; children were sleeping in doorways—the Prince thought this an odd thing to do on a November night.

The street lamps flitted by. His contentment was complete. They were beyond Long Acre now and for him this was an unknown world. All real ladies and gentlemen had been left far behind.

"Where's this, Trixie?"

"Tottenham Court Road, sir."

He had heard of it; there was a shopkeeper called Maple who had wormed his way into the Jockey Club. And now the Prince was almost dreaming—half asleep, half awake, savoring the warmth and the smells of the cab—a horsy rug round them both, stable straw under their feet, a scented girl, and brandy on his own breath.

"And this, Trixie?"

"Woburn Place, sir."

He closed his eyes. Woburn Place. Suddenly he seemed to remember who he was. He thought of a great ball, years and years ago, at Woburn. There had been a marvelous Viennese orchestra, but when they danced to the gavotte it had really been to the swirl and rustle of two hundred crinolines. It had been his first dance with Alix . . . but there had already been other women . . . he remembered still the Princess Bourbon Parma (so young and fresh) and the Duchess Caracciolo, the lovely mother of his Olga. Far-off days when he was first tasting free-

dom. And then he was back in the hansom with Trixie,
which, somehow, seemed better than all the glories.

Crossing Woburn Place they had seen an omnibus and
a few cabs—probably meeting the Irish Mail at Euston—
and then they had plunged into darker streets:
Bloomsbury, a seedy, down-at-heel sort of place, all as-
pidistras and "APARTMENT" cards, all lodging houses for
pale City clerks.

Then, quite suddenly, the lamps vanished entirely. The
hansom had been driven into complete darkness—a cob-
bled street without a light.

"Where's this, Trixie? Where are we?"

"My back door, sir. More private-like than the square.
It will be warm upstairs."

He helped her out of the cab, out into the dense yellow
fog. Clearly it was a mews; there was a four-wheeler
alongside them and a general smell of horses. The silence
was tense. He could hear nothing except the mare's
breath, and could see less.

"A strange place this, Trixie."

"As you say, sir, a very strange place."

Had he detected a change in her tone? She seemed
almost to be mocking him. He was handing up the fare to
the cabman when, suddenly, something, somebody,
knocked off his hat. He thought that the horse must have
shied. He saw his hat rolling on the cobbles . . . and then
there was something, something warm and suffocating—a
rug, a blanket, a coat—it was over his head—and men
were clasping his arms.

Nearly a quarter of a century later, coughing himself to
death in Buckingham Palace, he was glad that he could
be sure of two things—sure that Witch of the Air had won
at Kempton Park that afternoon, sure that neither Mama
nor the British people had ever been told of this night's
escapade.

He never knew where he was taken. The windows of
the four-wheeler had been soaped and the fog deadened
all sound. On leaving the mews he was almost sure—or so
he told the Home Secretary—that they had turned right,

which probably meant they had gone east. Later he certainly heard fog signals and ships' sirens out on the river. On and on they went—it seemed hours—sometimes clattering over granite blocks, sometimes slithering over tramlines. Once they all got out and used a most ornamental iron urinal, and then all climbed in again, but from that glimpse of the foggy night he learned nothing. He heard a clock strike four, so that weeks later he had to go with the police to see whether he could identify the chimes of Stepney or Rotherhithe—and much use that was. At one point the horse seemed to be toiling up a short steep slope, and then, with the brakes on, there was a short steep down slope. The detectives thought this might be the hump-backed bridge over Bow Creek into Canning Town —and much use that was.

They hardly spoke in the four-wheeler. As they drove through the night, along these silent and deserted fog-bound streets, they were all mute. It was only in the first few minutes that he had spoken to them.

"I must tell you, gentlemen, that I happen to be a man of high rank. You will pay very heavily indeed for this outrage. For your own sakes I advise you to release me immediately. . . ."

"Stow it, guvnor. We knows wot we're abart. Yer ain't goin' to come to no bloody 'arm—not you, yer ain't."

"Let me go now then, and no more will be said; I give you my word of honor, as an officer and a gentleman. I am no use to you. My pocket is not worth picking. I have a few sovereigns—five pounds at most—take them for God's sake."

He told them that he never carried much cash, that his "secretary"—he had nearly said "equerry"—handled his money.

"Take this sovereign purse, gentlemen; it's all I have . . . there's nothing else."

In fact there was his fob with his garnet; there were his black pearl studs and links; there was his signet ring with the plumes and the "Ich Dien"; there was also the cigar case, that very special present from Cesar Ritz. He prayed silently that these things would pass unnoticed. His prayer was answered. The Captain was in no mood to deal with such trifles.

"It's not yer rhino we're after, guvnor. We're not 'ere to talk 'igh finance. We're 'ere, believe it or not, to talk abart some bloody diamonds . . . Your Most Royal an' Mighty 'Ighness."

So they understood one another. From then on they traveled in silence—not a sound but the clip-clop of the hooves on the granite sets. He reckoned that it must have been about half past four when they stopped in a narrow court, with one lamp.

It was a room without chairs or tables, but it had been prepared for them: a stinking oil lamp on the floor and a blanket nailed over the window. That was all—a room borrowed for an hour. They had pushed him ahead of them into the house and up the stairs. They had put on harlequin masks. Mr. Wainwright and Daffodil had been left behind. They wanted no women, and as for Mr. Wainwright, the Prince had seen him too often at Windsor; even with a mask there was a risk. That left five of them: the Captain, Smith, Cabby, Shrimp and the Prince of Wales. They stood in a circle, their shadows thrown upward, rather weirdly, onto the filthy ceiling.

"There they are!"

With something of a flourish the Captain had taken a handkerchief from his poacher's pocket and laid the two twelve-pointed diamond stars on the bare boards. Five men stared down in silence.

"Well, gentlemen, what is all this about?"

"No good makin' speeches, 'Ighness; three-quarters of a million quid by Tuesday an' we'll take yer 'ome."

"This is ridiculous. This is damnable nonsense. Since you seem to know who I am, however, I might as well tell you that you have the wrong man."

"Nah, nah, none of that. We know yer."

"Oh yes, I'm the Prince of Wales—there's no doubt of that—but those diamonds are not mine. They belong to the nation. I cannot have any dealings with you. In any case the arm of the law is long . . . there is a murdered coachman to be revenged, and while I scarcely care what happens to me, this night's work, as you must surely know, is high treason—what the law would call 'assault upon a prince of the blood royal.' So you had better be thinking of the gallows instead of talking nonsense. I repeat, the arm of the law is long: you are already in a trap; my detectives shadow me everywhere."

The Prince had blundered. This was pure bluff. He never allowed detectives on his evening escapades. They all knew this—it was common talk—and the Prince could see that they knew it. His first bluff had been called. He was calm—he had been trained to be calm—but a vein in his neck was pulsating.

"We needn't talk balls, Yer 'Ighness. We're all men of the world, ain't we? The sooner we agree the sooner you'll be tucked up in yer li'l bed. Nah, come on, come on. We can't sell those blinkin' diamond stars—not *as* stars, that is—every diamond merchant in the 'ole world knows 'em. On the other 'and, if we break 'em up, they ain't worth ten tharsand quid . . . a tidy sum, I grant yer, but not really worth arl our bloody trouble . . . eh, lads?"

"Very well. I've no more to say, gentlemen. You will be arrested in the morning. We know who you are."

"Nah then guvnor, nah then, that's enough of yer bluff. We don't want to 'ang around 'ere arl noight, nor don't you. So, we'll break up the stars and get our ten tharsand quid. And then . . . why, then the 'ole bloody scandal can wash over yer, and over yer ol' mum . . . and down yer . . . plus a few spicy bits abart yer boy Eddy, dropped in the roight quarter. An' now yer can blinkin' well walk 'ome—eleven bloody miles in the bloody fog. You've enjoyed yer trip, I 'opes."

The Prince looked left and then right, as if in a trap. His hat had gone. The rug over his head had done him no good. His face had brushed against some cobwebs on the stairs. One false eyebrow had gone. The state of his shirt was unsuitable for the best-dressed man in Europe. Worse still, his famous *savoir faire* was crumbling. The Captain had got him where he wanted him, and knew it.

"Come now, 'Ighness, I'm a reasonable koind o' bloke . . . say 'alf a million. Fair's fair!"

"Hm! Even a prince, gentlemen, does not keep that much cash in his house. How, in heaven's name, do you think you could make the exchange? I could have you watched, followed and spied upon every hour of the day, and then . . . the condemned cell. However, I have a proposal. I admit I'm your prisoner. I will take the earrings—the diamond stars—now. Drive me to Marlborough House with them and, on my word of honor as a prince, I will, within ten minutes, give you a thousand pounds in cash at—well—let us say in the porch of Boodles . . . and there the matter will end, forever. Threats are quite useless, but that is a solemn engagement."

So he was prepared to drive some sort of bargain. He was broken, groggy, like a boxer on the ropes. Well, it had been bound to happen. Now they could put the screw on.

"Nah, nah, Prince, that's no bloody good at arl. Yer word of honor wouldn't count with the loikes of us . . . not on yer loife it wouldn't. Promises to crooks don't count. I know, I know. And Boodles . . . yah! with a couple of St. James's sentries in shoutin' distance. Now then, 'Ighness, our last word: 'alf a million by Tuesday . . . or yer don't go 'ome—not never. No, not tonight nor never. Got that?"

Who was bluffing now? Did they mean it? He could feel his own pulse. He knew his blood pressure was high—he was that kind of man—but this time it was dangerous because he was also frightened. Was this really the end, or was it possible that someone really was still bluffing? What was it to be—death, a long-drawn-out kidnaping, or a hard bargain? He knew that so far as he was concerned the game was up.

"Very well, gentlemen, I have given you a chance to get out of your mess. You have refused. In the end— whatever you may think now—you'll pay for that, probably with your lives. Meanwhile, you may as well state your terms."

"Good! Good! That's more loike it. That's wot I calls business. Shrimpo, my boy, go down and tell Mrs. D. to give yer foive mugs of 'ot coffee. We'll arl drink to this . . . what ho!"

"Your terms, gentlemen? I am waiting."

"Oh, no 'urry, no 'urry. Tike it or leave it—'ere's the plot. As I say, tike it or leave it . . . but you ain't got no bloody choice, really, 'ave yer? 'ave yer? Next Wednesday week, seein' as 'ow yer woife's in Denmark, yer goes up to bonny Scotland to see yer poor ol' Mum. Yer leaves King's Cross at 'alf past ten in the morning, *pre*cisely, with his blinkin' lordship the Proime Minister to keep yer company. They change yer engine at Grantham and again at Newcastle; at Edinburgh yer 'ave a red carpet kind of a do with wot they calls the Provost and a few toffs . . . arl correct, I trust."

The Prince had stiffened visibly. All his plans had been changed that very morning so that he could travel to Balmoral with the Salisburys . . . and already, within a few hours, these men knew every detail. This made the whole affair far more serious.

Shrimp now came clattering up the stairs with a tray of mugs. The Captain laced the lot from his flask and with a mock bow offered one to the Prince.

"Yes, Yer 'Ighness, yer go to Scotland on yer own train, jest 'alf an hour behind the Flyin' Scotsman so that if there's a bloody smash it will be the loikes of us as is killed, and not Yer 'Ighness, eh?"

"These arrangements are not of my making. For God's sake let us conduct our business quickly, and have done with it. I have yet to know why my journey should concern you. Pray tell me what it is all about. Again, I am waiting."

"Then yer need wait no longer. Listen, an' don't yer make no bleedin' mistakes, fer arl our bleedin' sakes. This is the plan . . . these are yer orders, an' if yer make jest one slip then it's all up with yer, an' with yer diamonds . . . so yer bloody well listen . . . now . . ."

6

Ten-thirty from King's Cross

Having emitted three loud puffs of steam and one flourish on its whistle, the Flying Scotsman had drawn out of King's Cross at ten o'clock precisely. In the calm that comes after bustle, the Station Master, a gardenia in his buttonhole, strolled nonchalantly to the Bay. Having got rid of what he prosaically called the "10:00 A.M. to Edinburgh," and having given his glossy topper an extra rub on his sleeve, he now turned to a more exacting task.

This particular royal journey being unannounced, there was no crowd worth speaking of except a crowd of policemen—about three times as many as usual. This was a mystery even to the Station Master. It piqued him: he should have been in the confidence of Marlborough House. At the barriers there was a mere handful of people, a few idlers who had spotted the red carpet. They were a drab lot except for one glamorous and golden-haired floozy. She had been hanging around for over an hour. The Inspector of Police—a Baptist—didn't care for the look of her but had decided there was nothing he could do about her . . . in any case the girl was unlikely to solicit at ten o'clock in the morning.

Here on the Bay, away from the other platforms, the Station Master could look upon the scene with pride. There was not only calm, there was a reverential silence, as in a church just before the coffin arrives. At the far end the big engine, eager to be off, was quietly putting out little jets of steam. There was no bustle, no luggage, no milk cans, no porters. The Marlborough House and Downing Street baggage, together with valets and ladies' maids, had been sent up in wagonettes an hour ago, and was already on board. From one edge of the platform to the other an expanse of crimson cloth was now an empty foreground for the maroon, gilded and emblazoned train.

Ten minutes to go . . . and a City messenger boy, smart and perky in his pill-box hat, was handing a black-edged envelope to the Inspector of Police at the barrier. The Inspector, blushing with self-importance at the sight of the crest, passed it to the Station Master. The glamorous floozy immediately left in a hansom. She had seen all she wanted.

One minute to go . . . At the entrance on Platform No. 1 there was a stir and a flurry, a procession of shiny toppers, of flowered and ospreyed bonnets and of spangled black mantles. The Prince of Wales, swinging his cane, was preceded by the Chairman of the Great Northern, and followed by his two detectives and a fox terrier. The suites, the ladies and gentlemen in waiting, the equerries and the secretaries, plus a repugnant German child in spectacles, velvet, lace and the kilt, all bore the usual self-conscious pose of mutual affability and the pretense that other people weren't there—a pose always to be seen in courtiers.

An acute observer might also have noted two rather more unusual things. First, buried unostentatiously among the various frock-coated gentlemen, were the Right Honorable Henry Mathews, P.C., Her Majesty's Principal Secretary of State for Home Affairs, and also—tremulous with age—General Sir Frederick Rogers, K.C.B., Chief Commissioner for Police. Alongside him, in a short jacket, was a dim, respectable and rather anonymous figure, a Mr. Crawford, a detective from Bow Street. Second, the acute observer might have remarked that although all luggage and impedimenta had long since been stowed on the train, an equerry—a Mr. Cyril Pumphrey—carried a cardboard box, a stout box such as Mr. Poole might use when delivering a suit to a customer. This was doubly odd, both because equerries do not carry cardboard boxes, and because a constable walked within one yard of Mr. Pumphrey's arm.

Everyone was at last collected upon the crimson cloth, now positively heraldic—courtiers sables on a field gules, all proper. The Station Master handed the messenger boy's black-edged envelope to the Prince's Secretary—reverentially.

"Sir Francis Knollys, sir . . . for His Royal Highness."

The envelope, bearing the Queen's crest, had been addressed with one of Ponsonby's new-fangled Windsor typewriters: HIS ROYAL HIGHNESS THE PRINCE OF WALES—EXTREMELY URGENT AND CONFIDENTIAL. The Prince ripped it open. His affability vanished. Very curtly he gave it back to Knollys.

"Take this. The bastards have got hold of Mama's private notepaper—the die must be changed of course—and they can't spell 'confidential.' However, I suppose the damned thing gives us our message. . . . Pass it on to Mathews immediately."

Then came the fuss of getting everyone into the right carriages—the usual conflict between protocol and corner seats. The train, as it pulled out at last into the autumn mist on its long journey north, had more dignity than its passengers. Within the central and emblazoned coach, among the palms and the electroliers, the Prince of Wales, the Marquis and Marchioness of Salisbury, the Honorable Mrs. George Keppel, Sir Francis Knollys, and Eddy relaxed in their tapestried chairs. Coffee, brandy and caviar sandwiches were served just before Kentish Town. The luncheon hampers would not be put on board until Peterborough, and one must keep up one's strength—it was, after all, an hour since breakfast.

As the train pulled out of King's Cross one would certainly have noted that the last coach was an "observation car." The observation car had a rear window from which, as the train sped northward, one could watch with fascination the receding perspective of railway lines, or—even more fascinating—the diminishing oval of light at

the end of tunnels. Such cars were normally used by
engineers for examining the track; this one had been
hurriedly supplied with armchairs, a carpet, provender
and a slop pail. Locked inside it were the Home Secretary, the Commissioner for Police and the dim and anonymous Mr. Crawford, together with the Honorable Cyril
Pumphrey and his cardboard box. While all this was
peculiar to a degree, all else was normal—a normal journey such as any royal creature might make to that ghastly castle upon Deeside where Buddha, the spider in the
web, was now waiting for her Prime Minister and her
eldest son.

From the window of the observation car the two great
iron arches of the King's Cross roof were already specks
in the distance. It was the Home Secretary who broke the
silence.

"Well, gentlemen, here we are, all locked in at any rate
until Edinburgh. So far these thugs have kept their word.
Here is the message they promised His Highness. It was
handed to him at the last moment. . . ."

"Surely the messenger was instantly apprehended, Mr.
Home Secretary?"

"The messenger, Mr. Pumphrey, was a small boy in
uniform from the Cheapside office of the City Messenger
Service. These men are not altogether fools, I imagine.
Anyway, here is the message, typewritten on the Queen's
Windsor Castle notepaper. . . ."

"By Jove, what damned cheek!"

"Quite, Mr. Pumphrey. Here it is: YOUR SIGNAL—A
WORKMAN ON THE LINE WILL MOP HIS BROW WITH A
YELLOW HANDKERCHIEF."

The Commissioner for Police, the aged Sir Frederick,
gave a hollow cackle.

"Really, ye know, I can hardly see the point of all this
nonsense. I suppose we must go through with it now, if
only to please His Royal Highness. If only my advice had
been sought sooner . . . this journey to Scotland, ye know,
at twenty-four hours' notice . . . all most inconvenient and

uncomfortable . . . and quite useless . . . not quite the thing, Mathews, for men in our position, what?"

"The call of duty, Sir Frederick . . ."

"Fiddlesticks! For Mr. Pumphrey here to throw half-a-million pounds onto the railway line—five bundles, you say, of a hundred bank notes each, and each for £1000—is really quite outrageous. I have no wish to be disloyal to His Highness but the thing seems quite farcical, if not criminal. One thing is certain—we shall lose the money and never get the diamonds."

"If those jewels are not delivered to Balmoral within a week, Sir Frederick, it is *you,* you know, who will have to start the biggest manhunt in history. On the other hand, once the diamonds *are* delivered, then the thieves have their money and also know, on the Prince's word of honor, that the matter is closed. They get off scot free, and the House of Coburg escapes a scandal . . . not a bad bargain."

"Very well, Mr. Home Secretary, look at the matter your way. I am only an old soldier but, by Gad, the thing sticks in my gullet . . . this supping with the devil. I abhor royal gossip, but, between ourselves, there is another matter: whence, pray, comes this half million? Popular rumor suggests that His Highness could hardly put his hands on such a sum. I only ask for information."

"Quite, Sir Frederick, quite. I understand that the Prince of Wales spent the weekend with the Rothschilds at Tring."

"Oh, I see, I see!"

Mr. Pumphrey also gave a long-drawn-out "Oh!" The silent Mr. Crawford was content to raise his eyebrows.

"That, of course, is strictly confidential."

"Of course, of course, Mr. Home Secretary . . . not a word to anyone."

"Very well then. Perhaps I may add that I dined at Marlborough House last night. I can assure you that the Prince is determined to avoid a scandal—if only for the Queen's sake. One can imagine the headlines—CROWN JEWELS STOLEN, perhaps; or worse still, QUEEN'S DIAMONDS FAKED. The thought of it is quite unbearable.

The institution of monarchy would never survive it, and that is something about which the Prince, for all his—er—conviviality, is much concerned, you know. So I think you may take it, Sir Frederick—as a strict secret—that it is the Baron Ferdy who has put up this vast sum (the actual bank notes were conveyed to Coutts from Threadneedle Street, but that means nothing) on condition that the diamond stars should pass quietly but absolutely to the House of Rothschild—at the Queen's death."

Mr. Cyril Pumphrey brightened visibly. "The Rothschilds, then, are confident that the gang will keep its side of the bargain. They may know something that we don't, but in any case that is surely a good point, Mr. Home Secretary. With all due respect to the Prince's own judgment—and Sir Frederick has just suggested that His Royal Highness is being profligate, reckless and irresponsible. . . ."

"Come, come, Mr. Pumphrey, I meant nothing of the kind. You twist my words, sir . . . really . . ."

"Well, whatever you may have meant, Sir Frederick, we can be jolly pleased that our operation has Rothschild backing. It puts a completely different complexion upon the whole show—what? Does it not, Mr. Home Secretary?"

"Oh, dear me, yes. Certainly, certainly . . . most reassuring."

"And of course the bank notes are all marked?"

"Really, really, Mr. Pumphrey. I have already told you that these men are not fools—desperadoes maybe, but not fools. Part of their bargain with the Prince—and remember that it was made under physical duress—was that the bank notes, now in that box, should be new packets from the Mint, with the seals unbroken. Of course we have their numbers, but what is the good of that? Within hours they will have bought scores of postal orders in a hundred different post offices and cashed them—or possibly changed all the notes at half-a-dozen different *bureaux de change,* in Brussels, Paris, Hamburg . . . who knows? Another part of the bargain is that we must not expect to receive the diamonds for a week—a week for them to change the bank notes and, if they choose, to leave the country."

"Clever devils, Mr. Home Secretary, clever devils!"

"I fear so, Mr. Pumphrey, I fear so. . . . But I see that we are already passing Stevenage. From now on we must be on the alert. Let me summarize our tasks. You, Mr. Pumphrey, must watch, as indeed we all will, for the workman with the yellow handkerchief. As soon as you see him you will open this window here and, as soon as I say 'Go,' will eject your package onto the permanent way. That is clear?"

"Couldn't be clearer, sir."

"That signal—the yellow handkerchief—may come anywhere between here and Aberdeen, or even on that last run up to Ballater. Vigilance must be maintained for every second. Now you, Sir Frederick, have made your dispositions. Kindly explain them."

"Oh, certainly. Positively a military operation. I have two thousand men, drawn from different police forces throughout the kingdom. They are in plain clothes of course. Two thousand may sound a great many, but it is, after all, barely four to the mile. That is enough. Fortunately the mist is thin—a real fog would have been disastrous. The entire track is under observation and if anyone picks up the box of bank notes after the train has passed, why then, upon my soul, an arrest is certain."

"I am glad you are so confident, Sir Frederick. Now you, Mr. Crawford, must watch everything and everybody with your—er—your trained eye. Above all you must have these binoculars at the ready so that when the moment comes we may depend upon you for an identification—some old lag perhaps, or well-known figure from the underworld. I am sure you won't let us down."

"I will do what I can, sir, but identification will be difficult. Our pace is terrific; seventy miles an hour or more. I suppose you will immediately pull the cord and stop the train."

"It was decided, Mr. Crawford, that we would not do that. We were advised that in any case a train of this weight and speed could not stop in much less than a mile.

Moreover, the incident might lead to undesirable reports in the newspapers—and all to no purpose. It would also give our protagonists an excuse to break their bargain. No, it would never do. I think we know best, Mr. Crawford."

Mr. Crawford felt he could have managed this affair rather better than either Sir Frederick or the Home Secretary. He also knew his place. He not only knew it, he felt that he was being kept in it, that he was no more than the hired detective. He gazed rather wistfully down the endless perspective of the Great Northern Line, drawn as with a ruler across the level fields of Hertfordshire.

"As you say, sir."

"Quite, Mr. Crawford, thank you. Now I, for my part, gentlemen, am ready to relieve any of you at any time. Meanwhile, I shall go on with what I am doing—ticking off the quarter-mile posts on this schedule of stations and distances. At this moment, for instance, we are precisely one and three-quarter miles north of Stevenage. When the crisis occurs we must be sure of our exact whereabouts— these thugs may have some local hideout or accomplices— someone to harbor them. And now let us all do our duty to the Queen and to the Prince. We have ample viands here, also several bottles of hock. We have an arduous day ahead, some nine hours to go; but my flask and cigar case are at your service . . . now, gentlemen."

They hurtled through St. Neots at nearly eighty. With the sun breaking up the mist, and with the Flying Scotsman ahead, acting almost as a pilot train, the driver barely glanced at his signals. He had surmounted the Potters Bar incline at over fifty—a good start—and was now making the most of these flat stretches of eastern England. He even allowed his bleary but sentimental eye to wander over Fenland spires and the far-off Isle of Ely. Then he looked down the line ahead and spoke to his fireman.

"Wot's up, Jack? They're guardin' the Prince very partikler like this morning, ain't they?"

" 'Ow's that?"

"There's blokes arl along the track—three or four to every mile. Plain-clothes coppers, I reckon."

"Gawd! D'ye think as 'ow it's train wreckers they're afeared of?"

"Nah, just a scare . . . nihilists or Fenians, or jest one of these 'ere dynamite hoaxes. Someone got the wind up. Blowed if I know . . ."

"Not our bloody business anyway."

"Nah. We're ahead of toime—that's our business. Lovely! Lovely! Shovel it on, Jack."

They ground to a halt at Peterborough: seventy-six miles in an hour and ten minutes. The platform had been cleared. The toppers and even the gold lace were paraded, but within the train not a soul stirred. Only the repulsive child in velvet bothered to look out the window. Twenty luncheon hampers were passed to the stewards at the door of the fourgon, and then, drinking their fashionable apéritifs, they were off again, this time through familiar hunting shires with nostalgic memories of runs with the Quorn and the Pytchely . . . and so up the long slope to Grantham. Within half an hour, and with a brand-new engine, they were over the Trent beyond Newark, and skirting the Dukeries—more nostalgic memories, this time of great house parties. And then, with everyone absorbed in the second course of luncheon, Doncaster, although it might have recalled the St. Leger and a night at Tranby Croft, flashed by unnoticed.

At Peterborough it had been possible to ignore the local gentry. York was different. One cannot ignore York. Even though York coincided with the coffee and cognac a moment had to be spared. Bertie and Eddy—successive heirs to the throne—stepped onto the red carpet. The Station Master presented the three Lords Lieutenant of the three Ridings. The North Riding remarked upon the miracle of modern travel; the East Riding said that the mist had cleared. The West Riding, more courageous, addressed himself to Eddy, who said that the mist had cleared. The ladies-in-waiting could be glimpsed in the corner seats of their steamy carriages, dozing over empty coffee cups, their bonnet strings flung back, their veils rolled up on their moist foreheads. It was only Mrs. Keppel who allowed herself a little powder, and a hat which gave cheer to all—a hat which was as if the spring had come. In the front coach four equerries could be seen playing whist; they were playing for ten-pound tricks. In the observation car, the Home Secretary, for reasons best known to himself, had pulled down the blinds—thus starting a fine hare that the dying Emperor Frederick of Germany was being carried north to say farewell to the Queen—perhaps to die in her arms. Then the whistle blew and on the long run up the vale between the Cleveland Hills and Swaledale they touched eighty. Nobody even noticed the towers of Durham.

As they crossed the High Level Bridge at Newcastle—one of the wonders of the age—they might also have beheld the most beautiful and most black of all these northern cities, yet another child of their own time; they snored or gambled.

The four men in the observation car, flushed with hock, struggled to remain alert. None of them spoke until they were past Morpeth. It was the detective who dared to break the silence.

"Excuse me, Mr. Home Secretary, but I think the next half hour is our last chance."

"Really, Crawford, what an extraordinary idea . . . another three or four hours yet, I think, to Ballater."

"The sun sets at Greenwich at 5:20, sir—rather earlier as far north as this."

"Gad, Sir Frederick, the man's right. It'll soon be dark. I never thought of that."

"Nor did I, Mr. Home Secretary, nor did I . . . but why should we? That's Crawford's job. Quite right to tell us, my man, but I can't for the life of me see that it makes a hap'orth of difference. After all, we can't see their damned yellow handkerchief in the dark, so why bother? The whole thing is a mare's nest anyway, eh, Pumphrey?"

"Oh, certainly, if you say so, Sir Frederick. Certainly."

"Of course it is—always said so. The diamonds—the earrings or whatever they call them—have gone anyway. That's that. The Prince must make up his mind to it, eh,

Mathews? He's spoilt, you know—between ourselves—
and it won't hurt him to have to admit defeat for once in
his life, eh, Mathews?"

"Possibly not, Sir Frederick; although the permanent
loss of the earrings will, surely, hardly redound to your
credit—as Commissioner of Police."

"Pooh! These things are bound to happen, my dear
chap. Don't talk stuff and nonsense."

"Anyway, it's not the Prince, it's Ferdy Rothschild
who'll be taking the rap. Not, of course, that he'll be
losing any sleep either. He will have had the whole thing
underwritten by the Sassoons, Barings and all that crowd.
They'll all have shares in this robbery, you know.
Damned profitable game. Underwritten all over again by
the small fry at Lloyd's. Overinsured at the top, underin-
sured at the bottom. The Ikeys will win—you can stake
your life on that."

"Ah! You know a lot, Home Secretary."

"I'm afraid it's true. Nobody is going to thank us, you
know, if we do catch these rogues. And I suppose when
Rothschilds get the insurance the Prince will take his
cut—a kind of commission—that's only fair. No, no, only
the Old Girl will be displeased."

"The Old Girl, sir?"

"The Queen, Crawford."

"Oh, yes, sir."

"If she's been told anything about it, that is. You see,
Sir Frederick, she doesn't want faked jewelry and she
doesn't want a scandal. . . . Everybody else stands to win
hands down."

Mr. Crawford was thinking that he would have to tell
Mrs. Crawford all this, in bed. He was profoundly
shocked. He was an experienced detective and yet it had
never occurred to him that people might actually make
money out of being robbed. . . . His mind reeled. Mr.
Pumphrey now looked around him—east and west.

"Hm, Crawford's right, you know. Sun's almost down.
It's jolly well all or nothing now, chaps. The whole thing
looks like being a 'no go.' Oh well, at least we'll be able to

put our feet up and booze a bit. By Jove we've earned it—what?"

It was almost dusk now, but nobody had thought of lighting the oil lamps in the roof of the observation car. They were running parallel with the Northumberland coast, a few miles inland, about a third of the way from Newcastle to Berwick. There was the occasional hill as at Alnwick, and the occasional rill running down to the sea, where they had to cross some little stream such as the Coquet.

Looking back down the long perspective of the double track, even in the failing light they could see three of Sir Frederick's plain-clothes policemen, widely spaced. Then, suddenly, there flashed into their field of vision a gang of three platelayers—all correct in corduroy trousers and checked shirts, and with the tools of their trade. As the men were on the "up" line they had no need to pause as the royal train roared past them. Two, in fact, kept their heads down. The third stood upright and mopped his brow with a large yellow handkerchief.

"Go . . . Pumphrey . . . Go! For God's sake! Crawford . . . your binoculars."

The cardboard box, heavy with crisp bank notes, whirled into space. Then . . . there was absolute blackness, utter darkness. They were in a quarter-mile-long tunnel.

"Bastards!"

"Bugger!"

"Light a match—for the love of Mike!"

"Damn their eyes!"

"Clever devils—I knew they were. Clever devils! So much, Sir Frederick, for your damned mare's nest!"

It had all been perfectly timed for the twilight. The platelayers, outside the tunnel, could now work on for a few more minutes, unsuspected by the plain-clothes policemen, until it was dark, and time to "go home from work." As for the cardboard box, it had finally thudded onto the line actually just within the darkness of the tunnel, only a few yards from the gang.

And now the train flashed out into daylight on the

other side. They had been inside the tunnel and now, quite suddenly, they were on a bridge—a small viaduct.

"Look, gentlemen, look—you see the trick."

Sixty feet below them, waiting in the road which wound up the glen—still just discernible in the dusk—was a gig, the driver looking up as they hurtled by far above him.

"Well, you see, Mr. Home Secretary, you see . . ."

"Of course I see, Sir Frederick. . . . I may be a fool but I'm not a bloody fool. Nor am I in my second childhood. Any identification, Crawford?"

"I do my best, sir, but I have not been trained to see in the dark."

"I didn't suppose you had. You realize, all of you, that that gang can go quietly working for another ten minutes or so, and Sir Frederick's 'sentries' won't have the slightest reason to suspect them. And then, when they stop work, one of them can nip into the tunnel, pick up the money, come through the tunnel and drop it over the viaduct to his friend in the gig. Most fortunately, however, as we left King's Cross we were told by Sir Frederick that, in the event of the box of bank notes being picked up, an arrest was certain . . . well?"

"Upon my soul, Mr. Home Secretary, you twist my words. Damn it, sir, you twist my words. Reasonably certain, maybe . . . but—er—not this, not this."

"Not what, Sir Frederick?"

"The tunnel . . . the tunnel. I never thought of a tunnel."

"I see. Well, gentlemen, as Her Majesty's Secretary of State, I must thank you for your cooperation. It has been a somewhat arduous day, I fear. It is unfortunate that neither the tunnel nor the dusk were foreseen. The whole affair—as I shall have to tell His Royal Highness—has been grossly mismanaged."

"Indeed, indeed . . . and mismanaged by whom, Mr. Home Secretary? Who, pray, is in charge of this—er—this operation?"

"I am, Sir Frederick; and, as you well know, a Minister of the Crown does not publicly blame his subordinates.

That may come later. Certainly a most searching inquiry seems to be indicated—an inquiry, Sir Frederick, into the administration of the police. Perhaps there are too many doddering old buffers in charge . . . we shall see, we shall see. Meanwhile we are being whirled toward Edinburgh. His Royal Highness alights for half an hour at the Waverley Station to take some refreshment with the Lord Provost, with the Duke of Buccleuch, the MacGregor of the MacGregor, and with the Lochiel of that ilk. I have, naturally, been invited to join them. You will remain here. The Prince will be impatient to hear my news. And this evening, at Balmoral, Sir Frederick, Her Majesty will doubtless wish to know how her police have acquitted themselves. I am a just man, I hope, but my task will be no easy one. You will now allow me, therefore, to compose my thoughts."

"Most necessary, I'm sure, Mr. Home Secretary, most necessary."

"Enough, Sir Frederick, enough."

Mr. Crawford was thinking that it must have been just like this after the Charge of the Light Brigade. Mr. Cyril Pumphrey noticed that they were now crossing the border: he could see the lights reflected in the river as they thundered over the bridge at Berwick. As a trained diplomat he attempted a *détente*.

"Well, well, let's all put our feet up. Still a couple of bottles left—shall we split one, Crawford?"

"Thank you, sir, that would be most welcome."

"Your first visit to Bonnie Scotland, Crawford?"

"Yes, sir; I am much looking forward to Deeside."

Sir Frederick, having been crushed by the Home Secretary, now saw his chance of vicarious revenge.

"I think, Mr. Pumphrey, that Crawford will be returning to his duties at Bow Street by the first train in the morning."

"I was hoping, Sir Frederick, for a glimpse of Balmoral."

"The Castle, Crawford, is not open to the public. I am sure, however, that the Railway Arms at Ballater will accommodate you. Bow Street is very busy just now—

footpads and burglars take advantage of these foggy nights—and a further day's leave would not be justified. And, Crawford . . ."

"Sir."

"I shall be enjoying Her Majesty's hospitality until Friday; you will make no report to your superiors until my return . . . is that clear?"

"Quite clear, sir."

"Hard cheese, Crawford—what?"

"Thank you, Mr. Pumphrey. I am sorry the trip has been such a failure."

"Oh, well, Crawford—not your fault, nor mine. These two must fight it out between them . . . and whitewash themselves if they can . . . glad we're not in their shoes, by Jove!"

Sir Frederick was now both choleric and purple. "Really, Mr. Pumphrey, you go too far. Speaking like that to a subordinate, and in front of the Home Secretary. Upon my soul, I can hardly contain myself."

"It's no good getting in a lather, Sir Frederick. Take it out of poor old Crawford, if you must, but *I'm* jolly well not your poodle, you know. Anyway, two things are now certain. One is that the Home Secretary will have to break the news to the Old Girl sooner or later, and also—in a few minutes when we get to Edinburgh—to our dear Bertie. The other thing is that half-a-million pounds' worth of Bank of England notes are being driven briskly over the Northumberland moors in a gig, and that Bloody Mary's Earrings have vanished forever from the Crown Jewels of England—if, indeed, they were ever there."

"And pray, Mr. Pumphrey, what is the meaning of that last remark?"

"Oh, nothing, Mr. Home Secretary. Only that you and Sir Frederick—both high servants of the Crown, what ho!—imagine yourselves as being given all available information, while I, being only a poor bloody equerry, hear all the gossip."

When they reached Edinburgh the station arc lights were blazing. At the border, at the precise moment of crossing the Tweed at Berwick, the Prince of Wales had taken off his trousers and donned the kilt. The crowd on the platform at Edinburgh, in their fustian—knowing only that the Prince played cards on Sunday—were not amused; the last Sassenach to behave in this bizarre way had been George IV, also no better than he should have been. The "do" with the Lord Provost, although oiled with whisky, was brief; the Prince walked back to the train, along the red carpet, with the Home Secretary.

"Well, Mathews, what news?"

"It happened this side of Newcastle, Your Highness, in the twilight. . . ."

"Go on."

"Three of them—they eluded Sir Frederick's men, sir, in a tunnel which, most regrettably, Sir Frederick had failed to foresee."

The Prince turned curtly on his heel, slamming the door of his coach. All the doors were slammed. The whistle blew. The train moved. The Home Secretary dived into a third-class compartment full of valets playing cribbage.

Outside the little station at Ballater, in the thick mist of a moorland night, eight carriages were drawn up, one with postilions, also wagonettes for luggage and servants. Gillies, on stout ponies, were ready to guide the cavalcade over the rough road to Balmoral. Four of the Black Watch bore blazing torches, their flickering light falling upon the reception committee—His Royal Highness Prince Alfred ("Affie") and Sir Henry Ponsonby, wet Inverness capes reflecting the torchlight, faces almost hidden between mufflers and deerstalkers. Four more highlanders, as the train steamed in, set up a grotesque wailing upon the pipes—a last agony for travelers surrounded by dark, drizzle and mist.

By some mysterious herd instinct everyone remained seated until Mrs. George Keppel had left the train, with her maid, and driven off in a closed brougham, with one outrider. Abergeldie Mains, a ghastly affair of granite, pine and bamboo furniture, was hers for a month. She could not visit Balmoral, a mile away, but the Prince could visit Abergeldie—a convenient arrangement.

Mrs. Keppel disposed of, the Prince of Wales, Eddy and the Salisburys could alight in order to be received by Affie and Ponsonby. The others followed—King's Cross worlds away, nothing ahead but the discomfort and discipline of Balmoral—a loathsome place.

Luncheon at Balmoral was more funereal than usual . . . the whole house, like the Blue Room at Windsor, was an eternal death chamber. The surrounding hills were scattered with cairns and plaques—the larger for Albert, the smaller for John Brown. And now, here at luncheon, in clear succession to Brown, was the Munshi, as catlike and sly as ever, passing round the *petits fours,* while the footmen dropped plates. Even the stags' heads, their glass eyes staring down from tartan walls, were more cheerful than these ladies in rusty black or these bearded gentlemen in kilts.

The dining room was icy. All the rooms at Balmoral were cold. Ponsonby, remembering the disaster of a previous visit, had smuggled an oil stove into the Salisburys' bedroom—those narrow iron bedsteads. "Cold is wholesome." That the Queen's end of the luncheon table should be gloomy was normal. But why, for two whole days, had the Prince of Wales looked like a thunder cloud? . . . "Something has come over Bertie." Hardly had the Prince swallowed his chilly coffee than he beckoned to the Prime Minister and to the Home Secretary. If only for a few minutes he had somehow or other to escape from that grotesque household where people communicated with each other only by notes. Thus, three men in huge overcoats stood on the terrace breathing the cold, damp air, gazing at the distant Cairngorms, white against a gray sky.

"Well, Matthews, this is a pretty kettle of fish. Sir Frederick has left Balmoral in dudgeon. The money's gone, the diamonds have gone . . . what do we do next?"

"I have taken steps, Your Highness, naturally."

"Indeed. I hope they will be successful. Pray explain them to us. The Prime Minister is as anxious as I am to avoid scandal. The House of Rothschild, I might add, are also anxious."

"Quite, sir. I can assure you that the gravity of the situation is not underestimated. Every post office in the realm will retain any person sending any sort of package to Balmoral. If such persons cannot immediately establish their credentials, then the police may retain them for further questioning. All this, sir, is within my powers. It should do the trick, I think."

"Hm! After that farce on the train you can hardly blame me, Mathews, for being skeptical."

"No, indeed, sir. Sir Frederick's conduct was quite incomprehensible. I have already told the Prime Minister that at the next Cabinet I shall demand an inquiry into the administration of the police—have I not, Mr. Prime Minister?"

"Oh, yes, you've told me all right; but by that time, ye know, there may be changes. We don't know, do we? who the Home Secretary may be. That's political life, Mathews—here today, gone tomorrow."

By some magic a footman had appeared at the Prince's elbow, his scarlet coat touched with flakes of snow.

"Yes, McTaggart, what is it?"

"His Grace the Duke of Argyll, sir. His carriage is in the forecourt. My orders are to say that his business with Your Highness is urgent."

"Ask him to join us here."

"Sir." Argyll was a few steps behind the footman.

"Well, my dear Argyll, this is an unexpected pleasure. You know the Prime Minister. This is Mr. Mathews, the Home Secretary. You have had a long drive . . . all the way from Inveraray?"

"Yes, Your Highness. I lay the night in the inn at Pitlochry. A wonderful drive through the glens. Loch Tay was splendid in her winter dress—bare birch trees, golden bracken and snow on the hills. . . ."

"Quite, Argyll, quite—most poetic, I'm sure. But what can we do for you?"

"It's all a little mysterious, sir. Yesterday morning a registered package arrived at Inveraray, with a Newcastle postmark. Inside the package, sir, was this smaller parcel, addressed to you. There was also a scrawled note, in an uneducated hand, asking me to deliver the parcel to you personally—and to trust it to nobody else. I felt it my duty to do this. . . . I trust, Your Highness, that neither of us has been duped by some hoaxer. Here, sir, is the parcel."

"Bastards, Salisbury, bastards! Swine! Clever devils! They'll beat you every time, Mathews . . . every time! Thank you, Argyll."

"Not at all, Your Highness; an honor to be of service. But, really, you know, I don't quite—er—understand. . . ."

"Come inside, all of you. We know what's in here, Argyll. They've used you as a postman—that's all. This damned parcel is worth half a million. At least I hope so. Come inside—you'll freeze here."

In the drawing room at Abergeldie Mains, embedded, as it were, in a great forest of palms, epergnes, easels, Landseers, raffia fans, antlers, pampas grass and bamboo, Mrs. George Keppel was pouring out tea for the heir to the throne. Her coiffure was superb, her complexion divine, her scent discreet. She wore a "tea gown" à la Japonaise. Her chaise longue was of wicker.

"Look, Alice, I want your help. You know such a lot about jewels and things of that kind."

"I should. Someone very kind has given me so many."

"Well, this is serious . . . really a sort of state secret . . . I can't tell you quite everything. Ponsonby and Knollys know less than nothing about jewels. Salisbury, for all his great possessions, is no better. Of course I could telegraph for Garrard's man, but—you know me, my dear: I'm always in a hurry. And I can trust you. Now, just look at these."

And there on the tea table, among the toast and the tea cakes and the scones and the baps and the *gâteaux* and the éclairs and the bread-and-butter and the sandwiches and the jams and the silver cream jugs and the Crown Derby tea cups, the Prince of Wales laid down the two twelve-pointed stars—the stars which the Duke of Argyll had just brought over the mountains and through the glens.

"These arrived today. What do you think of them?"

She barely glanced at them. She had a pretty laugh—a famous laugh—but for once it was also mocking.

"Really, my dear boy, you're not serious."

"I want your honest opinion."

"You shall have it then. The design is magnificent—Spanish of course. The 'diamonds' are quite good paste, better than cut glass. A theatrical costumer might give you a hundred pounds for them."

"Oh!"

"You had better give them to one of your little actress friends. I would expect something rather better."

"I only wanted your opinion, dearest. You are so clever. I never meant them as a present for you."

"I should think not indeed . . . complete rubbish, dear boy!"

7

The Osborne Conference

Skerret, the nonagenarian dresser, and Frau Güttmann, the octogenarian housekeeper—stiff collar and black gloves—were together at an attic window. On this cold, clear January morning, over the tops of cedars and deodars, they could look across an amethyst Solent to see the masts and crosstrees of the clippers in Portsmouth harbor. *Courageous* and *Lion,* lying off Calshot, were an assurance that, under God and the Royal Navy, this world would go on forever.

The two old women, however, were interested neither in clippers nor in ironclads; it was the carriages that puzzled them. One after another the broughams and the victorias, as well as a couple of hired vehicles from the livery stable, had crawled up the hill from Cowes, returning to the quay for a second load. It had been going on all the morning. Mystery was being added to mystery. For one thing, these people had no business at Osborne anyway—Osborne was for the family; and yet here they were—complete strangers—even before the Christmas trees had been dismantled. Why? Skerret and Güttmann had been told nothing.

As each carriage, gravel crunching under the wheels, trotted into the forecourt, disapproval grew. These visitors were not even ladies and gentlemen. They were, indeed, no ladies at all, and several of the men wore billycocks— quite common people. Once, it is true, Skerret thought she recognized the Baron Ferdinand, while Güttmann could swear to the Duke of Argyll . . . but then Güttmann, as Skerret often said, was getting confused in her old age and would swear to anything. Why, for instance, should the Dean of Windsor, not to mention Herr Mütter, the Castle librarian, be here at all? They did not belong—they were purely Windsor. And then, at last, below the window, there was a Field Marshal—in full rig. That was better: he might be hobbling on two sticks but at least he was part of the world they knew. It was something, but not enough; one Duke and one Field Marshal did not in themselves explain the use of the State Dining Room in January. Finally and above all, what was Prince William of Prussia doing here? . . . He must know perfectly well that he was not wanted until August—for the yachting.

The Queen took luncheon alone with the Princess Beatrice—a cup of Bengers, two biscuits and silence. Never had the Queen's mouth turned down quite so much. For three days now it had been one damned thing after another . . . only last night she had had to be told—it could be hidden no longer—that Prince Alfred's reputation in Coburg was unspeakable, and his debts astronomical. Prince Alfred—her dearest Affie—had become almost overnight her "greatest grief," Bertie, by comparison, being no more than "imprudent." It was hard on an old woman, already weighed down with such burdens as were hers. And now, on top of that, and without her permission, there was this absurd gathering of Bertie's in the State Rooms—rooms that were never opened in January, never until Cowes week. This was her house and she was told nothing—that was what hurt. . . .

Downstairs in the State Dining Room, dwarfed by the greatest of the Winterhalters, the Prince of Wales was at the head of the table. There was no hostess. There could be no hostess: this was the Queen's house. Alix, in any case, and as always lately, was in Denmark, while Beatrice was upstairs with Mama. The Prince explained to his guests, first, that this was a "business luncheon"—a most curious phrase—and that protocol might be ignored. Anyone might sit anywhere. This, of course, was nonsense. After a lot of jockeying Prince William got himself on Bertie's right, while Affie, after a tussle with Eddy, got himself on Bertie's left. After that Ponsonby told them all where to sit; it was so much simpler.

General Roderick Sparling, Master of the Royal Mews, was corseted, groomed and spurred to the nines with all accouterments. Field Marshal Lord Wilson, Constable of the Tower of London, sported his Waterloo medal—one up on Sparling—but was blinder, deafer and more arthritic than when Ponsonby had drunk his brandy six months ago. The Dean of Windsor—as always when Bertie was around—had been deprived of his only privilege, the right to say grace. The Marquis of Salisbury, his head as the dome of St. Paul's to other men's molehills, wondered why on earth he had come, but thanked God that, at any rate, it was not Balmoral. The Right Honorable Henry Mathews, looking more than ever like an ugly actor, had become a back-bencher almost overnight . . . as Cyril Pumphrey said, "Jolly decent of him to come at all." Pumphrey himself, having carefully inserted his monocle, did obscene doodles for the amusement of the Duke of Argyll. The Duke, having replaced the kilt with a frock coat, could hardly be recognized as the man who had driven through the glens with the diamond earrings. Sir Frederick Rogers, Commissioner for Police, expecting a wigging from the Prince, and in daily dread of a public inquiry, was more choleric than ever. Sir Francis Knollys simply fussed; he had to look after his master's guests but disapproved of the whole affair . . . totally unnecessary . . . utterly superfluous . . . most inopportune . . . the police could handle the matter . . . a fine body of men . . . second to none. The clichés dripped from him. Sir Henry Ponsonby, as the Queen's Secretary, was concerned with the Household service rather than with this damned conference. . . . The earrings had gone . . . and that was that. He glanced across the table at Rothschild—the Prince had forgotten no one. The Baron Ferdinand was as cool as a cucumber; he had all the figures he needed on a half sheet of notepaper; other men had Gladstone bags full of documents they hadn't read. Mary Ponsonby was really enjoying herself, chatting on her left to Herr Mütter about the Dürer drawings in the library at Windsor, and on her right to Mr. Friedman of Garrard's; he was telling her all the scandals among Regent Street shopkeepers— delicious.

Prince William, giving his mustaches a flourish, started off upon a high-flown oration concerning his beloved grandmother, the great Queen-Empress, and the need to protect her dear name from calumny. Bertie soon put a stop to that, explaining that there must be no discussion until coffee had been served. They would then move into the India Room, to be joined there by eight other witnesses now taking luncheon in the housekeeper's quarters.

When Benjamin Disraeli, in one of his more foolish flights of fancy, gave Victoria the title of "Queen-Empress," there were four things he did not foresee. One was that the Queen would take lessons in Hindustani; the second was that she would take the Munshi—the son of a common apothecary in Agra—and turn him into, first, her

personal servant and then her confidential secretary; the
third was that the Imperial title would last barely seventy
years; the fourth was that the Queen would create the
India Room at Osborne. The room became a great land-
mark in the history of English taste—symbolizing suffici-
ently its lowest point.

As the lunch, abominably served on Pomeranian porcelain, came to an end, the Prince of Wales led his
seventeen guests into the India Room. Princess Beatrice
quietly joined them—"Mama is resting." On a bench at
the far end were the eight men who had been fed in the
housekeeper's room. With a scraping of boots on the
Minton tile floor, they rose and bowed. There were two
frock coats—Mr. Quennell, the Station Master at Paddington, and Mr. Juniper, the Station Master at King's
Cross; they kept together, nursing a common resentment
about that housekeeper's room; after all they were in
charge of great London termini, not potty little stations
like Ballater and Wolferton. Mr. Archibald Bellow, the
house detective from Windsor, in a faintly tartan fawn,
puffed out his cheeks in annoyance—he, too, resented the
housekeeper's room, but, being inured to royalty's
rudeness, knew how to get his own back; only that morning he had raided the Windsor hothouse for a perfectly
splendid buttonhole—one up on everybody. Between
Chief Superintendent Chambers (Charlie Chambers of
the waxed mustaches) and Chief Detective Bertram Riddle (of the Dundreary whiskers) there was also a common bond: both having been on duty at Paddington on
June 19, they had been able to concert their evidence
while drinking in the bar of the Cowes ferry. Philpotts,
the Ponsonby coachman, sat rigidly to attention, his cockaded hat on his knees, his eyes on the ceiling. Mr. Crawford of Bow Street was enjoying his revenge for the Ballater trip: denied his glimpse of Balmoral he was now
feasting his eyes upon the polychromatic glories of Osborne
—and that nice Mr. Pumphrey had waved to him
across the room. Mr. Straw, manager of Lock's, the St.
James's Street hatters, was too absorbed in his old game
of picking out the real toffs from the dressy riff-raff to

bother himself overmuch as to why Mr. Friedman of Garrard's had lunched with the Prince—after all he and Friedman were both warrant holders. Mr. Straw, however, was philosophical about the gentry—he had learned to be. At the end of the bench, dim and anonymous, was Mr. Slattery, a Windsor footman, nervously turning his billycock round and round in his hands, in an agony of apprehension.

In front of the Prince, on an inlaid ebony and ivory and mother-of-pearl table from Mysore, were the two twelve-pointed diamond stars—those useless replicas which, only a month ago, the Duke of Argyll had borne across Scotland, and which the Prince had placed on Alice Keppel's bamboo tea table—to be told they were rubbish. And now, at a nod from the Prince, Francis Knollys gave a tap with his gavel . . . "Pray silence for His Royal Highness."

PRINCE OF WALES: You all know why we are here. Thank you for coming. Balmoral seemed to be inconveniently far away—it often is—whereas Osborne, although accessible, is withdrawn from prying eyes. Secrecy is everything. That, indeed, is why I have called this meeting instead of simply handing the whole horrible business to the Public Prosecutor. That would have let in the press. In effect, you are now behind locked doors. You all know, in a general way, the nature of our business. Six months ago, for one of the Jubilee dinners, Her Majesty decided to wear the famous Tudor Tiara, incorporating those priceless diamonds popularly known as Bloody Mary's Earrings. She therefore commanded her Secretary, Sir Henry Ponsonby, to convey the Tiara from the Tower of London, where it is normally kept with the Crown Jewels, to Windsor. In the course of Sir Henry's journey, by means of a Buckingham Palace carriage and the train, the diamonds were removed from either side of the Tiara and were replaced by clever but worthless replicas. Pray explain to us, Sir Henry, how you came to be robbed.

PONSONBY: Really, Your Highness, really! You embarrass me. With the greatest respect and loyalty I cannot accept your suggestion that I was robbed. Some other explanation must be found. I never betrayed my trust. The white hat box containing the Tiara was never out of my sight—not for a moment.

PUMPHREY: Get along with you, Ponsonby. Old Wilson here must have wined you well—eh, Wilson? Don't you ever go to the lavatory, Ponsonby, like the rest of the human race?

KNOLLYS: Order! Order! Mr. Pumphrey, you forget yourself. There are ladies present . . . the Princess. Dear me, dear me!

PUMPHREY: Oh, damn it all, Knollys, this is an inquiry, ye know, not a blasted levee.

KNOLLYS: There are ways of saying these things, Mr. Pumphrey . . . a man in your position . . . in the Household.

PRINCE OF WALES: Quite, Knollys, quite. You've made your point. All the same, my dear Ponsonby, perhaps you or Mr. Quennell, the Paddington Station Master, could tell us whether anything of that nature did in fact occur.

QUENNELL: Yes, Your Highness. When Sir Henry's brougham pulled up at the entrance to No. 1 platform, I had already held the Windsor train for some twenty minutes. When the footman opened the door, however, I observed that Sir Henry was—er—somewhat somnolent. It was a hot day. The footman had to tap him on the knee. Upon alighting he was also, quite clearly, in some—er—distress—in need of a lavatory. The hat box, therefore, was handed to Charlie—er—I beg your pardon—to Chief Superintendent Chambers, who, accompanied by four constables, conveyed same to Sir Henry's compartment on the Windsor train . . . Platform No. 4.

CHAMBERS: Correct, Your Highness, entirely correct . . . and at the compartment door we awaited Sir Henry and Mr. Quennell. There was no incident of any kind.

QUENNELL: Meanwhile, Your Highness, I had escorted Sir Henry to my office, where he partook of a thimbleful of the negus which I always keep upon my kettle ring. Then he brushed his clothes, gave his hat a shine, washed and—er—made himself comfortable.

PRINCE OF WALES: Thank you, Mr. Quennell. That is very clear. So, my dear Ponsonby, it would seem that there were in fact some ten minutes or so when the hat box *was* out of your sight. . . .

PONSONBY: Oh, well, sir, of course if you're going to take the matter as literally as all that . . . why, then, I suppose I must say 'Yes' . . . but really! Damn it, Your Highness, even for those few minutes the hat box was in the hands of a senior police officer, with an escort of constables. If that is all . . .

PRINCE OF WALES: It is not all, Ponsonby. It would seem that what with the heat of the day, and Field Marshal Lord Wilson's brandy, you were snoozing in the brougham. You were also attended by two bogus servants—never since apprehended—Fulleylove, the genuine footman, having been decoyed into the North of England, and Macdonald, the genuine coachman, having had his throat slit behind Paddington that morning—with no clues. Correct, General Sparling?

SPARLING: Yes, Your Highness—an unprecedented event in the history of the Royal Mews. I should point out, perhaps, that anyone can buy a fawn coat and then change the facings and buttons—the easiest thing in the world. The brougham was abandoned that evening outside Gorringe's. The two men, since they were wearing the Queen's livery, must have then decamped in a closed carriage which was presumably waiting for them. One suspects a gang.

PRINCE OF WALES: Exactly, Sparling; I have my own private reasons for agreeing with you on that point. And so, coming back to you, Ponsonby—slightly fuddled, you accepted the bogus footman and the bogus coachman without question. . . .

PONSONBY: I was not fuddled. The footman told me some sort of story about having been in service with Iddsleigh. I never saw the coachman's face. You say I took the men on trust—what would you have had me do?

PRINCE OF WALES: They were not the servants scheduled for your journey; you should have driven to the

Royal Mews and had the men checked—you had a million pounds in that brougham. Now, after the brandy and the negus, may we take it that you snoozed yet again in the train—including the stop at Slough where your coach was shunted?

PONSONBY: Utterly and completely irrelevant. My compartment was locked. I was locked in with the hat box and a tea basket. And that is that ... Your Highness.

PRINCE OF WALES: All the same, my dear Ponsonby, while you may not have betrayed your trust—and nobody is suggesting *that*—you seem to have executed it in an astonishing manner.

LADY PONSONBY: Your Royal Highness is wide of the mark. I beg you, sir, not to make a fool of yourself—that would do the monarchy far more harm than a few stolen diamonds. Someone might even point out that the heir to the throne has also been known to snooze after a stiff brandy ... or two, or even three. Anyway, it is as clear as daylight that my husband was robbed by the boy in the ginger suit.

PRINCE OF WALES (and others): What! What! Who?

PUMPHREY: By Jove, Mary! Now you've gone and done it. That was a corker for them.

PRINCE WILLIAM: A ginger suit! A ginger suit! What's all this? Really, Bertie, this is all most unseemly and most unroyal. In Prussia it would not be possible, but then in Prussia we have an excellent police force. And all this, Bertie, all this argument, this brawling ... you actually permit it. Great heavens! What would Grandmama think?

AFFIE: Shut up, Willy. That Tiara is worth a million ... more or less, according to Garrard's and Rothschilds ... and they're both here to speak for themselves. I could do with my share, I don't mind telling you. And before you start ordering us all about, just remember that you're not Emperor of Germany *yet,* and that one day you may be very glad of your mother's share of the Tiara money—so there!

PRINCE WILLIAM: Don't be squalid, Alfred. Stick to your violin.

PRINCE OF WALES: Silence, both of you, Now pray tell us, Lady Ponsonby, *who* . . . who on earth is the boy in the ginger suit?

LADY PONSONBY: I haven't the slightest idea—one of the gang, I suppose. The Windsor train, by the time Henry got into his compartment, was half an hour late. There wasn't another train for three-quarters of an hour. And yet Henry was followed onto the platform and into the train by "ginger suit" . . . with two large tartan carpet bags. Now, why?

PRINCE OF WALES: Now, Mr. Riddle, you were the detective on duty at Paddington. Have you anything to say about—er—"ginger suit"?

RIDDLE: I am unable to imagine, Your Highness, what on earth the lady is talking about. You mustn't take too much notice of the ladies, sir; if I may say so they get such fanciful ideas.

LADY PONSONBY: Riddle, Your Highness, was doubtless doing his duty—busy spotting Nihilists and Fenians, although how you recognize them when you see them, heaven knows. Common sense is what is needed. The whole detective service needs overhauling . . . in my fanciful opinion.

PUMPHREY: One in the eye for you, Sir Frederick.

SIR FREDERICK: Really, Pumphrey! Upon my soul, sir. Your Royal Highness, I wish to protest.

PRINCE OF WALES: We'll come to you later, Sir Frederick. Thank you, Lady Ponsonby, for your fascinating evidence.

LADY PONSONBY: And, of course, the detectives have told you there were two hat boxes.

PRINCE OF WALES (and others): What! Two!

LADY PONSONBY: Oh, dear me, yes. I've told Henry a dozen times but he never takes any notice—he doesn't think it's important. Oh, yes—two hat boxes. You may remember a footman at Windsor, sir, a man called Wainwright.

PRINCE OF WALES: Yes, yes, a decent enough fellow—but one could always smell the liquor. What of him, Lady Ponsonby?

LADY PONSONBY: . . . Decent enough fellow—Hm! He came over to the Norman Tower one day in the spring and said he had an order from Her Majesty to leave a message in Henry's dressing room—some nonsense about how to wear the K.C.B. ribbon, or something. I let him go upstairs, but thought it very odd. The Queen doesn't give orders to footmen—she "asks" the Princess to "tell someone"—but *you* know the rigmarole well enough. Of course, after the Tiara furor, I thought back, and became doubly suspicious. Henry wouldn't listen, so I invited Mr. Straw, of Lock's the hatters, to visit Windsor. That's why I wanted him here, at Osborne, today. Perhaps, Your Highness, he might speak for himself.

MR. STRAW: Deeply honored to be here, Your Royal Highness. For one in my humble station of life it is . . .

PUMPHREY: Oh, Christ!

MR. STRAW: . . . On June 25th last, Your Highness, Lady Ponsonby most kindly invited me to Windsor. She arranged that I should—er—hang about in the Castle until, as if by chance, I was confronted by this footman, a Mr. Wainwright. I immediately recognized him as a man who had visited my shop a few weeks earlier. . . .

PRINCE OF WALES: Many people visit your shop, Mr. Straw—I have done so myself. How can you be so sure . . .

MR. STRAW: Oh, I remember him very well indeed, Your Highness. I remember the fuss he made. Many customers, if I may say so with respect, are particular, and rightly so, but Mr. Wainwright was fussy, not about his hat—a very commonplace billycock—but about the box. We have white, black and striped boxes—normal, mourning and racing toppers respectively. This man not only insisted upon a white box, he made a great to-do about it. . . .

PRINCE OF WALES: I see. Obviously Wainwright must be cross-examined upon the matter. All most extraordinary . . .

LADY PONSONBY: Wainwright, Your Highness, within an hour of seeing Mr. Straw, had left Windsor forever. He had been with us for five years and I made Henry ask the Housekeeper for his papers. His testimonials, dated 1882, were absolutely impeccable; unfortunately they had been cleverly forged upon purloined notepaper. In one case the paper had been stolen from the library at Blenheim, and in the other case from Lady Sackville's boudoir at Knole. Nobody called Wainwright, as I soon found out, had ever served either the Marlboroughs or the Sackvilles.

PRINCE OF WALES: I see. Friend Wainwright seems to specialize in purloined notepaper. He wrote to me, as a matter of fact, on Her Majesty's private stationery—very clever. No doubt, Sir Frederick, your men are already hot on the trail. And now, my dear Ponsonby, let us come back to you. Can you tell us what happened when you got to the station at Windsor?

PONSONBY: Certainly, Your Highness. My own coachman met me and, walking at my side, carried the hat box to my own carriage in the station yard. To our amazement my horse—usually a very quiet animal—was rearing up upon her hind legs and foaming at the mouth. Fortunately—whatever my wife may think about him—the youth in the ginger suit was ahead of us and, very kindly, was already holding Black Beauty's head—hardly a criminal act. I suppose, however, on your excessively literal interpretation of my words, sir, I must admit that for a few seconds my eyes were not upon the hat box. I got into the carriage while Philpotts put the box on the pavement so that he could help "ginger suit" calm the horse. I gave the youth a gratuity, Philpotts put the box in the carriage and, within ten minutes or so, the Tudor Tiara was on the desk in my office. I had fulfilled my trust, Your Highness.

PRINCE OF WALES: Very explicit. You can confirm your master's statement, Philpotts.

PHILPOTTS: Yes, Your Highness. I can do that, sir, but should add, in duty, sir, that Black Beauty had been most maliciously injured. On returning to the stable I found the hock of her right foreleg had been cut—an incision with a sharp blade—enough to terrify any horse, Your Highness.

PRINCE OF WALES: Yes, indeed. Thank you, Philpotts. Everything seems to point to "ginger suit." Now, Sir Henry, kindly tell us the next incident in this—er—saga of the Tiara.

PONSONBY: On returning to Windsor, Your Highness, I found a message from Her Royal Highness the Princess Beatrice telling me that Her Majesty had commanded that the Tiara be displayed in the Corridor that evening for the delectation of her guests. With the help of Skerret, the senior dresser, I therefore arranged the Tiara on the onyx table. That would be about eight o'clock; I had been across to the Norman Tower to dress, leaving the Tiara in my office so that Your Highness might inspect it . . . you will remember that, sir. I then left a footman on guard in the Corridor with very strick injunctions to remain at his post at all costs. His name was Slattery. For some obscure reason—at my wife's request, I believe—he is here now.

PRINCE OF WALES: Slattery.

SLATTERY: Yer 'Ighness.

PRINCE OF WALES: Tell us, please, about the evening of June 19th at Windsor.

SLATTERY: Sir, Yer 'Ighness, with 'umble duty. Just after eight o'clock, when I 'ad come on for the evening, the major-domo told me as 'ow Sir 'Enery wanted me in the Corridor. Sir 'Enery 'ad put out this 'ere Tiara and told me as 'ow I was to guard it until 'e came back fer 'is dinner—and on no account ter leave my post. . . . Yer 'Ighness.

PRINCE OF WALES: And of course you obeyed orders.

SLATTERY: No, sir.

PRINCE OF WALES: What did you say?

SLATTERY: I said, "No, sir," sir.

PRINCE OF WALES: But that was most reprehensible, Slattery. Your position at Windsor will certainly have to be reconsidered.

SLATTERY: Thank yer, Yer 'Ighness.

PRINCE OF WALES: But why did you leave your post?

SLATTERY: I was ordered to, Yer 'Ighness. Wot my brother, Yer 'Ighness, wot is in the Royal Fusiliers, says as 'ow they calls "superior orders."

PRINCE OF WALES: Indeed, Slattery; and who, pray, gave you orders which you chose, without permission, to consider so—er—"superior"?

SLATTERY: Beggin' yer pardon, sir, it was 'Er Majesty.

PRINCE OF WALES: Oh! Oh, I see. I shall want your evidence confirmed, Slattery. Which of the ladies was in attendance?

SLATTERY: There wasn't no ladies, Yer 'Ighness. 'Er Majesty were alone.

PRINCE OF WALES: Alone in the Corridor, unattended, an hour before the service of dinner . . . most unlikely.

SLATTERY: But I'm sayin' as 'ow she was, sir.

KNOLLYS: You must not bandy words with His Highness, my man.

PRINCE OF WALES: Leave the room, Slattery.

SLATTERY: Thank yer . . . but I tells yer as 'ow 'Er Majesty was in the Corridor . . .

PRINCE OF WALES: I ordered you to leave the room. . . .

SLATTERY: An' she 'ad a bag . . . a big velvet bag . . . purple . . . I'm only a'tellin' yer. (Departs.)

PUMPHREY: Mary, if you have a pin, drop it . . . they'll think the *Courageous* is firing her guns.

PRINCE OF WALES: Knollys, we may need Slattery again. . . . See that he stays here tonight. Now, I think we should all forget what we have just heard . . . clearly a most insolent servant. . . .

LADY PONSONBY: He struck me, Your Highness, as an honest man in a difficult position.

PRINCE OF WALES: I flatter myself, Lady Ponsonby, that I am, if nothing else, a judge of men. Now, my dear Ponsonby, tell us—when you placed the Tiara in the Corridor you took it for granted, of course, that it was the real thing, *not* one of the replicas of which several had been made in 1851 for the provincial museums.

PONSONBY: Surely Your Highness is not suggesting that sometime between 1851 and today the Tower of London was robbed without anyone being aware of it . . . really, sir.

PRINCE OF WALES: Oh, dear me, no! But I must tell

you all that one of the guests at the Castle that night was His Highness the Maharajah of Kashgar—a world expert on gems. . . . You can confirm that, Mr. Friedman?

FRIEDMAN: Oh, certainly, Your Highness. We know him well at Garrard's. I would back his judgment against my own any day.

PRINCE OF WALES: Thank you. Now the Maharajah saw the Tudor Tiara in the Corridor. At the end of the evening he confided to Princess Beatrice—and again to me that next morning when walking in the garden—that while the Tiara itself might be the original, the precious diamonds were so much rubbish, mere paste replicas. So you see, Ponsonby . . .

PONSONBY: It is inexplicable, Your Highness. Or, rather, there are only three possible explanations. One is that the diamonds were tampered with on my journey from the Tower to Windsor; whatever one may choose to think of Mary's "boy in the ginger suit," I think I have shown that to have been utterly impossible. The second possibility which did occur to me was that the Maharajah's aide-de-camp—a Colonel Pinkerton, cashiered from the Indian Army and otherwise disgraced—might have switched the real diamonds for the sham ones. Perhaps, sir, I might ask Mr. Archibald Bellow, the Windsor Castle detective, to say a word on that.

BELLOW: Your Highness, I was assured by Sir Henry that the Maharajah's entire suite—whites and natives—would attend the Jubilee service in the Abbey. Accordingly I gave orders that while they were in London their luggage and rooms should be searched under my supervision. A needle in a haystack would not have escaped us. We drew a complete blank. Whether, of course, the diamonds were in the Abbey, concealed in the Maharani's stays, I don't know.

PRINCE OF WALES: Thank you, Mr. Bellow. Colonel Pinkerton had already been reported to me as being a most unsavory character. I don't think, however, that there is anything more we can do in that quarter. If, by now, the earrings are in India, then they have gone forever. I think, Ponsonby, you mentioned a third possibility.

PONSONBY: Yes, sir. It is this: is it not possible that the Tiara which was handed to me, in good faith of course, by Field Marshal Lord Wilson, was *not* the original which Sir Henry Cole took from the Crystal Palace to the Tower in 1851 . . . thirty-six years ago?

PRINCE OF WALES: Ah! Perhaps Field Marshal Lord Wilson would care to say a word?

WILSON (cupping his ear in his hand): Eh?

DUKE OF ARGYLL (yelling): HIS HIGHNESS SAYS, WAS THE TIARA YOU GAVE TO SIR HENRY PONSONBY THE ORIGINAL—THE 1851 VERSION?

WILSON: Of course it was . . . the man's talking balls.

KNOLLYS (also yelling): REALLY, FIELD MARSHAL, REALLY! YOU ARE ADDRESSING THE PRINCE OF WALES, YOU KNOW.

WILSON: He can be the Prince of Timbuctoo for all I care. He's talking absolute balls. Sir Henry Cole brought the Tiara from the Crystal Palace to the Tower himself, in a Black Maria . . . before my time of course . . . now where was I in '51? . . . let me see, now . . . let me see . . . ah, yes, I was on the Northwest Frontier . . . but about that blasted Tiara—it's all in the books, ye know.

PRINCE OF WALES: So, Field Marshal, we may take it that the 1851 Tiara, the original, never left the Tower until last June, when Sir Henry brought it to Windsor.

DUKE OF ARGYLL: THE 1851 TIARA NEVER LEFT THE TOWER?

WILSON: Of course it never left the Tower . . . bloody silly question . . . except of course in 1861, and then it came back in a few days.

PRINCE OF WALES: What! What's this? I've never heard of this!

DUKE OF ARGYLL: I THINK HIS ROYAL HIGHNESS WOULD LIKE FURTHER DETAILS OF THAT AMAZING STATEMENT, FIELD MARSHAL.

WILSON: Why? It was his own mother had the damned thing sent out to Windsor, or it may have been Buckingham Palace . . . can't remember . . . long time ago. Anyway, it was only her usual fuss, ye know. Ask her, ask her . . . she's still alive, isn't she?

PRINCE OF WALES: Great heavens! Oh, dear! Oh, dear! 1851 . . . 1861 . . . 1851 . . . am I going mad? Poor old chap . . . quite hopeless. But we've got to get to the bottom of it all. For God's sake, Argyll, ask him why the Queen had the original Tiara sent to her in 1861 . . . if she ever did.

DUKE OF ARGYLL: HIS HIGHNESS WANTS TO KNOW, FIELD MARSHAL, WHY THE TIARA WAS SENT TO THE QUEEN IN 1861.

WILSON: I've just told him, haven't I? It was his mother's fuss. Her husband had just died—Albert, ye know. She wanted a feller called Martin to write his life, and she wanted to show him every damned thing Albert had ever written or designed . . . this house, vases, mirrors, all kinds of nonsense. This Albert—I met him once—queer, solemn chap—very German—always mucking about with books and art and pottery . . . never rode to hounds . . . no red blood . . . not much use really . . .

KNOLLYS: MODERATE YOUR WORDS, FIELD MARSHAL. HE WAS THE PRINCE'S FATHER, SIR.

WILSON: Oh, I shouldn't think so. He may have been a blasted intellectual, but very strait-laced over women. I don't know who the hell you are, my good man, but you mustn't believe all you hear, ye know.

PRINCE OF WALES: Let it go, Knollys, let it go. *Non compos mentis,* poor old boy. But it does look as though the Queen may have had the Tiara back to show to Sir Theodore Martin when he was writing his *Life of the Prince Consort.* We shall never know.

PRINCESS BEATRICE: We may. I think I can help, Bertie.

PRINCE OF WALES: You, Beatrice . . . how?

PRINCESS BEATRICE: I was rather hoping to avoid this. It is all so—er—sacred to Mama's sad memories . . . but I do see that I must speak out. Well then, this is the truth. The original Tiara, with all the jewels and diamond earrings incorporated in it, was always—or at least as long as I can remember—locked in one of the big cupboards in the Blue Room. For those of you who may not know, that is the room at Windsor where my father died in 1861. Mama has kept the room quite unchanged—just as it was on that tragic winter night—but with certain precious souvenirs locked in the big cupboards, including the Tiara—Papa's finest design.

LADY PONSONBY: I can confirm that. Once, when Henry and I were bereaved, Her Majesty showed me everything in the Blue Room—including the Tiara.

DEAN OF WINDSOR: And I too . . . I used often to pray with Her Majesty at the late Prince Consort's bedside . . . most heart-rending.

PRINCE OF WALES: Quite, quite, Mr. Dean, but not very relevant. Our problem is still quite unsolved. If Mr. Cole, Chairman of the Commissioners of the Great Exhibition, took the Tiara to the Tower in 1851, how on earth did it get into the Blue Room ten years later?

PRINCESS BEATRICE: Be honest, Bertie, be honest. Face facts. Mama is a very emotional person; also very determined and very direct. What she wants, she gets. Why not say so? . . .

PRINCE WILLIAM: Because, my dearest Beatrice, several people are present who are quite outside our royal circle. All this would not be possible in our wonderful Prussia. It is unseemly . . . some things are better left unsaid. . . .

PRINCESS BEATRICE: Don't be foolish, Willy. As I was saying, Bertie, when Willy interrupted me, for heaven's sake face facts. Field Marshal Lord Wilson has told us exactly what happened. I was only four at the time but I said just now that the Tiara, the real Tiara—and Mama would have had nothing less for the Blue Room—has been at Windsor as long as I can remember. As the Field Marshal has told us, in 1861 the Tiara was sent to Mama . . .

PRINCE OF WALES: . . . And returned to the Tower within a few days.

PRINCESS BEATRICE: Was it? *What* was returned to the Tower? The original or one of these museum and art-school replicas of which no precise record exists? Clearly that is what happened. Mama kept the original, including the earrings, and put it in her beloved Blue Room. And, after all, why not? It was hers.

PONSONBY: Hm! If I might intervene, Your Highness, the late Prince Consort's will was by no means clear on that point. He had the Tiara placed with the Crown Jewels, the property of the nation. I suggest that the Solicitor-General . . .

PRINCE OF WALES: Oh, for God's sake, Ponsonby, forget all that. Stick to the point. After all, what does it really matter? It may even turn out to be a good thing. If Mama sent a replica back to the Tower in '61, in exchange for the real thing, without telling a soul, then that was all the Field Marshal had to give you last June. Moreover, it was all the "ginger suit" gang ever got for their pains when they switched the diamonds round while you were—er—snoozing in the train. However, no harm has been done. The original Tiara, complete with earrings, is safe and sound in the Blue Room at Windsor—as it has been ever since Papa's death in 1861.

PRINCESS BEATRICE: No. No. The Blue Room cupboard is empty. Apart from Mama, I am the only person with a key, and I know. The Tiara, the real Tiara, has vanished. It vanished on June 19th.

PONSONBY: Nonsense, if I may say so, Princess. It has vanished from the Blue Room only because it is now safely in the strong room. Her Majesty commanded me to put it there, under her seal, the day before her Jubilee. I haven't the remotest idea why . . . but she did and there it remains.

HERR MÜTTER: Nein, nein, nein! I am ze librarian only, and ze German secretary, but ze Queen, she trust her old Karl Mütter . . . it ees from Coburg I am. On ze Tuesday before zis Christmas Day—two veeks since only—she say to me, "Herr Mütter, get ze Tiara from ze strong room." Zat I do. I give eet to ze Fräulein Skerret for ze

baggage and now, zis very day, it ees here at Osborne . . .
oh jah, eet ees indeet!

PRINCE OF WALES: Oh, mein Gott! Mein Gott!

PRINCE WILLIAM: Quite so, Bertie. As I expected, we
have all been brought here for nothing. Perhaps, however,
now that your grandiose conference is over, you might
care to enlighten our curiosity. All the afternoon there
have been a couple of twelve-pointed diamond stars on
the table in front of you. Might I ask whether they have
any bearing upon our deliberations? I have no wish to
appear inquisitive. I only ask.

PRINCE OF WALES: Quite so, Willy. I was just coming
to these stars although, in fact, our discussion might seem
to have made them rather irrelevant. These stars are the
alleged earrings—mere paste and rubbish—which were
stolen from Sir Henry Ponsonby when he was—er—
snoozing . . . one set of replicas removed only to be
replaced by another set. . . .

PONSONBY: Quite impossible . . . and in any case you
have them back. I am utterly bewildered.

PRINCE OF WALES: On the contrary, my dear Pon-
sonby, these sham diamonds confirm everything. I too
now have something to reveal. I must tell you all that one
evening last November, after dinner at the Marlborough
Club, His Excellency the Russian Ambassador, the Baron
Serge de Staal, accompanied me on a stroll down Pall
Mall. I have not invited His Excellency here today be-
cause dear Serge always pretends that he can speak no
English . . . in private he speaks perfectly. Like all
Russians, he loves fireworks and it was Guy Fawks night.
That was why we ventured into the streets.

PUMPHREY: (A long, low whistle.)

PRINCE OF WALES: Thank you, Mr. Pumphrey; your
interventions have enlivened our afternoon . . . but
enough is enough. To continue with my own story . . . in
the course of our perambulations the Baron de Staal and I
were accosted by a small group of rough men. I need not
go into details. They satisfied me that they were what we
have been calling the "ginger suit gang." They even pro-

duced their—er—credentials in the form of these diamond stars. I had dispensed with my detective and was not in a strong position. I myself am a trifle stout, and I certainly could not involve the Czar's ambassador in a brawl. In the end, therefore—for a price, of course—I struck a bargain. Mama's name had to be protected at all costs— you would agree with me there, Willy. The money was paid over in such a way that the men could not be traced. . . .

MATHEWS (former Home Secretary): Ahem! Ahem!

PRINCE OF WALES: Surprisingly, Mr. Mathews, the men kept their bargain. These diamond stars were duly delivered to me at Balmoral, thanks to the mediation of His Grace the Duke of Argyll—I need not say more than that, Argyll—but of course the only diamonds the rogues *could* send me where the sham ones which they had stolen from that Tower of London Tiara, while Sir Henry was snoozing in the train.

PONSONBY: It pleases Your Highness to be very persistent on the point. . . .

PRINCE OF WALES: Oh, no offense, my dear Ponsonby— you mustn't be touchy. A lady who is very expert in gems happened, by a most extraordinary coincidence, to be staying at Abergeldie Mains, a mile or so from Balmoral— there is no need to keep whistling, Pumphrey, nor for you, Mathews, to keep clearing your throat—and I was able to consult her. She immediately confirmed my fears, that these diamonds are absolute rubbish—worth a hundred pounds at most, for the skill of the imitation. And that, I can assure you, is the whole story of my transaction with the gang—a very slight affair. And now, ladies and gentlemen, I am sure you are all exhausted. We may, however, congratulate ourselves that the Tiara, complete with Bloody Mary's Earrings, is safely here at Osborne.

ALL: Hear hear. Thank you, Your Highness . . . etc. etc.

PRINCE OF WALES: But, Mr. Prime Minister, we have not had a word from you all afternoon. Would you care to make a—er—a few valedictory remarks, as it were? . . .

MARQUIS OF SALISBURY: Thank you, Your Highness. An admirably conducted conference, if I may say so. I am glad you feel, sir, that it has also been successful and that the Tudor Tiara, complete with those famous diamond earrings, is now quite safe. I have no wish to dampen your pleasure, but may I remind you that the last two prime ministers of the Tudor dynasty were Cecils—the only distinguished members of my house. Consequently in the Monument Room at Hatfield we have the most complete Tudor records in the world—not least those of Queen Elizabeth when, as a princess, she was the prisoner of her half-sister, Bloody Mary. There are gaps and confusions in the record . . . but be careful, Your Highness . . . be very careful.

PRINCE OF WALES: Nonsense, my dear Prime Minister, nonsense. Those damned earrings went back to Spain with King Philip; but after the Peninsular War, when Spain was piling honors upon our own Iron Duke, they gave him the Holy Earrings, as they called them, and he gave them to my father specifically for the Tiara. There is no room for doubt there, Mr. Prime Minister. No, the time has come to congratulate ourselves, and to drink a toast. Knollys, I think we are all ready for the siphons and decanters.

KNOLLYS: Certainly, Your Highness; but I have just heard a knock on the door. I gave orders that we were not to be disturbed . . . but I suppose it can hardly matter now . . . we have finished our work.

Sir Francis Knollys unlocked the great double doors of the India Room. A footman confronted him—a footman whose face was as scarlet as his coat. Bowing slightly, he mouthed those syllables which the familiars of Windsor, Balmoral, Buckingham Palace and Osborne knew so well how to interpret; they signified quite soundlessly that "Her Majesty is on the way." And indeed she was not far behind. Everyone rose and bowed.

Even as she walked across the room they felt, as always, that in some inexplicable way this diminutive, dumpy and disagreeable widow dominated them all. For the moment there could be nobody else in the world.

"Thank you, Bertie. Sir Henry, a chair for the Prince. You may all sit."

They all sat.

"I have been alone for two hours with that awful Miss Phipps and Jane Ely. I am utterly exhausted."

She placed a large purple velvet bag upon the ivory-and-ebony table. Her mouth was more drawn down than ever. Her hooded eyes barely showed the whites—or, rather, the yellows. Her cheeks had been furrowed by tears. She was as white as her starched cap.

"I suppose you have all been chattering about the Tudor Tiara and those diamond earrings which my dearest husband so skillfully incorporated into its design."

"Yes, Mama."

"Well, instead of chattering and locking me out of my own State Apartments, you would have done better to ask my advice, and save your breath."

"Yes, Mama."

"Now . . ." and the mouth was set, the eyes closed ". . . now, let me tell you about something that happened some years ago. In 1839 I had a young and unmarried lady-in-waiting. She was accused of being *enceinte*. There was a tremendous scandal. It was all a wicked lie—she only had dropsy. I too was young and unmarried—possibly jealous. I was also very wicked: I supported the gossip and publicly dismissed the lady from my Court. I had to pay the price. In the end I had to admit that I was wrong; I had to apologize publicly—not easy for a young Queen. That was forty-eight years ago and the lady's family have still not forgiven me. Now I have come to tell you that once again—but this time in my old age—I have been deceitful and wicked. I have done wrong."

"Mama, must you . . . is this necessary?"

"Yes, Bertie . . . very necessary indeed."

She was sobbing now. The tiny lace handkerchief was wet with tears; the words came with difficulty.

"Nobody—nobody now living—can ever know how happy I was with my dear husband. Those far-off days in Scotland, the picnics and the expeditions, were paradise. The Great Exhibition—the Crystal Palace—was the epitome of his work."

"Dearest Mama, must you go on?"

"Let me be, Beatrice. In '61, when I was so utterly crushed, when all life had died in me, there was only one material thing that mattered—the objects, the clothes, the books, the jewels which my beloved husband had actually handled and touched. . . . I treasured them even more than my own children. I hoarded them in that dear, sacred Blue Room. Among them was one of the museum replicas of the Tudor Tiara. In the great cupboard this had a special place of honor. Within a few months of the tragedy, however, I sent for the real Tiara from the Tower. I wanted dear Albert's biographer, Mr. Theodore Martin, to see everything Albert had designed. So there, in the Blue Room, was the original Tiara, the one my beloved and I had seen made, that we had both touched, both looked at, in the Crystal Palace. I surrendered to temptation. I kept it. I sent the museum replica to the Tower of London. . . ."

"It was yours, Mama, to do what you liked with."

"Sir Henry thinks not—that it may belong to the nation. In any case it was very wrong and very deceitful of me, in my position, to change the tiaras round without telling anyone. For twenty-six years, you see, I have allowed the Tower of London to exhibit a forgery among the Crown Jewels."

"Well, at least, Mama, at the time you honestly thought it was yours."

"No. I was not sure. I should have taken advice. I was deceitful. In my overwhelming grief, with the tears often streaming down my cheeks, I did wrong."

"But is that all, Mama? It does not seem so very terrible. Is that all? . . ."

"No, it is not all. I have to tell you something else—something even more difficult for me to talk about."

It was almost dark now. No servant had dared to enter the room. The gaseliers were still unlit. There was only the blazing fire. The men on the bench—footmen, detectives and others—sat with mouths open; in the gloom they had been forgotten. Beatrice now stood with her arm around the Queen. Through the windows, far away, were the lights of Her Majesty's ironclads.

"And now the years have passed. One must love someone. Servants, secretaries, statesmen are not enough—not for someone as lonely as a Queen. There was my dear John Brown, there was dear Lord Beaconsfield—both gone now. In the end I came back to my own children. You, my dearest Bertie, are profligate and imprudent, so that the world thinks that I must disapprove of you. That is nonsense. You may be wayward but you are my son. Anyway, compared with most of our relations you are an archangel . . . you are a dear, good boy. Six months ago, two days before my Jubilee, and on that very evening when Sir Henry placed the Tiara on the onyx table in the Corridor, you came to my room. As usual it was about your debts. For once, however, you had a definite proposal—to ask Rothschilds for a loan on the Tiara. I said you were mad . . . then gradually, in my practical way, I saw the point. I agreed."

"You did, Mama. . . . I was very touched and grateful."

"Nonsense, Bertie. It was nothing more than a good stroke of business . . . both for the House of Coburg and for the House of Rothschild."

The Baron Ferdinand bowed his assent across the room.

"But what was I to do? You see, all the time, I knew that the Tiara which Sir Henry had placed in the Corridor was only the replica from the Tower. If the Constable of the Tower knew, he had never dared to say anything; Rothschilds, however, would not hesitate for a moment. I played for time, telling you not to touch the Tiara yourself but to send it to Hirsch, when I said the word, so that he could negotiate with Rothschilds in a proper manner . . . no hole-in-the-corner business at Tring or Waddesden."

"I see, Mama . . . I see now."

"Yes. From your point of view, Bertie, the wrong Tiara was in the Corridor. That evening, after our talk, I did a very wicked thing and, for me, a very hard thing. . . . I robbed the Blue Room."

"Mama . . . dearest."

"Yes, Bertie. I took the Tiara, the real Tiara, from the Blue Room cupboard, put it in this velvet bag, and then went to the Corridor. I dismissed the footman who was on guard. I was all alone in that huge gallery . . . there was still an hour to go before dinner, and the evening sunlight was streaming through the Venetian blinds. I then, quite deliberately, changed one Tiara for the other. Hirsch and Rothschild would now get the right one. It was very wicked and deceitful . . . but it was all for you, Bertie . . . there are so many calls on your purse, dear boy. A loan from Rothschilds . . . so wrong and yet so sensible. . . . I felt as if I was pawning the Crown Jewels. Above all, I had desecrated the Blue Room, the room where my dearest one had died . . . all for you, Bertie."

"You will feel better, Mama, for having told us all that. We shall also feel better for having been told everything. It is all over now."

"It is not all over. You have forgotten the Maharajah!"

"The Maharajah!"

"Of course—the Maharajah. Oh, I know that the silly man wanted the Garter, but that wouldn't really explain it, would it?"

"Explain what, Mama?"

"Beatrice, you should know. He spoke to you that evening, just after Sir Henry's little lecture. He told you, didn't he? that the diamonds on each side of the Tiara, Bloody Mary's Earrings, were so much rubbish."

"Yes, of course . . . we all know that, Mama."

"Well, don't you see? . . . that was after dinner, after I had changed round the Tiaras. It was the Blue Room and Crystal Palace Tiara, the one intended for Rothschilds, that the Maharajah had been looking at. And, according to him, its diamonds were false. For twenty-six years I had kept that wonderful object as a precious part of my private shrine . . . and now? I collapsed that night. Dear old Skerret had to give me brandy. That I should wear the Tiara at the Jubilee dinner was now, of course, out of the question. The very next morning I commanded Sir Henry to put it in the strong room, under my seal. But now, Bertie, just to round off your absurd Osborne conference, here it is for you all to look at—the genuine Tiara. . . ."

The old woman delved into her velvet bag. She extracted that rich, glittering hideous fountain of priceless stones which nobody had seen since that Windsor dinner party in June.

"There you are, my dear children, the real Taira . . . but . . . but . . . the Maharajah . . ."

Everyone rose and peered through the shadows at the grotesque object which, in its vulgarity, its intricacy and its excess, was so appropriate to that room. It was Knollys who rang for a footman. Nobody stirred until the blaze of gaslight was reflected from every stone in the Tiara.

For Mr. Friedman of Garrard's—although he had handled crowns and scepters—this was a historic moment. Every one of those stones was known to the trade. Behind his little pince-nez, as the Prince of Wales summoned him to the table, his eyes were popping. He spent only a few moments with his magnifying glass.

"May it please Your Majesty, Your Highnesses. On the basis of a superficial examination, I declare this to be the original Tudor Tiara with all its gems derived from famous items of sixteenth-century jewelry or costume. I regret to say, however, that the twelve-pointed diamond stars, so placed as to be just above the wearer's temples, are quite valueless . . . clever imitations of a very intricate Spanish design, but mere paste . . . value, say, one hundred pounds."

There was a long silence broken only by the Queen's sobs and then, at last, by Bertie's half-choked voice.

"So, Mama, we have all done our best. *We* have the Tiara . . . the gang have my money—or, rather, my dear Rothschild, *your* money . . . but where, oh, where the hell are Bloody Mary's Earrings?"

EDWARDIAN
EPILOGUE

Two of the peasant women crossed themselves. The sentries stood at ease. The street slowly emptied. The little Grand Duchess, one day to be the Princess Natasha Rostopochin, had entered a very cold and a very bitter world. . . . No wonder she yelled.

The Czar Alexander III had died horribly of Bright's disease. Through the November snows of 1894 his embalmed corpse, with priests and acolytes in the railway coach, traveled in easy stages the seven hundred miles from Sevastopol to Moscow. The corpse lay in state in the Cathedral of St. Basil, by the Kremlin Wall, and then on to Petersburg, to lie once again in the Fortress of St. Peter and St. Paul, by the frozen Neva. For the funeral Petersburg was filled with kings and princes—nearly all cousins, nearly all sharing each other's hereditary diseases. Punctiliously, day after day, they attended long and elaborate masses—punctiliously, although Lord Carrington noticed the curious ability of the Prince of Wales to sleep—like a horse—standing up as the holy taper in his hand burnt itself out. It was in the vast Anitchkoff Palace, where he was lodged, that the Prince first put on the uniform of the 27th Kiev Dragoons. It was in the vast Anitchkoff Palace that he first wondered why the courtyard, and indeed all Russia, was so full of policemen. It was in the Anitchkoff Palace that he first realized that for the new Czar and Czarina, for Alicky, the dearest of his hundred nieces, and for Nicky, nothing whatever could be done. They were hopeless. She was his "Sunny" and he was her "Little Boy Blue." They read aloud the worst of English novels, *East Lynne* and *Through the Postern Gate,* and on the day that the guards massacred a delegation from the Duma they wrote in their diary that they had "a nice picnic." They were too amiable, too inept, too weak, too hopeless, too credulous, ever to survive—let alone ever to rule over all the Russias. Clearly they were doomed.

It was in the vast Anitchkoff Palace—between one requiem mass and another—that the Prince of Wales first made love to Her Serene and Imperial Highness the

Princess Titania. He was really too stupid, too gross, for that very intelligent, very cultured and very beautiful daughter of the Romanovs—but then his attraction for women was always more difficult to understand than theirs for him. This very lonely woman—alone with the little Grand Duchess, her little Natasha, in those huge and echoing rooms—was in any case quite pathetically pleased that he should play with her child. Natasha was six now and the Prince gave her the very best toys in all Petersburg; he telegraphed to Paris for others. He gave her a black-and-silver sledge with two white ponies and red harness. He had always been fond of pretty little girls, and she reminded him of his own Olga at that age—far away in the villa at Dieppe.

The Princess Titania was so delighted that someone—someone other than peasants and servants—should notice little Natasha that one night she kissed the Prince very warmly, and then and there, in the vast and empty salon, allowed him to flirt with her. He was very pleased when she let him embrace her, more pleased than he would have expected to be. Perhaps, to start with, it was no more than a relief after all those requiem masses, but he suddenly found himself regretting that he had to go back to England so soon. And, in the end, when he looked out upon Russia, upon all those starving peasants and all those prisons and policemen, he told Titania—so very much alone in such a dangerous world—that she should bring her child to England before it was too late—too late because an oppressive doom overhung the whole land. He might be Titania's lover and Natasha's guardian, and he would certainly see to it that the mother and child, as well as their fortune and their jewels, would be well cared for. He could do nothing now for Alicky and Nicky—nothing. He knew that truly they were under sentence of death—it was only a matter of years. Quite irrevocably now they were part of Russia. Titania and her little girl were different; for them there might still be time.

The "Bertie" of his mother's Court had become the Englishman's "Teddy"—the King. Teddy was old and

Teddy was fat. In 1909, in the June sunshine, high above the valley of the River Test, the gray house was waiting for him. It waited for him in the full sunshine of an Edwardian England where everyone was rich and where it was always afternoon.

The house, in its own curious way, was Ned Lutyens's masterpiece. It was of gray stone flushed with pink. There were thick stone slabs on the roof and long ranges of mullion windows. There were enormous chimney stacks to match the open hearths within. From the carriage drive it was only the chimneys that one could see above the elms. It was on the southern side, with the valley and the winding stream at one's feet, that one beheld and understood the beauty of the place.

There were great flights of steps—a hint almost of Versailles—leading from the broad terraces to the garden. It was a garden that Miss Jekyll had contrived seven years ago for the Princess Titania, that remarkably beautiful woman who was still its mistress. On this Sunday in June the herbaceous borders, the great plat, the water garden, the lavender walks and the dark yew hedges seemed as mature as they were beautiful—they had been planted in the first year of the King's reign when Titania had brought her child from Petersburg.

It was one of those dreamlike houses built by the last generation of the aesthetic rich. After the South African War, having turned their swords into gold shares, they were now basking in the twilight of a culture—of sorts. They got themselves painted by Sargent and Orpen or even, in these latter days, by John; they got themselves dressed by Worth or Doucet; they bought pretty things from Fabergé, and bought each other presents from Cartier. And they got their houses built by Lutyens—the sort of houses where there were always ambassadors in the billiards room and Peter Pan in the nursery wing. This was Heartbreak House or Horseback Hall—Bernard Shaw's "cultured, leisured Europe before the War."

In the heat of the afternoon the three claret-colored Daimlers crackled over the gravel. One was for the King and for Reginald Brett Esher. One was for a couple of

equerries and for the scarlet dispatch boxes. The third
was for the valets and the luggage. Titania was on the
doorstep. Almost any woman seen against sunlight filtered
through the distended silk of a white parasol will seem
enchanting—and this woman was beautiful with the beauty of maturity, strangely beautiful in any light. If the mass
of dark gold hair, the small and freckled nose were rather
English—or at least Northern—the almond eyes and high
cheekbones were very wise and very Slav. The hair that
year was being worn thick on the nape of the neck so that
the flowered hat was tilted forward quite deliciously over
the forehead. He stood, not a little bewitched, with one
foot still on the running board of the car. If French had
been the first language of the Court of the Romanovs,
German had certainly been the first language of the children of Prince Albert; these two compromised happily
with their imperfect English. It had become a strange
relationship, the last one of his life—a relationship between a man of the world and a woman of the world—
both, in their way, people of many curious adventures.
She called him Teddy, which was something allowed to
nobody except his parrot. Of all the women he had loved
she was the only one who, however remotely, was of the
Family; she was allowed to take liberties and she took
them.

"Teddy."

"Titania. Charming, my dearest . . ."

"Maybe . . . but you have been neglecting me. Nearly
three weeks since you were here—I can't imagine what
you do."

"I'm sorry . . ."

"That's not much use . . . but still you've come now.
They're all waiting for you of course—out on the lawn—
and pretending not to be . . . of course."

"You're a genius, Titania. . . ."

"Don't flatter me; you know perfectly well it's no
use. . . ."

"But you are a genius, my dear, breaking the London
season with a June party down here in Hampshire. London is like an oven. My God, what a week! Two theaters,

four dinner parties, a sitting in the Lords, the Bridgewater House ball, two private views as well as the R.A., the garden party at Holland House and, to crown all, the suffragettes—as if that was *my* business . . . and then you say that you can't imagine what I do!"

"Poor, dear Teddy. Never mind. It's cool out on the lawn and there are lots and lots of perfectly charming people—quite a crowd. Only thirty sleeping here; but five carriages drove over from Broadlands this morning—almost all your friends, with just a soupçon of eccentrics to give the party flavor."

"Hm! Not artists and all that lot, I hope."

"Well, no, not quite . . . stage, not art."

"That's better. . . ."

"But I must warn you, Teddy, a very special sort of stage—not just your Gaiety lot and all that. There's a Monsieur Diaghilev from Petersburg. I am paying for him to bring his dancers here next year. He has a clever musician with him—a Monsieur Stravinsky, who may play for us later, and a quite enchanting and divine boy called Nijinsky."

"Oh. Oh, I see! Hm! And who else, pray?"

"Only my biggest catch of all. You must have met him in the Faubourg St. Germain . . . just think, Marcel Proust is out there on the lawn."

"No, never heard of him. Who else? Some ordinary people, I hope."

"Well, to start with there are the Morells—Phillip and Ottoline."

"She usually has a damned poet in tow."

"My dear Teddy, one must have a little culture, you know. It's done these days, and you really must not be such an old Philistine. It's bad for the arts. But there, don't worry: all your special friends are here too—Tennants and Wyndhams and Harcourts and Mitfords, and even old Cambon and—oh, yes—the Sassoons, with Sybil Rocksavage dripping with diamonds—just fancy, in the afternoon! And there's Dickie Fisher damning and blasting everything; and dear Lady Londonderry telling everyone she's had her legs tattooed . . . she's going to show them to me tonight. . . . Do you want—er—another private view?"

"Naturally. Your parties are always marvelous, Titania, and as long as you are there, my dearest, they always will be!"

He gave her a smacking kiss on each cheek. There was a laugh behind them. Natasha was standing at the top of the steps, half shaded by the big curved arch of the porch, looking even more beautiful than her mother. She was very like her mother, but, on this June afternoon, she was a nymph, a sylph of the air—the frills and the ribbons and the quite enormous hat somehow, but miraculously, did nothing to spoil it.

"Nunky—you've come! I just can't wait for my electric brougham—what a marvelous present. You're a dear, dear Nunky."

"Nothing is too good for you, Natasha . . . and I'm told these things are convenient for shopping."

And he kissed her as vigorously as, a moment before, he had kissed her mother.

A valet had approached them as softly as a cat. With rapid dexterity he stripped the King of his dust coat and motoring cap. Beneath was the pearly gray morning suit. The white topper was handed to him, and then together these three strolled through the sunken garden—paths of old mossy stone with cool water lapping their edges. They glanced at water lilies—water lilies worthy of Monet—and at curious exotic fish . . . and so to the great terrace on the other side of the house.

It was an English Sunday. The tennis courts, beyond the walled orchard, were out of use. Even the croquet hoops had been mysteriously whipped away at dawn. The white flannels of Saturday, the boaters and the blazers—blazing with the arms of Balliol and Trinity—had all gone; pale gray or black tails, white hats and spats, and lemon gloves had taken their place. The befrilled dresses, with their huge sleeves and trailing scarves, were all white, oleander or lavender, as were the long buttoned gloves and the twirling parasols. Everyone moved and revolved slowly across the lawns. These garments, this

correctitude, was a tribute either to the King or to the
Sabbath—nobody knew which. The Russian hostess had
issued no edict. It was all, quite simply, a tribal reaction—
something they all knew. Siberia or the mines of the
Donbass were further away than the moon—by a million
miles.

Tea was being served in the shade of the great elms.
Miracles of masculine agility and juggling were being
performed with cups and saucers and cucumber sandwiches and plates of strawberries and pairs of gloves; such
miracles were admired but it would have been improper
to mention them. And then, far away across the lawns,
three people could be seen coming down from the terraces—familiar figures. It was almost Chinese: the beautiful princess, the fat mandarin and Natasha—the little
Tanagra figurine.

He knew almost everyone; but a *cercle,* a conducted
tour—that he might miss nobody and that nobody might
miss him—was *de rigueur.* The curtsies on the lawn were
as if the petals of a white magnolia were slowly falling.
The removing of toppers was as if ordered by a drill
sergeant, or—to some—more reminiscent of the raising
and lowering of coronets, seven years ago in the Abbey.
The garden had until then been filled with the slow but
swirling movement of white and gray upon a green floor—
enchanting, casual and unordered. Now, quite suddenly,
everything had precision; the lawn had become a stage for
a corps-de-ballet. Only Diaghilev saw the dramatic beauty
of it all; he wished that Degas might be there to paint it,
or a choreographer to make it the beginning of an inspira-
tion. He caught Proust's eye and both men sighed at the
philistinism of these English who, alas, could not even see
themselves.

The intellectuals were given a royal nod. Mama had
been persuaded years ago to admit artists and actors to
Society—God knows why! It had been a great mistake.
She had even given Irving a knighthood—making honors
cheap. Such people were not much good anyway and—
worse still—they made one feel inferior. For everyone else
His Majesty had the right word, the right quip. For half a

century, after all, that had been his stock in trade. They would, every one of them, have taken almost anything from him: to be spoken to was more important than what was said. In fact he gave them all a moment of graciousness in which to wallow.

"Ah, my dear Wyndham, what is a party without you? A party without a Wyndham is unthinkable. And what have you to say? Has not dear Titania got an even more lovely house than your Clouds?"

"I could never admit that, sire, never, but the Princess would make any house beautiful of course—by her mere presence."

"You hear that, Titania. Ah, here is Cambon. *Bien, mon cher vieillerie*—what mischief is Your Excellency up to these days?"

"The mischief is yours, Your Majesty. Have you forgotten our beautiful Paris? . . . It is so long, so very long, since we saw you. Paris is quite *désolée* . . . without her King."

"My heart is there. It always will be. You know that, my dear Excellency . . . but my ministers, they work me to death. And now here is our Margot—your Royal Academy hat, my dear, was totally scandalous. How could you?"

"Sire, it was meant to be scandalous—what is life without scandal? You would agree with that, Your Majesty?"

"Never mind! You should be at Glen this weather . . . and yet what would London be without you? . . . And so this is our little Puffin. And here is General Booth—up to some good, I'll be bound, eh, General?"

"Your Majesty is very gracious."

"Ah, Your Eminence . . ." And it was for the King now to bow low in kissing the ring.

"And Emerald . . . well, well, dear Emerald. This seems to be *your* season. Truly, you know, we hear of nobody else."

"Majesty . . ." and a specially deep curtsy until Titania made the next presentation.

"And here, sire, is our surprise for you—something to make you really happy—the Baroness Meyer."

"Olga! My darling Olga! Yes, this is indeed a surprise. Why, we had tea together only yesterday, Titania, and she never even told me. . . ."

There were no curtsies now—just fond embraces. Everyone on that lawn knew that he took tea at Cadogan Gardens three times a week, but as the father kissed his child there was an inexplicable and slightly reverential silence. He moved on.

"Ah, Sassoon . . . you're entrenched in Park Lane now, I hear. I am told wondrous things about you. Tell me, Philip, when can I come from my house to visit your place?"

"If Your Majesty would deign . . ."

And so round the garden, from sun into shade and back into sunlight, until the dressing gong sounded on the terrace. These curious creatures dressed earlier nowadays. Dinner, it is true, got later and later, but the apéritif hour got more and more sacred. It was their assurance that they were cosmopolitan, that the *fin-de-siècle* was behind them . . . that they were something new . . . their assurance that the King's mother was dead.

The ruin of a great dinner is a marvelous sight. The lees and dregs in all the glasses, the shells of oysters or of plovers' eggs, the bones of quails, ortolans and *gelinottes* of carp soused in brandy or of crayfish in chablis, the last fragments of caviar, of truffles or *foie gras,* the ruins of iced puddings, collapsed mountains of meringue confections—all this lay littered across the table and through pantries.

Stravinsky had played his last chord. The roulette wheel had turned for the last time. The last card debt had been settled. The last apple-pie bed had been made. The last reputation had been torn to shreds. It was time to move into the "Big Room," time to dance far into the June dawn.

The Big Room ran the height of two stories. At one end, in the broad hearth—whether because the nights were cool or just the look of the thing—big logs were sparkling. The stone canopy above them soared into the roof, carved only with the two-headed eagle of the Romanovs.

"I can only dance quadrilles now, Titania. Long ago, you know, they used to say that I danced very well. Mama approved only of square dances, but later on, of course, there were the balls in the great houses . . . gavottes and polkas then . . . and after I was married, at Marlborough House, night after night we danced the Mandela *valse*. They are playing it now, but, alas, my dear, I am old and fat . . . and I puff. . . ."

"Nonsense, Teddy . . . portly, my boy, not fat. Anyway, I have made my decision. For my sake, and just for a very few minutes, you must start the first *valse* with Natasha."

And he did . . . very slowly they moved round the room . . . alone together on the empty floor . . . everyone watching them. The little Natasha looked up into his eyes. Those eyes were watching and he was looking at her very tenderly—the child of his dearest Titania. He looked into her face . . . he blinked to clear away the tears—again and again. Then, rather suddenly, Natasha knew that she must take him back to her mother. He had begun to cough. That was normal . . . until everybody realized that it was more than just the cough of a bronchial old man. His eyes, now—like oysters in a bath of blood—were bulging, dropping, almost, out of their sockets. The veins, great purple lines, were standing out on his forehead. He was trembling. He laid a trembling hand on Titania's arm.

"Take me away, Titania, take me away. Get me out of here. I'm ill, my dear, ill!"

Very gently she took him up to her boudoir, but he was not really ill—not really. He had had a very great shock.

"The Earrings, Titania, my love, the Holy Earrings! Bloody Mary's Earrings . . . the diamonds. Natasha's earrings . . . tell me."

"My dear Teddy, do be calm. It's nothing to get excited

about, or alarmed about. What on earth has upset you?"

"But where did you get them? Where on earth did you get them? Where? When? Why? How?"

"My dear boy, you don't think I could afford to buy diamonds like those—not in these days? I've always kept them hidden from Natasha—ready for the *valse* with you tonight. . . . I wouldn't even let her wear them at the dinner. She's never seen them until now, nor, I think, has anyone now living. You see, as kind of insurance I smuggled them out of Russia. I should be a very rich woman if I'd sold them, but, thanks largely to you, my dear, and to Hirsch, I've never had to use them. I've never even borrowed on them although I did think of taking them to Rothschild when I built this house. . . ."

"Good God! You would have given him the shock of his life. . . ."

"I can't see why. Anyway, I struggled through. There's no mystery about them. After all, the Romanovs have always had the finest jewels in the world. And they have always had the Holy Earrings, at any rate for centuries. . . ."

"Yes, yes. But where did the Romanovs get them? I want to know. I must know, Titania."

"Oh, very well, if you must know . . . but, for the life of me, I can't imagine why you're so upset. The story, oddly enough, does begin in England . . . more oddly still, a few miles away, in Winchester . . . nearly four hundred years ago."

"Yes, yes, yes, that's it. Tell me. . . ."

Very quietly Natasha had crept into her mother's boudoir—the little room with the white paneling, the scarlet curtains and the Paolo Uccello over the mantelpiece. She sat with her back to the candles; she was in shadow except that when she moved the candlelight glinted on the diamonds, first on one side of her head and then on the other. Her mother had lapsed into French now, as she was wont to do in times of emotion. Natasha and the King just listened, her hand on his knee.

"Very well, Teddy, if it will calm your mind, I'll tell

you. It's only one of those old stories—legends, call them
what you will—that we royals pick up as the years pass.
But, yes, if you must know, these really are the fabulous
and Holy Earrings which Philip of Spain gave to your
Mary Tudor...."

"I've guessed that much—that this was the end of a
long story. But why are they here tonight in Natasha's
little pearly ears? How did you come by them?"

"Well, Bloody Mary wore them at her wedding—at
Winchester, was it not?—her wedding with Philip of
Spain. You see, the earrings are very nearly home
again."

"Surely, but ..."

"Keep quiet. Let me tell you. Mary wore them in the
Cathedral and she was certain that she would wear them
again that night in bed, with Philip. But somehow or
other, after the banquet, the Holy Earrings vanished.
Mary always said, to the end of her tragic life, that *that*
was why she was childless ... she never bore a child, boy
or girl ... and God knows she tried. She blamed the loss
of the earrings...." Titania laughed a little. "... You see
these diamond stars perform miracles: they make barren
women fertile, and fertile with sons." She laughed
again.

"But, Titania, never mind that part. How did they
vanish?"

"I'm trying to tell you, Teddy. Do listen. You see,
everyone wanted the Holy Earrings. Philip thought that
once this plain English bitch was pregnant, the earrings
were too good for her; he wanted them back in the
Escorial. Mary, thinking God had sent them—that she
was blessed among women—wanted to put them forever
on the altar at Windsor ... Philip wasn't having that, you
know. And then the Imperial Ambassador, Renard,
wanted them for himself; he thought that Philip had been
pretty scurvy with him ... that he, Renard, had arranged
the marriage and that the earrings should be his perquisite
... certainly he deserved something, poor man. But
above all, it was the Princess Elizabeth, imprisoned at
Woodstock, who wanted them more than anyone. She

wanted them partly because she was, in any case, the
most avaricious woman who ever lived; she wanted them
because, when she became Queen, she would put them
among the Crown Jewels of England; but most of all she
wanted them to frustrate the miracle whereby Mary might
have a son—a Catholic heir—and because one day Elizabeth might need that miracle herself. Elizabeth's agents
arranged things so that before Philip and Mary could be
bedded that night (quite a ceremony in those days) the
Lady Clifford—an embittered and disappointed woman—
should put the Holy Earrings in a cloth and throw them
out the window . . . and she did."

"But Elizabeth never got the earrings. . . ."

"I haven't said she ever got them. She didn't. Something went wrong. There was a plot within the plot. All
these people were spies, remember, and all of them corrupt. There was a little hunchbacked girl . . . she was a nobody, but they called her 'Keeper of the Queen's Jewels.'
For all her grand title, she was consumed with hatred. She
was a crypto-Protestant anyway, and had been ridiculed
and ill-treated for her crooked back and legs. She altered
the clock that night and the Lady Clifford threw the
diamonds out the window half an hour too soon. Under
the window the little hunchback had placed her newfound
friend, Pétya—Philip's Russian valet, a man devoured by
greed as the hunchback was devoured by hate."

"So Philip of Spain had a Russian valet, did he? Russia
has come into the story. Go on, my dear, go on."

"Yes. The poor little hunchback, the Keeper of the
Queen's Jewels, had found a fellow creature in Pétya.
High up in the triforium of Winchester Cathedral, during
the wedding that morning, they had planned it all under
cover of the music. She gave Pétya the word and he was
there that night, under the window, to catch the Holy
Earrings. Needless to say he vanished immediately. It is
said that he joined some English gypsies. Anyway, he
made his way back to Russia, to Kiev where he had been
born—probably along the pilgrim routes. It may have
taken him years, but he got there all right. And he got a
very good price for his diamond stars—Bloody Mary's

Earrings. He went to Moscow and somehow wormed his way into the Kremlin. There was a Muscovite lord, a Romanov . . ."

"I see, I see . . . or I begin to see. Go on, Titania."

"This Romanov lord, or princeling or whatever he was, gave Pétya, so it is said, a million roubles. . . . And that, my dear Teddy, is how they come, this very night, to be in my little Natasha's pearly ears."

"So that was it. Madrid, Winchester, Moscow and now—almost back to Winchester. That was it . . . and to think . . . Papa and the Crystal Palace . . . Mama and the Blue Room . . . the Maharajah and old Ponsonby . . . the Captain and Trixie . . . and Shrimp in his ginger suit . . . and the real diamonds were never there at all. Oh, my dear, dear Titania!"

There was silence between them, and there were tears in his eyes.

"But, Titania, the story still doesn't really work, you know. It still doesn't hold water. What about the Holy Earrings that the Spanish Government gave to the Duke of Wellington, the Iron Duke, after the Peninsular War, and that he gave to Papa in 1851 for the Tiara in the Crystal Palace? . . . The story just doesn't work, my dear—the mystery is still unsolved."

She only laughed.

"My dear Teddy. Don't you see? . . . Poor Mary Tudor went nearly mad when the earrings vanished. God, she thought, must hate her. She was very near to death. To save her sanity Philip had some very perfect copies made. He then told her that they had got back the earrings, and they had caught the thief in Toledo and burnt him alive on a very slow fire. That made her extremely happy; and when Philip came back to England the next year she wore the copies in bed. . . . Ignorance was bliss."

"Well, I'm damned . . . and the Iron Duke?"

Titania only chortled.

"You simpleton. You don't really think, do you, that any Spanish Government there ever was would actually give a million pounds' worth of jewels to an English soldier? As a bribe perhaps—but to reward him *after* the

battle was won, that would be pointless. They gave the
Duke a couple of enormous estates—arid mountains actually; but diamonds—no. He was just an old buffer anyway who wouldn't know a diamond when he saw it. On
the other hand, by 1851 he was the greatest man in
England. Your good Papa had to take the diamonds on
trust—as, of course, did the Constable of the Tower."

"I see. So here are the Holy Earrings at last. Ye Gods!
No wonder we could never find them!"

He stood up and put his hands very gently on Natasha's ears, feeling the facets of the gems under his
fingers.

"Stolen property, Natasha, stolen property . . . Philip of
Spain gave them to the English Crown, and Pétya—bless
his heart—stole them. I suppose poor Eddy would have
liked them. . . . He's dead and gone now. . . . All for the
best; Georgie will make a better king, but wouldn't be
interested in diamonds. No, no, no . . . They are mine and
I give them to you. Keep them, my dear, keep them with
my love."

She stood up and kissed him.

"Yes, keep them, my dear. One day you may need
them."

"I shall always love them; but 'need them'—why?"

"Well, they are miraculous earrings and if, one day,
you were to wear them on your wedding night, then—for
certain—you would give the world a Prince."

It was late when Titania had finished her story. Natasha went back to the ball; up there in the boudoir they
could just hear the sound of the music, reminding them
that the guests must be missing both their hostess and the
King. The guests must wait a little longer. The sun was
above the Hampshire hills by the time the King had told
Titania his half of the story . . . the years came rushing
back . . . Windsor, Balmoral, Osborne and a slum somewhere east of Bow Creek. Twenty-two years had passed.
There were things he had almost forgotten. And then, at
the end, Titania had something more to say.

"I see . . . but what a pity your mother did not live to
see the end of the story."

"No. It's better as it is, Titania. Mama, you know, had very curious and very literal ideas about right and wrong, and also about property—not least Crown property. She would think Mary Tudor grossly careless to lose her diamonds like that and to appoint such unreliable ladies-in-waiting. As for Pétya—she would say that he knew perfectly well that he was doing wrong, and would be sorry that the man could no longer be hauled up at Bow Street. With Mama the years would make no difference. No. Bloody Mary's Earrings, my dear one, now belong to your little Natasha. That makes me very happy; but I can assure you that dear Mama would not have been at all amused . . . not in the very least."

Bibliography

BOLITHO, HECTOR, *Albert the Good*. Appleton, 1932.

CHURCHILL, WINSTON, *Lord Randolph Churchill*. Macmillan, 1906. 2 vols.

FULFORD, ROGER, ed., *Dearest Child: Letters between Queen Victoria and the Princess Royal*. Holt, 1965.

HOUSMAN, LAURENCE, *Victoria Regina*. Jonathan Cape, 1934.

LEE, SIDNEY, *King Edward VII*. Macmillan, 1925, 2 vols.

LONGFORD, ELIZABETH, *Queen Victoria, Born to Succeed*. Harper, 1965.

LUTYENS, MARY, ed., *Lady Lytton's Court Diary, 1895-1899*. Rupert Hart-Davis, 1961.

MAGNUS-ALLCROFT, PHILIP, *King Edward the Seventh*, Dutton, 1964.

MALLET, VICTOR, *Life with Queen Victoria: Marie Mallet's Letters from Court, 1887-1901*. Houghton Mifflin, 1968.

PONSONBY, ARTHUR, *Henry Ponsonby: Queen Victoria's Private Secretary*. Macmillan, 1942.

ROTH, CECIL, *The Magnificent Rothschilds*. Ryerson Press, 1939.

STRACHEY, LYTTON, *Queen Victoria*. Chatto & Windus, 1921.

VICTORIA, PRINCESS, *Queen Victoria at Windsor and Balmoral: Letters from Princess Victoria of Prussia*. Allen & Unwin, 1959.

VICTORIA, QUEEN, *Leaves from the Journal of Our Life in the Highlands from 1848 to 1861*. Smith Elder & Co., 1868.

————, *The Letters of Queen Victoria*. First Series, 1831-1861, 3 vols., edited by A. C. Benson and Viscount Esher. Second Series, 1862-1885, 3 vols., edited by George Earle Buckle. Third Series, 1886-1901, 3 vols., edited by George Earle Buckle. John Murray.

How to do almost everything

What are the latest time and money-saving shortcuts for painting, papering, and varnishing floors, walls, ceilings, furniture? (See pages 102-111 of HOW TO DO *Almost* EVERYTHING.) What are the mini-recipes and the new ways to make food—from appetizers through desserts—exciting and delicious? (See pages 165-283.) How-to-do-it ideas like these have made Bert Bacharach, father of the celebrated composer (Burt), one of the most popular columnists in America.

This remarkable new book, HOW TO DO *Almost* EVERYTHING, is a fact-filled collection of Bert Bacharach's practical aids, containing thousands of tips and hints—for keeping house, gardening, cooking, driving, working, traveling, caring for children. It will answer hundreds of your questions, briefly and lucidly.

How to do almost everything

is chock-full of useful information—information on almost everything you can think of, arranged by subject in short, easy-to-find tidbits, with an alphabetical index to help you find your way around—and written with the famed Bacharach touch.

SEND FOR YOUR FREE EXAMINATION COPY TODAY

We invite you to mail the coupon below. A copy of HOW TO DO *Almost* EVERYTHING will be sent to you at once. If at the end of ten days you do not feel that this book is one you will treasure, you may return it and owe nothing. Otherwise, we will bill you $6.95, plus postage and handling. At all bookstores, or write to Simon and Schuster, Dept. S-52, 630 Fifth Ave., New York, N.Y. 10020.

He stood naked and alone at the edge of the loch, its surface set aflame by the morning sun.

"D'ye have somethin' ye wanted to speak to me about? Or were ye plannin' on just starin' at me while I bathed?"

Kate thought hard about running then. But 'twas too late, he was already turning around to face her. She was thankful, at least, that half his body was covered in water. That is, until his eyes found hers.

How could they sear her flesh and chill her blood at the same time? They drew her in, inviting her onto a battlefield for which she had never practiced. Looking into them, she wondered what victory would gain her if she was braw enough to engage.

"Would ye care to join me?"

"Excellent writing and tantalizing romance."
—RomRevToday.com

"This novel captures the era, on both sides of the conflict, with masterful skill . . . a fine romance, plenty of action, and a few twists in this medieval tale."
—ARomanceReview.com

"Paula Quinn crafts a story in which the details combine to make you feel as if you are there with her characters. I sighed over the gentleness of the hero and the charm of the heroine. LORD OF SEDUCTION is not to be missed."
—Bookloons.com

"Bold and passionate medieval romance."
—FreshFiction.com

Lord of Temptation

"Features a sinfully sexy hero who meets his match in a strong-willed heroine . . . An excellent choice for readers who like powerful, passion-rich medieval romances."
—*Booklist*

"Will enchant and entertain . . . Passion, danger, treachery, and heartbreak fill the pages of this splendid novel . . . don't miss *Lord of Temptation*."
—RomRevToday.com

"Quinn's lively romance . . . offers two spirited protagonists as well as engaging minor characters . . . The sharp repartee and dramatic finale make this a pleasant read."
—*Publishers Weekly*

"Quinn wins readers' hearts with a light touch, even as she invokes strong themes of slavery, freedom, and the need for independence."
—*Romantic Times BOOKreviews Magazine*

"A truly magnificent tale . . . Dante is a perfect hero and lover and Gianelle is special—perfect for each other. The passion is fantastic—unbeatable!"
—*RomanceReviewsMag.com*

Lord of Desire

"Four stars! . . . Fast-paced and brimming with biting, sexy repartee, and a sensual cat-and-mouse game."
—*Romantic Times BOOKreviews Magazine*

"Gloriously passionate . . . boldly sensual . . . Quinn deftly enhances her debut with just enough historical details to give a vivid sense of time and place."
—*Booklist*

more . . .

Laird
of the
Mist

ALSO BY PAULA QUINN

Lord of Desire
Lord of Temptation
Lord of Seduction

Laird
of the
Mist

PAULA QUINN

FOREVER

NEW YORK   BOSTON

Cover illustration by Jon Paul
Hand lettering by David Gatti

Forever is a division of Grand Central Publishing.

The Forever name and logo is a trademark of Hachette Book Group USA, Inc.

The poem from page xiii is from *Children of the Mist* by Frank McNie. Reprinted by permission of Frank McNie.

Forever
Hachette Book Group USA
237 Park Avenue
New York, NY 10017
Visit our Web site at www.HachetteBookGroupUSA.com

Printed in the United States of America

First Printing: December 2007

10 9 8 7 6 5 4 3 2 1

For the MacGregors

"While there's leaves in the forest and foam on the river
MacGregor despite them shall flourish forever."

Acknowledgments

To MY HUSBAND, who patiently listened and learned about this brave clan and understood why their story made me cry. And to my children, who lovingly roll their eyes when I try (and fail) to speak with a Scottish burr.

To my editor, Michele Bidelspach, for each and every word of encouragement. Thank you for your insight and for helping me make this book all it should be.

To my agent, Andrea Somberg, who always makes me feel like I can do anything. Thank you for your faith in me.

To Rika, Gabrielle, Terra, Christy, Rabbit, Willow, Melissa, January, and Dublin, you make every page I sweat over worth it. Thank you for your support and your friendship.

And to God, for His grace in my life.

Children of the Mist
by Frank McNie

We're the children of the mist with no land to call home,
descended from kings but destined to roam.
We were honoured in battle then hunted like game,
but the proof of our mettle is we're still proud of our name.

They outlawed our clan and the mode of our dress,
but we never measured allegiance by chance of success.
Some things we're not proud of were circumstance led,
but what prince not a rogue to see his children are fed?

Our friendship was valued by high born and low,
our steadfast belief earned respect from our foe.
No great castles had we and our numbers were few
but our clansmen before us kept our legacy true.

Chapter One

GLEN ORCHY, SCOTLAND
SEVENTEENTH CENTURY

KATE CAMPBELL LOOKED her enemy square in his lifeless face and then swung. Her blade severed an arm, but the torso remained intact. Mindless of her uncle's men honing their battle skills around her, she lifted the ax she gripped in her other hand and grunted as it sank deep into her opponent's straw chest.

Swiping her hair away from her eyes, she spied her uncle Duncan crossing the small bailey of her holding. He had arrived in Glen Orchy a few days ago to bring her to Kildun Castle, in Inverary. He'd promised to bring her and her brother to his home when they were children, but at the end of each visit he left without them.

Their mother died giving Kate life. Their father was killed at Kildun twelve years after that, just before Duncan was named Earl of Argyll, and Kate and Robert's guardian.

Kate watched him stalk toward her, his equine legs encased in fine woolen breeches and boots of polished obsidian. His frame was slight, his shoulders narrow beneath an olive doublet. He was built more for priesting than for fighting, though he often bragged of his victories in battle. These battles kept him away from Kildun for months at a time, he'd reminded them many times during his visits, planting a kiss on their foreheads before heading for the doors. Soon he would come to bring them home with him. But he never did. Not even when her father's vassals began leaving, save for a small handful who raised them.

Kate met the earl's gaze briefly, and his gray eyes grew dark with intent that made her skin crawl. He may not have wanted her as a child, but he wanted her now.

"You brandish your weapons well, Katherine." He came up behind her and ducked to his right when she hefted her ax over her shoulder for another crushing swipe, this time to her enemy's thigh.

Aye, she and Robert had been made to practice day after day. "Amish and John taught us well."

Behind her, she heard a tight snort. "They have remained loyal soldiers to my brother these many years. But their duty to him is over now. I will see that they are rewarded." He leaned over her so that his whispered breath clung to her cheek. "It pleases me to know you would fight back should any man try to ravish you."

Kate clutched the handle of her ax and thought about flinging it over her shoulder. "Truly, Uncle, your concern for mine and Robert's well-being has always warmed my heart. Especially when you used to remind us how fortunate we were that it was the McColls who raided Glen Orchy every other fortnight, and not the murderous MacGregors." He hadn't cared that a Highlander might ravish her while she was growing up, or that there were but a handful of men left in the garrison to fight them if they did.

"When you were a child, the only thing the raiders wanted was sheep. I knew you were safe here. But now you are a woman and the Highlanders will take more than your livestock." His breath glided over her throat. Kate cringed and brought her ax down hard on her opponent, raining hay on their heads.

"I do not fear any man who thinks to come here to steal my virtue, Uncle."

"And if our enemy should fall upon you?"

Kate knew whom he meant. He'd spoken of them countless times over the years. "There are hardly any MacGregors left in Scotland worth fretting over. I'm certain I shall never meet one."

"There are enough of them left to continue to back the royalists' cause." The earl curled his finger around a raven lock that fell over her shoulder. "We must not forget how they joined forces with their Catholic Marquis of Montrose against us. Or how many of our kinsmen have died during their murderous rampages. Remember I told you how they massacred the Covenanters without mercy at Kilsyth? I will not let you fall to them, as well. You will do as I say and come home with me." He gave her hair a tug, as if to remind her that he would not let her refuse.

"This is my home," she said, stabbing her opponent in the throat.

"Not anymore." When she stiffened at his sharp retort, he softened his tone. "Robert is eager to see you. It has been near three months since he has set eyes on his beloved sister."

Kate missed her brother terribly, but he had chosen his path. "My brother has waited years to give his service to the realm, but I am content here, Uncle."

His laughter raked across her ear. "With a few old men and a handful of servants? What could you hope to do against the Devil, should he find you?"

Kate was certain he already had and was standing behind her at this very moment. Her uncle was trying his best to frighten her into leaving with him, by reminding her of the horrid MacGregors the way children taunt each other with tales of beasties. The most terrifying of them all: The Devil, who had killed over fifty Campbells six years ago in a massacre that had made him legend—and made her and Robert orphans.

Duncan hauled her closer and gritted his teeth. "Have you forgotten already that he killed my father and yours?"

"Nae," Kate answered without turning. "I have not forgotten." Indeed, Kate hated him, but she did not concern herself with legends or the foolishness of fearing them.

"And you do not fear such a blood-lustful man?" he demanded while she swung again.

"Nae, I will kill him if ever I meet him," she vowed, decapitating her enemy with her sword.

"You never will." The earl slid his hand down her arm until his fingers covered hers. He jabbed her blade into her lifeless opponent, a groan tangling in his throat as he pressed her back to his chest. "Tomorrow you will return with me to Kildun. Only there will you be safe from our enemy."

Kate stopped fighting and ground her teeth when he kissed the back of her head. "You are my enemy, as well," she murmured as he swaggered back to his men. She brought her ax upward instead of down; it struck and wedged tightly between her opponent's legs.

Leaving the ax where it landed, Kate sheathed her sword and walked off toward the meadow where her sheep grazed oblivious and innocent to the lusty wiles of men. It sickened her when she thought of why her uncle wanted her. She'd known of his depravity for some time but had never told Robert. She hadn't truly thought Duncan would come for her, even after Robert went to live with him, so there was no need. But now he was here and so anxious to get her out of Glen Orchy, she was certain he would drag her there tied to his horse if he had to. Did he think Robert would let him touch her once they arrived at Kildun? Fool. Her brother would slice off Duncan's hands, uncle or not. Robert was noble and valiant, with a strong sense of duty to protect his clan. It was he who taught her Malory and Monmouth's tales of Arthur Pendragon and his knights of the Round Table. And it was the terrible tales of the savage MacGregors that drove him to leave their home three months ago and join the other knights of Inverary.

Robert had begged her to go with him, but Kate did not want to leave her home, and she certainly did not want to live with her uncle. She was safe here. The raiders were bothersome but not terribly dangerous.

Amish had made her and her brother vow to never lift a weapon to the mountain men. Their raiding, he had told them, was a way of life. They did not come to kill, so long as they were not attacked. Not so the MacGregors. For over two centuries they were considered the scourge of Scotland: uncivilized barbarians with no regard for honor or a man's family. So heinous were their crimes against the Campbells and their allies that their name had been proscribed over fifty years ago.

Amish and John never spoke ill of them, though, even after the Devil killed her father. Hatred, they told her as her father had, was poison to the soul.

Kate wiped her fist across her ear, where the stale smell of her uncle's breath still lingered. Hatred might be poison, but if he ever touched her again he would feel the power of it when her blade sliced open his heart.

A thunderous cry from the braes above pierced her thoughts. Her face paled. Raiders! She turned, looking back at her uncle's men already drawing their swords. Nae! She sped toward them, praying as she ran that she could reach her uncle's men before the Highlanders did.

~

Callum MacGregor, clan chieftain of the MacGregors, reined in his mount atop the crest of a hill and watched the small battle taking place in the vale below. His dark brows creased over his eyes as he scanned the men engaged in the melee around the Campbell holding and those lying dead in the grass. Duncan Campbell was not among them.

"Looks like we've stumbled upon a raid by the Mc-Colls," said one of the four men flanking him.

"Ye said the Earl of Argyll would be here, Graham." The chieftain cut his gaze to his first in command.

"He's here," his commander assured confidently while he rotated the cap tilted jauntily atop his mane of honeyed curls to a backward position. If any man had reason to be so certain of his words, 'twas Graham Grant. After pretending to be a Campbell from Breadalbane and living in Kildun Castle for the last pair of months, Graham knew all there was to know about the Inverary Campbells and the tenth Earl of Argyll. "This was his brother Colin's homestead. He's come here to retrieve his niece." Graham pointed into the vale at the soldiers. "Campbell's men are here. Mayhap he hides in the keep. We know he lacks courage."

"Save fer when he's brandin' MacGregor women," said another man, a bit broader of shoulder than the rest. He popped the cork off a leather pouch dangling from his belt and raised it to his mouth.

"Can ye no' go anywhere wi'oot yer poison, Angus?"

Angus took a swig, belched, and then swiped his beefy knuckles across his thick auburn beard. "Brodie, ye know I like killin' Campbells wi' a bit o' auld Gillis's brew in me." He grinned at his cousin stationed beside him. "It fires up me innards."

Callum refused when Angus slapped the pouch of brew against his arm, offering his laird to take part. Callum did not need whiskey to fire his innards. Hating the Campbells was enough. They had taken much from his clan. But they had taken everything from him.

"The McColls are puttin' a quick end to the Campbells. They'll be less fer us."

"Dinna fret over it, Brodie," Angus said, corking his pouch. "We killed us enough o' the bastards already at Kildun before we got here."

"It will never be enough," their laird growled low in his throat.

"If Argyll is there, the McColls might get to him before

we do," Jamie Grant, Graham's younger brother and the youngest of Callum's men, pointed out.

"There's a lass fightin' among the men!"

"That's no' a lass, Brodie." Angus guzzled another swig of whiskey. " 'Tis a Campbell wi' mighty long hair."

Brodie flashed his larger cousin an incredulous scowl beneath his dark whiskers. " 'Tis a lass, ye dull-witted bastard."

Callum heard the side of Angus's sword smack against Brodie's head, and Brodie's subsequent oaths before he pounded his fist into Angus's chest. The chieftain ignored his kinsmen and observed the object of their disagreement. The mounted warrior certainly looked like a lass. He'd never seen a lass fight before, though many times he wished he had. His mother's screams still haunted his dreams. He'd been a lad when Duncan Campbell's father raided his village and his men raped and branded the women, though no hand had been lifted against the earl's men.

But here was a woman who had the spirit to actually fight to save her life.

" 'Tis a lass," he said, more to himself than to his men. "Mayhap Argyll's niece."

"Aye." Graham nodded, watching her lush raven mane swing around her shoulders while she whirled her horse around and deflected another mighty blow. "She tires against the McColls. I know she's a Campbell," he said with only a hint of regret, "but it looks like a good enough fight. Shall we aid her, Callum?"

Graham smiled at his friend's slight nod, and then he flicked his reins and took off a moment after Callum kicked his stallion's flanks and raced toward the melee.

The MacGregor chief cut a straight path to the lass, swiping his claymore through anyone in his way. His men fanned out around him, killing the rest. The closer he came to her, the harder he rode, his dark hair snapping behind him like a pennant. Her arms were growing weary. She was having difficulty lifting her blade to parry the flurry of strikes hammering down on her. He told himself, while he hacked at a McColl riding up behind her, that he was rushing to her defense to keep her alive so that she could tell him Duncan Campbell's whereabouts.

She whirled on him just as he reached her, and Callum felt something in his gut jolt. Her skin was pale alabaster against a spray of soft obsidian waves, dampened by exhaustion. Her eyes were beautiful as black satin, and when she looked up at him, they told Callum she had just lost hope in surviving this day.

He did not expect her to swing at him, looking as defeated as she did. For an instant, he merely gaped in stunned disbelief at the blood soaking his thigh. Then he lifted his claymore over his head and brought it down hard on another McColl. The lass turned away from the force of his deathblow, but a moment later she returned her gaze to his. Callum responded to the great relief in her expression by wheeling his mount around and calling out to his men to guard her on every side. There, they shielded her until the only men left in the yard, besides them, were dead or wounded.

When Callum turned his mount around to face her again, her sword slipped from her fingers. He glanced at it, then lifted his eyes to hers. "Are ye injured?"

She blinked as if emerging from a daze. Her breath still came heavy enough to part her lips.

"Are ye hurt?" he demanded again.

She shook her head nae. "Are you?" Her gaze slipped to his thigh. "My deepest apologies for wounding you. I did not know who you were, or—"

"Are ye Duncan Campbell's niece?" he interrupted.

She either didn't hear him or chose to ignore his query. "I must find Amish and John. They are old and—"

"Woman," he cut her off again, this time his voice hard enough to make her blink. "Are ye Argyll's niece?" When she nodded, his expression went hard. "Where is he?"

She looked around at the fallen, presenting him with the delicacy of her profile. "I had hoped he was here. But he must have run off with one of my sheep."

A hint of amusement crossed Callum's expression before he angled his head and barked out another order to the four men around her. "Brodie, check the keep with Angus and Jamie. If ye find Argyll, bring him oot to me."

"Who are you, that I may properly thank you for aiding me?"

Callum's gaze swung back to her. For an unsettling instant he lost all ability to reason, save that he knew he would be content to look at her for however many days he had left on the Earth. 'Twas not fear that made her bonny eyes appear so big, but reverence. Admiration from a Campbell! Since he had never saved the life of one before, he was not prepared for her awe. He shifted again, feeling damned uncomfortable and blaming her for it.

"I am Callum MacGregor." Best to get it over with sooner rather than later, though a part of him regretted having to watch that veneration turn to hatred when he spoke his name aloud. He was not disappointed. Her face paled to such a milky white he thought she might faint dead away and tumble from her horse.

His eyes were usually very quick, and on any other day Callum MacGregor would never have missed an enemy reaching for a weapon. But for a moment her beauty made him forget about fighting and hatred and blood. A moment was all it took for her to slip her hand beneath her belt and retrieve the small dagger she had hidden there.

The glimmer of surprise that sparked Callum's eyes belied his cold, impassive voice. "Ye have courage to point yer dagger at me." She swung, and he moved in a blur of speed, yanking her from her horse to his. Pressing her chest to his, he closed his arms around her, pinning her dagger securely behind her back. "Ye insult the laird of the clan MacGregor with such a meager weapon, lass."

"Let me go, vermin!" she hurled at him and spent the remainder of her energy kicking and wriggling, trying to free herself. "Let me go if you be a man, and let me fight you with my sword."

Callum glanced at Graham, mirroring the commander's expression of admiration at her furious promise. She was a fiery, braw lass, something all Highlanders valued.

But she was a Campbell.

"Is Argyll in the keep?" Callum asked her, barely straining a muscle against her attempts to be free of him.

"I told you I don't know where he is, but when you find him, take him to hell with you!"

Aye, now this was more like the reaction he expected from a Campbell. She was no more innocent than the rest. "Graham, get me some rope. The wench tires me."

Her fight came to an abrupt halt. She glared up at him with the promise of retribution frosting her eyes. "Will you prove yourself naught but a savage by raping me?"

Briefly, his gaze fell to her lips, then drifted over the rest of her body in a leisurely inspection of her feminine aspects, as if he were considering it. "Woman, I am much more than a savage."

Her nostrils flared. "I would cut off your—"

Over her shoulder, Callum saw one of her uncle's men exit from behind the house, cocked bow in hand. He had no time to shield her as the arrow whistled toward them and penetrated her right shoulder, just above her breast. Though it happened within the space of a breath, he watched it pierce her perfect form, watched the breath-taking spark of life grow dull in her eyes. As Graham raced toward the guardsman, Callum's eyes met hers again when she realized she'd been hit.

"Och, hell." Her breath was a ragged whisper, sweet against his chin. "That was likely meant for you."

Chapter Two

FIRE LANCED UP KATE'S ARM and seared her chest. Every inhalation of breath became more excruciating than the one before it. It wasn't helping that her captor still held her firmly pressed against his body.

On second thought, mayhap it was. For she couldn't move or flail about as agony gripped her. Her thoughts began to fade, but she fought to cling to consciousness. She had never fainted before, and she was not about to do so now whilst in the arms of a MacGregor!

"Be still with ye, lass."

"Dear God, it pains me," she groaned, covering her face in his shoulder.

"Let the pain settle." His pitch lowered to a comforting murmur. His arms loosened around her while she tried to slow her breathing. He turned to his men, who were exiting her home.

"Argyll isna inside," one of them called out. "We found only a few servants, nae old men among them."

"They must be there." Kate fought the MacGregor's

hold on her and then swooned as red-hot agony tore through her arm.

"Yer brew," the chieftain commanded to another one of his men, and then caught something in his hand. "Drink this." He held the nozzle of a small hide skin sack to her lips. "It'll dull the pain."

She glared at him with tears misting her eyes. "Did you kill Amish and John?"

He stared at her, unaffected by her sorrow. "I dinna kill old men. They are no' here. Now drink the brew." The intensity of his piercing gaze compelled her to obey.

She covered his hand with hers and took a long guzzle. Then she began to choke. Mother Mary! She had never tasted anything so foul! It was like drinking liquid fire. Her skin tinged green, and she shivered so violently her teeth rattled. She brought her hand to her mouth to stop herself from crying out . . . or from throwing up.

"It'll pass." Her captor moved slightly away and commanded her to look at him. When she did, his eyes fastened onto hers, and something in their ardent depths told her he did not expect to see weakness in her. She inhaled deeply. He would not find it.

"It's poison," she finally coughed.

"'Tis only whiskey." A smile lurked at the edges of his mouth, but that was the only evidence of softness in his striking features. An instant later, even that was gone. "Where is yer uncle?"

"For the last time, I don't know." Kate closed her eyes to stop herself from weeping all over her enemy. Amish and John had been like foster fathers to her and Robert. Dear God, where were they? Where was her uncle? "He was here earlier. We were to leave for Inverary tomorrow. He must have fled when he saw the McColls."

"True to his cowardly Campbell nature."

Kate looked up at him. Cowardly was killing old men, or slicing open her father's spine as one of this vermin's kin had done. "Take your filthy hands off me, MacGregor."

For a terrifying moment, Kate thought she might be looking at the Devil MacGregor himself. For his eyes were the color of fire: blue-gold embers that singed her flesh as they regarded her beneath the sable fringe of his lashes. Then his mouth crooked into a ruthless smirk as he opened his arms and released her.

Kate grasped his forearm to keep herself from slipping from his lap and crashing to the ground. She gritted her teeth as a fresh assault of withering pain ripped through her. "Damnation," she swore, narrowing her eyes on him through a haze of tears. "You bastard."

Her insult earned her a look of cool indifference. "Though ye look like ye could use some coddlin', I dinna have the heart fer it."

"I expected no less from a MacGregor," she countered, then stiffened and grimaced when his arm snapped around her again.

The pain was beginning to dull, along with her senses. Dear God, she'd never been wounded so. Damn the McColls. Raiding her cattle was one thing. Trying to kill her was another. They had never done the like before. But today, because her uncle's guardsmen had joined in the melee, the McColls had fought to kill. When two of the Highlanders swung at her, she'd had no choice but to unsheathe her blade and fight back. After over a quarter of an hour, her strength had been drained and she knew she could not hold them off much longer. She'd thought she was going to die. Though she had spent many years learning to wield a sword, no straw opponent could have prepared her for true fighting. She had been frightened many times in her life—three years ago, when the crop had failed and she'd thought her small family was going to starve. When her nursemaid Helen grew ill with the fever and did not recover. And after that, when Robert left and the wind howled and battered against her door at night, like a demon trying to enter. But she had never been as frightened as today, too weary to save her life, waiting for the strike of someone's cold blade to cut through her flesh. Then *he* came.

She was not afraid of the MacGregor laird, though when she had first laid eyes on him sitting atop his great warhorse, the hilt of a bloody claymore clutched in his hand and a dozen dead McColls around him, she had been certain her death was imminent. But instead of killing her, he saved her life. Even after she had wounded him, he fought to protect her. Why would a MacGregor do the like?

Her head suddenly felt too heavy to hold up. Just before her eyes closed, she gazed up at the warrior cradling her in his arms. He smelled of heather and mist. The scent covered her, going straight to her head. The sun hovered just behind him, splashing light over his shoulders like a golden mantle, reminding her of Robert's tales of Camelot. She smiled and then went limp in his arms.

⁓

Callum watched her head loll back, spilling her hair over his arm. His gaze fell across her throat, over the beguiling mound of her bosom pushed slightly upward by the brown bodice cinching her waist. God's fury, he must be going daft, but he found her completely mesmerizing. She fit so perfectly in his arms. Indeed, he had the feeling that they had been crafted this way and he hadn't known she was missing until this very day. Nae, he reminded himself, she was a Campbell, someone he was born to hate.

He had come here to kill the Earl of Argyll, not to save the bastard's niece. He looked away from her, and his eyes burned with frustration. "Gather the men and let us be away from here."

"And the lass?" Graham asked before turning to the others.

"Well, *I* dinna want her if she canna hold her whiskey." Coming up behind them, Angus laughed when his laird tossed him back his pouch.

She had held it better than most, Callum decided, unable to help himself from looking at her again. Others usually retched after just one sip of Gillis's potent brew. The way this woman had fought the whiskey's worst effect revealed the kind of strength he valued and had never expected to find in a Campbell.

"I'm takin' her," Callum said, raising his gaze back to his men. "If Argyll wants to see his niece alive again, he will have to find me and finally face me in battle."

"And if he finds our holding in Skye?" Graham asked.

"Let him." Callum's snarl was razor sharp. "He fears me and will nae doubt garner another army to bring with him. We will see them coming from ten leagues away and strike them doun as we did in Kildun. Argyll will die slowly, though."

"What if the lass dies before we reach Skye?" Jamie asked, dropping a small pink bud he'd been inspecting in exchange for the girl. Her skin was deathly pale and her breathing shallow.

"Ye dinna die from an arrow in yer shoulder," Brodie scoffed.

Angus swiped him in the chest with his fist. "How's he supposed to know that? We've never seen an arrow in a lass before."

"Women are more delicate than men," Graham agreed, tossing a lingering glance on the lass in Callum's arms. "She's a bonny one too."

"What in damnation does that have to do wi' anything?" Angus asked after another deep pull of his brew.

Callum glanced down at her again. "She will live. He shifted his arm to cradle her at a more comfortable angle when his thigh began to ache, and then scowled when she groaned—it sounded to his ears like a purring kitten after a healthy supper. She cuddled deeper against his chest, and his arms came up closer around her, mindful of the arrow jutting out of her shoulder. Here was something that certainly would have torn away his fierce reputation had anyone but his most loyal men witnessed it. A Campbell clutched in the crook of his arm!

"Should we no' take the arrow oot, Laird?" Jamie asked, keeping a close pace beside Callum as they rode out of the vale.

Callum had considered it, but the thought of causing her any more pain did not appeal to him. Still, he did not want his men thinking he was going soft, and over a Campbell, no less. "We'll take her to the Stewarts. They're no' far from here. Ennis's wife is a healer. Once the arrow is oot, the lass'll need herbs to fight infection. I'll need her alive if I'm to use her as leverage against her uncle."

"Ennis Stewart is a traitor," Graham reminded him. "He might not welcome MacGregors into his home."

"He will if he wants to live," Callum growled back at him.

Graham studied his best friend with a spark of amusement gleaming in his green eyes. "Here, let me take her. Ye seem more sour than usual since ye put her in yer arms."

"I've got her," Callum warned succinctly. "Stop gapin' at her."

"Aye, stop gapin' at her," Jamie intoned with a forced scowl aimed at his brother. "Callum fancies her and willna have his woman fallin' fer ye like them at Camlochlin."

"I dinna fancy her, Jamie," Callum corrected with an extra dose of disgust thrown in for the convincing. "She's a Campbell."

While Jamie often proved himself worthy to be ranked among the MacGregors' most fearsome men, his downy flaxen hair and large blue eyes rivaled those of the most innocent child. "So ye hate her, then?" Those huge eyes looked up to Callum.

Aye, Callum thought, he despised the blood that flowed in her veins. Her clan was responsible for killing almost every MacGregor laird for the past four generations without pause. They'd tortured the only person in his life he ever dared to love, until naught remained in him but anger, and darkness, and revenge. Aye, he hated her. But he could not find the stomach to utter it. He clenched his jaw tight instead and kicked his mount into a full gallop.

"Aye." Jamie nodded, and then took off after him. "He hates her aright."

Chapter Three

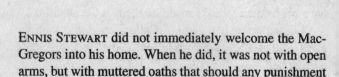

ENNIS STEWART did not immediately welcome the Mac-Gregors into his home. When he did, it was not with open arms, but with muttered oaths that should any punishment come upon his family for communicating with the outlawed clan, he would never forgive them.

"Ye're a MacGregor lest ye ferget, Ennis," Graham reminded the old warrior. "Yer name may have been changed, but yer blood is, and always will be, MacGregor blood."

Standing aside to allow them entry into his small bothy, Ennis mumbled a few more blasphemies, then poked his head outside after everyone entered. He looked left and right, then slammed the door shut and bolted it.

"M' faither was a MacGregor," Ennis acknowledged, turning to Graham. "M' brother and his family were killed because of it. Lest *ye* ferget, the name MacGregor is *proscribed*. I can be hanged fer aidin' ye." He went to his wife, who stood by a small table in the center of the room, wringing her hands together. Ennis put his arm around her and pulled her close as if the door were about to burst open and they be found guilty of harboring the rebels. "Yer defiance will get ye all killed." He turned to Callum and shook his head with the pity of it. "How long will ye continue yer war? Ye're strong and young. Life is no' so bad now. It willna be long before the monarchy is restored under Charles II. MacGregors have fought fer him. Surely he will remember it. Change yer name, fer the mercy of God, and live a peaceful life."

Angus stepped forward and towered over Ennis with a scowl as cold as a Highland winter night. "Mind yer tongue. 'Tis yer laird ye address."

Squaring his shoulders, Ennis tilted his head up to look the huge warrior straight in the eye. "M' laird is Connor Stewart now."

Angus regarded the old man with a look of disgust. "Ye're a coward, Ennis MacGregor."

"Nae! I protect m' family!"

"So do they!" Graham shouted at him. He stormed forward and slammed his fist on the table, ignoring Mae Stewart's startled leap back. "They protect their clan and their family name. I'm proud to say the Grants stand at their side."

"How are they protected?" Ennis demanded. He pushed his wife behind him and faced the group of warriors boldly. "D'ye protect them by arrogantly announcing yer names to yer enemies? How does that protect yer families?"

Now Callum moved forward. When he reached the table, he swept his arm across it, clearing it of bowls and a vase full of flowers. He bent forward, laying the woman in his arms across the surface. Straightening, he closed his fingers around the hilt of his sword.

"I protect them with this. Anyone who thinks to do harm to my clan will die by my sword, and the offense will never be forgotten. If I have sons, I'll train them to be warriors, as my faither taught me, so that when I die they'll protect the clan in my stead. And my clan is Mac-Gregor." His voice grew low with firm conviction. "I will no' hide my kin in the darkness of fear in order to protect them. If we die, then so be it. We die as MacGregors. Now, I've no' come here to d'ye harm, nor to shame ye fer what ye feel is right, Ennis. This lass is in need of yer wife's healin'. We'll be gone before the sun sets." He turned to Mae. "Will ye help her?"

"Aye." She nodded up at him. "Ye look in need of some of m' special salve yerself." She motioned to his leg, where blood had dripped and dried in thick rivulets down to his knee.

"I'd be most grateful," he said and watched while she began her examination of the woman on the table.

"Who did this to her?" Mae looked up from pulling the edge of the woman's bodice and shift off her shoulder.

"One of her uncle's guardsman," Callum told her, unable to look away from the smooth complexion of the lass's shoulder. She moaned, and he blinked his gaze away.

"Her uncle?" Ennis asked, his interest in her piqued. "Who is she, then?"

When Callum told him, Ennis tossed him a doubtful look. "Ye're aidin' a Campbell?"

"Aye, but he hates her." Jamie hastened to stand at his laird's defense.

"He doesna hate her, whelp." Brodie shoved his elbow into Jamie's gut.

"Ye're all going to have to wait ootside," Ennis's wife

declared, exasperated by the sudden bickering. Besides, she was going to have to undress the lass to get to the wound, and it was not proper for any man to see her. "Oot with ye now," she ordered, shooing them away.

"Ye see what ye did, Brodie?" Jamie hissed at him. "She thinks us barbarians because of ye."

"That's no' it." Brodie pushed him along. "She doesna want us to see the lass's breasts."

They were already heading in the direction of the door when Callum gave both men a harsh shove that catapulted them the rest of the way. "Mind yer mouths now and move yer arses."

Once the men left the bothy, Ennis looked over his shoulder every five breaths. Within ten, he had worked himself into a frenzy. Any moment now, someone was going to wander by to bid him a fine day, take one look at the five giant warriors, and go screaming throughout the holding that MacGregors were afoot. Then, Ennis thought, rubbing his forehead, he and his poor Mae would be cast out and left to starve to death on the moors.

Callum's hand on his shoulder startled him. "Dinna fret so, Ennis. Should anyone happen by, I'll put my sword to yer throat and ye can explain to yer laird that we forced ye to aid us."

Ennis knew the MacGregor was not berating him for his fears. The chieftain was indeed willing to lay his head on the block for anyone in his clan, even one who had chosen a different name to stay alive.

"I've thought aboot retreating to yer holding on the isle, laird." Ennis admitted, unable to help but respect the courage it took to stand firm against their subjugation. "But this is m' home now."

Callum nodded and patted his back. "Camlochlin will welcome ye if ye ever change yer mind."

Ennis finally managed a smile, but a moment later he resumed his pacing, scowling now and then at Brodie and the others while they hurled insults at each other.

"How did ye come to possess a Campbell?" Ennis asked the chieftain, to keep his mind off the panic rising in him.

Callum explained what had taken place in Glen Orchy.

"What d'ye intend to do with her?"

"I will hold her until Argyll comes fer her, then release her to her brother in Inverary." Callum ground his jaw, his penetrating gaze fixed on the heather-lined meadows before him. "The sooner I am away from the wench, the better."

"And the earl?"

Callum's eyes cooled to embers as he turned to his reluctant host. "He dies."

Ennis arched a bushy gray brow at him. "Will ye punish him fer what Liam Campbell did to ye, then?

"Aye," Callum nodded. "He will pay fer his faither's crimes, just as I paid fer mine. And he will suffer fer the MacGregors he has killed and the women's faces he has branded."

Ennis grew quiet. He'd heard about the women put to the iron by the Earl of Argyll. Damn pity 'twas, but 'twas naught out of the ordinary. The Campbells had been trying to tame the MacGregors since the time of Robert the Bruce, but to no avail.

Aye, Ennis knew that his clan was not entirely innocent. They were a bloodthirsty lot, killing Campbells for more years than Ennis could ever count. There were dozens of acts of Parliament's Privy Council against them, granting barons and other noblemen the right to pursue the outlaws with fire and sword. But when the MacGregors had massacred the Colquhouns at the battle of Glen Fruin fifty years ago, King James VI decreed them into extinction. Most Highlanders knew the Mac-Gregors did not deserve the punishment they'd received, for treachery amongst the Campbells and their allies abounded. But Callum and Margaret MacGregor had been innocent. That they had escaped Liam Campbell's dungeon at Kildun Castle was a miracle, everyone agreed. *How* they had done it, and what had become of Callum after that, was another matter entirely, depending on who was asked. Some called the laird of the mist braw, while to others he was a madman. One thing was certain, though. The MacGregor was a proud man, choosing, by his own words, never to hide in darkness. But as Ennis looked down at the leather cuffs encircling Callum's wrists, he wondered how long the young chieftain could hide behind those terrible years of his youth.

Ennis's thoughts were interrupted when his wife opened the front door and peeped her head out at the men standing around her doorway. She smiled when she met the MacGregor's gaze. "'Twas a clean injury. I've removed the arrow and dressed and bandaged her wound. She's awake, though a bit groggy from m' herbs. Probably why she asked fer the arrogant bas—" Mae caught herself from repeating what the Campbell lass had called him. She blushed and gave her chest a pat. "—man who raided her holding. I presume she's meanin' ye, laird."

Angus immediately puffed up his chest and stepped forward. "I believe she most likely meant me."

Chapter Four

⌐◦◦◦ↄ

KATE WAS RIPPED from her dreams of being cradled in the arms of her rescuer and came awake with a choking gasp. With painful clarity, she remembered being shot. She looked around the unfamiliar bothy, with understanding dawning on her that she'd been taken from her home, as well. And not by some knight of the realm, but by a MacGregor! There was little she could do now, fighting the dizzying effect of herbs, no doubt fed to her by the woman standing over her and wiping Kate's blood from her own hands with a small cloth. Or by that horrendous whiskey, as deadly as her rescuer . . . er . . . abductor. Good God, she'd been abducted! Where was her captor? She asked the woman, who gave her no answers, save for a reassuring pat before she hurried for the door. MacGregors! Kate's head reeled. Was it only this morn that her uncle was warning her about them? Pity she had wounded the laird in the leg. She ought to have sliced open his spine like they had done to her father.

She turned her face toward the door when she heard

someone enter. She hated this man's clan for terrorizing her kin for so many years, but she had to have been daft to lift a meager dagger against him. Why, he was even taller than Robert, and solidly built beneath a shirt of dyed saffron and belted plaid. He moved with the confidence of a conqueror. Two wide bands of brown hide encircled his wrists. Dried blood caked his bare knee and disappeared beneath the rim of his kidskin boot. But even the slight limp from his wound did naught to thwart his dominating presence. He paused for a moment, his eyes settling on her like a tempest, turbulent and dangerous.

Kate leaped from the table and stumbled back against the wall. Let all of Scotland fear the MacGregors. She would not! Her eyes darted around the room for something with which to hit him. She picked up a stool with her uninjured arm and raised it to ward him off. She fought a moment of sheer panic when he picked up his steps again. Pain resonated though her body, but she was not about to stand here and allow him to kill her without a fight. Gritting her teeth, she squeezed her eyes shut and swung.

When her stool came to a dead halt, she opened her eyes to find the chieftain's broad fingers closed around one wooden leg. He towered over her, so relentlessly compelling, his gaze on her so unforgiving.

"Ye will cease tryin' to do me bodily harm," he warned, taking a step even closer. "Or I'll be forced to confine ye."

"I mean to kill you." Kate stared up at him and gave the stool another tug.

Her would-be weapon flew across the room and crashed into the trivet with a mighty clang. Kate barely had time to startle before he swooped down and caught her in his arms. He lifted her to his chest, cradling her in a stone embrace. She struggled to free herself, but to no avail.

"Where are you taking me? Unhand me!" she demanded more forcefully when he did not answer right away.

"I'm bringin' ye to the bed."

Kate froze. Did he mean to ravish her? Aye, he had threatened to do the like earlier, had he not? She turned to look at the small mattress in the corner and fought to quell the drum of her heart. "If you dare touch me, I will rip out your heart."

"How might ye do that?" he asked, sounding somewhat amused. "With yer teeth?"

Kate wished she had the fortitude to do just that. She stiffened. It was true she could never overtake him with one arm. She reasoned she could not even fight him with two. She tried appealing to his sense of honor, hoping he possessed some. "I'm betrothed," she lied.

He peered down at her and then scowled for all he was worth, his eyes darkening to a smoky blue. "To whom?"

Kate drew the corner of her lower lip between her teeth, trying to come up with a name. She remembered one Amish had mentioned a time or two when he used to speak of his youthful days fighting the English. "To Lord Mortimer of Newbury. My uncle is very close to our lord protector, Cromwell, and I have been promised to Lord Newbury as an—"

"Newbury?" His scowl deepened into a glare that would have caused the most battle hardened warrior to blanch. "Ye're goin' to wed an Englishman?"

Kate glared right back at him as he crossed the room. "Aye, and I'm told he has an army two hundred strong."

The MacGregor snorted and shrugged his shoulders as if he didn't care if Lord Newbury's army numbered over a thousand. "I have nae intention' of dishonorin' ye, woman."

He laid her in the small bed, then sat at the edge, beside her. "'Tis bad enough ye're a Campbell. If ye considered weddin' an Englishman, ye're a fool, as well."

Kate lay there glowering at his profile. She had the mind to slap him, preferably with an ax! Still, he made no move to ravish her, which meant her lie had worked. Either that, or he hated her as much as she hated him. The latter seemed more likely, since every time he set his eyes on her, he frowned.

"Being a Campbell and a fool is better than being a MacGregor. *My* kinsmen never cut off a man's head and sent it to his sister, causing her to lose her mind."

He angled his head to look at her fully, his expression hard and unyielding. "Ye're correct. Yer kinsmen have done far worse."

Kate drew in a deep breath and forbade herself to tremble, though that trembling had less to do with fear and more with the rugged beauty of his visage. His dark hair swept past his shoulders. A strand on either side was braided at his temples and tied with thin leather strips. His jaw was shadowed with a few days' worth of whiskers, but not enough to conceal the alluring hint of a dimple in his chin. His nose was straight and noble, his lips full and sensual.

"Worse than carrying the head to a church and swearing on it to uphold the wicked deed in defiance of the king?" she demanded, pushing herself up into a sitting position. She tugged on his plaid when he began to turn away again.

He took a moment to let his gaze drift over her features, then riled her temper with a slow, slanted grin that made her feel like the biggest dimwit in Scotland. "Ye speak of the forester John Drummond, woman. The MacGregors killed him almost seventy years ago after he hung a number of them fer huntin' deer on their own land. Have ye nothin' more recent to remind me what ruthless bastards my kinsmen are?"

Kate blinked, and then her eyes flashed. "Aye, the worst among you killed my father and my grandfather."

His grin faded, but his voice still mocked her. "Are ye certain?"

The door burst open, stopping her from asking him what he meant. Angling her head around his arm, she surveyed the four men filing inside the small bothy, one in front of the other. They pushed and shoved their way toward her. Then the smallest of the bunch, a pleasant-looking young man with enormous blue eyes and pale yellow hair, stopped and grinned at her.

"Jamie Grant makes yer—"

The man behind him bumped into Jamie's back then swatted him across the back of the head. Another warrior, standing slightly to their left, took the opportunity to gracefully step around his comrades and bow to her.

"Graham Grant, of the clan Grant," he said, sweeping his midnight blue cap off his head.

Kate watched his mop of deep golden curls catch the light of the hearthfire as he straightened. He looked like an angel compared to the rest of them. An angel, she concluded an instant later, with a wickedly seductive smile.

"How do ye fare, Katherine?"

She arched a brow at him. "How do you know my name?"

"I spent the last pair of months with yer brother, Robert, in Inverary. He told me much about ye."

The mention of her brother drew a curious slant to her lips. He knew Robert? She had trouble believing her brother would consort with any friend of the clan responsible for killing their father. "Why would my brother tell you anything about me?"

"We were friends."

Kate offered him a suspicious smirk, certain he was lying.

"Ye see? She fancies him," Jamie pointed out, seeing her smile. "I told ye she meant Graham."

Graham reached for her hand and was about to lift it to his lips for a kiss, when the MacGregor snatched her wrist back and returned her hand to her lap. His fingers remained, covering hers possessively. He used his chin to gesture toward the rest of his men, ending any further charming introductions. "Brodie, Jamie, and Angus. There, now get the horses ready. Ennis and his wife have put themselves in harm's way long enough."

"Can she travel so soon?" the one named Angus asked. He was eyeing a barrel of what Kate imagined was whiskey. She suspected he was not really concerned for her well-being as much as he was about getting into that barrel. He was an enormous man with wavy red hair and a scar that laced his face from his left temple to his neck. When he looked at Kate, his expression softened and he reminded her of a fearsome dog she once had who used to lick her face clean after he'd chased raiders around her land, eager to take a bite out of one.

"I will not be traveling with you," Kate assured them.

The chieftain rose to his feet. "She can travel, Angus," he said as if she had not spoken at all. "She's a fit lass."

Kate glared up at him and pronounced each word clearly so that he understood her this time. "I'm staying right here until my brother comes for me, you callous swine."

His expression did not change as he bent to her and scooped her off the bed and into his arms once again, ignoring her protests. He stopped when he reached the elderly couple waiting at the door and offered them his thanks, muffling Kate's venomous insults with his hand over her mouth.

Mae Stewart looked ready to swoon when the Campbell lass took a bite out of one of his fingers. Callum MacGregor was a large man with a taste for blood that rivaled the kings of England. Mae shoved a small package into his hand, hoping to stay his temper before he struck the poor lass and killed her. "Her salve," she offered him nervously. "She can apply it to her chest, but she'll need help applyin' it on her back. Try no' to strangle her, laird, if ye be the one applyin' it." She rushed to a small shelf and picked up another package, this one larger than the one she offered Callum, and handed it to Graham. "Just some dried meat and black bread fer yer journey."

The men thanked her, though Angus continued eyeing the barrels like a man being torn from the presence of his only love. Graham shoved him out the door, and Ennis followed them outside.

"Remember," Callum told him, placing Kate on her feet hard enough to make her teeth knock together. He leaped into his saddle. "If ye're questioned, ye were forced to aid us."

He leaned down, fit his hands around Kate's waist, and lifted her sideways to his lap.

"Does yer arm pain ye much?" he asked her, a little too softly and close to her ear for her liking. She pushed herself away from him and nearly tumbled to the ground. He caught her, snaking one arm around her belly.

"Laird," Ennis entreated one last time. "Scotland is changin'. Leave the past where it belongs."

"I have tried," Callum answered solemnly. "But the past willna free me."

Ennis nodded and bid him farewell with a smack on the horse's rump. He stood in the grass, watching them leave, and offered up a silent prayer that the unruly bunch make it to Camlochlin alive.

Chapter Five

KATE CURSED HER SKILL for failing her and herself for not killing this MacGregor when she had the chance. She swore by the saints if he ever muzzled her again, she would bite his fingers completely off! Her arm throbbed in perfect rhythm with her heart. Where were they taking her? She fought the panic rising in her chest. Screaming would do no good. The miscreants would likely take great pleasure in her hysteria. She consoled herself with the knowledge that at least she had not been abducted by the Devil MacGregor. This chieftain might be the most arrogant man she had ever met, but he did not behave like a madman bent on killing Campbells. In fact, he had risked his life saving one. She relaxed a bit and shifted across his hard thighs, trying to gain a little more comfort if she was going to have to remain perched upon them all the way to . . .

"Where are you taking me?"

Before he answered her, he grunted something in

Gaelic, then pushed her dangling legs off his wounded thigh. "To Skye."

She swung around, hitting his chin with the top of her head. "Skye?" She hoped she hadn't heard him right. She wasn't exactly certain where Skye was, save that it was far from Glen Orchy, but its name conjured visions of some very far away, heaven-bound place. Mayhap where he sought absolution for whatever sins he had committed. And being a MacGregor, he surely had many.

Tilting her head back, she peered at his face. He kept his gaze fixed on the trees straight ahead. "Why are you taking me there? What do you intend to do with me?" Her eyes narrowed on his features, the indomitable set of his jaw. There was an air of cool detachment in his bearing that made Kate doubt he even cared about his transgressions. Well, she did not care about them, either. She wanted to go home.

He glanced down at her, weighing her with a dark, brief look of impatience. "I'll answer one of yer queries."

"Only one?" Kate quirked her mouth at his attempt to intimidate her. Why, this brute was even more arrogant than her uncle!

"Aye."

"Are you always so uncompromising?"

He inclined his head, giving her his full attention. Kate defied the urge to pull back at the virility in his bold gaze, the vivid beauty of flames fired with the power of some fervent purpose within. She met his strength of will head on—until his eyes swept over her face, lingering on her mouth and heating her cheeks.

"Verra well." He returned his gaze to hers. "To show

ye that I'm agreeable, I'll allow ye to choose which query ye want me to answer."

Kate's brows flew up at his haughty self-importance. "Two queries," she parried, challenging his amiability.

He conceded with a slight nod.

"Why are you bringing me to Skye?"

"Because there are over fifty dead bodies loiterin' on yer doorstep in Glen Orchy."

"Och." She blinked. "I see." She twisted her body forward and leaned back against his chest with a heavy sigh of relief. She had forgotten about the bloody battle on her front lawn. She certainly did not want to return to *that* alone. She would have to bury the bodies, unless her uncle returned to retrieve his men, which she could not fathom him doing. And there were the McColls to consider. They would seek revenge once they discovered what had become of their kin. "I confess, you have a point. It would not be wise to return home just yet." She turned toward him again and gave him a measured look. "I thought you were abducting me." His lips curled into a smile she suspected he'd used a hundred times before to frighten a horde of enemies. Kate's mouth tightened; she refused to yield so easily. "You are a MacGregor, after all." She shrugged her shoulders and her expression relaxed. "But you did save me, and I don't want you to think that I—"

"I dinna trouble myself with thinkin' of ye at all."

His curt insult grated on her last nerve. "Of course." She shifted her position again and brought her legs down with resounding thumps on his injured thigh. His body went rigid, but he did not move her.

"What do you intend to do with me?"

"Slicin' off yer head would be a good beginnin'," he ground out through clenched teeth.

"Och, but then who would you practice your frightful scowls on?"

Her bravery to mock him right to his face fired his blood. "Yer kin."

Oh, what Kate wouldn't have done for her sword at that moment. "Alas, then, you would frighten no one." To prove her point, she didn't turn away when his eyes swept over her face. She should have, though, because the smile that graced his lips made her heart quicken.

"What are your plans for me?" she asked again, turning away.

"I have no' decided that yet."

Kate prayed she hadn't heard him right. He had not decided yet? What did that mean? Was he going to return her to her brother, safe and sound? Or was he going to kill her?

"Well, I'd rather go home than to Skye," she informed him, deciding that he was simply trying to frighten her again. "So I've made your decision for you."

Dear God, how could she find a MacGregor so dangerously appealing? Damn her, but the indulgent slant of his mouth made her knees go soft.

"Thank ye. That is exactly what I will do."

Her eyes widened. "What?"

"Return ye home to yer brother."

"To Inverary?"

"That is where he lives."

She lowered her gaze lest he see the trepidation in her eyes. She didn't want to live with her uncle. Oh, why had Robert left Glen Orchy?

The chieftain leaned forward, and his breath caressed her temple when he spoke. "Ye have made it clear that ye dinna care fer yer uncle. Why?"

She raised her eyes to his, unable to find the sudden concern in his voice any less noble than that of the most gallant knight. She shook her head at herself. Was she daft? This was no knight, but a savage outlaw. Kin to the beast who murdered her father. She could be thrown into the tower for finding him anything but vile. But he had rushed headlong into a melee of swinging swords and saved her from certain death. He had not abducted her. He had carried her all the way to the Stewarts' homestead to remove her arrow, when he could have easily left her to tend to herself. He had held her and comforted her when the pain of her wound was unbearable. And most important, he meant to deliver her to the safety of her brother. Of course, she had not forgotten how he'd let her almost fall off his horse when she had demanded he release her. Or the way he had clamped his strong hand over her mouth at the Stewarts'. He was an overbearing brute, to be certain, but he had not harmed her.

"My uncle means little to me." She offered him a slight pat on the arm to ease his obvious concern. "But I fear he would punish Robert for befriending you."

He severed their gaze and straightened, moving his body further away from hers. "Nae more talkin'."

Kate's nostrils flared as she inwardly scolded herself for fancying him to be anything more than an obstinate worm. She prayed the man didn't have a wife waiting for him in Skye. Poor wretched thing she must be if he did. "Though I owe you my life, I find you immensely dislikable."

He arched an eyebrow at her and gave her a measuring look. "Come, Campbell," he challenged with a slow, rapier smirk. "Be the first of yer ilk braw enough to tell me what I've done to provoke yer scorn."

"Your kin," she accused without hesitation, "murdered my father and left my brother and me orphaned to a man who did not want us."

The laird's hard expression faltered, but his voice was firm, his gaze steady on hers. "'Twasna I who killed him."

Kate nodded. "I'm thankful for that."

Jamie watched them curiously from a few feet away, momentarily distracted from his examination of a particular patch of powder-blue blossoms. The lass was bonny, aright. Fer a Campbell, that is. But did she think she could make his laird like her by staring up at him with that trusting look in her eyes? He reined in a bit closer. "You willna make him like ye. His mind's made up. He hates ye," he said.

Callum would have whacked the young warrior right off his horse, but he could not tear his eyes away from Katherine Campbell—a discomfiting condition he'd suffered from more than once since first laying eyes on her. He dipped his gaze from her large coal eyes to the luscious contours of her clenched mouth. Hell, he didn't know which was more dangerous of the two. Fortunately for him, she turned away, her spine stiff.

"Then my enemy and I have something in common," she replied coolly.

Callum shifted uneasily, wanting to say something. But what? Could he deny Jamie's charge—or her own? They were enemies, her name as hated as his was worthless.

He bent forward slightly and inhaled the scent of her hair. He shouldn't want her. But he did. And every time he looked at her, each time her body yielded against him, he wanted her more.

Her braw spirit tempted him with unbidden images of her in his bed, just as fiery. She could wield a sword, that much was evident by the throbbing in his thigh, but hell, her tongue was even sharper. Twice he was torn between grinning at her saucy mouth and kissing the belligerence off her lips.

He was daft. She was a Campbell, and he could not wait to be rid of her.

Chapter Six

THEY RODE THROUGHOUT THE NIGHT without stopping and traveled alongside the still waters of Loch Leven the next afternoon. They passed grand mountain ranges whose summits were hidden by swirling clouds and vast verdant fields where grouse basked beneath the sun. Kate took in every detail of the new landscape around her. With such raw splendor surrounding her, her awareness of the man behind her intensified. The sleek strength of his arms around her waist. The knotted steel of his thighs beneath her. Had these MacGregors somehow convinced Robert not to kill them? She simply could not believe her brother would consort with MacGregors. Had they come to Glen Orchy to kill her uncle? Why had they protected her? Had Robert asked them to do it? Had he somehow discovered his uncle's true intentions for her? And why would he risk his life by trusting MacGregors?

Dear God, had her brother betrayed them? Nae! She would never believe it. She pushed the thought out of her mind and replaced it with a dozen others. There were so many questions, and she was too sleepy to think on them all now. She leaned against the chieftain's chest, mindful of her sore shoulder, yawned, and made a mental note to question him about it more later.

Callum's muscles flexed involuntarily when her body sank into him. The lass was bone weary, and he didn't fancy the notion of her sleeping on him again. They would have to stop. Sleeping outdoors anywhere but in Skye was unwise, but he would rather travel a few more leagues north, into friendlier territory. There were some who knew him by sight and would risk all for a chance to take his head. 'Twas not safe to stop, but more dangerous was the pleasure he took from her ease with him, the softness of her curves, the scent of peat lacing her feathery curls when they blew across his face. He shifted back, separating himself from her.

He reined in his mount at the crest of a windswept ridge and scanned the dense patches of pine nestled in the glen below. "We'll stop there fer the night."

Stopping beside him, Graham studied his profile with concern creasing his brow. "Ye look pained. Yer wound needs closing."

The only sign that Callum had heard him was the tightening of his jaw. His commander was correct. His leg was stiff, and every time the lass in his lap inhaled, it felt like she was digging a dagger into his flesh. The slice had to be closed before fever set in. He'd had many injuries put to the fire in the past, but the mind simply could not prepare for the brand.

When they reached the trees, Callum set Kate down first and then glared at her after a painful dismount.

"I apologized for wounding you!" she charged, though

he hadn't said a word. His brows dipped over his eyes, but she didn't shrink away from his blackest scowl. "You should have called out! I didn't know you had come to aid me."

He peered down at her for a moment, looking like he wanted to say something. But then he turned without a word and snatched Angus's pouch from the warrior's lips.

"We need a fire," he called out to Jamie and limped away.

Callum stopped when he reached a tall pine, leaned his back against it, and tipped the pouch of brew to his mouth. When he spotted the lass storming toward him, he raised his eyes to the heavens.

"Why did you not have your friend's wife tend to your leg?" She reached for the hem of his plaid to take a peek at his thigh. He swatted her hand away.

"Get some rest, Katherine. I willna—"

"It's Kate."

He stared at her with eyes a heart-stopping shade of stormy blue, then took another swig of whiskey.

"I willna have ye sleepin' on me, *Kate*." He closed his eyes, letting the potent brew warm his muscles. When he opened them again, she was gone. Against his will, his gaze scanned the campsite until he found her again, sitting on the ground a few feet away, her knees drawn up to her chest. She watched Jamie start the small fire between them and shook her head when Angus offered her some of Mae Stewart's black bread. Callum studied the shape of her face, the bonny luminance of her deep, dark eyes, the sensual fullness of her mouth. Fire flushed through his veins. Damned whiskey. He ran his hand over his stubbled jaw. He would never compromise his convictions by bedding one of his enemies. No matter how enticing she'd felt nestled between his thighs for the past day and night. When she rubbed her arm, he felt a sharp sting of pity for her. She had not complained once about her wound, though he knew it pained her. He quaffed another long drink from the pouch, determined to douse the embers of desire and mercy she ignited in him. If he had any sense at all, he would leave her here in the morn.

Her eyes shimmered like the gabbro of the Cuillins when Jamie's flames finally sprang to life. As if sensing his silent vigil, she shifted her gaze to his. Callum's knees buckled beneath him. Of course, his weakened state could be blamed on the whiskey he'd consumed and not on the tender look she aimed at him. Damn her, where was the seething contempt in her eyes? She was a Campbell, for hell's sake! Why was she looking at him like he was anything but her worst enemy? If she hurled a few oaths at him, cursed his clan to hell, he might not find her so pleasing. His back slid down against the trunk, and he landed with a heavy thump that rattled his teeth. God help him, he felt like grinning at her.

"A few more swigs of me brew and ye willna feel a thing," Angus chuckled. Callum leaned his head back, preferring not to watch Graham's sword heat to bright orange.

"You are not going to . . ."

Callum heard Kate's voice and closed his eyes again. He liked the sound of her, the dulcet huskiness that carried an undercurrent of strength so deeply rooted, she did not even fear the Devil.

"You cannot mean to sear his flesh with *that!*" she

screeched, causing Callum's shoulders to bunch up around his ears.

"Sit ye down, lass," Graham said softly. "There's naught else to be done."

Callum looked at them and blinked at the three scalding swords in Graham's hands. One. He dragged his hand across his eyes. His friend held only one sword. One glowing, sizzling iron rod that would soon . . . He guzzled more brew and braced himself for what was to come.

"Well? What are ye waitin' fer?" he demanded a moment later when Graham simply stood there staring down at him.

"I'm thinking I should tie yer hands first," Graham admitted.

"Do it."

And still Graham hesitated. Callum MacGregor was mighty indeed. If he swung that fist and made contact with Graham's face, the commander was sure he would not awaken for a se'nnight. Years of hard labor and torture had made Callum stronger than any man Graham knew, but 'twas the torture he had endured and the scars that still marred his body that made Graham hate the task at hand.

"Graham," Callum warned impatiently.

The blade descended. For a moment, the entire world went black. Callum clenched his teeth and threw his head back, but he did not make a sound.

Kate stood aghast, unable to move while the sickening smell of burning flesh wafted through her nostrils. Graham dropped his sword and strode away, swearing as he went. The instant he was gone, Kate bolted forward.

When Callum opened his eyes, he was not sure if he

couldn't form a rational thought because of the pain ripping through his entire body, or because of the beautiful goddess kneeling before him, looking like she was about to weep all over him.

Without warning, she snatched the pouch from his fingers and dumped a goodly amount of its contents over his leg.

Callum reacted instantly. His eyes widened and blazed with both fury and agony that made him writhe. He clutched her shoulders and fought the urge to fling her across the campsite. "Christ!" he shouted between gasping breaths. "What the hell did ye do to me?"

"The whiskey will cleanse the wound," she explained, but Brodie yanked her from Callum's arms and hauled her to her feet.

"Ye will stay away from him." His dark hair eclipsed even darker eyes that impaled her while he pulled a dagger from his belt. "Have ye no' done enough damage to him? Will ye no' be satisfied until ye have killed him?"

"Nae!" Kate took a step back, feeling her mettle begin to fade for the first time. These men surrounding her were warriors of the most savage ilk. Their laird meant to deliver her to safety, but they looked only too eager to hang her from the nearest tree. "I did not mean to cause him injury. I saw him riding toward me and I thought he was coming to fight on the side of the McColls."

"Why in hell would we fight on the side o' the bloody McColls?" Brodie raised his voice at her. "Are ye daft?"

The mighty chieftain hiccuped. " 'Tis understandable. She's a Campbell."

"Aye, she's a Campbell." Angus agreed and spat in

disgust. "Stick a knife into a MacGregor's guts as quick as her men kin would."

"Treacherous she is."

That insult was enough to strengthen Kate's mettle back to full force. "I did not stick a knife into his guts, but his thigh. And as for my men kin, at least they are not cowards who slice men from behind like your kinsmen did to my father. They do not go around raping and pillaging innocent people and starting wars that last for centuries."

"We didna rape anyone innocent," Angus argued.

"Shut up, Angus." Callum groaned against the tree. He rubbed his forehead. "And what in blazes is in this brew? I feel like my head's floatin' off my shoulders." He attempted to stand, held on to the tree for a moment until the ground stopped moving, then tried again. He nearly fell on top of Kate. Grasping her waist to right himself, his heavy body almost caused her to fall with him. He groaned when a bolt of pain shot through his leg.

"And we wouldna kill a Campbell from behind." Brodie moved closer to them, his voice hard as steel. "We would look him in the eye and—"

"Brodie, step back before I take my sword to ye," Callum warned, trying to fight the effects of Angus's whiskey.

Angus caught his laird when Kate took a step toward Brodie and Callum teetered on his feet.

"Look him in the eye, you say?" she asked quietly, her voice seething with emotion. "Do you take that much joy in killing that you want to see your victim's last breath?"

"If they're Campbells, aye."

Kate shook her head with disgust. "I see now why my

uncle's hatred for your clan is so profound. Why he always warned us about the MacGregors. You defy kings and kill earls for little reason other than you enjoy it."

"Little reason?"

They all turned toward Callum, who was hanging over Angus's shoulder and looking more lucid than he did a moment ago. His eyes glittered against the firelight when they locked on Kate. His nostrils flared with anger. He did not blink. He seemed not to breathe. "Did I hear ye right?"

The forest went deathly still; even the crickets seemed to hush awaiting Kate's reply. She looked at the other men around her. Each wore the same expression of cold, hard contempt. Her heart leapt with fear. She did not doubt in that moment that should she say the wrong thing, they might just kill her after all. "I didn't mean . . . I know it must be difficult to lose the right to bear your name, but surely you understand that—"

"Nae, ye dinna know anything aboot losin' yer name," Callum cut her off. He pushed himself off Angus and closed the distance between them in two strides. "Ye know nothin' aboot us save half-truths that took place over half a century ago. Ye have no' lost yer land, or yer—"

"I lost my family."

His jaw tightened around something more he wanted to say. The fury in his eyes faded, leaving him with a resigned look as his gaze dropped to the pulse at her throat. Kate had the urge the lift her hand to shield her flesh from him. For he looked as if he could stop the beating of her heart if he but thought about it.

"Then ye have good reason to hate us, Katherine Campbell." He began to turn away. "Try no' to ferget it."

"You make the task easy, MacGregor," she hurled at his back. "If I had my sword I would show you."

"Ye're a Campbell." Callum tossed her a dry smirk over his shoulder. "I wouldna expect anything less from ye. Angus," he snapped. "Come here."

The largest of Callum's men took a step forward just as his laird's knees buckled under him.

"Ye fokin' poisoned him," Brodie accused the burly warrior while Angus dragged his unconscious laird back to the tree.

"'Tis the whiskey," Angus defended. "Auld Gillis said 'twas stronger than any man. I'm guessin' he was right."

Kate watched Callum slump to the ground and begin to snore. Even in his dead stupor he appeared to be brooding. By the saints, his conviction to hate her was even stronger than her uncle's was to hate the MacGregors. She wanted to hate him, too. She did hate him! But when he let out a low moan, she found herself moving in his direction. She almost reached him when Brodie stepped in front of her, blocking her path.

"Ye'll be away from him now." His voice was low, warning her not to argue.

"But I—"

"Sleep over there." He pointed, then cupped her elbow to move her along.

"Let her be, Brodie. She's not going to stab him in his sleep, are ye, lass?"

Kate looked up into Graham's warm gaze and shook her head. He smiled, revealing a dimple as devastating as Callum's sword.

"Callum could use a woman's gentle touch during the night," she heard him tell Brodie as he led the grumbling Highlander to the fire.

Kate turned back to their laird. She had no intention of touching him. She simply wanted to make sure his wound had been closed properly. *Savages,* she thought, cringing again at the memory of his sizzling flesh. Sitting beside him, she carefully lifted the edge of his plaid off his thigh, then nearly retched. The skin was black and blistered, but the wound was sealed. Her gaze drifted over the rest of him. Heavens, he was big, his legs well muscled and long. She blinked away, covering his thigh, and looked at his hands instead. She remembered how skilled they were at wielding his great claymore against the Mc-Colls and, she realized now, her uncle's men. She'd been so busy praying for her own life, she hadn't even looked up to see who he was killing. They were born enemies, but she could not forget the strength in his arm or the murderous glint in his eyes when he stopped a McColl blade from cutting her down the middle. He had the look of a savage, garbed in his plaid and leather wrist cuffs instead of clean breeches and polished boots like her uncle wore. But he hadn't tried to ravish her. In fact, his touch was so gentle when he held her in his saddle, the very thought of it drew a sigh from her lips. She closed her eyes and settled against the tree beside him, thanking God that it was Callum MacGregor who found her, and not the monster who had murdered her father.

Chapter Seven

DUNCAN CAMPBELL SLOWED his mount as he approached Kildun Castle. Something was amiss. Silence clung to the land like scum on a pond. Beneath clouds of rolling charcoal, the high battlements stood empty. He looked around and wiped the sheen of sweat from his brow. He was alone. He'd cursed his men the entire way back to Inverary for falling so easily to McColl blades. He hadn't been there to see how it had happened. Why should he have risked losing his life to raiders? But now, with a growing sense of panic knotting his innards, it dawned on him who his men must have fought. He had feared the MacGregors would go to Glen Orchy to take revenge on his niece for what he'd done to one of their women a fortnight ago. He wanted to get Kate away before they found her, believing she would be safe in Kildun. The rebel chieftain would never return here. He had been so sure of it.

When he reached the lowered drawbridge, he dismounted and drew his sword. The wind howled through the deserted entryway, sending a chill over his flesh and the acrid scent of blood to his nostrils. Images of another day much like this one flooded his memory. Fearing what he would find when he reached the bailey, and fighting the urge to run the other way, he stepped cautiously past the gatehouse.

Over a hundred of his men scattered the bloodstained ground, flies swarming around their hewn bodies. Dread and fury produced a faint groan from the back of Duncan's throat. He had seen this kind of destruction six years ago—when the Devil had left Kildun. Duncan had never forgotten that day. It was forged in his memory, branded into his dreams.

Alerted by the screams of his comrades, he and twenty of his men had rushed down the narrow stone stairs that led to the dungeon. When he arrived there he wanted to flee back up the way he had come. He had covered his mouth to keep from retching. Dismembered bodies littered the stony ground, all of them ravaged by a single sword. Duncan's eyes followed that blade, glinting red in the torchlight, as it descended on Donald Stuart, his father's first in command, and near cut him in half.

At first, Duncan had feared God had finally sought vengeance against his father's sins and had set Satan loose upon Kildun. Blood dripped from the creature's long, limp hair barring his face. His eyes shone beneath like brimstone against the torchlight, striking terror in the hearts of the men around him. The beast's shoulders were slightly hunched forward and massive, providing him with unearthly strength.

Just beside him, one of Duncan's men screamed and fell to the floor. Duncan's body shook as he gripped his hilt with both hands. He'd managed to swing his blade, but it whooshed across empty air. Something whistled just in front of him an instant later and another guard crumbled to his knees, clutching the fatal gash across his belly.

Ten breaths had passed while Duncan stood alone in the paralyzing silence of his father's dungeon. Someone whimpered. A lass's voice. Duncan's eyes darted to the eastern wall, knowing who it had to be. Still, he staggered backward when he saw that MacGregor was gone, and with him the chains that had held him. Young Margaret MacGregor's confines lay crushed on the ground in a heap of twisted steel.

Impossible—Duncan remembered thinking—until the murderer stood before him.

"Fer now, ye will live to tell yer faither I will return fer him."

Duncan took another swing at him, determined not to die cowering at a prisoner's feet. His blade was met in midair by a crushing blow that sent fire up his arm. Mac-Gregor's sword ground against his until the tip was only inches from his eye.

Strewn over her brother's shoulder, Margaret MacGregor cried out, halting the blade's deadly course.

"Dinna force yer death. It will come soon enough," MacGregor had promised him before he fled, taking his sister with him and vanishing into the mists.

Duncan wished the bastard had killed him instead of leaving him to face his father. It was the first time Liam Campbell had ever struck his son. Would that he had never stopped. It would have been more merciful than the contempt hardening his father's eyes from that day hence.

Duncan surveyed the gruesome scene around him

now. The Devil had finally returned to Inverary, and with the same fury. A sound from beyond the western curtain wall startled him. He spun on his heel, his sword at the ready to send the MacGregor straight back to hell this time.

He waited, hearing naught again but the wind. He inched forward toward the heavy portcullis that led to the inner bailey, drawing up his nerves to face his most formidable enemy once again.

Instead, he came upon his nephew, tied securely with rope, to the half-raised thick iron gate.

Robert Campbell stared down at his uncle and felt a tight knot rise in his throat. His great relief at being rescued vanished from his eyes as he noted the absence of any man at mount beside his returning uncle. The knot thickened, threatening to suffocate him if the strip of plaid tied over his mouth was not removed posthaste!

It took far too long for the earl to lower the gate and cut the cloth away from his face. "Where's Kate?" Robert erupted.

Duncan did not answer him right away but looked around the deserted grounds, then continued cutting the rest of him loose. "Did he kill everyone, then?"

"Nae, anyone who did not lift a weapon was put in the dungeon," Robert told him quickly. "They need be released. But first, Uncle, where is my sister? Why does she not ride with you?" Panic and nausea vied for his attention. Robert refused them both. The moment one hand was free, he used it to grip his uncle's doublet. "Give me your reply!"

Eyes of forged steel finally fastened on his, narrowing slightly and stilling any further movement from Robert, despite his freedom. "Why do you fear for her so, Robert? You do not even consider that I might have left her unharmed in the care of my guardsmen in Glen Orchy?"

Robert had spent days helplessly secured to a wrought-iron gate, praying for an act of God to free him so he could save his sister. He prayed now again that it was not too late.

"Because the men you took with you to Glen Orchy are all dead, as these men are. I beg you tell me my sister is not among them."

Now Duncan gripped his nephew's tunic and yanked him closer. "How do you know the others are dead? It was the MacGregor, was it not? And you told him where to find me." His eyes seared into Robert's. "You chose to give them my life in exchange for yours," he accused, then pushed his nephew away. "Here you are alive and well while your sister is their captive. You are a coward, Robert." He nodded at his own words while Robert went pale. "Your grandfather would toss you from Kildun."

"I did not tell them where to find you," Robert flung at him before turning for the stable. "You did."

"I?" Duncan stormed after him and stopped him by closing his fingers around Robert's wrist. "I told no one but you where I was going!"

"And Graham Campbell," his nephew informed him. "Or rather, Graham Grant, commander of the Devil Mac-Gregor's men. Aye, they made certain I knew whose eyes I was staring into ten breaths after we were led past the gates by the traitor that *you* took in as your kin after I arrived here."

"Nae." Duncan reeled back, stunned. He shook his

head, refusing to believe he had been so easily fooled. "Graham Campbell drank with me, sat at my table."

"And with me," Robert agreed, his voice trembling with fury at the man he had come to think of as his friend. "He deceived us all. He led us outside the protection of the castle on the pretense that a band of MacGregors, led by the Devil himself, had captured you and were holding you just beyond Loch Awe. He led us directly into the swords of our enemies, at least two hundred strong." Robert's gaze swept over the bodies around him. Bodies he had been left to stare at for days. "We did not stand a chance against the wave of destruction which came upon us. Quickly our men were slain. Without mercy or pause were their bodies torn asunder and trampled." He returned his gaze to his uncle, checking back the emotion in his voice. "The Devil and his men came here to kill you, but you were gone. Grant told him you were in Glen Orchy. They were on their way there when they left."

"And they left you alive." Duncan's tone dripped with the accusation of betrayal.

"The fighting was over. My sword had been wrested from my hands. After the MacGregor instructed the bulk of his men to take your cattle to his holding, he ordered Grant to hang me, charging you with doing the same to his kinsmen."

"And hang you he did." Duncan smiled dryly. "But MacGregor let you live. You were fortunate. When the Devil strikes, he leaves no Campbell alive."

Robert's eyes narrowed on his uncle. "How then did you escape him?"

Duncan lifted his shoulders in a hesitant shrug, but he looked away from his nephew when he spoke. "I had gone for a morning ride after helping your sister with her swordplay. When I returned, your father's land looked much like this. Katherine was gone."

"And Amish and John?" Robert asked, drawing both hands down his face in an effort to calm his frantic heart. "Were they killed, as well?"

"I don't know what became of them. They were not among the dead."

"We must send word to the lord protector."

Duncan shook his head. "Cromwell will do nothing. He sent over four hundred men to hunt the Devil after he killed my father. Most of those men were killed by Highlanders who side with the MacGregors. He will not tax his army so again. That is why he leaves the duty of killing the outlaws to the noblemen of Scotland."

"But you are his vassal, uncle. Your entire garrison was killed. Surely he will send reinforcements."

"It will take time."

"Then I will find her myself," Robert vowed.

"Where do you propose to look first?" Duncan did naught to conceal his mocking smirk. "This man holds no patch of ground in Glen Orchy, Glenstrae, or Rannoch. He left the banks of Lammond long ago and disappeared into the north. Since then, he has been as difficult to capture as the mists that hide him. If Cromwell's army could not find him, you certainly won't."

Robert's expression hardened, reminding Duncan of the lad's father when Colin had set out to find the MacGregor after he had escaped. Liam Campbell had been pleased. At least, he had accused, one of his sons did not shyt his breeches in the face of a common outlaw. But

Duncan had known the truth of it, even if his father was too blind to see.

Colin had been well loved by their father. He was tall and well muscled compared to Duncan's scrawny physique. His dark good looks had also earned him the favor of the castle wenches at Glen Orchy. Robert's resemblance to his father was a bit unnerving. Their eyes were the same, light brown flecked with gray and green and glinting with determination. But the similarities between father and son ended with their physical appearance. Robert Campbell was no coward.

"I know in which direction to ride," Robert said stiffly.

"And when you come upon him," Duncan challenged, "how will you succeed in gaining your sister back when you could not even keep your sword in your fists the first time you faced him? I fear you will not escape his wrath a second time."

"I do not care if he kills me. I will free my sister from him first."

"Braw words." Duncan searched his nephew's eyes and was pleased at the raw resolve lighting their depths. The Devil had to be stopped, but Duncan had decided long ago that he would not give his life simply to avenge those who perished at the fiend's hands. His father might have thought him a fool, but he was not fool enough to think he could live through an encounter with Callum MacGregor. Nae, but he enjoyed taunting the beast. The law was on his side when it came to hanging the rebellious Highlanders and branding their women. But he had not thought the Devil would ever return here. MacGregor had to be completely mad to slaughter Kildun's garrison a second time.

"Callum MacGregor needs to be dead."

"If he has harmed my sister, he will be."

"If?" Duncan tempered his query with a withering sigh. He would never make the same error his father had made in allowing doubt to grow in the heart of his kin. Robert had to know and understand well that the Mac-Gregors were their enemies. Doubting the like gave room for pity, and pity bred sympathy. Nae, Duncan would nurture Robert's fury and mayhap the lad would succeed in ridding them of the Devil once and for all. "Lad, I've no doubt he will violate her. Let us pray he does not kill her." He smiled tightly when Robert rushed for the stables again. "We will need more men!" he called out.

His nephew slowed to a halt and looked over his shoulder at him. "You said it would take time."

"Not if they come from Scotland," Duncan promised. "I can assemble at least one hundred within a few days. But Robert," his uncle added when Robert turned to face him fully. "When we find the bastard we will employ a more effective strategy than charging his holding."

"What do you mean?"

Duncan looked toward the castle doors, returning once again to that day—and the only thing that had stopped MacGregor from killing him. "He has a weakness. And I know what it is."

Chapter Eight

"GOD CURSE YOU!"

Kate's eyes darted to the right to see who had hurled the offense, but the dozens of faces staring back at her all looked equally guilty.

Beside her, Callum lowered his gaze, avoiding the accusation and anger thick in the air. He knew he was not welcome in Roderick Cameron's village. They were afraid of him. 'Twas why he had dismounted before he entered the village and commanded his men to do the same. Leading his warhorse by the bridle gave him a less intimidating appearance.

"Go back to the hell that spawned ye!"

These people wanted peace, no matter what it cost them.

"Why do they hate you?" Kate tugged on his plaid. "I thought you said their laird was your friend."

When Callum lifted his eyes and met her incensed gaze, the sudden urge to smile near overwhelmed him. It astonished him that even while he was being so painfully reminded of what he had become, the indignation Kate felt over his rebuke could soften his black heart.

"They dinna all hate me. 'Tis only the MacGregors who curse me."

She stopped walking, stopping him, as well, with her hand still on his plaid. Her eyes opened wider, and Callum allowed himself a moment to bask in the knowledge that she truly didn't know who he was. As far as she was concerned he was simply a MacGregor laird, guilty of the same as any other. And some traitorous part of him gloried in it. She didn't know of the blood that covered his hands. That covered all of him. He should tell her the truth, but the truth was too harsh and ugly, and it would change the way she looked at him.

"Your own kin hate you? Why?" she demanded to know.

A glossy curl obscured the alluring curve of her cheekbone. The tilt of her chin tempted him to lean down and kiss her until she went weak in his arms.

"Many of these people have changed their names and live here now as Camerons. They want the world to ferget us. I keep reminding the world that we still exist."

"How do you remind them?"

"By keeping our name alive and avenging the wrongs done to my kin." Hell, she tempted him as no one had ever done before to give account of what his name meant to him.

Her expression on him softened briefly, and he was the one who felt weak. "You sound more like their hero than their enemy."

For an instant, he wanted to stay in that moment forever. But the lives he'd taken for his name, and in the name of vengeance, were too great an iniquity to be forgiven. He ground his jaw and picked up his steps again. He was an outlaw, a murderer, the most feared MacGregor in Scotland, and the one with the largest price on his head. He was not a hero.

"Come," he said, grasping her hand as he cut toward the stone keep overlooking the village. "I must be granted permission before we go further."

They were met just outside the fortress by Roderick Cameron. He was an imposing man with thick gray hair plaited on either side of his weathered face. The plaid draping his expansive shoulders and belted low on his waist was fashioned of many colors. His eyes were the shade of a stormy sea, but when they settled on Callum they softened with fondness.

"How d'ye fare, MacGregor?" He slid his gaze to Kate and smiled in a way that told her he thought Callum was faring rather well. He swept his arm across the threshold to usher them inside the keep. "Enjoy the comforts of my home as is afforded to friends."

Callum placed his hand on the chieftain's shoulder. "I must refuse yer generous offer. I would chance nae further peril to yer people. I wish only to see the woman."

"Verra well." The Cameron held his palm up to stop two of his men when they stepped forward to accompany him. "This way." He led Callum and his small troop toward a cottage at the farthest edge of the village.

Kate fell in behind the two lairds and found her pace even with Graham's. All around her, the inhabitants stepped outside their doors, drawn by the presence of the tall, dark laird accompanying their own. Kate regarded none of them, for their stares were hard, fearful, and mistrusting.

She knew both the Campbells and the MacGregors had their enemies, but she wasn't sure whom these people regarded with more contempt, her or Callum. "What wrongs have been done to them, and how has he avenged them?" she asked Graham softly, though her gaze remained fastened on Callum's back.

"I fear ye're about to find out, lass."

She tilted her face up to look at him just as they reached the cottage. Graham swept his cap off his head and moved to the side of the entrance, after Callum and Roderick disappeared within. His hand reached for Kate when she moved to follow them.

"Mayhap 'twould be best fer ye to wait here with me." His words were firm, as was his hand on her arm, but the gentle entreaty in his green eyes told her his request was given for her own good.

Kate brushed his hand away and stepped inside. A small fire burned beneath a trivet in the center of the outer room. Firelight mingled with that of the sun's rays spilling across the rushes from the window.

Callum stood with the Cameron and another man, slightly smaller in stature, his palms resting on the shoulders of a boy with large, doleful eyes and a dirt-streaked face.

"'Tis yer laird, boy," the man said, looking as wide-eyed as his son. Kate could not tell which of the two chieftains the man referred. "Pay him the homage he deserves." He pushed the child to a kneeling position in front of Callum, but Callum raised his palm to stop him.

"Tell me aboot the attack."

The man pushed his son away with a quiet order to leave the cottage. He waited until the boy was gone before he spoke. " 'Twas a band of Menzies who did this to m' Rhona."

Callum's jaw twisted around a low curse battering against his teeth.

"We've had nae quarrel with the Menzies fer years." Cameron assured him. "These men acted on their own. No' under any command of their laird."

"They marked m' wife's face in accordance with the law!" The man stepped closer to Callum, his eyes gleaming with defiance and fury. "They are Argyll's dogs, fer they spoke of their reward as they burned oot her eye."

A sharp gasp drew the men's attention to where Kate stood at the door, her face ashen and her hands trembling as they twisted the woolen folds of her skirts. "What has my uncle to do with this?"

"Yer uncle?" the man asked, sounding as horrified as Kate looked. His expression changed quickly to loathing as he drew a small dagger from a fold in his plaid. "Have ye come to finish what yer kin began, then?"

Before he took a step in her direction, Callum blocked his path and snatched the dagger from his hand.

"I will avenge m' wife," the man insisted.

Callum's rigid gaze stilled the remainder of his protests. "No' on her." The thread of warning in his softly spoken words was unmistakable. "Bring me to yer wife. I've tarried here long enough."

The man did as he was commanded without sparing Kate another glance. "M' Rhona is here," he said, pulling away the curtain that separated the outer room from the sleeping quarters. "Her sister is changin' the dressin' to her wound."

Kate watched him lead Callum inside. The Cameron did not follow. When they were alone, the older chieftain turned to her, a deep frown drawing his gray brows over his eyes.

"A Campbell," he whispered.

Kate turned to him, still horrified that her uncle was responsible for branding a woman. "You needn't worry that I'll tell my uncle you are friends with Callum."

He stared at her, looking somewhat perplexed by her casual use of the laird's name. Then he shrugged his massive shoulders. "I dinna care what ye tell him, lass. The MacGregor saved my life."

Kate smiled, glad to hear it. "He saved mine, as well."

Now the Cameron stared outright at her, his jaw going slack an instant before his scowl returned full force. "The Devil has never spared a Campbell's life, let alone saved one. Surely he has ye too frightened to speak the truth."

Kate's feet took root in her spot. *The Devil?* Nae. Och, God, nae! Fear and anger warred within her, stopping her from running out the door or charging through the curtain. It was Callum who killed her father! Her grandfather! He had lied to her. He was the Devil MacGregor! *He has never spared a Campbell's life.* Dear God, was Robert dead, as well? She swayed on her heavy feet, feeling ill, her breath growing tight. She had smiled at the murderer, likened him to a knight of old! Now his cold regard made perfect sense. He had no heart.

The curtain snapped open. Callum stood in the doorway. His expression bore the remnants of horror but hardened with each breath into a mask of barely contained control. His eyes blazed with fury, hatred, revenge. Kate took an involuntary step backward when he stormed across the rushes. It was easy to see now how he had gained such a worthy title.

"Devil," she whispered as he passed her, heading for the door.

His scorching gaze swung to her, halting her drumming heart. He moved toward her before she could run, and closed his fingers around her arm. Without a word, he dragged her back to the curtained doorway and then left her there gaping at the sight within. She heard his determined footfalls as he left the cottage. His coarse command for his men to await his return two leagues outside the village faded against the gurgled wheeze of a woman's breath and the mournful sobs of her sister as she applied more ointment to the charred flesh beneath her fingers.

Chapter Nine

KATE STARED SILENTLY into the growing flames, fed by Brodie's careful attendance. Vaguely, she was aware of Jamie covering her shoulders with a thick plaid of coarse wool. Sitting beside her, his dark eyes flickering against the firelight, Angus held out his pouch of brew to her. When she refused it, he tapped it against her arm.

"Drink. There's a deep chill in the air this night. The whiskey will keep ye warm."

Indeed, the cold seeped into her marrow, but the weather was not to blame. Callum was out here, somewhere, alone. Roderick Cameron had told her where Callum had gone. What he intended to do. She was not afraid for Callum's life, or for the lives of the men who had branded Rhona MacGregor's beautiful face. Nae, if their judgment was about to come upon them, it was a righteous one. The chill that iced her blood came from the memory of looking into their executioner's eyes. He was going to hunt them down. He would show them no mercy, for there was none in him to give.

He never left a Campbell alive. Her grandfather. All the men of Kildun's garrison.

Her father.

She looked up at Graham when he folded his legs and sat opposite her.

"Is my brother dead?" Her quavering voice shattered the silence around them.

Graham pulled off his cap, tucked it into his plaid, and raked a golden lock of hair out of his eyes. "Nae." He shook his head when Angus held up his pouch. But for the pop of a thin branch burning in the fire, quiet had once again descended on the campsite.

Please God, Kate wanted to believe him. If the Devil killed Robert, too, she would cut his throat while he slept.

"Is it only Campbells he kills?" she asked coolly.

Jamie shifted closer to the fire. Brodie spat into it and then lay down, closing his eyes for the night. Graham's gaze, though, never wavered from hers.

"Nae, lass. He kills friends of the Campbells, as well."

Kate's blood drained from her face at the indifference in the commander's voice. Her uncle deserved to be flogged for his part in Rhona MacGregor's branding, but how could life mean so little to these men? She knew she could never understand, for she cared even for the lives of her cattle. "Why? Why all the killing? I know our clans have been warring for centuries, but what is behind it all? A woman? What offense did my clan commit so long ago that cost my father his life and still brings such scorn to all your faces?"

No one answered her right away. Brodie opened his eyes and cast her a narrowed look before closing them again and shaking his head.

Graham poked a long stick into the embers, his handsome face growing pensive. "Would that this war was about a lass," he said. "Fer nae matter how fine she was, it would have ended before it ever touched Callum and Maggie." He caught a small piece of dried meat that Angus tossed him and took a bite. He chewed for a moment, then continued. "This war began three centuries ago. Callum was born with its purpose already flowing in his veins."

"Aye, I know of the battles," Kate told him. "But I don't understand what sort of men would fight them for so long?"

Graham's eyes glittered at hers across the firelight. "Men who are the sons of kings," he said, his words weighted with the measure of respect and affection he felt for them of whom he spoke. "Ye want the full tale of it, then?" When she nodded, he pulled in a deep breath and threw the remainder of the meat into the fire, as if the telling of it ruined his appetite. "The MacGregors are a royal race, descended from King MacAlpine. Their territories were once vast and held by the old ways—by right of sword. A fierce and mighty clan, they fought at the side of Robert the Bruce. But they were betrayed, and their land in Glen Orchy was given over to the Campbells, who had gained influence in the royal court." His voice was soft and deep, compelling even Brodie to sit up again and listen. "The MacGregors found themselves reduced to the position of tenants on the lands that were once theirs."

"Taken from us by cunnin' and devious schemes that continued until yer ancestors had gained it all," Angus added solemnly and produced another pouch from a heavy fold in his plaid.

"The MacGregors fought back, of course," Graham said. "Naturally, they directed their attacks against those who had wrested their land and their livestock from them. They were brutal and feared by all. They killed and slaughtered many until their oppressors were forced to obtain royal assistance in putting an end to the troublesome tribe. Given noble titles and the right to hunt their enemies with dogs, the Campbells and some others provoked the MacGregors into more acts of violence, and the formidable clan was only too happy to oblige."

"Driven from Glen Orchy, the MacGregor chiefs lived at Stronmelochan at the foot of Glenstrae," Brodie added. "While the Campbells expanded eastward into Breadalbane."

"Aye," Graham agreed. "'Twas up to the Glenstrae MacGregors to carry on the resistance, but their chiefs were hunted down and murdered, their sons along with them, and their land taken, also. When the Protestant parliament, many of whom are Campbells, declared it illegal to be a Catholic, many Highlanders joined the Gordon clan chieftain in his fight against the realm. But the chieftain was beheaded, and the clans who backed him were pursued with fire and sword."

"To this day, we are considered papist heretics," Jamie muttered quietly.

"After a particularly bloody battle at Glen Fruin, a half century ago, the clan was proscribed," Graham continued. "The name MacGregor, abolished. They are forbidden to bear it."

Kate nodded, knowing a little about their proscription

and what it meant. "All lieges are prohibited from bearing them aid," she said, repeating the creed she'd heard her uncle say many times.

"Aye," Graham confirmed and then added, "They have been stripped of every basic human need, including the right to bear arms and the right to gather together in one place. They are hunted, men, women, and children alike, and their heads are used as pardon fer the most vicious of crimes. Care of the aged and the sick is still refused to them. Even the sacraments of baptism, marriage, and burial are denied. And yet the MacGregors remain, despite everything."

They were to be forgotten.

Jamie tore a hunk of bread away from his loaf and offered it to Kate, breaking her thoughts. She'd known the MacGregors were forbidden to bear their name, but she'd believed they had forfeited that right by defying every decree set forth by the realm. She had no idea their proscription had stripped them of so much more. Did her kin truly have so much to do with the annihilation of an entire clan? It was difficult to believe. Why hadn't Amish or John ever told her any of this? Mayhap they were afraid of contradicting her uncle. They never judged the MacGregors, even knowing they killed her father. She closed her eyes and inhaled, gathering the strength to ask her next query and the courage to hear the reply.

"Is this why Callum killed my grandfather? What did my father do to deserve his wrath?"

"I do not know anything about yer father, lass," Graham answered her and untied his belt, settling more comfortably into his plaid. "But Callum did not kill yer grandfather."

"But everyone knows the Devil—"

"They know only what yer uncle believes to be true. Mayhap yer father and yer grandfather fought. We Highlanders know Colin Campbell did not agree with his father's tactics against the MacGregors. Mayhap he—"

Kate rose to her feet and held up her palm to stop him. She was not about to listen to such treachery against her father. "Has the Devil convinced you of this?"

"Nae," he said, never flinching at her challenge. "Callum does not pretend to know what happened. But he did not kill Liam Campbell."

"How do you know?" Kate demanded.

"I know because I was with Callum in Skye when he learned of yer grandfather's death. He near went mad again."

"Again?" Kate asked, barely able to breathe.

"Aye. The revenge was his to take. He earned it." Graham did not give the full meaning of his words time to seep in before he spoke again. "When Callum was a lad, yer grandfather and his army rode into his village and killed everyone in it, including the laird Dougal MacGregor and his wife. The chieftain, 'twas rumored, had begun a new rebellion and had been known to declare his name openly. Yer grandfather had them all slaughtered, save fer Dougal's young son and daughter. To them, he delivered a harsher punishment than death. Callum and his sister grew to maturity below the belly of Kildun Castle, where they paid fer their father's crime."

"Maggie was but five summers auld when they took her." Jamie's voice was low and riddled with anger Kate had not heard in it before.

She stared at him through a heavy haze of tears. She

wanted to shout at them all that what they told her was false. Her grandfather would never have done such a vile thing. Her father surely knew naught of it. He had children of his own! He would have done something. My God, *had* he done something? Did Colin Campbell kill his own father, mayhap in the heat of an argument? Nae! Never! She refused to believe any of it. She did not come from such merciless ilk. She wanted to tell Graham, but the sob poised behind her lips stopped her from opening her mouth. She willed her feet to move. She needed to be away from them, away from the contempt she saw in their eyes when they looked at her. Now she understood it better. She turned, ready to make her way to a tree closer to the shadows. But she stopped, unwilling to run away from them as her uncle had. What could she say to them? If all this was true, what could she possibly say?

"I am sorry for what my kin have done. I know it is not enough, but I would have you know it just the same."

Graham smiled, turning to watch her as she settled down for the night a few feet away from them. "That's the first Campbell who has ever apologized to a MacGregor."

"Aye." Brodie nodded, then smiled with him. Angus chuckled, thinking the apology was even more satisfying than his brew.

"Is it aright if I like her?" Jamie asked in all seriousness, and he knew that it was when the others burst into hearty laughter.

Chapter Ten

KATE WAS AWAKE when Callum returned to them early the next morn. How could she sleep when images of women's branded faces and children living out their lives in a dungeon invaded her every thought?

Quietly, she watched him dismount and look around, making certain they were all there, safe. His men still slept, rolled in their plaids, scattered around the dying embers of their campfire. When he saw her, he dropped his gaze to the ground, then turned to tie his reins to a nearby tree.

"Did you kill my father?" she asked him, needing to know the truth. Her grandfather may have deserved Callum's wrath, but her father did not.

"I never knew yer faither."

God, she needed to believe him. "Are you injured?" she asked, rising to go to him. Blood stained his plaid and smudged his jaw, but it was clearly not his own. For while his voice fell heavily on her ears, the unbending steel of his emotions remained.

"Dinna concern yerself with me, Kate," he answered before turning to leave, this time on foot into the trees.

She watched him go, and though she knew he had been victorious in his endeavors the night before, he walked with the weariness of a man defeated. Was he simply a heartless rebel, bent on killing Campbells because he felt they'd treated his clan unfairly? Or was the Devil a man with a greater cause? *Keeping our name alive and avenging the wrongs done to my kin.* She recalled his words at the Cameron holding. God's mercy, he fought to avenge too much. She picked up her steps and followed him, wanting, needing to know if her grandfather had truly kept him locked away in a dungeon when he was a child. And if so, how far would he go to right *that* wrong?

Coming upon him a few moments later, she studied him from between the tangle of branches that separated them. He stood naked and alone at the edge of a loch, its surface set aflame by the morning sun. His plaid and tunic, along with one crumpled boot, lay in a heap at his feet. His left boot flew over his shoulder and just missed Kate's head when she left the sanctuary of the trees, her gaze fastened on his bare back. Though every muscle that fashioned him was honed and defined by years of toil and battle, it was not the sheer beauty of him that drew her closer but the ugliness of long, jagged scars covering one end of his expansive shoulders to the other.

They were deep, angry imperfections carved into stone. The sight of them brought tears to Kate's eyes. How old was he when he had received them? Had it been her grandfather's hands that had produced them? In that moment, Callum MacGregor became more than an avenging warrior to her. He was a man who had lived through the merciless torture of a barbarian. His purpose was made even stronger by his pain.

Paralyzed by the poignant power before her, she watched him stalk into the sun-dappled current like Poseidon returning home from war. She had felt his body against hers, hard as granite. But never had she seen a naked man before, and never one so finely made. She did not blink as the water caressed his shapely calves, then rose upward to his thighs as he waded deeper into the loch. Mesmerized by his sheer masculine glory, her gaze continued up over the perfect roundness of his buttocks. Her mouth went dry, and her heart pounded so loud in her chest she feared he might hear it.

He tilted his face toward the sun. The splay of muscles in his upper arms rolled under his skin as he spread his arms at his sides, skimming his palms over the cool, satiny surface. It was then, while she stared almost longingly at the length of his fingers, that she noticed he had removed the leather cuffs that normally covered his wrists. She lifted her hands to her mouth to still a sob welling in her throat. Pocked skin, almost worn down to the bone, bore evidence of the irons that had held him captive.

"D'ye have somethin' ye wanted to speak to me aboot? Or were ye plannin' on just starin' at me while I bathed?"

Kate thought hard about running then. But it was too late; he was already turning around to face her. She was thankful, at least, that half his body was covered in water. That is, until his eyes found hers.

How could they chill her blood and sear her flesh at

the same time? They drew her in, inviting her onto a battlefield for which she had never practiced. Looking into them, she wondered what victory would gain her if she was braw enough to engage.

"Would ye care to join me?"

Her heart near beat right out of her mouth with the thought of it. She felt her face burn and almost turned away, but he seemed to be enjoying her discomposure. She suspected he was quite used to terrifying everyone around him. But she was not everyone.

Folding her arms across her chest, she forced herself to look him straight in the eye. "Nae, I would not care to join you. But I do appreciate the consideration you afford me by bathing. It would be better for us to speak when you are not covered in blood."

He said nothing but continued to trace the curves of her body with his bemused gaze. Kate thought he might be trying to provoke her anger. She was certain he had no idea how he was making her insides tremble.

"Well?" he asked after another moment passed with her staring at him.

She blinked. "Well what?"

"What is it ye want, besides me to look more appealin' fer ye?"

"I can assure you I care not how you look, MacGregor," Kate argued, irritated now that he had turned her meaning into something entirely different. "Were you beaten for your pride?"

He nodded, and though the slight humor hovering around his lips was arrogant indeed, Kate was dreadfully sorry for her words the moment she spoke them.

Finally she lowered her eyes. "I did not mean—"

"Speak yer mind, Kate Campbell," he drawled and lay back into water, exposing his sculpted chest to the sun. "If my scars please ye, then say it and let us be honest enemies."

Kate took a step forward. Her hand came to her chest. "Please me?"

He lifted his head to squint at her. "Aye."

"They horrify me!" She watched him paddle away from her on his back and was tempted to reach her hand out to bring him back. "Why didn't you tell me you were the Devil MacGregor?"

"Ye didna ask," he called back.

Oh, the man was completely insufferable. Kate looked around for a rock to fling at him while he swam farther away. "MacGregor," she called out. "Did my grandfather truly . . ." God, she couldn't bring herself to ask him, to even think of it. It didn't matter. He had no intention of answering her. She moved closer to the edge of the loch.

"Did you kill him for what he did to you?" She gritted her teeth when he continued to swim away. "I am trying to talk to you!" she shouted.

Still nothing.

"If you would just . . . MacGregor!" she called out louder while he drifted. "I believe you did not kill my father. Are we to remain enemies simply because of our names?"

" 'Tis the only reason we need," he called back, sunning himself.

Kate's blood boiled. She was tired of hating him. Or trying to. And besides, if what Graham told her was true, her reasons to hate him were completely unjustified. But Callum's weren't. She took another step forward. She didn't want him to hate her, no matter what had been done to him. He was swimming farther away from her, and the more he swam, the angrier she became. She refused to fight with him ever again, and she was determined to prove it to him, even if it killed her. Before she could think clearly enough to stop herself, she unfastened her kirtle and kicked it away. She stepped into the loch and swam toward the belligerent chieftain in her shift and hose.

He heard her splashing behind him but did not bother to turn around, which infuriated Kate all the more. When she was close enough to reach out and touch him, a strange comfort washed over her. She had traveled in his embrace since the moment they met. His closeness was becoming familiar to her, enjoyable, safe.

"Why are you running away from me?" she asked, frowning at him, and at the dull pain beginning to throb in her shoulder.

He turned and opened his eyes to look at her. His long hair swept over his forehead, gleaming black down his shoulders. Droplets clung to his long lashes, giving more potency to his hard blue-green gaze. "I'm no' runnin', lass. I'm floatin'."

"Do I frighten you, then?" she charged, fueled by his nonchalance. For in truth, she knew she was the one who was afraid. Not of his strength that could overpower her so easily, but of her own maddening attraction to him.

"How could a wee thing like yerself frighten me?" He turned and swam away again.

Kate swatted the surface and gritted her teeth. "You're afraid of Campbells, then!"

It was definitely the wrong thing to say, she realized when he pivoted around and impaled her with his angry glare. He rose out of the water, looming over her and blocking out the sun. She had to fight to keep herself from withering in her spot. "Woman," he said very slowly, the word rumbling on that bear's voice. "I've crushed more Campbells than ye'll ever know, and I'll go to my grave with a Campbell's heart clutched within my fingers."

Kate tipped her head back. The intensity in his gaze held her still, but her heart roared within her chest. His face was so hard, so unforgiving. She wanted to look away, for she knew now the passion that burned within. How deeply was his hatred emblazoned on his heart? He'd had a lifetime to nurture it. He would die hating her. Nae. She did not want it to be so. She raised her eyes to the dark, damp strands of his hair falling around his shoulders, the faint trace of blood not completely washed away by the water. She should fear him, but there was more to him than anger and malevolence. She had sliced open his leg, and he had not sliced off her head in return. Even when she fired his fury, he had not put his hands to her. His eyes were sharp and hard, but sometimes, when he looked at her, his gaze grew tender, as if he could not sustain his resolve to hate her.

"Will that heart be mine, my laird?" she asked quietly.

"It might," he answered, pulling her gaze back to his.

"Nae." She shook her head. "If you hate me so much, why did you save me? I do not believe you would hurt me."

Callum wanted to mock this trust she so freely granted him. Trust that poured from her lips, from her eyes every time she set them on him. Trust he did not deserve. But instead, he found himself enraptured by it. "Ye dinna know anything aboot me." His voice rumbled like thunder, a low growl of warning, and something else . . .

"I know what people call you," she said. "But mayhap they are wrong. Mayhap you are more like Sir Gawain or Percivale than Satan."

Callum reached for her then and slid one arm around her waist. Drawing the lower half of his body flush against hers, he leaned toward her, his long, sable lashes swept downward. "Ye dinna know me, Kate." His velvet baritone was an erotic caress as seductive as the smirk that curled his lips when she struggled to free herself. "Or what I'm capable of doin'." Her flesh felt warm and soft beneath her wet shift, igniting a fire that blazed through his veins. He kept her still while he spread his palm over her belly, then upward, slowly, deliberately between her breasts and over her collarbone. Her lips parted on a sigh that mingled their breath even as she fought him. Hell, how easy it would be to take her. He lowered his head and covered her mouth with his. Her protests ended instantly, provoking him to taste her more fully. He swept his tongue inside her, then out again as he slanted his lips to take her at an even deeper angle. His kiss was fierce, possessive, his tongue probing, stroking her with sweet, hot, melting desire until she groaned and looped her arms around his neck.

When Callum felt her tongue flick against his, he grew hard against her. He could tear the thin barrier between them away and with one forceful surge impale her to the hilt. He wanted to show her that he was not the gentle man her eyes hoped for. He was no knight on a quest to save bonny damsels, though, by God, she was the most beautiful of them all. He could take her now, shatter her fanciful notions of him. God knew he could do it, for she tempted him beyond reason. But he knew the harsh reality of the world, and what would become of her if he took her. For her own good he had to keep her heart out of his hands.

He broke their kiss, letting his mouth hover over hers. "I am the MacGregor," he whispered on a growl that sounded harsh to his own ears. "The most feared enemy of yer clan. Dinna ferget it, Kate."

With every ounce of control he possessed, he released her and leaned back in the water. He was a murderer, aye, not a violator of women. "D'ye want to know why I saved ye?"

She shook her head no. But he saw the new spark of fear in her eyes even before he gave her his reason. He forced a thin smile. She deserved to know what a ruthless bastard he was, though at present he hated himself more than when he was Liam Campbell's prisoner. "Ye are more valuable to me alive than dead."

Kate's arm stung, along with her heart. She felt tears slowly rising to the rims of her lashes and grew angry with herself for letting him see the effect of his words.

"I want yer uncle's head," he continued, "and when he comes fer ye, I will take it with nae mercy—his and those of any others who come with him."

Kate's heart lurched. Terror washed over her, as frigid as the water beginning to numb her limbs. Her uncle had already proven her value to him when he fled against the McColls. He would not come for her. But her brother would. Robert would search for her. "You said Robert was your friend."

"Nae, I never said I was friend to any Campbell."

He was going to kill her brother! She had to do something. She could not allow Robert to die for her.

"I fear you've made a terrible error," she said, doing her best not to weep. It would do no good against his hardened heart. "My uncle will not come for me."

"Aye, he will." Slowly, Callum treaded toward her again. When he reached her, he lifted his fingers to a tear spilling down her cheek. "I know he will, because I would come fer ye." She broke away from his touch and swam back to the shore. He watched her snatch her kirtle from the ground and then flee, satisfied that he crushed any hope she had placed in him.

"Aye, Kate, if ye were mine and someone took ye, I would follow him to the ends of the Earth until I got ye back."

Chapter Eleven

KATE BURST INTO THE CAMP, clutching her kirtle to her chest. She stopped for a moment to look at the four faces staring up at her from their pouches of dried mutton and bread, then rushed to Callum's horse. She had to find Robert before he found her. Her chest burned. Her muscles felt frozen, save for the throbbing in her arm. She tried to pull herself up into the saddle, but a bolt of pain shot through her and almost made her retch.

A large pair of hands caught her by the waist and steadied her.

"Now, where do ye think ye're going, lass?" When Graham turned Kate around to have a look at her, his expression changed to concern. "Hell, yer wound is bleeding. What in blazes did ye do?"

"She looks like she had a bath," Angus offered, coming up behind Graham to see what the fuss was about.

"Did Callum toss ye into the water, then?" Jamie passed the others and rushed to her side.

"Jamie, why the hell would he toss her into the water,

ye lackwit?" Brodie smacked the younger warrior on the side of the head, hoping to knock some sense into him.

Jamie glared at him. "Because she's a Campbell, why else?"

Kate shook Graham to gain his attention from the others. "You knew I was bait to bring my uncle to Callum. I must go to Kildun!" Her teeth began to chatter, and Jamie near barreled over Brodie to retrieve a plaid from the ground to cover her.

"We cannot let ye do that, lass," Graham said gently.

"But he is a loathsome coward," she argued, trying desperately to make them understand. "My brother will be the one to die!" She leaned against Callum's horse when another wave of pain washed over her.

"Who is a loathsome coward?" Jamie asked, thoroughly confused.

"Callum is," Brodie answered.

Jamie's shoulders straightened. "I take offense to that."

Angus snickered, then guzzled some brew from another pouch he had hidden beneath his plaid.

"Kate." She heard Graham speak her name. She dabbed her head with the back of her hand, wondering when the air had turned so warm. "Yer wound has opened, lass."

"Hell, she's bleedin' all over m' plaid," Brodie complained, sincerely upset.

Angus belched, then swiped his hand across his mouth. "Since when d'ye mind someone else's blood on yer plaid?"

"Please!" Kate shouted at the men. "You do not understand. My brother . . . he will look for me. You must let me go! I will not let him die because of me!"

Callum was securing his plaid over his shoulder when he stepped out from within the trees. He stopped as her plea reached him and pierced him like an arrow. He'd meant to frighten her, to open her eyes to the truth, but her desperation to save her brother's life was too familiar to his own. Despite the darkness that consumed him, he clung to one love. That of his sister. He defied the law in honor of his name, but he had given up his soul in exchange for Maggie's life. He would not force Kate to do the same. He was glad he had listened to Graham and not killed Robert Campbell.

Callum called her name. She turned, along with the others, as he picked up his steps again and moved slowly toward her.

"I willna harm yer brother." Aye, 'twas his voice he heard promising to spare the young Campbell's life yet again. His voice that sounded uncommonly gentle to his ears. "I willna kill him. I swear it," he repeated, reaching her.

"Even if he comes to fight you?" Kate questioned, needing to be certain.

"I vow he will walk away unscathed." His gaze dropped to the blood seeping through her shift. "Come." He pressed his hand to hers, thankful that she did not pull away. Her confidence in his word produced a warm smile he could not resist giving her. "Yer wound needs tendin'."

Her expression went from appreciative to terrified in an instant. "You will not attempt to burn it, will you?"

Callum bit down on his words. He would not lie to her. He closed his fingers around hers instead. "I'll no' do anything that'll pain ye overmuch."

He turned to Angus. "Give me yer brew."

The hulking warrior gaped at him. "All of it?"

A seething glare from his laird stilled the remainder of Angus's protests, and he handed the pouch over.

Callum cut a quick glance to Graham next. The commander nodded, knowing what needed to be done. He pulled a small dagger from his belt and headed for the cooled campfire, motioning for Jamie to gather more leaves.

"She needs to come oot o' her undergarment. She'll catch a wicked fever soaked through like that," Brodie muttered with a tight smirk when Callum walked past him.

His cousin spoke true. She needed to change into her dry kirtle before she was unable to do it herself. Of course, Callum was not opposed to undressing her. But his control was already on the brink of shattering from just looking at her in her wet shift, her dark waves clinging to her fluid curves.

"I would know what you mean to do," Kate demanded weakly while he led her toward the trees.

He knew exactly what she meant. She was worried about how he was going to tend to her arm. He did not think it wise to tell her just yet. Best to keep her mind off the blade, mayhap even rile her a bit. "I mean to offer ye the privacy ye denied me while ye get oot of that shift."

"You did not seem too bothered by my watching," Kate couldn't help but parry, as ill as she felt.

"Aye," he conceded with a long, repentant sigh while he placed her behind the nearest tree. "Devils have nae honor."

"But knights who offer a lady her privacy do."

He stared after her, unable to look away as he had promised. Knights. He almost laughed. What did he know of them? Those noble heroes who brandished their swords against injustice. His blade was stained only with vengeance. The lass was daft. But hell, he felt more human around her. More like a man than a monster.

"You're looking!" Kate shrieked at him from her hiding place.

Grinding his jaw, he turned swiftly away. He was enjoying very manly thoughts when she came up behind him a few moments later and tapped him on the shoulder. He turned and looked down at her pale face with the residue of longing still heavy in his gaze.

"Drink this. It'll keep ye warm." He pushed Angus's pouch between them before he was tempted to drag her into his embrace and do the like himself.

She accepted the whiskey and drank. Immediately a crimson blush streaked across her cheeks, just before the color changed to a greenish hue.

"Ye've forgotten to apply yer ointment," he stated firmly, taking hold of her shoulder.

"I—och hell . . ." She squeezed her eyes shut and trembled all the way down to her toes. "I could not apply it to my back." She swayed on her feet, but Callum caught her and sat her down gently on the ground.

He eased her kirtle off her shoulder with careful fingers. "'Tis no' so bad," he said, squatting over her and examining the wound. When she tried to look, he cupped her hand in his and brought the pouch to her lips for another drink. When he returned to his ministrations, his hands shook and he cursed himself. He'd tended to hundreds of wounds to keep his men alive. This was no different. But it was. Kate's skin was cool silk, milky white, and no matter how hard he tried, his littlest finger kept brushing against the swell of her breast while he tried as gently as he could to remove the packing Mae Stewart had used on her.

Kate remained still until she saw Graham approaching with a glowing dagger pointing straight at her. "Nae!" She struggled to gain her feet, but Callum's hold on her remained firm.

He lowered his lips to her ear, closing his eyes when her intoxicating scent wafted through his nostrils. "Come, Katie lass," he whispered. "Ye have faced doun the Devil. Ye willna turn Campbell on me now, will ye?"

She clutched fistfuls of his plaid and smothered her face into his chest when Graham came closer. "Do not burn me!"

Warding off Graham momentarily, Callum held her, knowing firsthand how badly this was going to hurt. "Another drink, Kate. It needs be done. I willna have ye die on me."

"Aye, I'm of more value to you alive." She pushed away from him, glared at Graham, then squeezed her eyes shut.

She did not remember Graham leaving, or if she screamed. Just Callum's arm around her, cradling her while he sealed her wound shut with Graham's blade. She was certain he asked her forgiveness a time or two while the hot metal seared her flesh. She was also acutely aware of the warmth of his muscles and the controlled strength he used to hold her still. So close, she took in the angle of his jaw tightening beneath a dark dusting of facial hair. His mouth, so firm and decadently shaped.

"You kissed me in the water."

"Aye."

"Think you might ever do it again?"

He stopped tending to her arm and looked down into her drowsy gaze, wanting to kiss her now. "I'm afraid I might."

"Will you make certain you are dressed next time?"

Her words were slurred enough to make Callum smile as he went about finishing his task. "If I must."

"You really should smile more."

When his brilliant blue eyes settled on hers again, she tried to show him how it was done, slanting her lips just before she belched loudly enough to rival Angus on his drunkest day.

"There, you see? Just like that." Her eyelids drifted closed, but she fought to stay awake. "Aye, you are quite a handsome man when you smile. Though you are handsome when you frown, as well, Clalum MacKreglor. Damn it, that hurts." She cried out softly when he poured some of Angus's brew over her shoulder, as she had done to his leg.

"I'm done, Kate." Tenderly, he adjusted her kirtle so that the fabric did not touch her flesh. His fingers grazed her face and then paused when she moved closer to his touch.

"Thank you for not killing my brother."

Callum did not move his hand away but stroked her temple with the backs of his fingers.

She opened her eyes, addling him thoroughly. "I see two of you." She smiled again but then grew serious.

"Clalum?"

"Aye, lass?"

"If you did not kill my father, then who did?"

Chapter Twelve

KATE WOKE UP many hours later, propped against Callum's chest while he kept his horse at a slow pace and his arms closed loosely around her. Her head ached from front to back. The bouncing up and down did not help, and she silently cursed his horse and every other horse in creation while they trotted along a rocky incline. She was trying to find a more comfortable position when she remembered that her knight was her captor and she was nothing more to him than bait to catch a jackal. She tried to sit up, but her head felt like it was going to teeter off her shoulders and careen to the ground.

"How do ye fare, Kate?"

The deep voice behind her ears boomed through her head and made her cringe.

"Must you shout?"

"I'm whisperin'."

"Do not whisper so loudly, then," she groaned. "I feel like I'm dying."

Behind her, Callum nodded sympathetically, familiar

with the agonizing aftereffects of Gillis's brew. He laid his hand on top of her head and eased her back against his chest. "Just be still."

Kate knew he did not like her, but once again, he was comforting her. His hand, one that had killed more Campbells than she cared to ponder, was so achingly gentle when he touched her that it almost made her doubt the conviction of his hatred. She did as her captor ordered and leaned against him, squinting in the daylight at the land around her.

Slopes were fast becoming mountains that rose like great granite curtains around her. When she inhaled, her nostrils tingled. The air was getting thinner. She had never traveled outside of Glen Orchy before, and she began to realize just how much she had missed. The Highlands were an uncharted place, vast and wild with untouched foliage and men who hid atop jagged cliffs, unseen in the mist. It was an untamed land of bursting color. The heather grew here in lush splendor, decorating the braes in rich purple majesty. But there was something more. 'Twas gray. The color of strength. An endless line of mountains rose boldly toward a vast blue sky that hovered so close one would wager his best horse that he merely need lift his hand to the sky to touch it. It was as if the very heavens descended upon this land. Kate decided the Highlands were the most breathtaking, soul-stirring place in creation.

Somewhere overhead, a hawk released a cry that echoed for leagues through deep glens and over rolling moorlands. Kate closed her eyes and snuggled deeper into Callum's body.

Hard, tight muscles caressed her back. The weight of

his shoulders slowly relaxed over hers, enfolding her. Thighs nestled and caressed her now instead of feeling like stones against her hips.

Callum sighed when Kate let out a wee snore under his chin. He had always considered himself hard, not pillow soft or cushioned with clouds. But hell, he was fast becoming this woman's bed! She was a Campbell. And a nuisance. He tightened his arm around her and stroked her belly with the pad of his thumb. Acts of both protection and possession, he realized, praying for God to grant him strength to keep his wits about him. Protecting her was one thing, but possessing her would be deadly. Deadly for them both. Still, when the wind blew her curls against his face, he closed his eyes and inhaled. He had always thought nothing in the world could ever smell better than the Highlands. He was wrong.

He accepted a wedge of cheese from Brodie, who rode up beside him. They chewed in silence for a few moments before Callum turned toward him. "Brodie, stop starin' at me and speak yer mind."

Brodie shrugged his shoulders and tossed back the strands of dark hair that fell over his eyes. "I was just thinkin' how even-tempered ye have become since takin' the lass." He let his eyes rove over her form. "'Tis plain to see that she pleases ye," he continued, even though Callum glared at him. "I was wantin' to know if ye are thinkin' o' claimin' her."

"I'll claim nae Campbell," Callum answered him, tight-lipped.

"She fancies ye, laird," Brodie went on. "Listen how she purrs like a kitten all wrapped up in yer arms." The way Callum tightened his hold on her did not go unnoticed by Brodie. "Have ye no' considered a way to torture the Earl of Argyll before killin' him?"

"Nae, but I'm sure ye have thought of naught else," Callum replied. Brodie was a most ruthless warrior, loyal in battle, but a bit overly bloodthirsty.

"The lass." Brodie smiled, pointing his chin at her.

"What aboot her?"

"Bed her, and bed her thoroughly. What could be worse fer The Campbell than to have a MacGregor growin' in his niece's belly?"

Callum went still on his mount. He hadn't thought of anything but bedding her for the past se'nnight. 'Twas true, 'twould be satisfying to tell Argyll that MacGregor seed grew in his niece, before Callum killed him. And if he took her to his bed, there would be no marriage between her and the English lord of Newbury. Aye, that thought pleased him well enough. But there was something more to consider.

"And what would become of her when she's returned to her brother carryin' my bairn? Ye saw what was done to Rhona MacGregor just fer bearin' our name."

"Aye, there is nae mercy fer sympathizers," Brodie agreed quietly, then eyed Kate pressed so intimately against his laird. "Mayhap, then, 'tis best ye dinna give her back. Fer I fear it may be too late."

~

Since she had slept most of the day, Kate was wide awake when Callum and his men settled into their plaids that night. Lying down was fruitless. She blamed the stars for keeping her eyes open, the sound of the leaves rustling for keeping her ears alert. But it was the man sleeping across the campfire who made her heart feel restless. No matter how she tried, she could not stop thinking about his kiss. Lord, but he was dangerous. She hadn't been able to move in his iron embrace while he touched her so intimately, as if he owned her. And then she didn't want him to let her go. He'd ravished her, all right, but she couldn't seem to muster even the slightest bit of anger over it. His mouth took her with ruthless mastery. His hot tongue sliding over hers made her so weak and willing, it frightened her thinking how far she would have let him go had he not stopped on his own.

God's mercy, he had warned her twice to remember who he was, and she needed to do just that. It was one thing to liken Callum to a champion of his people—for saving her from death—but caring for any MacGregor was considered treason. And the Devil was the most forbidden of them all. She sat up, cursing her wakefulness under her breath, and turned toward the sleeping laird.

Callum was not sleeping but sat propped against a tree, his legs outstretched before him and crossed at the ankles, his eyes on her.

She cast him a diffident smile. "Sleep eludes me."

He did not move, but his expression appeared to soften beyond the glimmering firelight.

He was a stranger to her, and yet the chill of midnight tempted Kate to move closer to the familiar warmth of his body. She drew in an uneven breath instead. "I fear I will never sleep at night again if I keep sleeping in the day."

"A burden, to be sure," he agreed, his voice light and teasing. "But if the restive sparkle in yer eyes tells the tale true, 'tis one less troublesome than the one I will be sufferin' again on the morrow."

Kate's eyes flashed at him, and a hint of a smile etched her lips to match his. "Suffering indeed. If you had to endure the tedium of traveling with an insolent ogre day after day, you, too, would bless unconsciousness when it came to claim you."

His eyebrows rose with surprise, but instead of scowling at her as she expected, he grinned and set her heart to pounding. "Have ye always been so braw, Kate Campbell?"

"Nae," she assured him. She tucked her legs beneath her and turned her gaze to the flames. "When I was a child I was very much afraid of thunder. The ground rumbled much the same way when the Highlanders raided. But Robert always promised to protect me. He was quite gallant, even as a boy." She smiled, remembering. "My father often mused that my mother should have named her son Galahad."

"One of King Arthur's knights who fought against the Picts."

Kate slanted her gaze at him. "You know of them?"

Callum nodded, "Graham once spoke of them. Men whose armor shone with the radiance of righteousness."

"Aye." Kate met his steady gaze. "They believed in what they fought for. Robert used to tell me it is not the victory but why a man fights the battle which makes him a hero."

Callum regarded her in silence. A play of the light across her eyes it was not: he saw himself, and who he might have been, in their shimmering reflection. He cast his glance downward. "I have naught in common with such men. 'Tis late." He folded his arms across his chest and closed his eyes. "One of us needs to sleep, else we'll ride my horse into a tree."

Kate lay back down and stared up at the treetops. A moment of silence passed before she broke it again. "Robert used to tell me tales when I could not sleep."

"I am no' yer brother."

She sighed and turned to her side to find a more comfortable position, then . . .

"My faither was a hero. He led the *Griogaraich* against his enemies with Hamish Grant at his side fer many years before he was killed. When we were lads, Graham and I once . . ."

Kate closed her eyes and let the sound of his rich, lilting voice carry her away to her dreams.

Chapter Thirteen

WHEN THEY STOPPED at an inn two nights later, Kate was so deliriously happy at the thought of sleeping in a bed, she didn't notice the possessive way Callum kept his fingers clenched around her wrist after they dismounted.

Callum had agreed to stop here because they were at the edge of MacDonnell country, and though none were permitted to aid the MacGregors, most Highlanders did. His men could use a hot meal, and mayhap if Kate slept in a bed this night, she would cease falling asleep in his arms. Every time she pressed her cheek against his chest, as if she belonged there—or when she looked into his eyes like he was her champion—she tempted him to forget all he lost in her grandfather's dungeon and imagine that something new and wonderful was still possible in his life. Hell, he was going daft, and the dulcet sound of her breath, the achingly sweet comfort she found in his embrace were to blame. He had to find a horse for her to ride and get her out of his arms. And fast.

But this night he kept her close to him because even

though the innkeeper, Ferguson MacDonnell, was his friend, the price on a MacGregor head was too high for some to resist. And since Kate traveled with him, she was considered his. Her life, forfeit.

He could have entered the inn with caution, but if there were enemies inside, their fear of him would keep Kate alive. So, feeding what they knew of The Devil, he brandished his sword and kicked open the door. He stood beneath the entryway like a wraith freed upon the swirling mist. The inn grew silent while he raked his powerful gaze over every face, warning death swift yet painful should any come against him.

Angus let out a loud belch, stepped around his laird, and entered the inn first. He sauntered over to a large trestle table where a group of ruffians sat, their cups paused in midair at their lips. He hovered over them with dark, bloodshot eyes. "What ails ye, ye bunch o' sorry knaves? Have ye never seen a MacGregor before?"

"Aye, we have," said the leader of the group. "But none as ugly as you, Angus MacGregor."

"Archie MacPherson, I thought ye were dead." Angus laughed and grabbed hold of the man's forearm to haul him out of his seat and into his arms. " 'Tis good to see ye, old friend."

Flanked on all sides by Callum and the rest of his men, Kate watched, relieved that the men were not enemies, for one would have to be a fool to cross the mighty brutes surrounding her. She was also surprised to find more friends of the MacGregors. It pleased and comforted her to know they were not hunted everywhere.

Now that the threat of bloodshed was over, she relaxed and took in the sights around her. The inn was more like a tavern, with rooms above stairs to accommodate patrons and the wenches who served them with coy giggles on their lips. The scent of ale and sweet wine flooded Kate's lungs and made her gag at first, but then, oddly enough, the place began to smell cozy.

"M'laird, welcome," a small man with a bulbous nose and thick, unruly red hair greeted when he reached them. He turned his pale green eyes on Kate, giving her a hungry looking over that made her shift closer to Callum.

His response was to toss his arm around her and drag her to him. "MacDonnell." Callum's voice was an octave above a growl. "If ye dinna quit starin' at her, I'll be forced to stop ye myself."

The innkeeper's eyes darted back to Callum. "My apologies," he said, offering a swift, repentant smile. "I didna mean . . . I'll have me Robena prepare a room fer ye right away."

"That will be two rooms, innkeeper," Kate corrected him as he turned to find his wife.

"My apologies again," MacDonnell offered her, then glanced back at Callum. "I thought she was yers."

"Nae," Callum said then tugged her back to him when she tried to pull away. "But we'll be needin' only one room."

"I am not staying in the . . ." Kate's vehement refusal faded from her lips when Callum set his cool cobalt gaze on her. She felt like she'd been hit with a large stone. She cursed herself and squared her shoulders. It astounded her that she could battle a whole legion of sword-swinging McColls but one look from this man could set her heart to racing.

"Is she under yer protection, then?" MacDonnell asked, unsure of what to do.

Callum nodded. "Aye, she is."

To be used as bait, Kate corrected him silently. His ransom until he had her uncle. She said nothing in front of the innkeeper, but she planned on setting Callum Mac-Gregor straight the moment they were alone.

Which was about to be any moment. Kate swallowed audibly when Callum clutched her hand and pulled her toward the stairs.

"Make certain you request extra bedding from your friend the innkeeper," she demanded on the way up. "I wish him to know that you will be sleeping on the floor and not in the same bed with me. I am not a trollop."

Callum ignored her. When he reached the room, he flung the door open and stepped inside, leaving her to follow.

Kate glowered at his lack of chivalry and stepped past him to survey the small room. As she had suspected, there was only one bed. Callum knew his way around the inn, that much was obvious. She eyed the old fur blanket on the bed and wondered how many times he had tumbled a maid upon it. The thought of it brought heat rushing to her face and a sharp prick of anger to her heart.

"I'll have Ferguson's wife bring ye somethin' to eat."

"And where will you be?" Kate asked, turning to him.

"Below stairs, sharin' a drink with my men."

Her brow rose sharply. Of course, he didn't want her around while he guzzled his brew and dragged any number of willing wenches to his lap. Well, she certainly was not about to spoil his eve. Let him bed them all, what did she care?

"I dinna want ye—"

"Och, I know perfectly well what you want," she accused him. "Just do not bring your women back here with you. The door will be barred."

His only answer was a slow smile that dared her to do it. "Dinna leave this room," he warned as he left, shutting the door behind him.

Kate stared at the door, and then snapped her mouth shut. Did he truly believe he could order her about because she was his captive? He was a fool if he did. And an even bigger fool to believe she would obey him.

~

An hour later, seated at a long table with his men, Callum lifted a tankard of ale to his lips. Many of the inn's patrons had retired above stairs, but the tavern was still crowded enough for Callum to almost miss Kate's entrance. Graham sat beside him, telling him about a wench he planned on meeting later that night, but Callum did not hear a word, so arrested was he by the sight of Kate standing in the doorway. A snood of dyed ruby ribbon was fastened beneath her hair and tied in a bow on top. Long, lustrous blue-black curls fell down her back, almost to her waist. She wore a kirtle of indigo wool, given to her, no doubt, by Ferguson's wife. A shawl of deep ruby draped her shoulders. It was not the sight of her drawing her full lower lip between her teeth when she could not find her captors, or even her wide, searching eyes, that made his heart pause, but the stubborn tilt of her chin when her gaze finally found his. She knew he would be angry that she had defied him, but she was not afraid. Damn him, but her fearlessness pleased him.

"Saints, she's breathtaking," Callum heard Graham say. Callum nodded as he stared at her with helpless admiration. She was the stark beauty of a winter night shrouded in the soft crimson of the setting sun.

He swallowed hard, and then his expression hardened, as well. Hell! Any one of these rogue patrons would think naught of causing her harm. Did she not understand his clan was outlawed, that the MacGregors were considered lower than slaves to many Scots? It did not matter that she looked more bonny than ever before; she was a daft fool who would get them all killed.

He almost knocked his chair over when he stood up as she made her way toward his table. She paused for a moment seeing his fierce scowl but then squared her shoulders and continued on. Jamie reached her before she reached the table and snatched her arm to escort her safely to the bench.

Kate sat directly across from the glowering laird, which earned her another deep-throated grumble. She toyed with the idea of commenting on his constant sour mood, but he looked about ready to leap over the table and throttle her, so she simply smiled at him instead, though it took enormous effort.

"Good eve, my laird."

"Return to yer room, Kate," he warned in a quiet, menacing tone.

"I cannot," she replied sweetly. "I am hungry. Dear Robena went to so much bother bathing and dressing me, I felt it unkind to ask her to feed me, as well. I would much rather dine here, with you."

Callum considered dragging her back above stairs, but doing so would most likely cause a brawl. He looked around at the patrons, his jaw tightening. Many of the men were already staring at her. They looked away when they caught his murderous gaze.

"Verra well," he conceded, motioning to a serving wench before returning his gaze to Kate. "Eat, and be quick aboot it."

"I hope I didn't spoil your merriment for the eve." Kate offered him a cheeky smile that said the opposite, then glanced up at the buxom blonde laying a trencher of steaming mutton stew before her. When the wench threw herself into Graham's lap and not Callum's, Kate didn't know whether to feel relieved or angry with herself for being possessive of him. That's why she'd defied him and came down here, wasn't it? She hated the thought of him enjoying his evening with a pretty wench. But it was clear Callum MacGregor did not allow himself much merriment.

"Just eat and dinna concern yerself with me." Callum tore at his bread and shoved it into his mouth, seeming to forget about her.

"Very well." Kate fought the urge to fling her trencher at him. She may have been wrong about him wanting a wench with his supper, but he was a callous bastard nonetheless. She decided not to spare him another thought. Heavens, she was starving! She lowered her head to inhale the delicious aromas of her supper. When a loud belch exploded through Angus's lips, she lifted her thick lashes from her food.

"What a perfect tribute to so fine a meal, Angus."

The burly brute roared with laughter, but it was the sound of Kate's mirth that made Callum lift his gaze to her once again. He stared at the slender curve of her jaw, the soft crinkle of her nose when she laughed. He felt en-

tranced by the way her eyes danced. For a moment, he
relished the sound of her joy. She made him think of
hope. She made him want things he never thought about
wanting before. It had taken him years to build Camlochlin. 'Twas his fortress, his sanctuary, second in his
heart only to his name. 'Twas all he had and all he ever
wanted, hoping for nothing more because he'd probably
be dead in a few years. And he did not mind dying, so
long as it was on his terms and not the Campbells', and
with bravery in battle. He had never considered having a
family, though he would like to have sons to carry on the
MacGregor name. He had never hoped to listen to the
music of a woman's tinkling laughter echoing off the steep
mountain walls, satisfied in knowing 'twas he who gave
her joy. He would not hope for it now.

"To Brodie." Angus raised his tankard, breaking Callum's thoughts, "May the bairn his lovely wife Netta
carries fer him look like its mother and not Graham."

Graham tossed Brodie a smug wink, which Brodie answered by punching him in the arm. Soon the merriment
around them grew. The men swore oaths that would have
made any other woman at the table blush and rebuke
them. But, damn her, she continued to laugh, addling Callum's brain thoroughly. Callum did not join in the song,
nor in the raucous laughter that followed. He was, for the
time being, content to sit and study Kate—when she
wasn't looking at him.

He watched her so closely he did not notice the man
approaching their table from behind her. No one noticed
him until he slammed a coin down directly in front of her.
Laughter stopped abruptly, and every eye rose to meet
those of the stranger, including Callum's.

"Ye have had her long enough," the knave announced to Callum. "And ye've done naught but gape at her like a fresh-faced whelp. Now I want her."

The only sign of Callum's fury was the slight clenching of his jaw. No other muscle moved. "Take yer coin and leave before 'tis too late to do so." His voice was nothing more than a low growl. Kate found herself unable to take her eyes off him.

"Tonight I'll have a MacGregor bitch in my bed," the man behind her mocked.

Everything happened so quickly in the instant that followed, Kate had no time to react. The stranger's hand clamped on her sore shoulder, making her cry out as he hauled her to her feet. Callum stood up simultaneously, seeming to defy time as he drew his massive sword. He whirled it over his head and brought it down with such force it smashed into splinters the thick wooden table that separated him from the stranger, sending food and drinks crashing to the floor. Callum leaped over the cleaved wood and held the point of his blade against the man's throat. His calm expression had dissolved into a storm of black rage.

"Think well aboot yer next breath. It'll be yer last."

Silence descended upon the tavern, every eye pinned to the man still gripping Kate. Every eye, that is, but Kate's. Try as she might, she could not tear her gaze away from Callum MacGregor. He seemed to have grown five more inches in height. The breadth of his shoulders cast dark shadows over her and her would-be attacker. As she gazed up at him, her breath went still by the power and steady strength of his arm, the promise of destruction in his piercing glare. She knew why this man had never been caught.

"Ease yer sword, MacGregor. Ease yer sword." The stranger released Kate and took a step back. He was three shades paler than when he first arrived at the table. His Adam's apple danced, swallowing an audible gulp the moment his throat was clear of Callum's blade. Brodie crunched into a juicy pear. The sound propelled the man to turn and run. Before Callum could sheathe his weapon, the stranger was gone.

Kate blinked. A hand clasped her wrist tightly. It took a moment for her to realize it was Callum who held her, and when she did, she opened her mouth to speak.

"Bid good eve to my men," he ordered, cutting her off. Then, before she could do as he commanded, he dragged her toward the stairs.

"Let me go!" She tried to pull her hand away from him, but she didn't even slow his pace.

"That's twice I saved yer life." Callum said tightly without turning to face her. "Dinna give me yer cheek."

When he reached the room, he shoved the door open and fair flung her inside, then slammed the door shut behind them.

Kate rounded on him, her eyes sparked with fury. "You will tell me what I've done to cause your wrath against me! And do not tell me it's because I'm a Campbell. I did nothing to you!"

Callum stared at her when she shouted at him. A battle played across his features. He didn't know whether he wanted to throttle her or drag her into his arms, grateful that he was here tonight to save her. Anger lit his eyes like lightning and his jaw clenched with fury, but when he opened his mouth to tell her, he found that he had no words. He turned and stormed toward the window. When he reached it, he whirled on his heel again and raked his gaze boldly over her.

Kate went still. He was touching her. The longing in his eyes shocked her and made her tremble. Never in her life had she felt such a maze of emotions. She was angry with him, and she wanted to run into his arms so badly her legs almost ached with the need. She knew he would not turn her away again. For while his expression was hard, his eyes gleamed with warmth and the promise of complete possession. He wanted her. A flame ignited somewhere in her belly at the thought. God help her, but he was so terribly handsome standing there heaving like a dark dragon on the verge of plundering a village.

"Callum." She whispered his name, breaking the silence that seemed to stretch on endlessly. "I don't want to be your enemy anymore. I . . ."

If her plea softened him at all, he made no show of it. His expression was no more forgiving than it had been a moment before. "D'ye no' understand that my clan has been proscribed?"

"I thought we were safe here," she tried to explain, but her words faded when he took a step closer to her.

"We? Yer no' a MacGregor. Ye dinna know what it means to be one, or the dangers of being a friend to one."

"Aye, I do," she assured him, understanding now why he'd demanded she stay in the room. He had tried to protect her. "No one may aid you—"

"Upon death or branding!" Callum's voice erupted into a roar.

Kate turned away. She had to. He was telling her that

they could not even be friends, and just looking at him made her want more than that. God, protect her neck from the gallows, she wanted so much more.

"We have been declared worthless, nonhuman. A price has been placed on the heads of our men, women, and children! Our lands are free to any taker."

Tears gathered over the rims of Kate's eyes as she understood fully the depth of his pride and the reason for it. "It is as if you no longer exist." She brought her gaze back to his. "You feel forsaken, even by God. Callum, I do understand. And I am so sorry."

"I dinna want yer pity," he said, cursing himself inwardly. He should rebuke her, shake her, push her away until she was so afraid of him her fear and hatred destroyed whatever else she felt. "I'll no' allow ye to shed tears fer my clan. Ye dinna understand the danger in it."

She did understand, but at that moment she didn't care. God's mercy, she doubted even Robert would forgive her for siding with The Devil, but she wanted Callum to kiss her again. She didn't want their names to matter anymore. She wanted to touch him and forget laws and proscriptions. But could he ever forget his past and what her family had done to him?

She was sure he could hear her heart pounding. She wanted to tell him how she felt, but her mind had ceased to think of anything save the sheer size of him, the smell of sweat and fury lingering about his flesh, and the longing in his eyes for something unattainable.

He moved toward her, but a knock at the door made him pause and ushered a low growl from his throat.

Kate did not turn to follow his path to the door but closed her eyes instead and chewed her lower lip. She listened while he argued with Ferguson MacDonnell about payment for the table he had smashed. Then she near leaped out of her flesh when the door slammed shut again.

She could feel his eyes on her. Hard, dangerous eyes that had sworn vengeance upon her entire clan. Hot, burning eyes that ached with hunger for her.

"Take the bed," he snapped.

Turning to him, Kate scowled, frustrated by his deep conviction to despise her no matter how hard she tried to make him like her. "You make it difficult to ignore the true reason you saved my life."

His expression on her hardened, as if she'd just given him a great insult. "I would no' have let ye die, even if I killed yer uncle."

Kate was relieved to hear him say it. She was right about him all along. But . . . "Sometimes it's difficult to believe you care for my safety when you continue to look at me as if I were your worst enemy."

"Lass," he said, and the silken depth of raw desire in his voice made her stagger. "If I cared naught fer yer safety, ye would no' be standing there."

Kate's nostrils flared as she folded her hands into fists at her sides. "Where would I be, then?"

"Ye would be spread across that bed, beneath me."

Kate's face burned at the thought. In fact, she felt as if her entire body was about to go up in flames. "Your threats are empty," she challenged, refusing to believe he would force himself on her. "As would be your eye sockets if you dared touch me uninvited."

He actually chuckled, mocking her warning as he crossed the room.

She backed away when the distance between them shortened. "Besides," she said, hastily employing a different tactic to ensure that he remained chivalrous. "You would be making *love* to a *Campbell*."

He walked past her, a slight slant of his lips making her palms moisten and her knees go soft. "Nae, I would merely be havin' my way with one, which in our case would be just as dangerous."

Kate said nothing more but climbed into the bed fully clothed. She pulled the coverlet up to her chin and watched him settle down beside the hearth for the night.

Soft firelight danced along the walls. The room was silent save for the crackle of firewood being devoured by flames, along with Callum's crude promise drumming in her head. Fate was cruel to have cast her into the care of such a cold man, and crueler still because she liked the brute. He despised her, making it perfectly clear that his desire for her was naught more than pure lust in its most basic form.

"You've nae more need to treat me cruelly, MacGregor," she spoke softly in the darkness. "I will do my best to remember who you are from this night on."

There was a movement from where Callum lay on the floor, and then, like a mad war god rising from the bowels of the Earth, he rose to his feet and stormed out the door.

Chapter Fourteen

~~~~~~~~~~~

KATE ROAMED THE DIM HALLS of the inn, praying that no male patrons were lurking about looking for a wench to warm their beds. She held a small candle to light her way past endless doors behind which laughter and the sounds of harsh groaning echoed and made her cheeks burn.

Logic told her to leave Callum alone. He had every right to want to be as far away from her as he could get. And if she had any wits left at all, she would be glad he stayed away from her. But after the moments spent waiting for him to return had stretched into an hour, she knew her heart was the true culprit, the direst danger to her well being. She sighed tightly, trying to resolve herself to the bare fact that she was obsessed with the man accused of killing her father. *Stop it, Kate,* she chastised herself, holding the candle in front of her to illuminate a path toward the stairs. *He did not kill your father. But he is going to kill your uncle. And then they will kill him. Get him out of your mind.*

A woman's laughter seeped from behind a door to her

left, halting Kate's steps. What if he was in one of these rooms bedding some wench? Visions of his naked body poised over a heated smile assaulted her. What if he was whispering tender words of love into someone's ear while he . . .

A door opened and Kate almost fled, not wanting to see him exiting the room. The wench exiting the room was a bonny lass with flaxen hair that fell in limp coils around her cherubic face and over the mounds of round, milky breasts she worked lazily to conceal. She offered Kate a pleasant smile while she tied the laces of her gown, then hurried past her and disappeared down the stairs. Kate almost fainted with relief when Graham appeared at the doorway next, adjusting his plaid. She blushed when he grinned at her, a pair of roguish dimples slashing his cheeks, his hazy emerald gaze hooded with spent satisfaction.

"Greetings, lass," he said and leaned his shoulder against the doorframe. "I never would have believed he tossed ye out."

"He did not toss me out," Kate advised the strapping Highlander with an inquisitive smile of her own. She liked this man. His joy came easily and his brash style was strangely attractive. "Is there a line of women waiting to get into this room, Graham?" she continued when his eyes lit on her in amusement. "How many wenches have you entertained so far this eve?"

"Och, but ye have a sharp tongue, lass." He laughed, making Kate realize that she missed the sound terribly. She studied him for a moment, understanding why the women in the tavern sought his company, for he was fair of face with sunlit hair and a lithe body. Aye, he was quite handsome in a roguish way, she decided. His smile wasn't as devastating as Callum's, but it was certainly charming enough.

"What are ye doing roaming the halls at this ungodly hour?" He shoved a thin twig between his teeth and chewed on it. "It's not safe fer such a lass as yerself."

She shrugged. "Callum left the room earlier and I . . ." She bit her lip and looked at the doors framing her on either side.

Graham lifted a curious eyebrow at her as understanding washed over him. "A night's pleasure would do him good. But fear not, he is not inside any of these rooms. Fer come morn, naught will change fer him."

The candle flame quivered when Kate's hand shook slightly. She should have been relieved by Graham's words, but she felt worse than before. "What did my grandfather do to him? Tell me. Please, Graham."

Graham studied her for a moment, then drew out a long sigh. "He was shackled to a wall fer nine years, sometimes fer weeks at a time without pause, without a day in the sun."

Kate took a step back and lifted her hand to her mouth. "My God," she choked on a woeful sob. "He was a child. His scars . . . his wrists . . ."

Graham nodded. "He fought to free himself. He finally did when . . ."

But Kate couldn't bear to hear another word. She fled down the stairs, needing to find Callum. She rounded a sharp corner and almost bounced off a wall that stood in her way. The candle flickered out, and for a moment she was engulfed in darkness. Then she heard the crackle of fire and slowly turned around. She was in the tavern section of the inn. Light from the great hearth fire just behind another wall sifted through the archway, dimly lighting another path. She followed it, though a voice in her head told her to flee back up the stairs.

Callum slept in a heavy wooden chair in front of the hearth, an empty tankard strewn in the rushes beneath his dangling hand. Kate took a step closer to him until she could see his perfect features in the coppery candescence. He was a warrior, but asleep, the vulnerable tilt of his lips drew her closer. He took her breath away. She let her eyes drift over the broad expanse of his chest, the sleek, smooth sinew that shaped his arms. Her gaze traveled down the length of his body, lingering for a breath on his lean hips and then continuing, with a stifled moan, to his long, muscular legs sprawled out before him. God's teeth, there was so much of him.

Suddenly, he cried out. "Nae!" He jerked his hands forward, and Kate's eyes fell to his leather-bound wrists. Was he dreaming of her grandfather's dungeon? The terror and torment in his voice almost felled her to her knees. Without thinking, she reached for him, wanting to ease his pain and wake him from his nightmare. When her fingertips brushed his wrist, his eyes shot open. His hand snapped up and gripped her arm with such force she bit her lip not to cry out. He pulled her down, almost on top of him, and stared into her eyes with a mixture of anguish and haunting fear, the likes of which she had never seen before and would not soon forget.

"Callum," she breathed, too afraid to utter anything more.

The wall fell away from his eyes. His dream was over. As quickly as he had yanked her to him, he eased his hold

on her arm. But he did not let her go. Her face was close
to his, so close she could feel the heat of his uneven
breath upon her lips. But it was his eyes that paralyzed
her. No longer were they dark with resolve to hate, no
longer were they smoldering blue orbs of forbidden desire. Kate's heart wrenched within her at the stark sorrow
staring back at her, consuming her soul, as it did his.

She whispered his name again as the weight of his unguarded gaze struck her full in the heart. Before she
could stop herself, she threw herself against his chest and
held him.

"I'm sorry for what he did to you."

He did not answer her right away. First his arms came
around her, slowly, as if he feared he might break her. He
ran his palm over the length of her hair, down her back,
holding her head closer. With her ear pressed so closely
to him, she had no trouble hearing the fierce pounding of
his heart.

"What are ye doin' here, lass?" her asked her. Then, as
if he realized what he was doing, he gently pushed her
away.

Now she did fall to her knees beside his chair. The
shadows returned, drifting across the surface of his eyes
as he stared down at her. She fought to hold on to whatever gentleness and vulnerability she had just seen in him
before it completely disappeared again. She could reach
him, mayhap touch him if he would only release his
anger and hatred for just a moment.

"I was looking for you," she told him softly, clinging
to the trace of tenderness in his tone.

His features softened again, but he looked away from

her and into the flames of the hearth fire. "Return to yer bed, Kate."

Even against the soft golden hue of firelight, his profile was all hard, harsh planes. Even his eyes gave naught away now about the torment he had suffered. Still, Kate ached to hold him. Part of her knew it would be like reaching her hand toward a ravenous lion. Her fingers could very easily be bitten off. Och, but to touch such a magnificent beast, to touch him and not be eaten alive.

Slowly, casting off her fear, she lifted her fingers to his wrist and touched the leather cuff that covered scars too horrible to look upon. He turned and looked at her and her heart stopped, ready to be devoured. She drew in a deep, quivering breath and straightened her fingers to stroke his wrist. "Do you wear these to remember?"

"Nae, I wear them to ferget."

Kate squeezed her eyes shut, hoping to trap the tears she would shed so unabashedly for him. But they came nonetheless. She expected him to pull away, but he turned his hand in hers until their palms met. Then he closed his fingers around hers. His touch was gentle, whisper soft.

"Cease yer cryin' fer me. It willna change a moment of the past."

But she wished she could change it. Even more than that, she wanted to change his future. She wanted him to let go of his hatred and . . . and what? Kate bit her bottom lip, keeping her eyes fastened on his fingers. What did she want? God's fury, what did it matter? He was a MacGregor and she a Campbell. Their destiny was already written in the law, carved into his flesh. There was naught she could do to change it.

"I dinna want yer sympathy." The roughness of his voice only intensified the plea beneath.

"But it is mine to give, my laird."

Above her, Callum closed his eyes. His fingers moved over hers, stroking, caressing. Her hand was so small, so soft. He should send her back to the room before the sight and scent of her drove him completely mad. Then again, mayhap madness would be a welcome respite from the constant darkness inside him.

His heart went soft when he looked down at her bent head. She looked like an angel kneeling beside him, so ready to offer him atonement for what she did not know. "Mayhap," he murmured, "I should accept what ye offer me."

Kate did not understand what he meant, but she remembered the heated emotion in his eyes before the innkeeper interrupted them earlier that night. She tried to pull her hand away, but his fingers closed around hers more tightly. Kate's head reeled. She had the feeling of falling off one of his giant Highland cliffs, and his hand, so strong and steady, was all that could save her.

"You frighten me," she told him, still not daring to meet his gaze. "Yet I feel safer with you than anyone in my life. How can that be?"

"I wouldna hurt ye, Kate." The husky timbre of his voice felt so tender to her ears.

With breath held, she lifted her head and set her eyes on his. He held her searching gaze for a moment before she found the strength to speak again. "Do you like me, then?"

Before she had a chance to guard her heart against it, Callum's smile washed over her. It hit her full force and she felt dizzy, muddleheaded. She was almost glad that he smiled so rarely, for surely she would lose her heart to him completely, clutched in his vengeful fingers.

"Aye, I do like ye, Kate Campbell. I must be daft, but I do."

"Truly?" And then she grinned at him and watched, delighted and tingling all the way down to her ankles as his smile widened into a torturously resplendent grin of his own. A new spark of hope lit Kate's eyes. "Does this mean you will forget about killing my uncle?" When his grin vanished and he turned away, she tugged on his hand. "They would never stop hunting you."

"'Tis late," he said and stood to his feet. "We're leavin' at first light, so ye best get some sleep."

He pulled her to her feet and took up his steps behind her when she headed back toward the stairs. He couldn't take his eyes off her. The gentle sway of her hips as she climbed the steps drove him to distraction. She was the granddaughter of the man who destroyed everything Callum was. He should feel naught but contempt for her. Instead, he found himself aching to hold her again. To tell her of the dreams he had given up years ago. Kate Campbell was carving her way through his flesh as deeply as the gouges that encircled his wrists, and he had to stop it. He would never allow her to reach his heart the way the cold, cutting metal of Liam Campbell's shackles had. Still, when she turned to look at him over her shoulder, he felt his heart quicken.

She entered the dimly lit room first and then turned to him while he bolted the door. "Callum, I . . ."

"What?" He looked at her, taking in the spark of apprehension she tried to conceal beneath her veil of dark lashes. He had to use all his strength of will not to gather her up in his arms and kiss her senseless. When she took a step toward him, he gritted his teeth and held up his palm. "Would ye set yer life to ruin, Kate?"

She shook her head, ignoring his attempt to keep her at a distance. "I would talk to you, comfort you from your memories."

His smile mocked her, but the sorrow that haunted him was evident in his husky voice. "I fear nae one can do that. No' even ye." But she could. She did, even now.

"When I was little I was told that hatred was poison." She moved closer still, until her intoxicating scent filled his lungs. He clenched his fingers in an effort to stop him from taking hold of her. "I see the truth of it now." Her fingers shook as she raised them to his face, touching him, stroking him as if he were a beast she meant to soothe. "I would stop it before it kills you."

"Kate." He uttered her name as if it pained him to speak it. As surely as her sword had pierced his flesh, her trusting, worshipful eyes caused him to take leave of his senses. He had been a villain for so long, he no longer knew what it felt like to be anything else. Until she looked at him. "Ye shouldna care aboot such things."

She nodded and began to turn away from him. "But I do."

His fingers closed around hers and he pulled her back, capturing her waist with his other arm. He swept her off her feet before he even kissed her. Covering her small hand with his, he brought her fingers back to his face as he lowered his mouth to hers.

Chapter Fifteen

⌒

HIS KISS WAS HOT, passionate, his tongue a fiery brand exploring the deepest recesses of her mouth. He was hungry and hard, and Kate felt a thread of fear course through her. When his hand cupped her buttocks and razed her against his stiff erection, she arched her back to end their kiss. He bent with her, cupping her body with even more intimacy. His ragged breath along her throat thrilled the fear right out of her. His large, rough hand untying the laces of her gown made her forget everything but the feel of him, the scent of him. She didn't want to think about consequences. She didn't care about them.

Her breast came loose, and he moaned, taking it in his hand. The raw desire in his hooded gaze when he broke their kiss to draw her nipple into his mouth made her groin ache for something she didn't understand. Something only he could satisfy.

He carried her to the bed, gently biting her nipple until it grew as tight as the rest of her. They fell to the mattress. His body covered hers, but his weight did not crush her.

She opened her mouth to him again and clenched her fingers in his hair, pulling him closer while he kissed her. His hands tore at her gown, pulling the thick folds up over her knees. Then his fingers slipped beneath. His breath was ragged, heavy with desire. Kate went rigid when his palms grazed her inner thigh. His hand lingered there while he spread the pad of his thumb over the hard nub of her passion. Red-hot pleasure bolted through her and she squeezed her legs together. He spread her apart again with his knees, slid his hand behind her rump, and sank down onto her.

Kate knew they should stop. But the feel of his arousal between her thighs was so basely erotic, so insatiably intimate, instead of fighting him, she moved against him. He was long, and thick, and so very hard he made her melt into pool of liquid passion. He growled low in her ear and then whispered what he was going to do to her, with words that made her blush.

With one final tug, Callum pulled her skirts over her waist and rose up above her. He looked down at her, wild to taste her while his hand swept beneath his plaid and closed around his shaft. His gaze met hers a moment after his plaid rose over the tip of his swollen head. Her eyes opened wide, and she pushed herself up toward the headboard to be away from him.

It gave him a moment to consider what he was about to do, and to remember what would become of her if he did.

He yanked her skirts down and climbed off her.

Kate didn't move. She didn't breathe while he sat at the edge of the bed and rubbed his hand down his face. She didn't try to stop him when he left the room, though she wanted to. She had never been intimate with a man before, but Callum's touch, his kiss, his voice, everything about him ignited her. Every nerve in her body screamed for him, but she let him go. She had to. Not because of his name, but because of hers. He would never see her as anything more than his enemy.

She wasn't angry that he tried to bed her. Dear God, she would have let him do it if he hadn't stopped. Nor could she fault him for the anger that hauled him off her. She would never forget the disgust that twisted his features when he looked at her face. She wondered, pulling the coverlet up around her neck and wiping her eyes, if Callum would truly release her after he killed her uncle. She reasoned that if he tossed her into the pit, it was a fair trade. He wouldn't touch her again, of that she was certain. It was better that way, she told herself even while her body ached for him. Hell, but the size of him frightened her. She knew enough about mating from raising livestock to know that she could have been carrying his bairn tomorrow if he had not stopped. How would she explain *that* to her brother?

Staring up at the ceiling, she tried to remember her life before the Devil MacGregor had charged into it and changed everything. Had she been happy in her fields tending her sheep, listening to her brother's tales of brave, noble men? Aye, she had. For she'd been oblivious to the searing, aching need to be kissed by such a man. She imagined the torture of living with Callum in the future, seeing his face every day and knowing she would never be anything more than a pawn of revenge. It would be painful indeed, but she was willing to suffer it. At least she wouldn't be shackled to a wall until it became so unbearable that carving off her hands would be a better option.

God's mercy, what did she know of sorrow, of anger? Nothing! She sniffed and wiped her nose, bracing her shoulders against the soft mattress beneath her. The wonderful men in her life had taught her how to fight. Now was not the time to surrender. She must conquer her attraction to Callum MacGregor. But no matter how much he despised her, she would never hate him again. And she was going to stop him from hating her, even if it killed her.

Chapter Sixteen

WHEN KATE AWOKE the next morn, she was still alone in the room. Her pulse quickened when she sat up in her bed and stared at the empty place before the hearth. Callum hadn't returned. Was he gone? Would he have left her alone here? Had he taken Graham and the others and gone to his holding without her? She looked around the small room while her heart pounded madly in her chest. She knew he did not want her company, but would he just abandon her here in this . . . this . . . brothel? She whipped the blanket off her body and sprang from the bed. Cold rushes pricked her toes when she ran across the floor and threw open the shutters on the window.

Sunshine exploded in her eyes and spilled over her face and down her hair. She heard the shouts of men directly below and leaned out the small window to get a better view. When she saw Callum and his men, relief filled her. Brodie and Angus packed food into their leather saddlebags while Jamie surveyed a nearby patch of purple thistle.

She couldn't help but admire Callum while he bent to saddle his mount. Damnation, the more she looked at him, the more handsome he became. Two strands of his dark hair were fastened at the back of his head, while the rest fell over his plaid. He was a tumultuous, rebellious warrior, she decided, gazing at him, and though she was the object of his contempt, she couldn't help but admire his resolve to keep his name alive. Surely even Robert would see the honor in his fight. When he turned and looked up at her window, she waved at him.

"D'ye plan on sleepin' all day?" he called up to her with a fierce frown Kate was growing quite accustomed to.

She'd decided to ignore what happened between them the evening before. He didn't take her, so no harm was done. It was better if they both put it out of their minds.

Without saying a word, she disappeared from the window, combed her fingers through her hair, and snatched her shawl from where it hung over a chair. Within seconds of peeking out the window, she dashed down the stairs and out the door.

"Good morn," she greeted, tilting her face up to Callum's when she reached him, and then blushing to her roots. So much for putting their last encounter out of her mind.

A breeze blew a strand of dark hair across his face. The lock swept across his unshaven jaw and he did nothing to remove it, which only made Kate ache to do it herself. He stared down at her for a moment, long enough to make her insides melt. He possessed the confidence to conquer, the intoxicating power to thoroughly seduce her, and the strength to resist doing either.

"I purchased a horse fer ye. Can ye ride?" he asked.

"Aye." Kate's smile deepened, already seduced by his coarse charm and the full suppleness of his lips. "But I tell you, I will not get a wink of sleep."

She flashed her dark eyes at him and spun on her heel before he could reply, which would have been nothing more than a grunt by the look on his face.

Callum stood by his mount and watched the gentle sway of her hips as she made her way toward Jamie and her new mount. A moment later he swore under his breath and chased after her.

"'Tis already saddled," he said, coming up behind her. "I did it while ye slept."

"Ah, my thanks." Kate turned and graced him with yet another tender smile. "'Tis a fine horse, too." She lifted her hands to the saddle horn to mount but felt strong hands span her waist and lift her up. Her heart lurched at the gentleness of his touch.

Once seated, she stared down into his face. Something had changed in his expression. He was looking at her with such raw yearning she bit her lip and almost made it bleed. Seconds passed, and he did not turn away from her. His eyes revealed thoughts he wanted to utter, ways he wanted to touch her, not cruelly, but curiously, tenderly. Could she have been wrong about why he stopped last eve?

"Last eve was . . ." He ground his jaw then began again. "I was no' thinkin' clearly."

Kate blinked, then forced her smile to remain. "Of course, nor was I."

And then, as suddenly as his emotions appeared on his face, they vanished once again and he strode away from her.

Beside them, Jamie watched with astonishment, and then a knowing smile crept over his face.

Graham finally moseyed out of the inn a few moments later with yet another wench attached to his arm. He bid the lass farewell and joined Callum, ignoring the lethal glare his friend tossed him because he was tardy.

The troop traveled for the rest of the day with merry song echoing across the glens and lochs. The mood among the men was light on their way back to their beloved home, and Kate could not help but revel in their cheer. The land grew more beautiful with each league they traveled. The air was fragranced with heather and linseed. But the view that held Kate enthralled was that of her rescuer's broad back a few feet ahead of her. It seemed that after every fifth breath, Callum turned to look at her as if to reassure himself that she still rode with his band. She thought about riding at his elbow to save him the trouble but decided she rather liked the fact that he was concerned she would run off.

Graham took up his pace beside Kate's mount and explained to her how some MacGregors came to live on the Isle of Mist.

"We found a more peaceful life in Skye. Even the Campbells do not bother to travel so far to hunt us. After Callum escaped yer grandfather's prison, he fled to the isle and was welcomed by the MacLeods, and even the MacKinnons and MacDonalds. Many of them helped him build Camlochlin. When we heard where he was, some of us left our homes and came to live with him and fight by his side."

Kate brushed a strand of her hair out of her eyes and

narrowed her gaze on Callum's back. "Think you he will ever stop killing Campbells?"

"He already has, lass." When she turned to him he slanted his gaze to her and winked. "'Tis a start, aye?"

~

The next morning, they traveled onward to Glenelg, toward the Isle of Skye, crossing the narrows by boat. The captain, Seamus MacRae, was a slim man of medium height and with dark hair as long as Kate's, his bound at the nape. His laughter was quick and robust. Of course, that could be attributed to the three swigs of whiskey he'd consumed at the start of their journey.

"Ye brought a wife back wi' this time, eh, MacGregor?" the captain hollered over his shoulder to where Callum stood resting against the bowsprit, sharing a word with Graham. "She'll give ye bonny bairns." He lifted his boot to a crate and leaned on his bent knee to study Kate more closely. "Aye, bonny indeed."

Kate's eyes darted to Callum when he straightened and began walking toward them. Och, how she wished their names were different. A touch of flame stole across her cheeks at the notion of being wed to so fine a man. She knew in that moment that should he look into her eyes he would see the quickening of her heart. Her vision took in every splendid detail of him, from his dusty calves to the flare of his shoulders. Not a devil, but a man in whose arms she had found warmth and protection. A man whose kisses made her forget who he was, whose smile was more glorious than Lucifer's, and rarer, as well.

"She's no' my wife, MacRae," Callum announced upon reaching them. "I took her from her home against her will, and I bear the evidence of her capture upon my thigh." He pulled the edge of his plaid over his knee to expose his wound. He nodded his head in agreement when the captain grew pale and gaped at her. "She's a hell-witch, and were I you"—his gaze darkened with warning—"I wouldna stare at her so boldly."

"As ye say." Seamus took a step back, still unable to believe that a mere lass had inflicted injury to the mighty MacGregor chieftain. "I have some rope in m' quarters should ye need it."

"Aye," Kate rounded on her captor, her eyes blazing. Had she thought him warm? Fool! "You could hang yourself with it!"

Her angry retort earned her a slow, devastating smile from the MacGregor chieftain.

"Och, but she has ballocks the size of the Cuillins," Seamus MacRae laughed and turned away. "I'll leave the wench to ye, Devil. Some might say ye deserve it."

When they were alone, Callum's smile deepened, making Kate's toes curl and her teeth clench. "Ye're learnin' well, Kate."

"Learning what?" Though her question was curt, she sighed miserably immediately after she asked it. "That every moment you spend with this hell-witch is a sacrifice you suffer for the name MacGregor?" He opened his mouth to speak, but Kate cut him off, holding up her palm. "That you intend to declare your hatred of me to all of Scotland?"

She turned away, leaving Callum to stare at her profile. The wind blew her dark waves across her face, compelling him to lift his hand to her cheek. When his fingertips touched her flesh, the need to touch more of her

Chapter Seventeen

"HOW DO WE KNOW the gel is not a sympathizer?"

Robert Campbell ceased pacing and watched his uncle leap to his feet, lean across the table, and snatch the man who spoke by the throat.

"My niece is no sympathizer," Duncan snarled.

The man nodded, then rubbed his neck when the earl released him.

Robert continued his worn path in the rushes of Hugh Menzie's great hall. He raked his fingers through the dark strands of hair falling over his forehead. He aimed a frustrated glance at his uncle, who was reclining once again at one of three long trestle tables. Neither Duncan nor the rowdy group of Menzies sharing their ale with him paid Robert any heed. It had been over a se'nnight since the MacGregors had abducted his sister, and they were no closer to finding her than they had been the day she was taken. They had gathered men from Breadalbane to Rannoch. They had enough to face MacGregor and his men if they caught up with him now.

Robert had reminded his uncle that the miscreant laird had sent almost all of his men back to his homestead. He traveled now with only four others. They had to catch up with the MacGregors before they returned to the Devil's lair, where they would face his army. But Hugh Menzie, laird of the Menzie clan, had news for the Earl of Argyll, and hence Robert found himself, at present, mumbling blasphemies meant only for the vilest tongue. He did not care.

"Uncle." He stiffened his arms at his side. "Uncle!" he called more forcefully when no one looked up. "I must insist that we leave here at once and take up our search." He almost faltered at the murderous gleam in his uncle's eyes when Duncan finally, slowly set them on him.

"We know all we need to know," Robert continued, refusing to be moved. He had cowered once already when he first faced Callum MacGregor, and it may have cost his sister her life. "The Devil attacked and killed seven of Laird Menzie's kin just a few nights past. Let us make haste while his tracks are still fresh."

"The lad is right!" a rough-looking man with hair the color of charcoal agreed. Another followed, slamming his cup on the table and rising to his feet.

Duncan's lips hooked into a sinuous smile that he cast at his nephew before he raised his cup to the others. "Let us be off, then."

~

Robert's hopes of finding Kate began to falter two days later when they hadn't found so much as a broken twig to keep them on the right path. How had the MacGregors disappeared without a trace? None of the men traveling

with him and his uncle knew where the Devil's holding
was. It could be leagues away, or just beyond the next
hill. Surveying the rocky peaks and rolling hillocks
around him, Robert could not help but wonder if they
were not being watched. Could he and his meager army
of forty men survive an ambush of five? Hadn't all but
those five killed fifty of Duncan's men in Glen Orchy?
No one would aid them if they were attacked. The Highlanders they had questioned along the way had told them
nothing. Even those the earl had beaten and threatened to
hang claimed to know nothing of Callum MacGregor. If
his sister's life were not at stake, Robert would have admired such loyalty. The Highlanders did not seem frightened of the Devil, but of his uncle. And from what Robert
had witnessed thus far, they had good reason to be.

When Graham Grant had first told him about the Mac-
Gregor laird's imprisonment in his grandfather's dungeon, Robert had refused to believe him. He had barely
known Liam Campbell, for their father rarely took them
to Inverary. But Robert was certain no man of his ilk
could be so vile. But after what he'd witnessed so far
when his uncle questioned the Highlanders, he was no
longer so sure. Aye, Robert knew Duncan Campbell was
a warrior. The earl had reminded him of it often enough
when Robert was a boy. There was no shame in shedding
blood for the good of the country. But where was the
honor in torturing one's countrymen because they did not
give him the answers he desired?

Once Kate was returned to them safely, there would be
much to consider about remaining in his uncle's service.
As much as Robert hated to admit it, mayhap he was not
cut out for the coldhearted, underhanded business of

warring. He had certainly been deceived easily enough by the traitor, Grant. Damnation, why had he not suspected something amiss when Grant had informed him that the Devil had captured his uncle?

Like any other Campbell, Graham had known much about the centuries-long battle with the MacGregors. Robert wondered now if it was the subtle inflection of admiration lacing Graham's voice that had almost convinced *him* to admire the proscribed clan. The man pretending to be his kin had not denied that the one the Highlanders called the "Laird of the Mist" had massacred Liam Campbell's garrison. But he claimed to know for certain that the laird did not kill his grandfather, though Graham told him he would have had the right to do so. Robert had found it odd at the time to hear such unprejudiced talk from a Campbell, but Graham had assured him that his Breadalbane kin did not hold the same disdain for the MacGregors. He should have asked Graham how he knew the tale of his grandfather's dungeon was true. Instead, he let Kildun's guardsmen ride directly into the swords of their enemies.

A cold numbness trickled down Robert's spine, even now, at the memory of what had happened next. He'd been spared and brought before the warrior who led the battle. Stunned and shaken, he had turned to see that the man binding his wrists was Graham. Robert had fought against his tight hold, until he felt the tip of MacGregor's blade at his throat. But it wasn't the warm, wet metal on his flesh that halted his movements, and almost his heart. It was how badly MacGregor wanted him dead. It was clear in his eyes, in the cold snarl curling his mouth.

"Tell me where Argyll hides before I remove yer head."

Behind him, Graham had spoken quickly, dragging the chieftain's attention back to him. He spoke at first in Gaelic, causing the MacGregor's expression to darken, then informed him that the earl had gone to Glen Orchy, to the home of his dead brother.

Robert would have preferred that they kill him instead of tying him to the gate and leaving him alive to contemplate what they were going to do to Kate when they found her.

It was his fault. He had left her. He had been too eager to become a knight of the realm.

He had to find her. He prayed his sister was still alive, despite his uncle's belief to the contrary. Kate had to be alive, else not honor or even God would stop him from killing the Devil.

Chapter Eighteen

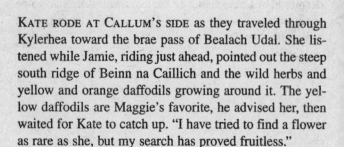

KATE RODE AT CALLUM'S SIDE as they traveled through Kylerhea toward the brae pass of Bealach Udal. She listened while Jamie, riding just ahead, pointed out the steep south ridge of Beinn na Caillich and the wild herbs and yellow and orange daffodils growing around it. The yellow daffodils are Maggie's favorite, he advised her, then waited for Kate to catch up. "I have tried to find a flower as rare as she, but my search has proved fruitless."

Kate's heart lurched at such sweet gallantry. "Margaret MacGregor must be quite a lady to invoke such tenderness in a man," she told him, wishing she knew how to do the same.

"A lady!" Brodie snorted to their right. "Why, Maggie is as much a hellion as her Devil brother."

Jamie's expression grew serious instantly. He gave his mount's flanks a hard kick that delivered him directly in front of Brodie. "I take offense to that! She is as innocent as a newly born lamb."

Brodie merely looked heavenward, and then at Kate.

"The wee hellion's protector. Some think she's a bit simple, what wi' all them years o' pain, but I tell ye, cross her and she's got a tongue as sharp as m' blade."

"Off yer horse!" Kate heard Jamie's demand and Brodie's subsequent laughter as she turned to follow Callum when he passed her.

The laird had cantered to the top of the low summit and was looking out over the landscape when Kate reached him. She came up slowly, mesmerized by the perfect image of some battle-hardened king of old returning home to his kingdom.

"Your sister has a champion."

Callum smiled, bemused by her fanciful notions and determined to rid her of them as he turned to look over his shoulder at Jamie. "'Tis his duty to guard her, nothing more."

Och, but was he so consumed with one thing that he failed to see something as large as one of his men in love with his sister? Or could he simply no longer recognize love at all?

"Does my uncle know where your home is?" she asked as they climbed the next pass.

"We dinna hide. If Argyll wants to find me, 'tis easy enough."

"And you hope that he will. Because of me." When he nodded, she drew out a wistful sigh. "Pity, it would be enjoyable here without him." She cocked her brow at him when he cast her a bewildered look. "What?"

"Ye possess a way about ye that makes significant things seem . . . no' important at all."

"You mean our names?" She dismissed his impression of her with a shrug. "They are only as important as others make them. I refuse to waste another moment being afraid of the consequences of associating with you. You will find that I don't frighten easily."

Beside her, Callum smiled, already knowing her declaration to be true.

"Take you, for instance. My uncle tried desperately to make me fear the terrible Devil MacGregor, but I barely spared you a thought."

"No' a thought?" He flashed her a winsome grin that made her senses reel. Nothing she had seen thus far matched its beauty.

"Barely one." She did her best to keep her composure and offered him a teasing smile of her own. "Of course, I did not know it was you at the time."

"And now that ye know me, d'ye find me worthy of more than a passin' thought?"

She blushed, hating herself for doing it. "I think of you from time to time, I admit."

His grin softened into a smile so intimate, so shockingly sensual her mouth went dry. She licked her lips to keep them from sticking together. His eyes followed the path of her tongue. His expression darkened with desire. He wanted to kiss her, and she wanted him to. Dear God, she knew she would go willingly to him if he but spoke the request, hanging be damned! She wanted to taste his mouth, his breath. She wanted to be in his arms again, to feel his hardness against her breasts, his skillful hands holding her, exploring her, caressing her while he told her . . .

"Are there many people in Camlochlin?" she asked, forcing from her mind the foolish notion that he would ever care for her.

"There are enough." He watched her guide her horse up another steep incline, making certain her mount did not slip. "There are more of us in Rannoch."

But Kate did not hear him. From the top, her gaze spread over the breathtaking panorama of a world set apart from the rest. Black mountain ranges, their jagged peaks swathed in silver mist, cut across an endless horizon as if painted there by a mad artist bent on intimidating visitors. She could have been looking at the sacred isle of Arthur Pendragon's burial place, for Skye appeared timeless, ancient, untouched.

"It is Heaven," she spoke on a shallow breath, not wanting to move from her spot, wanting never to leave this place.

"Nae, but 'tis as close as I'll ever come to it."

She turned to him, disquiet marring her brow. "Can you not forget what haunts you, even here?"

He shook his head and continued onward. " 'Tis here where I remember."

⁓

They traveled for the rest of the day in silence, save for Angus's gravelly voice filling the braes with old Highland ballads and Brodie's intermittent groaning.

As they passed through the small village of Torrin, the black mountain range—or the Cuillins, as Jamie had called them—loomed closer in the distance, a force of nature as harsh and unyielding as the warrior chieftain riding toward them. They skirted round Loch Slapin and followed a path that brought them directly below the mountain brae.

Kate doubted any view could be more splendid than

the one she had seen at Glen Arroch. But she was wrong. The road they traveled rose above a sun-dappled loch toward the honeycombed cliffs of Elgol. Every step was more treacherous than the one before it, but the view alone was worth every heart-stopping turn. Following closely behind Callum, they winded around another curve, at whose edge Kate was forced to stop. She was certain they had arrived at the end of the world or the beginning of time, for the brutal grandeur that unfolded before her stilled her breath. The entire horizon was a chiseled masterpiece of jagged, shadowy mountaintops and white, swirling mist. Her heart wrenched at the intense loneliness of such a savage landscape. Who could survive here, and who could survive without it once they had seen it?

They continued on while salt tang filled her nostrils and the sound of crashing waves below played like music on the moist breeze. This land was as tumultuous as the sea and just as dangerous, with mossy peaks and crannies, and slippery slopes that promised certain death with one wrong turn.

Finally the cliffs fell away, leaving the troop on a grassy crest overlooking a remote haven nestled beneath the giant slopes of Sgurr Na Stri and the craggy bulk of Bla Bheinn to the north. Directly below them were rolling moors carpeted in lush lavender heather. Sheep dotted the sunlit vale, and cattle grazed amid cozy thatched-roof bothys strewn across the grass. To the west of the glen, a wide loch spewed small frothy caps along a pebbled beach where children played.

"Camlochlin Castle." Callum reined his mount closer to Kate and pointed down into the glen.

The fortress must have been built of the same stone as the mountain behind it, for it blended into the landscape so neatly she doubted she would have even noticed it there had Callum not pointed it out to her.

Kate longed to push on ahead and enter this vast, separated land Callum called his home. The men did not move toward it, and just when she was about to question them about why they were not rushing home, the sun began its short descent. Golden rays of light were captured in the mist above the mountains. The sky exploded into flames of bronze and yellow, while the curtain wall before her grew even darker, casting shadows over the land. Splashes of gold fell upon the loch, turning white caps a frothy ochroid.

"I want to go there," Kate breathed on a longing sigh, then turned to Callum. "Now."

Callum held her gaze with his own and wondered at the way she worked at chiseling away his defenses. He'd never planned on bringing a woman here to share his life. He had neither the time nor the heart for such watery notions. But if he was going to entertain thoughts of taking a wife, she would be a woman who loved his home as much as he did. A woman who could see beyond the veil of the unyielding and the impenetrable and appreciate the beauty of a land that spoke to the heart alone. Aye, and mayhap she would even be able to see something good in him beneath the beast he had become.

He swallowed back the unwanted desires Kate Campbell stirred in him, but they returned full force when she slanted her smile at him and then kicked her mount into a full gallop.

The men followed her down the steep heather incline,

but before Callum let loose his reins, he watched the back of Kate's slight form racing toward his home as if it were her own.

With a heart that felt lighter than it had in years, he set his eyes on his castle and his heels to his mount. Within seconds he thundered past Kate and his men as if they were pausing to admire the scenery.

The celebration of their return began even before Kate and the others reached the castle, when Angus popped the cork off a fresh pouch of brew and, in an uncommon gesture of generosity, passed it around. After a long swig of the potent spirit, Kate shuddered all the way to her kneecaps, then set her eyes on Camlochlin's laird. He had reined in just before entering the pasture and then turned his horse back toward the others, his smile wide and beautiful, his long hair streaming across his shoulders.

There was happiness in Callum's life, and it was here. Kate was thankful for it. She wanted to be a part of it.

Aye, Callum was happy to return home, but 'twas the joy in Kate's eyes and the tenderness of her smile that exhilarated him.

He lived his life with a single purpose, to avenge what had been done to him, his clan, his sister. He'd hated who he had become—until he saw himself through Kate's eyes. He despised the memories that haunted him, but just looking at her made him forget. At first he had fought her effect on him because she was a Campbell. Then he fought it because she could never be his—and live. Hell, leaving her in that bed at the inn had nearly driven him mad. But they were far away from the world now, far from the law. Somehow she had come to mean more to him than revenge, more than a quick tumble to quench his desire. His heart longed for the redemption she offered him. His body ached to hold her. He looked over his shoulder at Camlochlin. His sanctuary. But so much was missing from his life. He had no notion of how to find what would make him whole again, or even if 'twere possible. He was an outlaw, a murderer, a monster. But Kate Campbell saw something more.

He flicked his reins.

When he reached her, he leaned forward in his saddle, coiled his arm around her waist, and heaved her onto his lap. He offered her no explanation as he gazed deep into her questioning eyes. He could barely think at all. Instead, he stroked the soft contour of her cheek, then slipped his hand behind her nape and bent his mouth to hers. She did not resist him. He knew she wouldn't. Her lips parted on a sigh of sweet surrender that made his whole body go rigid and melt at the same time. His tongue swept deeply, intimately into her mouth, tasting her and letting her taste him in return. Plunging his hand within her hair, he tilted back her head while the other drew her closer. He kissed her with exquisite thoroughness, ravishing her softness until she fell back, limp in his arms.

He lifted his head and slid his gaze over her glorious face while she hiccupped and smiled at him. And all at once he knew 'twas not only her heart with which he should have been more careful.

Chapter Nineteen

CALLUM COULD NOT HELP but smile as he stepped into Camlochlin with Kate clutched to his arm. He should be angry with Angus for feeding her Gillis's poison, but he liked the way she pressed herself against him. He knew she held on so tightly to keep herself from stumbling, for the whiskey was potent indeed. But her rather submissive position would also work at easing some of the tension sure to come when he told Camlochlin's inhabitants who she was.

He looked around at the squires and vassals rushing to help his men disarm. Baths were already being prepared to wash away weeks of dirt and grime, and somewhere close by, Callum heard Old Keddy the cook shouting for a dozen fat hens to be slaughtered in celebration of the laird's return. Brodie's wife, Netta, heavy with child, came barreling down the long stairway and near leapt into her husband's arms. Graham was besotted with kisses from Rabbie the tanner's twin daughters, Glenna and Lizabeth.

Callum drank in the sights and sounds of his home like a man parched by the sun. He knew the face of every man, woman, and bairn who greeted him. Familiar scents of smoky peat and burning tallow wax fragranced his nostrils. He drew in a deeper breath, letting it comfort his restless spirit. Aye, Heaven.

His gaze dropped to Kate. 'Twould not be Heaven for her. When his kin learned that she was a Campbell, and naught but a captive to him, they would treat her unkindly. Some might even try to cause her harm. At the thought of it, his heart seized with the need to protect and shelter what was his. But she was not his, his mind reminded him.

"Who's the lass, then, Laird?" someone called out as if to drive the truth of it home.

Best to get it the hell over with, Callum thought, involuntarily pulling Kate closer. "This is Katherine Campbell," he shouted so that all could hear. People stopped what they were doing and gathered 'round him, some already whispering offense at her name. Callum's expression went hard. "She'll be brought nae harm here, understood?"

The mumbling soon died down, but there were questions aplenty. Callum felt Kate slip against his arm and wondered if she was even aware of all the faces staring at her.

"Did ye snatch her from her home, Laird?"

"What d'ye plan to do wi' her?"

Hell, she wasn't completely oblivious to what was being said, Callum realized when she lifted her head from his arm.

"She looks dimwitted. Is she simple, then?"

"Nae," Callum replied succinctly while he carefully fit his hand over Kate's mouth. He'd felt the slight tightening of her shoulders and knew she was about to let his clan find out what a fearless little hellion she was. No MacGregor took kindly to being insulted, and especially by a Campbell. "She's drunk."

Suddenly he jerked his hand back and shook it as if he'd been burned. "Christ, ye near took off my finger!" he bellowed at her.

"She bit him!" someone shouted. A dozen men moved forward ready to protect their laird. The rest simply stood there gaping.

"Stand doun," Brodie warned, stepping in front of the men before they reached Kate. " 'Tis no' the first time she's wounded him, and I'm guessin' 'twillna be the last."

"Aye." Kate's glassy eyes blazed at Callum. "And if he ever muzzles me again"—she paused to lift her fingers to her lips and burp—"I shall do more than bite him."

"She's a fiery wench," a male inhabitant called from the crowd.

"Will ye be claimin' a Campbell, Laird?"

"Nae, I willna be," Callum called out over the sudden throng of dissatisfied voices.

"Of course he won't," Kate responded in kind. "I am already betrothed to a lovely man." She tossed Callum a pert smile when he scowled at her.

"A *lovely* man?" Even Angus had to question that.

"He's English," Callum explained.

"I love him!"

Callum didn't actually smile in front of his clan, but his eyes warmed considerably at Kate's announcement.

"Good, then ye'll be pleased when yer brother returns ye to him." He did not give her the opportunity to reply but called to one of the lasses hanging off Graham's arm. "Glenna, take her to a room."

He watched Kate reluctantly leave the hall, turning over her shoulder to glare at him one more time. Hell, she was spitting mad.

Callum grinned.

Brodie snickered while Angus pushed through the dispersing crowd and headed for the buttery.

Callum looked around the hall as the people returned to their duties. He hadn't seen her among the faces, and he turned toward the doors to check the barn.

"Brother?"

He heard her voice, slight and soft behind him, and his heart slowed as he turned.

Margaret MacGregor's frame was small, almost frail compared to her brother's brawn. Her back was slightly hunched. Her short, pitch-black hair pointed out in all directions and was littered with straw.

"Greetins, fair lass." Callum bowed slightly to his sister. When he stood to his full height a moment later, his eyes grazed over the top of her head. "I see ye were lyin' in the barn again."

She did not return his smile, but Callum knew she was happy to see him by the tears glistening over the tips of her long, dark lashes.

"Did you find him?"

"Nae," Callum told her, knowing who she meant. "He fled."

She nodded and scratched her small, dirty nose. "Why did you bring her here?"

"She is his niece."

His sister looked toward the stairs, pondering his words. After a moment she turned her enormous blue eyes on him, knowing his reason. "So he will come to ye."

Callum nodded and looked away. For she saw who he was. She had seen what became of him when he gave up his soul to take her from hell. She hated the thought of him killing anyone, even a Campbell. "It will end with him, Maggie."

She lifted one small hand to his face and the other to the tears streaking her cheeks. "Nae, it will end with ye," she said, wiping her face.

Callum took her hand and kissed it. He did not bother telling her that was what he meant. When Argyll was dead he would stop warring with the Campbells. He would explain it all to her later.

"Jaime's been pickin' flowers fer ye again," he said, wanting to lighten the mood of their reunion. He crooked her arm through his and led her toward the great hall. "When last I saw him, he was headin' fer yer chambers with an armful of daffodils. Those are yer favorites, nae?" he teased and was rewarded with a scowl as dark as his own.

"Ye know they aren't, Callum. Why did ye not tell him that my favorites are orchids?"

"Orchids dinna grow well in the north."

"That is why I like them best. They are delicate."

"Like ye," Callum said, smiling at her.

Margaret quirked her lips, looking much like the imp their mother used to call her. "What flower would ye pick for Katherine Campbell?"

Callum snorted. "I wouldna pick flowers."

"Ye let her take a bite out of ye." Maggie looked up at him, then cut him off when he opened his mouth to speak. "Ye fancy her. What flower would ye pick for her?"

"Tulips," he mumbled, ignoring her knowing smirk. "Come, let us get somethin' to eat."

She shook her head. "I'm not hungry. You go, brother, and then please share a word or two with Keddy about keeping ducks off the supper trenchers."

"He's already agreed to keep mutton off them," Callum reminded her.

"I know, but it upsets Matilda." She smiled when he finally promised to speak to the cook.

Chapter Twenty

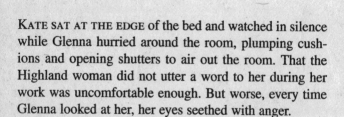

KATE SAT AT THE EDGE of the bed and watched in silence while Glenna hurried around the room, plumping cushions and opening shutters to air out the room. That the Highland woman did not utter a word to her during her work was uncomfortable enough. But worse, every time Glenna looked at her, her eyes seethed with anger.

Kate knew why. She was as unwanted a guest at Camlochlin as the English were in Scotland. Damnation, she was tired of people despising her because of her name.

Her head was beginning to pound. Hadn't she vowed never to drink Angus's whiskey again? Och, she was no good at keeping promises. But Callum surely was. Unfortunately, the effect of Angus's brew had worn off enough for her to recall Callum's smug reply to her when she said she loved lord whatever his damned name was. She also remembered the way he had kissed her before they entered the castle. She touched her fingers to her lips. It was even better than before, if that were possible. His mouth had caressed hers, his gaze so gentle and full of meaning.

Almost as if he . . . *Och, stop it, Kate. You were drunk, you fool!*

She slammed her palm down on the mattress, and Glenna looked up from filling a basin with fresh water and glowered at her.

Kate offered her a repentant smile. "I was pondering something. I did not mean to startle you."

"I'm no' afeared o' Campbells," Glenna snapped.

"Of course not. That isn't what I . . ." Kate shook her throbbing head and began again. She'd never fought with a woman before and didn't fancy the thought of having her eyes clawed from her head. "You fancy Graham," she said instead, hoping to steer the young maiden toward more pleasant conversation, since she was finally talking. "He's quite handsome and—"

Glenna dropped the basin to floor. In truth, she delivered it to the rushes with a vigorous smash.

"Keep yer hands off him. He'd never touch the likes of ye."

Kate's mouth fell open, but before she could form a fit reply, someone else spoke behind her.

"Glenna, go fetch some rags to clean up your mess. Graham is already occupied with Lizbeth, so there's nae need to make haste."

Kate turned to the dulcet voice as Glenna strode out of the room. What she saw nearly made her recoil.

"She believes Graham is in love with her." The woman hunched beneath the doorway turned to watch Glenna leave. She sighed and shook her head with pity. "And they say I'm dense."

Kate was still reeling from the sight of her when the woman—or was she a child?—she was certainly small enough to be one—turned to her. Whatever she was, she was surprisingly beautiful. Kate wasn't certain if it was the dirty streaks covering parts of her round face that made her eyes glimmer like clear blue ice, or if it was their size that made them so stunning.

"I am Margaret. But I prefer to be called Maggie. I already know who ye are."

Kate's stomach twisted with sorrow and then shame. God's mercy, this was Callum's sister. Her hair was a mass of dark tangles and her spine, misshapen and bent like that of an old woman. Was her grandfather responsible for this? Kate could barely stop the disgust in her heart from spilling forth. Unfortunately, Maggie took notice.

Those brilliant eyes narrowed on Kate, and then, with a scowl as fierce as her brother's, Maggie turned to leave. "My brother awaits ye in the great hall after ye freshen up."

Stunned and saddened by Margaret's appearance, and sorry that the poor lass had misread her contempt, Kate bolted to her feet and rushed after her when Maggie left.

"Please, wait!"

Maggie didn't even pause in her steps but continued straight down the hall and into another room. Kate followed her, coming to an abrupt halt at the entrance.

The room was large! There was a heavy wooden bed against the south wall big enough to fit three people, but by the crisp look of it, no one slept in it. Daffodils, fresh and old, festooned every table, every window niche. The walls were painted with lush green vines, and in the corner was a small tent fashioned of dyed leather, long sticks, and heavy rope.

Maggie pushed the flap away from the opening of the tent and disappeared inside.

For a moment, Kate had no idea what to do. The room, the tent, Maggie's appearance . . . everything overwhelmed her. But she had to apologize for hurting Maggie's feelings. She went to the tent and knelt beside it.

"Please come out," she prodded gently. "I didn't mean you any insult."

"Callum awaits ye in the great hall. Off with ye."

Kate wrung her hands together trying to find a way to make her come out so that she could speak to her. "I . . . I feel as if I know you already." She leaned closer to the flap. "Jamie has told me much about you."

Maggie's face appeared where the flap was, momentarily startling Kate. "What did he tell ye?"

"That you like yellow daffodils."

Maggie rolled her eyes heavenward. "Mother Mary, I do not like them. I like orchids." She crawled out of the tent and sat facing Kate. "I told him I like daffodils because he picks so many for me."

Kate had the sudden urge to smile, but first she needed to apologize. "It was a long journey here. I did not mean to treat you unkindly."

Maggie studied her for a moment, and then arrived at some conclusion that softened her features with a smile. She lifted her fingers to wipe a smudge of dirt from Kate's brow even while her own face was streaked with it. "Ye were not hurt, were ye? Callum would never let ye be hurt."

"I was not hurt," Kate assured her. She could not keep herself from thinking about the years Maggie had spent in a dungeon, and what had happened to her there. Amazingly, though, there was tenderness and innocence in Maggie's eyes that Callum lacked. "You said you already knew who I was. Then you know I'm a Campbell?" Kate added hesitantly. When Maggie nodded, Kate pushed on. "And you don't hate me?"

Maggie patted her cheek, then stood up. "My brother has enough hate in him for both of us. D'ye want to come to the barn with me?"

The change in topic was so abrupt Kate didn't answer her right away. Then, "The barn?"

"Aye, it's verra peaceful there."

Kate smiled and rose to her feet, accepting Maggie's outstretched hand.

Though her body was bent, Maggie MacGregor had no trouble almost racing down the stairs, still clutching Kate's hand, of course. The delicious aroma of food wafting through the air made Kate's stomach ache. Panic filled her suddenly when she realized that Maggie was leading her to the great hall. Hell, Callum and his entire clan would probably be there and she had not even washed her face. It didn't matter that they had all seen her less than an hour ago. Surely they expected her to wash the grime from her body after traveling for so long. Och, she must look like a village wench! She ran her free hand through her hair and yanked at some of the tangles, but it was no use. She was a mess. She also realized that this was the first time in her life she was concerned with her appearance. The idea pleased and disturbed her at the same time. It was wonderful to want to look pleasing, and even more wonderful to have someone to look pleasing for. Sadly, the man she wanted to please didn't even like her. But he certainly had not kissed her like a man who held her in contempt . . . unless he was just so happy to be home.

His home. God's teeth, what would her uncle think if he knew she was in the MacGregor holding? She looked around, soaking up the thick tapestries that provided warmth to the castle. The long corridors were illuminated in the soft glow of sconced torches. The furniture was plain but tremendously big. Exactly what a wondrously big man like Callum would choose, although poor Maggie likely ceased to exist when she sat in one of the carved walnut chairs sprinkled throughout the halls.

The two women rounded a corner that opened into an endlessly long great hall with a vaulted ceiling that rose upward two full landings. Kate's face paled when she saw dozens of ladies, all with clean, untangled hair and unwrinkled gowns, seated at the long trestle table with Callum's men. The light from the central hearth did not help her position, either. Every eye seemed to fall on her curiously being led by the hand by a wee hunched-back woman. Self-consciously, Kate ran her hand over her gown to smooth it and then wondered if breaking free of Maggie's surprisingly strong grip and running for the doors would make her look even more foolish.

She spotted the object of her affliction and forgot everything else. Callum MacGregor stood a good head taller than the other men, save Angus. His long, dark hair was neatly combed and hung loose over his shoulders, the shadow of stubble gone now from his ruggedly chiseled features. He wore a loose-fitting white tunic unlaced at the neck and tucked at his waist beneath his folded plaid. He stood with Graham and a female of ample bosom and sultry green eyes.

Kate tightened her grip on Maggie's hand, not wanting to go any further.

When he looked up from the flaxen-haired wench's coy smile, Kate knew it was too late to flee, though she was no longer sure she wanted to. Callum looked pleased to see her. That is to say, he was not scowling. His eyes swept over her, his gaze a tender caress. But Maggie had stepped in front of her, and Kate wondered if he was looking at her or his sister.

"Greetings, Callum!"

Callum lifted his goblet and finished off its contents in one swallow, then returned his sister's greeting.

"Did ye drag Kate oot of her room before she could bathe?"

Kate's smiled vanished. If Maggie weren't holding her hand so tightly she would have fled the hall and Camlochlin itself.

"She does not need to bathe," his sister huffed. "She needs friends, so I am going to introduce her to Matilda and the others."

Callum looked over her head at Kate. "Mayhap Kate would like somethin' to eat first."

Kate was torn between smiling like a dreamy dimwit into his beautiful eyes, or smashing a trencher over his head for not even caring if she was in love with an Englishman.

"Later." Maggie tugged on her hand, pulling her away from Callum. "I'm sure she will not want to eat Keddy's supper after she meets Henry and the others."

Kate felt Callum's eyes on her, but she did not turn around as they exited through a small door at the other end of the hall. They entered the kitchen, and Maggie threw the burly, chubby-faced cook a glare as menacing as her brother's on his angriest day. Kate plucked an apple from the chopping table just before she was hauled through another door. She completely missed Keddy's scathing glare.

A cool, salty breeze whipped through Kate's hair when they stepped outside. But for the distant roar of whitecaps forging toward the shore, the only sound in the utter stillness of the surrounding mist was Kate's own breath.

"It is beautiful here," she said, gazing at the twilight wonder around her. "But we should go back inside. It's too difficult to see."

Maggie yanked on her hand. "Follow me."

A few more steps and Maggie pulled on another door just off the eastern wall of the castle. The wood creaked, weathered on its hinges. Kate followed her inside what she assumed was the barn, if the sounds of squawking made by various farm animals were any indication. Finally Maggie released her hand and reached up to retrieve a small lantern hanging low on a wooden rafter. She lit the candlewick inside, and Kate drew in a short gasp. It was a barn, but like none she had ever seen before. Fresh hay littered the floor, and bags of oats and nuts hung from hooks on the walls. There were no cages to house the animals. Instead, they roamed freely, nibbling at scattered cornmeal and sliced apples strewn along the floor. There were not many animals here. A duck was either very happy to see the two women or quite displeased, for she waddled at them honking loud enough to wake the dead. A pig followed the duck in hot pursuit, snorting just as loudly. An old horse crunched on a carrot in the corner, and he, too, looked up when Maggie and Kate entered. A gray and white cat leapt from the rafters and startled Kate.

"Bertrid, this is Kate, my friend," Maggie informed the purring cat and then sat down on the floor. "Well?" She glanced up at Kate. "Are ye not going to say hullo back?"

"Greetings to you, Bertrid," Kate replied politely, feeling silly. She felt a tug on her skirt.

"Come doun here. 'Tis less threatening to them. They do not know ye yet, Kate."

Kate bit into her apple and glanced around at the corn strings decorating the barn from rafter to rafter. Crisscrossing the corn were strings of blackberry, elderberry, and various nuts. Animals were carved into the wood, and dried daffodils fragranced the air. It was positively enchanting. "You did all this?"

"Jamie did it for me. Now sit."

Kate obeyed and waited for the next introduction.

"This is Henry." Maggie became the perfect chatelaine as she introduced the snorting pig to her newest friend. "He likes to be pet behind the ears. And that's Matilda. She honks aplenty, and though I vow she rants louder than Angus, 'tis but her declaration of love. That's Ahern. He was Callum's best warhorse. He once belonged to the Earl of Argyll, but Callum took him when we left. Ahern is verra braw, but he's old now."

By now, Henry the pig had curled up into in Kate's lap like a well-loved puppy, and to her surprise Kate felt a sense of calm wash over her, be it from the comforting, gentle tones of Maggie's lilting voice or from Henry's slow, rhythmic breathing. She liked it here, and she was glad to be away from all the eyes in the great hall.

The barn door opened, and Matilda spread her wings and honked out a few more oaths as wind blew the hay on the floor into circles around the small group.

"We are fine, Jamie," Maggie called out without turning. Then she looked at Kate through the corner of her eye and explained in a low voice, "My brother always sends him to watch over me as if I were a hapless child."

Kate was about to turn around to greet him when she heard Callum's thick, velvet voice behind her.

"Yer brother only wants to be assured of yer safety. Should we flog him fer that?" His tone was light, and when he reached them he folded his long legs and sat down in the hay beside Kate.

"Och, ye've been flogged before and it did not help a bit," his sister replied tartly.

Kate shot her an incredulous look. How could they jest about such a thing when Callum bore those terrible scars all across his back? She felt his gaze on her and turned to find she was right. His eyes flickered in the light like embers. When he spoke, the husky cadence of his voice made Kate's spine tingle.

"How d'ye like my sister's friends?"

"I think I like Henry best." She lowered her gaze to the sleeping pig in her lap.

Callum watched her stroke the swine and imagined what it would be like to have her touch him with such care.

"Ye have no' met Sarah yet, then?" he asked, rising to his feet again. He crossed the barn and bent into the shadows. When he came into the light again, he was carrying a small lamb in his arms.

Unabashedly, Kate watched him. She loved how he walked, proud but not arrogant, with the grace of a king and the quiet strength of a leader. He squatted before Maggie and handed the lamb to her, then sat down near Kate again.

"She's a bonny babe!" Kate cooed and slipped her fingers beneath Sarah's woolly chin. "What big brown eyes she has."

Maggie seemed to melt, caressing the lamb to her chest. She closed her eyes and lavished Sarah's head with kisses. "Sarah must stay here now since she was trampled by the other sheep," Maggie told her, her kisses unceasing. "Keddy wanted to make stew of her."

Kate gasped.

"Aye," agreed Maggie. "But I bit him and asked him how he liked it."

Biting her tongue to stifle a giggle, Kate was thankful for the dim lighting. She was sure Maggie was perfectly serious, and Kate did not want to insult her by laughing.

"I will never eat even a morsel of meat," Callum's sister declared lovingly.

Callum grumbled something, but his sister seemed not to notice as she threw herself down in the hay and lay there on her back with Sarah atop her belly.

An hour later, Kate and Maggie both lay on the barn floor. Callum had requested that they return to the castle, but both women refused. Sprawled on their backs and staring up at the low rafters, they talked quietly while Callum sat propped against one wall, his long legs stretched out before him and crossed at the ankles. Both of them giggled when he began to snore.

"Did Callum tell ye about our imprisonment?"

The question was so sudden and unexpected that Kate took a moment to answer. Then, "Nae, he has not spoken of it."

"He never does." Maggie looked toward him. "I do not remember much before we were taken captive. They put the sword to my papa, and then did bad things to mama before they killt her, too. Callum tried to fight them, but he was just a lad. Och, he grew strong later, though." She paused. Her eyes drifted off to the past for an instant, and then she blinked and began to breathe again. "He did everything they demanded, but they still beat him."

Lying still beside her, Kate turned to gaze upon Callum's sleeping face while his sister spoke.

"He is so stubborn, though." Maggie yawned and her eyelids grew heavy, but she continued speaking. "Each time they beat him he vowed to kill them. They mocked his promise, until one morn when he pretended to be asleep. A guard stepped closer to him and my brother killt him with just his forehead. Callum knew they would kill us because of what he had done."

The barn was so quiet Kate heard the sound of her drumming heartbeat. She wanted to scream for Maggie to cease, but she could say nothing. She poured her eyes over her knight, aching to climb into his lap the way Henry had climbed into hers. She wanted to kiss his face and soothe his cold heart. But he would never let her. The thought made her moan.

"They came for me first. But Callum broke free." Though Maggie's voice was but a whisper, Callum's eyes opened as if he were hearing her words in his sleep.

He rose from his place against the wall and stood over them. "Come, to bed with ye now," he said gently and picked Maggie up in his arms.

"Och, but were they not surprised at that, Callum? Were they not surprised at how ye killt them all?" Maggie said, and then closed her eyes.

Callum's expression twisted with some emotion so painful Kate doubted she would ever recover from seeing it.

As she settled into bed that night, Kate's thoughts were plagued with images she prayed hard to forget. But first, she prayed that the two people who lived through the horrible tale could forget them, as well.

Chapter Twenty-One

⌒

THE MORNING SUN BLAZED like a dragon's breath through the wide, unshuttered windows of Kate's room. Golden light splashed over her hair while Maggie brushed it until Kate's scalp began to ache. Callum's sister had insisted on bathing her new friend after they shared a hearty meal of cooked oats. Kate's skin still tingled from the scrubbing she received at Maggie's strong hands, but it felt wonderful to finally smell better than a fortnight's worth of dirt.

She had so wanted to brush Maggie's hair, but the lass refused. But after Kate commented on how Jamie might be tempted to plant a kiss on her cheek if it was clean, she did agree to wash her face.

At Callum's request, a handmaiden named Aileen had delivered an earasaid and an armful of kirtles and shifts to Kate's room earlier, all of which were tried on until Kate finally chose one with a sleeveless bodice of sapphire wool. The cut was low, the laces ending just beneath her breasts. She wore a cream-colored shift beneath with long bloused sleeves. Maggie had helped her don her earasaid of patterned scarlet and saffron, pleating it around her waist with a belt and wrapping the spare material around her shoulders. She'd secured the plaid with a round brooch of hammered bronze.

"Kate?" Maggie asked now, brushing one of Kate's curls around her finger. "Is yer uncle very skilled with a blade?"

Kate heard the distress in her voice and knew what Maggie was really asking her. "I've never seen him in battle, but he often boasted of his skill." When Maggie expelled a little groan, Kate hastily continued. "Whereas I have seen Callum wield a sword, and I do not believe any man could stand against him."

"Are ye verra frightened for yer uncle, then?"

Kate shifted in her seat. She was not worried for him at all. In fact, she did her best not to even think of him. But she couldn't tell that to Maggie without the girl thinking she was as coldhearted as her grandfather. "I don't want Callum to kill him," she finally said, leaving it at that.

"Nor do I."

Kate turned to her, surprised. "How is it that you suffered with your brother at the hands of my kin and you don't wish them dead, as Callum does?"

Maggie's huge eyes shimmered with tears when they settled on Kate. "How much longer will my brother live if he keeps killing them? Sooner or later they will come for him. Just like they did at Kildun."

Kate nodded slowly and turned back around. Her heart beat madly in her chest. She knew Maggie was right. She had even tried to tell him at the inn. This war would never end if the killing continued, and Callum would surely die. "We must stop him."

"How?" Maggie asked. A dash of hope tinged her voice. "D'ye think he will listen to ye? He did say he would give ye tulips."

"Tulips?" Kate turned to her again with a befuddled look. The lass had the most peculiar way of switching topics right in the middle of a conversation.

"Aye, he would pick tulips for ye."

Kate almost laughed. "Your brother would never pick flowers."

"That's what he said, but then he said tulips. I think he fancies ye. So will ye speak to him?"

"Aye." Kate nodded, rising from her chair. Tulips? Whatever made him choose that particular flower? She touched her fingers to her mouth. And why would Maggie think he fancied her? He had kissed her, aye. He had even wanted to bed her. But it was lust—he had all but told her so. He could never bring himself to care for a Campbell. Could he?

"Kate?"

"Aye?"

"What are ye waiting for?"

⁓

"I don't think this is a good time," Kate whispered out of the corner of her mouth to Maggie as they headed down the stairs.

"Why not? You look verra bonny in yer earasaid."

"Look." Kate pointed to the faces staring up at her from the bottom landing. There were only one or two at first but, emboldened by the rest, more of Camlochlin's inhabitants gathered at the foot of the stairs until Kate and Maggie faced a small crowd of mumbling Highlanders. Kate paled, noticing that each face bore the same expression of hardened contempt for her.

"Where is Callum?" Maggie demanded, recognizing the anger, as well.

One man stepped forward from the crowd. He wore a heavy woolen tunic beneath his plaid. His legs were bare, his boots dusty and tattered. "Why d'ye stand beside a wretched Campbell as if she were yer friend, Maggie? Send her back from whence she came."

Maggie stepped around Kate's shocked face and wagged her finger at the man. "Iain, ye'll not speak of her that way. She is my friend, Campbell or nae. And Callum's, as well."

"Our laird would ne'er befriend our enemy," someone shouted.

"Aye, he had to rob her to force her uncle to face his fate."

"Toss her oot on her arse!"

Kate took a step back as the crowd grew larger. Many of them were shouting now, demanding that she leave Camlochlin and ignoring Maggie's small fist when she shook it at them. Someone took a step forward, and Kate backed further away until her heels bumped the stairs. Then she heard the shout of a loud, resonating voice, and every head in the hall turned in the direction from which it came.

Graham stood in the doorway leading to the great hall, arms at his sides, ready to draw his sword. Beside him, Angus appeared bigger and more menacing than ever. Brodie was there also and slid his dagger across a small whetting stone clenched in his fist. Jamie stood at his side, his usual innocent expression exchanged for one far more threatening.

"What in blazes is going on here?" Graham demanded. "Did I hear ye all right? This fair lady is not welcome in our home?" The crowd was silent for a moment, and then someone muttered the name Campbell and the rest began to nod.

"We dinna care what her name is," Jamie warned in a low growl. "Callum's orders are that nae harm be brought to her. Now step back."

Maggie tugged at Kate's sleeve. "Jamie's verra braw, nae?" She let out a little sigh and then went back to glaring at the crowd.

"The MacGregor's taken leave of his senses to bring a Campbell here," another thick Highland voice called out, and the others agreed until their voices rose again. Brodie and Jamie hurried to Kate's side while Graham unsheathed his sword, prepared to fight.

He did not have to. Dead silence fell upon Camlochlin after the doors behind the angry crowd slammed shut. Slowly, the sea of heads turned toward the entrance. The only sound to be heard was that of Brodie's muttered oath at the sight of his laird.

Callum paused at the doors for just a moment, taking in the scene before him. 'Twas clear by the expressions on Brodie and Jamie's faces, and by Graham's unsheathed blade, what was going on. When he took a step forward, the crowd moved backward like a great waning wave. His eyes, so piercing and deadly, slid to Kate. "Are ye well?"

She nodded, unable to do more. He spoke quietly, but

he looked more dangerous than he had the night at the inn when he cleaved a table in two. He moved slowly, his hands at his sides. Every face found by his wintry gaze paled before turning away. He circled the crowd until he came to stand before Kate. When he took her hand in his, his frown deepened at her trembling.

"My senses"—he raked a lethal glare over each face until he found who he was looking for—"left me long ago, Alasdair. And while I'm more inclined to kill Campbells, I'm no' entirely opposed to killin' MacGregors if the need arises." His burr was thick with suppressed fury, and if Kate was not so terrified for them all, she would have sighed at the sound of him, the safety she felt being with him.

"I've kept ye all protected here. But I warn ye if one of ye speaks unkindly to her, ye'll leave Camlochlin. One way or another." He turned to face her, and Kate was sure he hadn't meant to let his eyes drift over her features so tenderly. They were supposed to be enemies, and after meeting Maggie and hearing of their life in her grandfather's dungeon, Kate understood why Callum would never give her his heart. But here he was protecting her from his own clan. Did he do so because she was more valuable to him alive, or for another reason entirely?

The crowd dispersed with one final and far less dangerous glare bestowed on them by their laird. Brodie sauntered away, digging his sharpened blade into a pear as he went. Angus and Graham left the castle to practice their swordplay, the larger of the two throwing his head back to laugh when Graham threatened to whack him all the way to England.

Maggie tugged on Kate's earasaid and whispered in

her ear when Kate bent to her, and then announced that she was going for a walk. Her brother motioned to Jamie to go with her, a command the young warrior was only too eager to obey.

"Ye look verra bonny, this morn," Kate heard Jamie tell Maggie while he strode out the door behind her.

When they were alone, Callum's gaze drifted over Kate from foot to crown. "Ye look fine, as well." He lifted his fingers to the shiny curls draping her shoulders. "And yer hair." He paused to frown and dropped his gaze to the floor as if fighting some deep emotion. Kate rejoiced when he lost that battle and returned his gaze to her tresses. "Yer hair is pleasin' to look at," he finished quickly.

Kate curtseyed and did her best to conceal her amusement over his loss of composure. "Thank you, Callum."

She tilted her face to study his profile as they began to walk together toward the great hall. He was so tall, so broad compared to her. When he slid his eyes to her and caught her obvious awe, she blushed a true shade of crimson.

"I'm still angry with you," she said in defense of the teasing smile slanting his mouth.

"Truly?" He traced her profile with his bemused gaze. "Ye look rather joyous to me."

Kate shrugged her shoulders. "That is because soon I will be reunited with my beloved betrothed."

"Aye." Callum nodded. "His name has slipped from my memory. Lord Newton of Manchester, is it?"

Kate almost paused in her steps. Hell, what was the name she had given him? It wasn't Newton, was it? "His name is of no importance," she said haughtily, not about to confess that she didn't remember. "There is a more pressing matter I wish to discuss with you."

"Ye have my ear," he said, keeping his gaze ahead.

"It is about my uncle." She cut him a quick side glance, expecting him to scowl or mayhap storm away. He did neither. "I am concerned for you."

"Ye insult me."

"I don't really care." Och, he was scowling now. "Insult will not kill you; Cromwell's army will."

Callum's mouth hooked into an arrogant half smile that made her insides burn. "If his army finds me and comes here, they will die at the hands of MacGregors, MacLeods, and MacKinnons. I intend to kill Argyll, Kate. Nae one will stop me. No' even ye."

"What about Maggie? She does not want you to kill him, either."

He was quiet for a moment, but then he shook his head. When he spoke again, the hard edge in his voice told her this conversation was about to end. "My sister knows who I am."

What in damnation did that mean? "Will you at least consider—"

"Nae."

Och, but he was a stubborn man. "You are making it terribly difficult to like you, MacGregor."

"You like me well enough, Campbell."

She heard the smile in his voice and turned to look up at him. Her steps faltered at the warmth of his gaze. His mask was gone, momentarily tantalizing her with the bare truth of his emotions. His expression darkened with unspoken yearning so replete she drew closer to him, wanting to fling herself into his arms.

" 'Tis a burden, to be sure," he said, "but I am willin' to suffer it."

Kate's brow rose sharply, the slow curl of her lips a direct challenge to his beguiling grin. If he insisted on keeping up his air of detachment, which his eyes told her was a facade, she was not going to make it easy for him. With her heart racing, she reached for him, fitting her hand into his much larger one. She hid her satisfaction when his composure seemed to desert him again, and she leaned in closer to him.

"Though your suffering might be great, I will grant you no pity."

Instead of pulling away, he twined his fingers through hers, binding her to him more intimately. "Ye're a fierce opponent, lass. I'll grant ye that." He took his time looking her over, letting his smile carve into a slow, seductive smirk. "But I'll no' be beaten by a Campbell."

Blast him, but he would not give up! "Aye, as your scarred leg can testify," she replied tartly.

He actually threw his head back and chuckled. Kate stopped walking and gave his hand a tug. Now he stung her pride. If there was one thing she was good at, it was wielding a sword.

"Why do you laugh, Callum? Do you not think I fight well?"

"Aye, I'll admit ye fight well, fer a lass. I saw ye fight against the McColls."

"For a lass?" She snatched back her hand and folded her arms across her chest, drumming her fingers on her elbows. "I could beat you, Callum MacGregor."

Humor danced across his handsome features. Even

though it made Kate angry that he found her amusing, she couldn't help but smile at the sight of his arrogant mirth.

"Let me out of this heavy plaid and meet me outside."

"Och, nae, lass. If I injured ye, I'd never fergive myself."

He was an overbearing ruffian, indeed. But his gentleness with her was what made her move toward him. She missed his arms around her. Blast him again for not missing it, as well. She took another step closer until their toes touched, then tilted her head to meet his gaze. His mouth was so close when he bent his head to her that she felt his breath warm against her lips. "Are you afraid of me, then, MacGregor?" she whispered against his chin and cautiously laid her hands on his chest.

She felt his body respond almost instantly. His muscles tightened. His heart accelerated. Kate rejoiced. She did affect him! It was enough to make her want to kiss him again, though in truth, she had thought of naught else since the first time he laid his mouth on hers. He lifted his arms, ready to enfold her. His breath pulled on a low, ragged groan as his hands touched her back and sank into her curls.

She stepped back, using all her will to do so. She wanted more from him than his kiss, and if she had to battle him to get it, she would. "To the yard, then. And make sure your sword is ready."

He watched her disappear above stairs and ground his teeth at the wonderful agony hardening his loins. "Och, lass, my sword is ready. That's no' a problem."

Chapter Twenty-Two

CALLUM WAS NOT A MAN to waste his time while he waited for Kate to meet him in the practice yard, and that was why Brodie found himself beneath the tip of his laird's sword three different times in the space of two breaths. When Callum finally spotted Kate making her way to him, he waved his cousin away, stabbed the ground with his blade, and leaned on the hilt to admire her. Her skirts flared around her ankles, narrowing at her hips. The bodice she wore revealed her feminine beauty. Her hair, he noticed with a smile that darkened his eyes with desire, was still unbound, whipping across her fearless smile.

"Are you ready for me?" she called out before she reached him, then waved happily to Brodie and Angus, before accepting a lighter sword from Brodie.

"Aye." Callum's eyes drank in every inch of her while his lips curled into something feral. "I'm ready fer ye."

When she faced him, he shook his head at her and

stepped back. "Wait, lass, ye'll wear some protection. Brodie, go fetch—"

Kate's sword glittered in the sun as it descended upon Callum's head. His reflexes were instantaneous, and, yanking his blade from the ground, he deflected the blow, paused, and sent her a stunned glare. She grinned in return and parried his next swing.

"I'd prefer it if ye wore some armor, lass," he said and swiped his blade across her belly.

She leaped backward, easily avoiding the blow. "It hinders me. And I would prefer it if you were not so careful with me." Slinging her sword over her head to gain more momentum, she swung left, then right, then chopped at his flanks. "I can . . ." Her sword met his in a clash of sparks. ". . . defend . . ." She sliced low at his legs. ". . . myself."

"The lass is beatin' his arse!" Angus roared with laughter, then yelped when Brodie cracked him broadside against his temple with the flat of his sword.

"D'ye intend to run me through, Kate?" Callum inquired with a provocative growl that sent fire down Kate's spine.

God's blood, she had to focus her thoughts on fighting him and not on the wickedly erotic grin on his face, the fire in his eyes. He was excited, his senses heightened. He was thoroughly enjoying himself. He looked so physically arousing, she found herself wondering what it would have been like to bed him that eve at the inn. She swung. And missed. His arm shot out and coiled around her waist. With a flick of his wrist, he spun her on her heels and hauled her back against his chest. One hand splayed across her belly, holding her close, while the other held the edge of his blade pressed to her throat. "Yer no' concentratin', Katie lass."

The throaty tangle of his voice against her ear made her nipples spring to life and press against her shift. She fought the titillating effect of him behind her and rammed the hilt of her blade into his ribs.

He released her and bent over slightly, holding his side. Kate leapt away and blew a lock of hair off her cheek.

"I intend to lay you flat on your back, Devil." She gripped her hilt in both hands and readied herself for his next assault. She countered his advance with a strike to his thigh, which he blocked almost too effortlessly. He shook his head, lowering it just a fraction to impale her with his gaze.

"And what will ye do to me when ye get me there, woman?" His voice thickened around that one word, as if to remind her that he could take her, dominate her, possess her. His lusty smile told her he wanted to do just that.

She brought her blade down hard. He leaped to the right, whirled on his boots, and whacked her backside with the flat of his blade. His grin widened when she glowered at him. He moved backward without even bothering to swing while she advanced, slicing at him viciously. "Did I say somethin' that distracted ye again, lass?"

Kate quirked her brow at him, beginning to understand the tactic he chose to employ. The rogue would resort to anything! Devil, indeed. Well, she could be just as devious. "Aye, Callum, the thought of me atop you distracted me." She sliced over his head, and almost took it off. "Or mayhap"—she moved forward, their blades clanging hard with each matched blow—"I would prefer you on your knees."

She attacked. And caught him.

He touched his fingers to the blood staining his shirtsleeve, then let his smile shine on her fully. "Well done."

"Och, Callum, forgive me!" She lowered her sword, dreadfully sorry that she'd wounded him—again. Before she had time to leap away, he was upon her, clipping the sword from her hands.

"Never show mercy to yer enemy, Katie." His heavy voice enveloped her like smoke. He spoke so tenderly her bones near melted to the marrow.

"I have nae enemy here, my laird MacGregor."

He reached her in one more stride, curled his arm around her waist, and lifted her off her feet into his crushing embrace. He dragged her mouth to his, claiming her with a long, hard, demanding kiss. His broad hand along her back molded her even closer to his rigid angles than she thought possible. His tongue plunged into her mouth, marauding her, stroking her in a dance so seductive she went weak against him. He pulled back from their kiss slowly, his eyes half-closed and burning. "I want ye."

Angus and Brodie had ceased fighting and stared open-mouthed at their laird and the lass clutched in his arms. Then Angus elbowed his smaller companion and the two moved to leave them in privacy. They stopped in midstride when Maggie's screams pierced the heated air.

～

Callum was the first to reach the barn. Panic coursed through him while his sister's screams echoed through a chamber of his heart he prayed every day to forget. He spotted her crouched behind a bale of hay beside Ahern's stall. She covered her face with her arms and did not look up even when her brother called her name. She wasn't injured, Callum knew by her position—by her terror. She had seen blood.

Kate rushed into the barn next, with Angus and the others. Hearing them enter, Callum turned and lifted his finger to his lips for silence, then motioned for Angus to search the barn. Something had triggered his sister's terror. Where the hell was Jamie?

Callum moved toward Maggie so softly his boots made no sound. When he reached her, he did not touch her but squatted before her. "Maggie, 'tis Callum," he said, his voice riddled with love and tenderness. If she heard him, she made no show of it but sank deeper into the shadows, a low moan vying with Matilda's honking.

Callum looked away from her only once to watch Angus hoist an unconscious Jamie out of the barn. Maggie's dear champion appeared to have fallen from the rafters. A trickle of blood covered his face, but Angus assured them with a quiet nod that the lad was still breathing.

"'Tis all right now, lass." Callum returned his attention to his sister. He knew she was in another place. And he knew where that place was.

"Callum?" her delicate voice touched him so profoundly it pulled a sob from the back of his throat.

He picked her up and cradled her body close to his chest, then turned and almost walked straight into Kate.

"Let's get her to bed," he whispered, holding Maggie closer. He closed his eyes and kissed the top of Maggie's head, then left the barn.

Chapter Twenty-Three

$\sim$

KATE LEANED against the doorframe of Maggie's chambers in silence. As she watched Callum bend to place his sister inside her tent, Kate's heart broke so completely for both of them that it numbed her. She felt the tears burning behind her eyes, but she was careful to hold them in check, for fear they would never stop falling. Her kin had done this—her own grandfather. When Callum rose to his feet, he turned and looked away from Kate's sorrow-filled gaze. He did not want pity. Kate knew it, but it was all she felt at that moment . . . besides the certain knowledge that she had fallen in love with the Devil MacGregor.

"She's asleep," Callum told her and ran his hand through his hair. "Hopefully she will sleep through the night."

"What happened to her today?" Kate asked when he turned to go to the window. "Please. Speak to me about it. What frightened her so, Callum?"

He looked out, remaining silent until Kate thought he would not tell her. Or he could not bring himself to. Then, with a muffled groan that seemed to wilt his broad shoulders, he finally spoke. "She is afraid of blood. It covered her, smothered her . . ." He turned to look at the tent again and swallowed back a well of emotions Kate feared he might never release. "Ye would think she'd abhor the confines of such a wee place, but it comforts her." Slowly, he faced Kate, ready to tell her what he had wished, had prayed to forget since the day they had escaped six years ago. "Liam Campbell kept my sister in a cage suspended just a stone's throw away from me." He forced himself to go on even though the horror on Kate's face clearly made him want to cease. "At first, I thought she would go mad. She was just a babe. Imagine what it must have been like cramped in a prison an inch larger than yer crumpled body." He ran his palm over the soft leather of Maggie's haven, his voice a loving whisper. "Argyll's men used to come and drag her oot and stretch her until she screamed from the agony of it." His haunted gaze found Kate's again. "I had to kill them, Kate," he said, moving toward her. "I butchered them. I killed them all with my sister clingin' to my back. I could no' stop, even knowin' what I forced her to witness."

"I understand," Kate told him softly, barely able to breathe. She suspected he was asking for her absolution. She gave it.

He took her hand and sat on the bed, pulling her down gently to sit beside him. "Nae, lass, ye dinna understand. D'ye know what she saw? 'Twas ugly, Kate. So ugly she makes herself ferget. But sometimes . . ." he paused, looking like he could not go on. "Sometimes she awakens from her dreams and she remembers."

It was then that Kate saw in his eyes the thing that

plagued him, that had utterly destroyed him. It was not the years of horror spent in a dungeon but guilt and self-reproach at what his sister had watched him do to escape it that twisted his features and dulled his eyes to a lifeless blue. "My sister would rather go back to the cage than to that one day and the blood I poured upon her. Yer uncle is right to call me a devil."

~

Kate walked along the shoreline, letting the frothy surf soak her feet. She barely felt the water chilling her flesh. Her thoughts were fixed on the dark, foreboding fortress before her, and on the man inside.

Callum MacGregor had survived the abyss of hell. He saved his sister from it, but what he had to become in the process near brought Kate to her knees.

Her tears fell heavy into the waves rolling beneath her feet. She could not weep this way in front of Callum, for his shoulders already carried enough, so she had left him and wept with unabashed abandon until the sun dipped below the loch. He had killed the men of her grandfather's garrison in a massacre that had made him a legend, and he believed it cost him the only thing he'd ever had the chance to love. His sister.

But Maggie *did* love him. Dear God, if Robert had saved her from such a cruel existence, Kate never would consider him anything less than the bravest of men. Maggie had many evils from her past with which to live, but Kate was certain that Callum was not among them.

Chapter Twenty-Four

CALLUM WAS NOT in Maggie's room when Kate returned. Aileen sat by the bed, working a small piece of embroidery by the light of a single candle. She looked up when she heard Kate enter.

"I'm to call Callum when she awakens," the handmaiden advised her, laying the embroidery in her lap. "Mayhap 'twould be wise if she did not see ye when she . . ." Her voice faded as she set her eyes on the tent. "Ye are a Campbell, after all."

Kate squared her shoulders and crossed the room to stand in front of her. "I will not leave. Whether you like it or not, I care for her."

Aileen peered at her through narrowed eyes, and Kate braced herself for the contempt bequeathed to her because of her name.

"Ye wield a sword right fine, ye do," Aileen complimented instead. "Even Graham is impressed with ye."

"My brother taught me." Kate began to smile, but then

her eyes opened wide. "Oh, heavens, I did not clean Callum's wound!"

"Aye, everyone's talkin' aboot how ye clipped the laird." Aileen's deep blue eyes fair glimmered in the soft firelight of the chambers. "Would ye teach me to fight like that?"

"Of course, but it was not my intention to hurt him, I assure you." Kate began looking around the room for what she would need to tend to Callum. She found a small basin of water and a strip of cloth beside Maggie's bed. "But I should tend to him. Aileen, please send him to me posthaste."

"Aye, m'lady." Aileen gathered her things, offered Kate a swift curtsey, then headed for the door.

When Aileen left the room, Kate crossed the rushes and crouched before the tent. She peeked inside. The wee lass was sound asleep, snoring, in fact. Kate gently removed a piece of straw from Maggie's hair and sighed. "Bless you, sweeting."

She waited for Callum, growing more apprehensive as the moments passed. Why did she send for him, she asked herself, dipping the cloth into the bowl. He had probably cleaned the wound himself. Why did she tell Aileen to make haste? God help her, she loved him. She lifted her hands to her throat. Loving him would most likely get her killed . . . or branded. Nae, Robert would never allow it. But what in damnation would become of her? Callum didn't love her. She was going back to Glen Orchy, or to Kildun. Once her uncle was dead she would never see Callum again. Her use to him would be over. She remembered his kisses and patted her flushed cheek with her wet hand. Callum MacGregor was passionate in his hatred—and his kisses. Her gaze drifted over the bed, and she quivered. She wrung the cloth until it was almost dry again. "God's breath, he makes me feel feverish."

"I hope the 'he' ye refer to is me, lass."

Kate whirled around, nearly knocking over the bowl of water. Callum stood in the doorway, blocking out the light from the hall. When he stepped inside he wore a smile that was becoming as familiar to her as his fearsome scowls, and even more mesmerizing. He closed the door behind him, coiling Kate's nerves into a springy mess. "Ye sent fer me?" he asked when she didn't answer his first query.

"I . . . I remembered your wound and meant to clean it."

His eyes fell to her trembling hands when she plunged them in the water again and snatched the cloth. She held it up, dripping water down her elbow. "See?"

He raised one dark brow and nodded, then crossed the room. Kate watched him check on his sister as she had. When he turned to face her, his expression unguarded and achingly tender, Kate saw the victory in this battle. She wanted it. She would have it.

"Where d'ye want me?"

"Closer." She let her heart speak for her.

"Careful, woman," he warned, his voice a deep-throated rasp. "Ye tempt me to throw ye on that bed and kiss ye until ye faint in my arms."

"I fear," she said, casting all she had left to win him to the battle winds, "if you do not kiss me, I will faint that much faster."

He was already moving toward her, helpless to resist. Cupping her face in his hands, he tilted her head upward. He gazed deep into her eyes, laying bare the tortured remnants of his heart while he swept his thumb over the delicate curve of her lower lip, parting her lips to receive him. He covered her mouth with his, caressing her, breathing her, consuming her, surrendering to her.

Kate opened her mouth to take him fully, clutching his plaid in both hands as his kiss deepened with barely checked desire. His arms closed around her, enfolding her in his protection, his strength, his desire. Here was what she longed for, to be here with him, just like this, cherished and treasured.

"I love you," she whispered when he pulled back slowly, searing her nerves with his hungry gaze. "I cannot stop myself, no matter what our names are. No matter who protests it."

He withdrew from her, and she watched in sorrow as he closed his eyes, distancing himself from her again. "It was difficult." She fought to keep her voice light. "You are not an easy man to care for, Callum. And Maggie loves you, as well. How can you not know that? Let us love you and prove you are no devil."

A low-pitched moan drew Kate's gaze back to the tent.

The flap opened, and Maggie left the comfort of her safe haven. She stopped upon seeing her brother. Kate paled at the hollow, vacant look in Maggie's large eyes. Maggie stared at Callum but didn't seem to see him at all.

A moment later, Kate knew the horrible truth of it. Maggie did see him, and she was afraid. She was terrified.

"They were dead," she said in a quivering voice that teetered on the edge of madness. "All of them were dead."

Callum did not blink. In fact, Kate was stunned to find his gaze on his sister almost as empty as Maggie's.

"His head. His head fell away."

"Kate?" At the sound of Callum's voice speaking her

name, Kate near leaped off the floor. "Ye should leave now."

"Nae."

"Callum." Maggie's voice shattered on a throaty sob. She swiped her hands over her face. "The blood was on me!"

"Aye, Maggie, I know," her brother whispered on a strangled moan of his own.

"Nae more!" she shouted. Huge tears teetered on her lashes, and her bottom lip trembled. "'Twas on my hands." Suddenly she ran to her brother and he caught her up in his arms. "Ye must cease! Please, cease!"

Callum held her, but he did not speak, and Kate knew it was his own guilt that silenced him. He had caused this terror.

"Cease, Callum!" Maggie screamed, and he closed his eyes, helpless to do anything more.

"Oh, dear God." Kate breathed, seeing the images of what happened that day. Callum had carried his tiny sister over his shoulder while he hacked at men from every direction. Nine years of torture, of watching his sister suffer, of hearing her scream, helpless to stop it. He lived in hell and had become a monster painted red with the blood of his victims.

"Please . . . nae more." Maggie's wails faded into a muffled sob. "Or they will surely kill ye."

"I'm sorry, Maggie, m'love." Callum groaned into her hair. He was only faintly aware of Kate slipping quietly from the room.

Chapter Twenty-Five

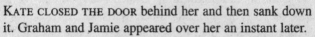

KATE CLOSED THE DOOR behind her and then sank down it. Graham and Jamie appeared over her an instant later.

"Come away," Graham urged gently while Jamie stared at the door, anguished by the sounds coming from inside, a slightly bloodstained bandage wrapped around his flaxen head. "All will be well with them."

Kate buried her face in her hands and wept softly. "If my grandfather was not already dead, I vow I would kill him myself."

Graham knelt beside her and then helped her to her feet. "Ye look like ye could use a warm cup of mead." He called over his shoulder as he led her away. "Come, Jamie, leave Maggie to her brother."

"I'll stay," Jamie called back, still staring at the door.

Graham brought Kate to the solar rather than to the great hall, since many of the men would be settling down for the eve. The only drink in the solar was whiskey, so Graham warmed it by the hearth fire and poured her a cup. Cool night air chilled the room. He pulled two oversized chairs closer to the fire and covered her shoulders with a blanket.

Kate folded her legs under her and sipped her brew. When she blanched, Graham laughed and warned her to go easy, lest she singe her insides.

"It does burn going down, doesn't it?"

" 'Tis another of old Gillis's concoctions," he told her, settling into the chair opposite her. " 'Twill warm ye fer certain."

She took another sip, slower this time, and stared into the flames. "Will it help me forget what my grandfather did to them? I do not blame Callum if he killed him."

"Callum did not kill him," Graham assured her. "If he had, mayhap he would have been satisfied."

Kate nodded, then looked at him beneath the veil of her lashes, too ashamed to look at him directly. "Did my father know of this?"

"I don't know."

Kate drank more of her brew and thought about everything. After a few moments, she spoke again. "Callum thinks he is a monster in Maggie's eyes. But she is not afraid of him, Graham. She's afraid *for* him. She wants him to stop fighting his war."

The commander swallowed a mouthful of whiskey, then closed his eyes as fire lanced through him. "I am afraid fer him, too," he admitted and leaned back in his chair. "He's determined to kill yer uncle. When he does, I fear the full power of the realm will come down upon him. Argyll knows it, as well, and taunts Callum with his cruelties against MacGregor women."

Kate shivered beneath her blanket. She knew her uncle was depraved. "He never came for us when we were children, though he promised to. He left us for the servants and my father's guardsmen to raise. As I grew older, he paid more attention to me than to Robert. I found out why last winter when he tried to kiss me."

Graham leaned forward in his chair and set his flagon on the floor. His gaze on Kate was unblinking, his voice low with controlled anger. "Does Robert know?"

"I never told him," Kate said. "I hope Duncan never finds us," she added into her cup.

"Us?"

When she looked at him, Graham was watching her with a mixture of concern and admiration sparking his gaze.

"'Tis a dangerous thing to align yerself with *us*, Kate." Graham's expression softened when she hiccupped. "Feeling better, are ye?"

She nodded and focused her attention on him. With the firelight softening his beguiling features and pouty mouth, he looked more angelic than even his younger brother. "I'm glad to see Jamie has recovered."

"Aye. 'Twas a minor wound. He fell from the rafters saving Maggie's cat."

"Who taught him such chivalry?" Kate smiled at Graham and cuddled deeper into her blanket.

The commander poured her more brew, his roguish grin proving to Kate it was not him who taught his brother such noble ideals. "Jamie is young."

"He cares so for Maggie."

"Then he is foolish, as well."

Kate regarded him while he smiled into his cup, his dimples twinkling in the flickering light. She was quite fond of Graham. From the moment they met he had treated her kindly. Though he was fiercely devoted to

Callum, he had never shown her contempt because of her name. He was kind and terribly charming. With that halo of curls falling carelessly over eyes of deep emerald, and a sinful smile that could melt the heart of the most stoic matron at twenty paces, it was not surprising that almost every woman in Camlochlin sought his attention.

"Love is not foolish, Commander."

He looked up. "I was bred fer war. 'Tis the only thing lasting and constant in this life. Love is fleeting."

"I see you laughing quite often with Aileen," Kate pointed out, "Do you mean to tell me you feel nothing for her?"

"Aye, I care fer her deeply. She is my sister."

"Och, forgive my hasty assumption." Kate blushed all the way to her roots.

"My sisters Sineag, Murron, and Mary live in the bothys outside the castle with their husbands and bairns."

Kate's eyes widened. "How many sisters have you here?"

"Just the four. But I have eleven sisters in all."

"How wonderful to grow up in a large family."

"Nae." He laughed. "I learned more about women than I'll ever need to know. The rest live in Edinburgh and Moray. One has even taken a Campbell fer a husband." He nodded when Kate raised an eyebrow. "This feud began long ago, and though it wasn't our feud to fight, the Grants have always been good friends to the MacGregors. Yer grandsire was a cruel man, but not all Campbells are like him. Ye, fer one, are quite enchanting." He couldn't help but grin at the delicate flush painting her cheeks. "And I did grow fond of Robert during my stay at Kildun."

Kate's eyes grew misty upon hearing about her

brother. It felt like centuries since last she saw him. "How is he, Graham? I miss him terribly. Tell me, how did you come to know him?"

The commander dipped his eyes to his drink and then quaffed the remainder of its contents before he spoke. "I was sent to Kildun to befriend yer uncle and gain his trust."

"Why?"

"Because Callum could not infiltrate Kildun. I was to lead Argyll's men to—"

Angus and Brodie saved him from having to continue by crashing open the solar door. "There ye are, ye knave." Angus entered first, a flagon of brew clutched in his giant paw. When Kate belched and waved at them, the brutish Highlander smiled like a puppy that had just been petted behind the ears.

"I guessed Graham was spendin' his night wi' a bonny lass. I was right."

"That makes one time in yer accursed life." Brodie snickered and moseyed inside. He found a seat, fell into it, and closed his eyes.

"Brodie, why are ye not in bed with yer wife?" Graham asked him, ignoring the string of oaths muttered by Angus while he searched for a place to sit.

"Because there's nae room fer me in our bloody bed. If Netta doesna deliver soon, I'm leavin' her."

Angus howled with laughter, but Kate frowned at them all. She wanted to chastise them, and she knew she should. She just could not remember what for. She did suddenly remember her conversation with Graham, though, and turned back to him.

"Did Robert send you all to Glen Orchy?"

"Nae," Graham said. "In truth, he was against our going."

"Think ye he's still wrapped aroond that gate ye tied him to?" asked Brodie, opening one eye.

"Tied . . . to a gate?" Slowly, Kate turned to fasten her eyes on Graham. "You tied my brother to a gate?"

"Brodie, ye bleedin' whoreson," Angus barked at him. "Ye made her weep." He looked around the solar. "Where are all the fokin' chairs?"

"Angus, mind yer damn tongue," Brodie admonished him sternly.

"Well, did you?" Kate demanded, untangling herself from the blanket. She would have leaped from her chair, but she felt dizzy and clutched the arms instead to keep from spinning. "Was he not your friend?"

Graham was about to tell her when the door opened again and Callum filled the doorway. His eyes fired with something so dangerous, Graham instinctively bolted to his feet. Callum's gaze wandered over each of them in turn and then came to rest on Kate.

"Ye'll tell me where yer goin' from now on, Kate."

"And you will never speak to me again, you heartless ruffian." She yanked the blanket completely off and sprang to her feet. Then almost toppled over. Graham caught her by the elbows. She didn't take her eyes off Callum while she righted herself. "You tied my brother to a *gate?*"

"Nae, Graham did," Callum told her.

She opened her mouth to tell him what she thought of him and burped instead.

In his chair, Brodie leaned his head back, closed his eyes, and smiled.

"Which one of ye gave her the brew?" Callum demanded, suspecting Angus.

"Graham did," Kate told him. "And though he is a very sweet man, I shall never forgive him for tying my brother to a gate."

"Ye should be thankin' him, lass," Angus said before downing the contents of his flagon. " 'Twas Graham who convinced Callum to spare the lad's life."

Callum shot Angus a murderous glare, which Angus answered by stepping behind Brodie's chair.

Kate blinked up at the commander and then took a step toward him. Graham moved back, unsure if she meant to hug him or rake out his eyes. She swayed on her feet for a moment, then turned her green-tinted face to Callum. "I feel ill."

Callum watched her pass out in Graham's arms, then sent his friend a scorching look before he snatched her from him and tossed her over his shoulder.

"Send Aileen back to Maggie's room," he commanded. "And if ye ever feed Gillis's brew to her again, I'll remove the teeth from yer head." He narrowed his eyes on the other two before he left. "Ye'll watch what ye say in front of her, or I'll take ye both to the fields and thrash yer godforsaken hides."

When he stormed out, slamming the door behind him, Brodie looked up at Angus and then both men roared with laughter. "Our laird is turnin' soft!"

"Aye." Graham felt his mouth hook into a smile while he stared at the door. "Finally."

Chapter Twenty-Six

KATE SLEPT SOUNDLY nestled beneath the warm furs on Callum's bed while he watched her well into the night. At first he paced before the bed, torn between his body aching for her and his heart aching to send her away. Dear Christ, she loved him. Was she daft? Didn't she understand that it was a death sentence for her? God's blood, it was his fault. He knew she didn't hate him. He had done nothing to stop her tender smiles. He let her think him a hero of sorts. He'd kissed her and more, knowing . . . He should have done all to protect her, for he was the gravest danger to her well-being. He'd even brought her to his bed! God, he wanted her there. He could not even think properly around her. And now, in her innocence, she had fallen in love with him. He might as well have killed her.

After the first hour of pacing like an anguished lion, he finally sat in the corner in a chair hidden by shadows. Flames from the hearth lit Kate's sleeping face and he watched her while another hour passed away. He already knew every contour of her features, every bonny curve that shaped her. He longed to know more of her. But the cost was too great. She had fallen into his arms, pierced by an arrow meant for him. How was he to know at the time that she would wreak such havoc on his heart? He was so sure of his defenses he hadn't bothered to guard them. And in so doing, he allowed her entrance into his hell. He had dragged her to his fortress and scribed the word *death* onto her forehead.

He clenched his teeth, his fists. He tossed his head back, needing to curse the heavens. He had hauled Maggie through the gates of damnation to save her. From what? He had become the very demons he sought to kill. And now he did the same thing to Kate. Death to MacGregor sympathizers. 'Twas the motto of the realm. *God, nae.* He knew he had no right to ask the Almighty for anything. *But please, just this one thing.* "Please," he whispered. "Strengthen me."

He stood up, determined to do what he must. She was forced. Taken against her will. Aye, 'twas all she had to tell them. He had not taken her. She remained unblemished. There was only sympathy. And sympathy was easy to destroy.

He walked to the edge of the bed and squatted, bringing his face close to hers. She was his redemption for sins he thought too foul to be forgiven. But he could not accept her gracious gift without putting her in mortal peril. His hatred ran deep, with no room for love. He would make her believe it. He would do it in order to save her life.

"I'll no' love ye, Kate Campbell. No' ever." He rose to

his feet, vowing to himself that she would never know
what a tortured liar he was.

～

Kate dragged her eyelids open and then slammed them
shut again at the ray of sunshine blaring like a herald's
trumpet through the window. Lifting her hand to her
head, she released a groan that sounded to her poor ears
like she was dying. And she felt like she was doing just
that. She willed herself not to move, since even the mer-
est breath shot bolts of pain to her head. Damn old Gillis
and his poison. After a few moments of reeling, she
slowly lifted her lids again.

God's blood, what happened to the window coverings?
She shifted as cautiously as her body would allow in
order to escape the blinding beam of light. Thick cobwebs tangled her thoughts and muddled her brain, and
then, like a curtain being drawn, she realized she was in
an unfamiliar room, a strange bed. Still too pained to
move her head, her eyes darted left and right. The ceiling
offered her no answers, so with great effort she sat up,
still holding her head to keep it in place.

She was in a man's room, that much was clear to her.
Everything in the room was carved of dark waxed wood.
Even the walls were paneled with thick slabs of it, making all the furniture in the room blend into an enormous
view of deep magenta brown. An intricately carved
wardrobe, taller even then Callum, stood between two
great chairs that could seat at least two people each.
There were three tables set up to house everything from
tankards of whiskey to a carved wooden chess set and as-
sorted weapons. A silver bowl for hand and face washing

rested on another table, along with a small candlestand. No tapestries decorated the walls; neither shield nor banner offered cheer. The windows were bare, and the absence of draperies around the poster bed told Kate that whoever slept here cared nothing about privacy. Yet despite the absence of color and fabric to offer warmth, the cavernous chamber heated Kate to the deepest corners of her heart. Of course, there was the giant alcoved hearth with its roaring fire to warm the bones, but Kate knew instinctively what made her feel like she belonged here all her life. It smelled like Callum, of wild heather and mist. *Aye,* she thought, closing her eyes to draw him to her. This was his chamber, his bed.

She was still smiling when Callum entered the room.

The sight of Kate sitting in his bed, her lush ebony curls tumbling around her shoulders and arms, set Callum's heart to pounding. He experienced a sudden rush of something so strong he near doubled over. When she turned her head and aimed her heady smile at him, he had the urge to drop to his knees and pay her the homage she deserved. He almost smiled.

Death to MacGregor sympathizers.

He scowled so fiercely at her it wiped the smile clean off her face. Propelling himself forward, he avoided her gaze while he crossed the chamber and stopped at the window.

"Is all well with you?" she asked, sensing by his cold, hard gaze that it wasn't. Her voice was low, pained, but Callum did not turn to look at her.

"Nae," he answered tightly. He gazed out the window at the distant heather. "There's a Campbell in my castle."

Kate's mouth fell open, and her heart drummed so

violently she felt it in her belly. She didn't hear him right. She couldn't have. "But I had hoped . . . Callum, you kissed me."

Now he looked at her over his shoulder. His eyes glimmered like cold cobalt glass against the sun. "Poor judgment on my part, nothin' more."

Kate sat, numb. Tears pooled her eyes and dripped over her lashes when she blinked at him. His eyes hardened on her. "Ye're leavin', Kate. My men will escort ye to the Stewarts' home on the morrow. Once ye arrive, ye'll tell their laird that ye escaped the clutches of the fearsome MacGregors. Tell him the truth, that the Devil abducted ye. Ask him to send fer yer brother. He will come fer ye, I've nae doubt. If ye see yer uncle alive, tell him I will come fer him."

"Why?" It was all Kate trusted herself to say. Her throat ached from the burden of smothering her sobs.

He turned back to the window and folded his hands behind his back. "I dinna need to give ye a reason."

"I want one!" she shouted at him. That her shout sounded more like a withered screech did not surprise her. Her head exploded with the aftereffects of Gillis's brew, and her heart ached to leap from her chest and into Callum's arms.

"Verra well, Kate. I'm weary of ye. I admit 'twas curious to have a Campbell in my midst that I didna want to kill. But I realize now that I canna . . ." He paused and closed his eyes, then gritted his teeth. "I canna stand the sight of ye. Leave my bed. Leave my castle. I dinna want ye here anymore."

Callum thought she would weep. He prepared himself for it. She loved him, 'twas obvious by the way she looked at him, spoke to him. She lit up like a brilliant morning sky when he entered a room, and he had just stomped the light out. He expected her to weep, to carry on the way a woman would. But when she rose from his bed and left him without a word to wither her dignity, he clenched his teeth to stop himself from shouting her name and ordering her to come back to him.

~

Kate ran directly to the garderobe, where she promptly expelled what was left in her stomach. Callum's cruel words echoed mercilessly through her mind. Over and over again she was forced to relive his rebuke. He had stood by that window like a warlord cast in stone, his back set straight like an arrow. God help her, but she understood why he hated her so. She did not blame him. She had hated the MacGregors, and she had not gone through one day of torture. He had every right to throw her out of Camlochlin. He had told her from the beginning that he would return her to her brother. She knew he could never love her, but she thought . . . She had hoped . . . Nae, she wept. It was her own fault for falling in love with him, for loving his home, and aye, she would declare proudly, his kin.

To Graham, who stood on the other side of the garderobe door, Kate sounded anything but proud. His heart wrenched at the rawness of her sobs, and for the first time in all the years he had known his dearest friend, he cursed the terrible beast who did this to her.

Chapter Twenty-Seven

KATE SPENT THE MORNING of her expulsion from Camlochlin alone. She refused Graham's offer to speak with Callum about his decision for her to leave. She didn't answer when Maggie knocked at her door, pleading with her to eat something. Kate didn't want food. She wanted to be someone else. She wanted to be a MacGregor. His woman, his love. But Callum had no love to give her. He seemed at times to be made only of hatred and anger. But there was more to him, she knew. There was humor and tenderness, and passion. A man whose eyes fired with pride and purpose when he spoke his name. A champion to his sister, and to her.

God, she didn't want to leave and never see his face again.

But she had pride, also, and she sat up finally and wiped her eyes. She would not spend her last day with this proud clan weeping with self-pity. She would let them know that not all Campbells were afraid to face their fate.

Callum stood on the battlements an hour later, heedless of the cold air blowing off Sgurr Na Stri. His eyes fastened on the woman in the training field with Jamie below, bracing her body as she slipped an arrow into its bow. She aimed, mindless of the satiny tendrils blowing across her face, and let the arrow fly. Callum's lips lifted into a slight smile of victory on her behalf.

He heard Graham's footfalls behind him long before the commander reached him. He did not turn around, nor did he take his eyes off Kate when Graham cleared his throat to announce his presence.

Reaching him, Graham leaned his elbows on the wall and followed Callum's gaze. "Brodie said ye changed yer mind about hunting this morn."

"Aye."

When Callum said nothing more and continued to watch Kate, Graham exhaled a slight sigh. "Yer eyes are verra telling, brother. Why do ye send her away when ye do not want her to go?"

"She's a Campbell." Callum slid his gaze to Graham for a moment before returning it to Kate. "She doesna belong here."

"That may be so, but it is not the reason you do this," Graham argued. "Are ye in love with her, Callum?"

"Nae."

"Aye, that's good to know." Graham gave him a pat on the back while he let his gaze rove over the woman below. "Because she's quite bonny and were it me, I'd not be able to think of anything but her in her betrothed's bed."

Callum whirled around and stormed away from him.

Graham heard the furious pacing behind him and smiled. Callum did care for the lass. Why, he was as jealous as a squire who just found his milkmaid in the hay with someone else. The commander decided to use that jealousy to convince his friend how foolish he was being. "I hope fer her sake her husband is not old. Someone as braw as she deserves a man who can satisfy her spirited appetite."

"What d'ye want, Graham?" Callum clenched his teeth at Graham's back.

"Want?" Graham turned and offered him an innocent shrug. "I want her to be happy. I like her. I pray to the saints the bastard does not beat her."

Callum's glacial glare was enough to make Graham clamp his mouth shut. "I know what yer thinkin', Graham. But I dinna love her, so cease yer games with me. She's a Campbell, my enemy, and she belongs with her kin."

"She is not yer enemy, Callum. She's in love with ye," Graham insisted quietly, more serious now.

"Then she's a fool!" Callum's voice exploded into a thunderous roar.

Ah, Graham thought, understanding finally. "Yer heart is set on protecting her, but think. She is *in love* with you. She is no longer safe anywhere but beside you."

Callum shook his head, refusing to be moved. "She knows the law. She will ferget me soon enough."

Graham held his palm up in surrender. "Verra well, then." He'd had enough and pushed himself off the wall. "I do not know who ye are anymore, if there's even a heart in ye left to save. But hear me, Callum MacGregor, if there be any part of ye that's still human." At his words, Callum blinked as though he'd been struck. "I'll have no part in delivering her into the hands of her uncle. And I'll pray that when she's returned she will have the sense to keep her true feelings silent. But fer hell's sake, look at her!" He set his eyes on her, obeying his own command. "She's as open and honest as a babe. They'll know her heart the moment they speak yer name."

"Then I must make certain her heart is against me."

Graham heard Callum's footfalls and turned to see where his friend was going, but Callum was already gone.

~

Callum charged down the stairs, taking three and four at a time. Let Graham think what he would of him, Callum was going to make Kate hate him.

When she came into his sight, his lips hardened into a tight line across his face, and his eyes glittered like a winter's night.

Kate stepped back when she saw him, then returned her attention to Jamie and motioned with her sword to continue practicing. But six feet, three inches of brawny male moving swiftly toward her was difficult to ignore. She bit her lip and almost lost a finger when Jamie swung at her.

Callum snatched Jamie's sword from his hand and shoved him away, all in one fluid motion. He rounded on Kate, a giant warrior with the cold promise of death in his gaze. "Ready yerself, Kate, or there will be one less Campbell in Scotland."

"Callum, I . . ." She began to tell him that she did not want to practice with him. She was frightened by his rage. But he swung, and the thunderclash of his blade against hers near knocked her off her feet.

At first Kate could only stare at him, in stunned disbelief that he would strike her with such force. Then he lifted his sword over his head, gripping the hilt with both hands, and she knew he was going to kill her if she did not fight back. She forced herself to stop thinking like a woman and act as a warrior. She parried another bone-crunching blow. Leaping backward, she braced her legs for his oncoming assault. Completely on the defense, she managed to block three more swings.

Just a few moments later she was gasping for breath, her hair damp with sweat and her muscles burning and quivering with spent strength. Even the McColls had not exhausted her this quickly. Then it was over. One hammering clash that rattled her teeth, and then one more that sent her heavy blade careening to the ground.

Callum advanced one step and pointed the tip of his flashing claymore at her throat. "How does it feel to be so close to death, Kate?" With the metal cold against her throat, he moved his body closer to hers and leaned down until his their noses almost touched. When he spoke, his voice lowered to a bear's growl. "Remember this day and the fear that suffocates ye. Ye might believe yer ready to face death fer noble reasons, but when the time comes, nothin' will matter but yer life. Remember this and dinna be a fool."

Kate closed her eyes, unable to breathe. He clutched her heart in his hand as he had promised. Why didn't he just kill her and be done with it? Was he so cruel that he would torture and tease her first? Nae, she had seen him comfort his sister. She saw the terrible pain in his eyes when he became Maggie's beast. He wasn't any of the things so many people believed him to be. He was proud and possessive, a defiant rebel who had given his clan a home and kept their name alive. He was a man who had become a monster to protect what he loved.

"Love is the noblest cause of all, Callum MacGregor," she said as defiantly as he spoke his name.

He shook his head at her. The flash of emotion that colored his eyes absorbed most of the hard edge in his voice. "Nae, 'tis poison to us both."

He walked away, pleading with God that she could hate him. If she couldn't, he would butcher any who punished her—and everyone else, until he drowned in their blood and ceased to exist altogether.

Chapter Twenty-Eight

KATE WATCHED HIM walk away. Every muscle in her body convulsed with the need to go after him. But she did not dare move. He had made his feelings for her more than clear. She could not bear to suffer them again.

She hugged herself to drive out the chill of a coming storm and swept her gaze across the wild moorlands and jagged mountain ridges swathed in mist. She had thought it beautiful here when she first arrived. But now Camlochlin felt harsh and infinitely lonely. It was a land as battle-scarred and unforgiving as her MacGregor. She would never touch him. Finally, she surrendered. She wanted to go home. She wanted her brother.

She scanned the surrounding hills. Was Robert close? Or at the other end of the Earth?

She was going to be taken back to Kildun, but Robert would not be there. She knew with her whole heart that her brother was searching for her. She had been so preoccupied living in her new pretend kingdom that she had not thought about what would happen if he found her.

Now the reality of it beat against her heart. If he came here, Callum would surely kill him. He had promised not to harm her brother, but Callum's hatred for her clan was too strong. He could scarcely stop himself from killing *her.* Robert would not fare any better if he found her on her way back to the Stewarts'. Chivalry would dictate that he fight for her honor. He might be able to kill one of Callum's men, but he would fall swiftly after that. Kate did not want her brother or any of Callum's men to die.

There was only one way to stop it.

～

Robert Campbell gritted his teeth as each bone-crunching blow Kevin Menzie delivered to Roderick Cameron resounded off the keep walls. One more and Robert would put a stop to it. He cut his gaze to his uncle standing a few inches away. The man was grinning!

"The Devil was here," Kevin spat, clutching the laird's plaid in his fists. "Ye'll tell us where he went, or we'll put fire to the whole fokin' village."

"I have no' seen him," Cameron said for the fourth time, blood dripping from his mouth and nose.

"He killed seven of my kinsmen!" Kevin lifted his fist to strike him again.

The blow was halted in midair by Robert's hand. "Cease this!" he shouted.

Kevin spun around, ready to strike him instead, but the murderous glint in Robert's eyes gave him pause. Then he smiled. "Or what? What will ye do? Go back to Glen Orchy and rut yer sheep. Ye have no stomach fer violence."

Robert's scorching gaze was unflinching. "Touch me and find out."

"Nephew." his uncle's voice dipped with mocking iciness as he took a step forward. Robert did not look at Duncan while he spoke, but at the Cameron laird. What honor was there in tying an old warrior to a chair and beating him senseless? "This man hinders us from finding your sister. Why do you seek to protect him? Allow Kevin to finish his questions so that we can save Katherine before the Devil kills her, if he hasn't done so already."

Robert caught the subtle look the Cameron gave him beneath his swollen eyelid. Kate was not dead. "I wish to speak to the chieftain alone."

"Nae," Duncan refused.

Now Robert turned to look at him. "Aye, or I will set my steed toward England and bring this matter to Cromwell, as it should have been done from the beginning."

For a moment their gazes locked in battle. The challenge in Duncan's cool gray eyes was unmistakable, but Robert would not be swayed. Finally, his uncle nodded and motioned for the Menzies to leave.

The instant they were alone, Robert bent to the laird and clutched his shoulders. "You have seen my sister. Tell me, was she harmed?"

"Nae."

"Where has he taken her?" When Cameron didn't answer, Robert shook him. "You give your loyalty to a man who butchered Menzies."

"Ask your uncle why the Devil killed them," Cameron replied weakly. "Better yet, go see fer yerself at Stuart MacGregor's cottage."

Robert pulled away from him and raked his hands through his hair. Hell, he didn't want to see. He'd waited his whole life to serve the realm, to fight at his uncle's side. But this was not fighting. This was something else entirely.

"Go to the cottage, young Campbell, and see what made yer sister weep."

"First you will tell me where he took her, and then I will see."

~

Robert left Rhona MacGregor's bedside, stepped out of the bothy, and summoned every ounce of strength he had in him not to retch. Instead, he set his eyes on his uncle staring at him from atop his mount.

"Why was she branded?"

"She broke the law, as did her husband and child. All Scotsmen have the authority to hold MacGregors to the law in any way they see fit. You know this."

Aye, Robert knew it, but seeing how the proscription was enforced was quite different than hearing about it. Infection festered in Rhona MacGregor's flesh. She would not live another se'nnight. And for what? Because of her name?

"You do not hold sympathy for them, eh, Robert?" his uncle asked him, his eyes as sharp as twin blades. "The Devil, and any other MacGregor chieftain, would cut off your limbs and scatter them to the four winds just to satisfy their bloodlust. This is the only way to keep them under control. It has been this way for many years. Now tell me where he has taken Katherine. I grow weary of your curiosity."

Robert strode toward his mount, spitting the foul taste from his mouth as he went. "East." He told his uncle what Cameron had said. "The Devil took her east toward Badenoch."

Chapter Twenty-Nine

"COME INSIDE WITH YE, Maggie. 'Tis goin' to rain." Callum knelt over his sister lying on her back in the cool heather not far from the castle.

She opened her eyes and smiled at him. Then she scowled, making no move to obey his gentle command. "Why did ye send Kate away? Jamie says ye hate her."

Callum blew out an explosive sigh and lifted his eyes to the hills so as not to meet his sister's accusing stare. He did not want to be discussing Kate. Not when the very thought of her made his arms ache with the need to hold her. He was doing the right thing, he told himself. Finally. "I dinna hate her," he answered. "But 'tis no' safe fer her to be here with us . . . with me."

When he looked at her again, she caught and held his gaze. Her brows quirked curiously at him. "Is it true, then, Callum?"

"Is what true?"

"Do ye think ye are so dangerous that even I fear ye?"

Her question was so unexpected, Callum simply stared

at her, unsure of how to answer. His sending Kate away had naught to do with him. Or did it? He was the Devil MacGregor, and all of hell would descend on the Campbells if Kate was harmed. Aye, what he could become frightened him. If anyone should understand that, 'twas his sister.

"Kate spoke true, then," Maggie said when the memories that haunted him darkened his expression. "Ye're no devil, brother. But ye are a fool," she scolded, though her voice was as tender as his had always been to her. "Ye took me away from that terrible place. Ye gave me back my life."

Callum had never hoped for absolution such as this. He had also never wept a day in his life, and he damn well was not about to begin now. "But yer dreams . . . the terror I caused you . . ."

"Aye," she agreed. "And each time ye leave Camlochlin to seek yer revenge, and I do not know if ye will return, the verra same terror grips me. This will end only with yer death."

He took her hand in his as understanding washed over him. Understanding he would have fought to deny, even now, if he had never seen something other than a monster in Kate's eyes. "I am a fool." He smiled, then cleared his throat when his eyes stung.

"Now will ye bring Kate back?"

"She hasna left yet, Maggie. But I canna—"

"She has so left!" she insisted, yanking her hand from his so she could slap her thigh. "She took Ahern and bade me call to the guards to allow her departure. I think Graham should have gone with her."

Callum tried to calm the fierce pounding in his chest

but failed as he leaped to his feet. "Nae! She could no' have left. No' alone!"

"I tell ye, she did," Maggie said adamantly while she rose.

"Christ!" He raked his fingers through his hair as if he meant to yank out every strand. His eyes searched toward Elgol. "When did she go?" He whirled around, dropped to one knee, and gripped his sister's shoulders. "Maggie, think hard. How long ago did Kate leave?"

"Och, 'twas long ago, Callum. 'Twas before I fed Matilda."

Since he had no idea when that was, he groaned, released his sister, then took off toward the stable, calling over his shoulder that she return to the castle. He was grateful to find Maggie finally doing what he asked when he flew past her on his mount.

Callum cursed on the wind that tore his hair away from his face while he thundered out of the glen. Why the hell would Kate do such a foolish thing? He snapped the reins, driving his steed faster. He was to blame. He had pushed her so hard she could not wait another day to be away from him. Driven by fear of what might become of her, he kicked his mount's flanks harder, urging the horse to fly.

He plundered toward Elgol just as the sky tore open above him. His eyes scanned the darkened cliffs and countryside, searching. She could not have been gone from the castle for any length of time without him noticing, he told himself, trying to remain calm—to contain his rawest emotions. Surely she could not have gone far with old Ahern beneath her. Praying she had not already reached the treacherous cliffs, Callum gritted his teeth to keep from crying out the name that had somehow become more important to him than his own.

～

Kate reached Elgol just before the heavens darkened and poured out their wrath upon the land. She was sure it was wrath, for the rain battered her flesh, saturating her bones until the cold numbed her limbs. The torrent obscured her vision and she slowed Ahern's pace, fearing she might lead them blindly over the cliffs. A few feet up ahead, a shadowy figure crossed her path. She pulled the old horse to a halt and swiped the rain from her eyes. The hair along her neck rose. A warning sounded in her head. Someone was watching her. She cursed herself for not bringing a sword, or at least a dagger, for protection on her journey. She heard the sound of feet pounding the muddy ground and turned, panic accelerating her heartbeat.

The man was upon her almost instantly. His fist caught her in the ribs, doubling her over. He yanked on her hair, pulling her off Ahern's back. She was too shocked by the sudden assault and too cold to fight back while she was dragged off the path and hurled against a wall of rock that separated the minty fragrance of forest from the briny scent of the sea.

Kate reeled backward and fell hard against a large boulder, one sharp edge barely missing the back of her head. Red, searing pain flared across her shoulder and then sent a numbing tingle down her arm, to her finger-tips. She gasped back the breath that was knocked out of her and pushed herself to her feet to face two men, their dark hair plastered to their satisfied faces. She clawed the rain from her eyes, trying to gain some control over her trembling fingers. The whitecaps behind her pitched and crashed hard against the rocks that lined the shore. Above her, the vast heavens deepened to charcoal gray and the rolling roar of thunder resonated through her bones.

"She's a bonny wench, Clyde. Are ye certain she's a MacGregor?" the first one said, sweeping his eyes over the length of her body. So lewd was his gaze, Kate almost looked away. These two would not kill her right away.

"Aye, she comes from the path to Camlochlin," Clyde sneered. "I dinna know if m' stomach can stand ruttin' a MacGregor."

Kate's fear faded into rage. She tossed each man a glare that would have made Callum proud, had he been there to see it. "Touch me and I'll rake your eyes out and toss them into the sea, you filthy son of a—"

Clyde took a step forward and cracked her hard across the mouth. She fell backward again, landing on her backside against the rock. "I see we're goin' to have to beat some courtesy into ye before we sell ye."

"What think ye we'll get fer her? She's bonny, she is." The other stared at the blood dripping over her bottom lip and licked his own mouth.

"No' much, Ewan. The barons dinna pay much fer MacGregor women, and even less if she be wi' child."

"Mayhap she's a MacLeod. Should we no' be certain first?"

Kate listened on in horror. They spoke of her as if she was naught more than a cesspit rat. This was what it meant to be a MacGregor. No honor, no dignity. No place was safe, not even here in Callum's own kingdom. Her life was worth nothing simply because they believed her name to be MacGregor.

"Ye'll tell me who yer laird is before I have m' way with ye, wench." Clyde grabbed a fistful of her hair and dragged her forward.

How difficult would it be to tell them who her uncle was? To simply deny a name?

It wasn't difficult at all.

It was impossible.

She was not a MacGregor, but it did not matter to her. Here was the noble fight of heroes. Would she cower to Callum's enemies by denouncing everything he fought to keep alive?

"Will I be defilin' m' body by touchin' ye?" Clyde demanded.

To do so meant more than just forgetting Callum's bravery and Maggie's suffering. It meant stripping away the existence of an entire clan. A clan that belonged to Scotland. And Kate was sure now that each time a MacGregor was killed or denied the right to bear his name, the very hills screamed out at the injustice of it. Yet the heather still grew in all its glory, the mists still lingered over the mountaintops, exploding into golden brilliance with the setting of the sun, as if reminding her children to never give up.

Kate lifted her gaze to her captors and wiped her mouth. "It is you who defile the name MacGregor when it falls from your loathsome lips."

Clyde raised his hand to strike her again, but Kate ducked low, picked up a rock, and smashed it against his temple. Clyde swayed on his feet, then staggered backward. A look of astonishment animated his face at being wounded by this waif of a gel who now stood ready to fight.

His companion charged her like a wild boar and caught her square on the jaw with his fist. Kate crumbled to the ground, unconscious even before she reached her destination.

A peal of thunder bellowed its rage, quaking the earth and its foundations. But 'twas the sound that followed that caused Clyde and Ewan to turn. 'Twas the sound of death. Ewan wanted to run, but sheer terror rooted his feet to the ground. Blindly, for he could not tear his terrified gaze from the direction of the unholy wail just beyond the fog, he reached out to where Clyde stood equally still, and clutched his companion's sleeve.

"Good God in heaven, 'tis him." Clyde's voice rattled with the certain knowledge of his imminent death. Many had heard of the fiend, MacGregor, but not so many had actually ever seen him. Tales were told about the laird of the mist around bonfires when the moon hung low in the sky and the wind howled like the souls of his victims. As elusive as a nimbus mist, he had been hunted for years but never caught. 'Twas whispered his was the blackest soul ever to walk the Earth. But Clyde swore by his poor mother's grave that the Earth itself lent to the beast's foul existence. For the heavens blackened, and out of a rising mist he rode like a demon ascending from the sooty vapors of hell.

He did not cut them down instantly, but leaped from the heaving creature snorting beneath him. For an instant he did naught but stare at the woman lying in the sand while the rain washed blood from her face into a thin rivulet beside her.

He groaned. The sound tore the last meager fibers of

courage from her attackers. Their death was swift. Both heads fell to the ground with one mighty blow.

Callum sank to his knees beside Kate, biting back another forceful groan. Reaching his hand out, he closed his eyes and touched her throat to discover if she lived. He sighed with such relief his shoulders sagged to his chest. He scooped her up into his arms and held her close before he kissed her cherished brow. She shivered, unconscious in his embrace, and he cursed the rain for soaking her so. Ahern was nowhere to be found, but had the old horse been standing beside him, it would have made no difference. Kate was freezing, and Camlochlin was leagues away.

The cave was easy to find. There were many carved into the jagged cliff walls of Elgol. Callum built a roaring fire out of dry driftwood found deeper within the rocky crevice and some dried seaweed, which he used to cushion the cold ground before he laid Kate upon it. He undressed her, getting her out of her dripping clothes, and then he, too, stripped naked and lay down beside her. Her teeth chattered, but still she did not awaken, making Callum pray the bastards had not struck her with anything more serious than their fists.

"Nae, ye just find it pleasin' to sleep aroond me, dinna ye, Katie, my love," he whispered while he soaked his vision with her. Now that she was back safely in his arms, he knew he had to have been daft to ever let her go. He wrapped one long leg over her hips and dragged her closer against his warmth. Facing her, he used his large hands to rub the cold from each limb. He did not stop until her flesh grew warm. She moaned and nuzzled closer to him. He closed his eyes to stop the wave of emo-

tion aching to be released, and the rush of silken heat that
having her naked body against his made him feel. "Och,
lass, what have ye done to this poor fool of a man? I
shouldna keep ye with me, and 'tis makin' me so daft I
canna think straight." He smoothed wet curls over her
forehead, watching her—watching her until he knew that
not being able to do so would be worse than being shackled to any dungeon wall. "God have mercy on ye, Katie,
but I love ye."

~

Kate's eyes drifted open an hour later. Thick cobwebs
settled over her like a warm woolen blanket. A very warm
blanket. She snuggled deeper beneath it and faded back
to sleep. She dreamed of Callum's handsome face so
close to hers, sleeping beside her, his strong arms clinging to her as if his survival depended on her. Somewhere
deep within her, her heart told her it did.

Chapter Thirty

~

KATE OPENED HER EYES. For a moment she thought she was still dreaming. But, and God help her, that face was real. The warm, spicy breath falling on her cheek was real. He had come for her, saved her from . . . She lifted her hand off Callum's chest and brought it to her swollen lip. An instant later, her gaze slipped back to him.

His bare chest.

She looked down and squeaked. She was naked! He was naked! Instinct made her jerk away from him, but his arm curled around her more firmly and then hauled her into an embrace that snatched the breath from her body. She gasped. He snored. Her bones went pliant against him. What was this? How had he found her? Why had he found her?

She would ask him why later; right now she was too occupied with the task of trying to still her beating heart, for it rejoiced with such a loud thumping she was sure it was what had awakened him. For when she looked at his face again, his gentle gaze made her tingle all the way down to her toenails. She smiled and then blushed.

Callum was sure his poor heart would never recover.

"Where are our clothes?" she whispered, lowering her gaze modestly.

"Dryin'. Ye were freezin' and I had to keep ye warm."

He still had not released her, and she did not want him to. Not ever again. "Why did you come for me?"

He pulled her closer into the steel of his arms. "I didna want to send ye away, Katie."

"They were going to sell me." She closed her eyes and pressed her cheek to his chest. "And all I could think of was you."

Callum's jaw danced beneath his flesh. God help him, how could he ever live without her? "Dinna fear, lass. They'll no' be comin' back."

Kate did not hear the terrible beast in his voice, only the hollowed guilt of a man who knew killing was the sole way to survive and wished it wasn't.

She stared up into the flames of his eyes, blue-gold kilns where his passion for life, for hope, for revenge, and for redemption burned. He had killed many. He had become something detestable, and his cause had ceased to be an honorable one in his own eyes. But nowhere in that powerful gaze was there hatred. She smiled, suddenly understanding why he had sent her away. He became a monster to save what he loved.

"You rescued me again."

God's mercy, would she always look at him as if he were a hero? Callum wondered. Even when he tried to enlighten her about his black heart, she refused to see it. "Kate." he almost didn't want to utter it. Damn it, he had to admit to himself that he quite honestly loved being a hero to her. But he was not a knight. He was not a hero. "I'm naught but a coldhearted bastard. I—"

She shook her head. "You are more than I ever dreamed of. What you do, you have been forced to do to protect those you love, to save your clan from extinction. Sometimes I can do naught more than ask the Lord what I have done to deserve meeting a man such as you, my laird MacGregor."

His gaze ravaged her with a need so profound she felt her heart stall. He brought his fingertips to her lips and angled his head toward hers. "Yer bruised." The husky warmth of his voice singed her nerve endings. "Does it pain ye?"

"Aye," she barely whispered.

He kissed her mouth softly. "Still?" When she nodded, he kissed her again, gentle, meaningful kisses that made her head spin. "How aboot now?"

"I fear it is bruised mightily, my laird." Her long lashes fluttered against his cheek. She parted her lips, waiting.

He did not make her wait, but rose up over her and watched her surrender beneath him. His breath was heavy, ragged. He looked like he wanted to say something—something that might rip his heart from his chest. He grazed his lips over hers and kissed each one with worshipful appreciation. The length and breadth of him descended full upon her. He parted her lips with his fingertips and then licked the seam of her mouth. 'Twas not the powerful control he possessed that made him so exquisitely thorough in the claiming of her mouth, but the need to savor every moment of touching her.

She opened easily to his plunging tongue and moaned into his mouth as he tasted her. She felt his rigid flesh against her untried body, but it did not frighten her. He was her knight. A savage in his own right, but his hands moved over her like silken flames, so utterly tender she thought she might go mad. When those hands found her breasts, a low sob of need escaped her. She arched her back to meet his hungry mouth sooner, and the wondrous agony of his warm lips caressing hers sent a titillating explosion of fire down her belly and between her legs.

When he broke their kiss to stare into her eyes, she smiled at him, loving him and wanting to be with him this way. "Kate," he whispered, and the desire in his eyes changed into something more pleading. "If we do this, ye'll be a MacGregor and nothin' will be able to change it."

She heard the fear for her well-being in his voice and stroked her fingers along his tight jaw. "I am already one, and nothing can change it. Nothing." She pulled him down, without having to use much force, and kissed him until he felt her whole heart in it.

He molded her breasts with delicate mastery, suckling and nibbling until he had her writhing beneath him. "Ye taste fine." Closing his lips around her sensitive crest, he sucked and brushed his tongue hard across her nipple.

Kate tunneled her fingers through his hair and held him to her. She wanted him never to stop, but the heated ache in her loins demanded to be satisfied. When he laved his tongue down her belly, Kate pushed herself up on her elbows to see just what he was going to do. His tongue fluttered over her skin, revealing his intentions. She had the urge to pull away, but the thought of his mouth *there* was too arousing to deny. Just when she thought she might swoon if she didn't feel him soon, he looked up at her from beneath his dark brows and the sexual fire blazing his eyes was enough to make Kate's legs spread wider. He dipped his face. Kate held her breath. His kiss was like a flame that spread out of control through her blood. He took his time laving, feasting on her fully. Then, taking both her ankles, he lifted her legs and opened her wider, exposing her fully to his hungry mouth.

Kate groaned and licked her lips as searing jolts of ecstasy wracked her body. She felt wicked clutching fistfuls of his hair while he pleasured her beyond endurance. Craving release, she cried out his name and watched him rise up on his knees, still holding her legs apart. Her vision drank in the full glory of him above her, so powerful, so acutely male.

She watched him enter her slowly, sensually. She was sleek enough from his mouth and her passion for him to glide halfway into her, despite her body's tight resistance. His thighs flexed on the verge of burying him into her fully. He was going to take her, and she was helpless to stop him.

She lifted her arms over her head and undulated her hips, snapping his control. The initial pain was naught in comparison to the sizzling friction of his powerful shaft dipping in and then out of her. He grew still and asked her not to move, not to speak. The muscles along his arms shuddered as passion's talons gripped him and he resisted. He released her legs and bent his head to kiss her, then lowered his weight to hers. He angled his hips and surged against her hard, hot crux.

He made love to her slowly, and with such tenderness, Kate felt as if time slowed just for them, so they could both relish every moment, every touch. Taking her fill, she slid her fingertips across the breadth of his scarred shoulders, down the dip of his spine. She looked at him to find his eyes already on her face, taking her in as if the very sight of her gave him breath. She basked in him, as he did in her with every long, deep thrust.

Her sheath tight around his length, she spread her palms over his tense thighs to feel each plunge. Pleasure heightened to its pinnacle; her muscles convulsed beneath him. He answered by driving into her with slow, deliberate strokes until her fingers clenched his buttocks and rapture engulfed her. She watched, as if in some erotic, clandestine dream, his sensuous mouth curl into the wickedest of smiles before he lifted his head and erupted inside her.

Later, she lay nestled in the place that had become more familiar to her than her home. Callum's arms would always be here to hold her, to protect her. She was certain of it, as certain as any young woman in love could be. She kissed his chest, then ran her fingers over the rippling planes of his abdomen.

He captured her hand in his and brought it to his lips. But he remained silent for so long Kate raised her head to look at him.

"What troubles you? Tell me, please."

In the amber glow of firelight, his gaze was open and his heart exposed. Would she ever get used to the way his eyes tried to speak to her from beyond the darkness that plagued him? She ran her fingers over the shadowy dimple in his chin.

"What is it, Callum?"

"The world," he told her, "suddenly seems perfect." She nodded, but an instant later he exhaled a great, deep sigh. "But 'tis no' perfect, Kate. Mayhap Ennis has it aright. I dinna know anymore."

"Ennis Stewart?"

"MacGregor. Ennis MacGregor. He changed his name."

Kate bolted upright. Callum had to smile at the beauty of her sitting there all pale and ready for a battle, her dark tresses tumbling down her bare shoulders. She was his, and it made him happier than he could ever remember being. Being here with her like this—why, it could make him forget everything else in the world.

"Callum, you would even consider such a thing?"

He dragged his gaze away from her breasts and grinned into her storming ebony eyes. "No' until that day I was sealin' yer wound and ye called me Clalum MacKreglor."

"I would never allow you to do it!" she admonished him. "I would never allow you to deny what you love."

He reached up and cupped her cheek in his palm. "Even if it meant yer life?"

Kate choked back a sob. She had become another responsibility to him. Dear God, she wanted to give him rest. She wanted to reassure him that no matter what happened, no matter what became of her, it was her choice. "I would give my life for you."

Callum closed his eyes, unable and unwilling to bear the thought. "Kate," he said, looking at her again, his voice a warm caress. "D'ye think lovin' someone makes dyin' fer them easier?"

She nodded. "Aye. Aye, I do, Callum." When he shook his head and turned away from her, she touched his jaw, bringing his gaze back to her. "Or do you think you are the only one worthy to be willing to give your life for something you love?"

Callum's heart pounded in his ears. Of course, he understood that any true MacGregor would be willing to die for his name. But he would not let her die for it.

He wanted her, needed her in his life. Every time she looked at him, every word she spoke to him, all worked at making him forget the injustices he and his clan suffered. How could he be angry at the world, when the world had given him Kate Campbell?

But she could be taken from him.

The thought chilled his soul and stirred the beast. She already loved him. She already declared herself a Mac-Gregor. He'd made love to her, spilled his seed into her. But all hope was not lost. Nae, mayhap if he kept his heart silent, if faced with a choice for her life, she would choose to live. "I willna let ye die fer me, Kate."

Well, it wasn't a declaration of love, but he cared for her. She knew he did. She would worry him about it no more. She gave him a sympathetic pat on the hand and rose to gather her clothes. "I do not intend to die. When I return to my brother, I will—"

He snatched her wrist and pulled her back until she was sprawled over his chest. "Ye're no' returnin' to him."

"I'm not?" she asked.

"Nae." He traced her features with his smoldering gaze, then drew his fingers over her parted lips. "Ye're mine and ye'll be stayin' with me."

"But I worry for my—"

"Katie?"

"Aye?" She smiled at the sound of her name spoken so sweetly from his lips.

"Ye talk too much, lass." He devoured her mouth, capturing anything further she wished to say while his hands slid down her back and over her soft buttocks.

Chapter Thirty-One

⁓

THEY RODE BACK to Camlochlin with Kate comfortably nestled between Callum's thighs. They did not ride on the wind, but he kept his mount at a slow trot, enjoying the feel of her against his heart. It had been a long, torturous eternity since he held anyone so close to that sacred place. When he had told her he would die clutching a Campbell heart in his hands, he truly had no idea that heart would be hers. He had not been prepared, and doubted he ever would have been, to hand his heart over to her in return. Aye, he had tried to make her loathe him in order to save her life. For her life meant more to him than his home, his kin, his name. He had no doubt he would give up all for her. But 'twas his soul he had been trying to protect, also. He had lost it once because he loved. To lose it again terrified him.

Losing Kate terrified him even more.

Along the coastline on which they traveled, frothy whitecaps crashed in a rolling crescendo against the low, jagged cliffs, launching sea spray twenty feet into the air. Kate watched it, thinking how very much Callum was like the ocean, all turbulent and raging and powerful. She clutched his hand at her belly and leaned her head back against his chest, enjoying the wonderment of the day. The rains had ended and the sun shone like an orb of fire in the pale sky, but a brisk chill remained in the air, making everything smell clean and crisp and new.

A new day. Callum enfolded her deeper into his embrace and bent his face to the crook of her neck. He kissed her curls. She heard him inhale deeply, and the brawn of his body surged up against her like the waves to her left.

Kate sighed softly on an exhilarated breath. Her eyes slid to the east, where the forest had just begun to fall away in place of fallow fields where woolly cattle grazed with sluggish indifference on overgrown grass. Before her, the Cuillins rose up—a stone behemoth shielding its children beneath its vast black wings. A mist rolled over the sharp peaks and drifted downward toward the earth like a gossamer avalanche. Everywhere Kate looked she beheld power and beauty, land so achingly feral and beautiful it was almost painful for a mere mortal to gaze upon it overlong. Skies so vast she had the urge to spread her arms and bask in the freedom flying would bring. The Highlands and the people who inhabited them belonged to each other. Never was it clearer to Kate. She doubted one could survive without the other and wondered at the same time if this untamed land compelled its people to fight against attempts to subdue them, or if the people's untamed will and stubborn resilience made the land so wildly breathtaking.

"Will we have children together, Callum?" she asked wistfully, suddenly wanting to bear all his bairns here.

"Aye. I want many sons."

She turned to give him a haughty look. "Think you, you would allow me to bear some daughters?"

Humor fanned the flames of his eyes. "I would allow it only after a son."

"Humph." Kate swung around to conceal her smile, only to quiver in his arms a moment later when he parted the curls at her nape and spread his hot breath there.

"We could stop right here and continue our effort to make one."

"I think not," she said. "We are not even wed. And now that you mention it, I remember hearing Aileen and some of the other women talking at the castle, and they said that if a man wishes to have a son, he and his wife must wait until the waxing of the full moon. I think that is . . ." She counted on her fingers, then nodded. "Aye. A fortnight away."

Callum's head snapped up from its thorough ravishing of her neck, and he glowered at her raven curls. "I willna be denied fer a full bloody fortnight, Kate."

"Och, but ye will, Callum MacGregor." She imitated his thick Highland burr.

"Are ye makin' sport of my speech, woman?" he asked, sincerely surprised that she would do so.

She laughed, a rich, beautiful sound. "I find your speech quite enchanting."

Appeased, he allowed himself a smile. "There's much to learn aboot the MacGregors."

"Such as?"

"Such as the men, especially the laird, will no' be black-mailed." He yanked his plaid over his hard cock and, dropping the reins, curled one arm around her waist and lifted her gown over her hips with the other. He slipped his hand over her throat and pulled her close to rake his teeth across her skin. "I've wanted to take ye like this fer too long now," he whispered huskily in her ear, then lifted her enough to thrust his silken lance deep within her without breaking stride.

His big hands on her hips guided her up and down on his steel shaft, making her feel every inch. His low groans along her flesh sent flames up her spine. When Kate looped her arms around his neck behind her, he shoved her down hard, then swept his palm over her belly and lifted her again. He dipped his fingers to her swollen bud and stroked her until she pitched against his chest.

"I say son." He smiled into her nape and lurched upward. "What say you, Katie?"

"Twins," she bargained and then laughed with him. He grew serious an instant later when he whispered how he felt inside her. Then he showed her by cupping her from front to back in his hands and sliding her up, almost over his thick, sensitive head, then back down to his hilt.

To say that he was gentle in his lovemaking this time would be sheer folly on Kate's part. Her breasts ached, her neck felt delightfully bruised by his wicked teeth, and the backs of her thighs would surely bear the truth of his passion before the day's end.

Sometime later, when his four most loyal warriors came upon them just before they reached the crest of Camlochlin's glen, Kate's hair looked as if she had been caught in a violent Highland storm, her cheeks were flushed, and her gown twisted almost backward on her shoulders.

Brodie grinned from one ear to the other. Angus belched and nodded his head as if his approval was all that was needed to complete this pair's binding. Graham pulled up short on the reins and regarded Callum and the suddenly bashful woman in his arms with a measured look. Jamie was the only one in the group scratching his head, befuddled by their appearance.

"Where are ye all off to?" Callum looked each one of them over, adding a well-deserved scowl to Brodie's knowing wink.

"Maggie told us ye barreled out of here like there was a fire on yer arse," Graham told him, still unsure if his instinct was deceiving him. He had tumbled enough wenches to recognize when they'd been thoroughly tumbled. "What the hell happened to ye, Kate?" he asked her while she inconspicuously patted the last of her unruly curls into place.

Her cheeks went crimson almost instantly, and Graham would have smiled if the sight of her bruised face hadn't made his blood go cold.

"Graham, if ye have a question to ask, ye'll ask me." Callum aimed his fierce glare on his commander.

"Verra well." Graham switched his attention to Callum. "What the hell happened to her face?"

How had he forgotten that? "She was attacked on the road." When they demanded the full tale, he told them. "I killed the whoresons."

"Callum." The braw tilt of Jamie's chin struck Callum in the gut, and the laird arched his eyebrow and waited for Jamie to continue. "Ye canna be so careless to let her oot of yer sight again. I think I should watch over her when ye're angry with her."

Kate almost wept. She would have leapt off Callum's horse and hugged the young warrior had he not visibly cringed when Callum inched his mount closer to his.

"So ye're her champion now, are ye, Jamie? What of Maggie?"

Whatever resolve Jamie possessed a moment ago fair

dripped off his shoulders until they slumped in defeat. 'Twas too late—he had started this, and now he knew he must finish it. He swallowed audibly, then cleared his throat. "Ye know that I would never let harm come to Maggie. But Kate needs . . . She needs . . ." Callum waited patiently while the young warrior fought to girdle up his loins again. "She needs . . . someone . . . to . . . to protect her," he finally spat out.

Callum nodded and thought about it, taking his time and trying to subdue his amusement. "Verra well, Jamie. Yer duty is now to guard my sister and Kate when I'm unable to do so. But"—he leaned forward, fastened his piercing gaze on each of them, and then, miracle of miracles, began to smile—"there will be only one Sir Galahan fer this lady at Camlochlin. And that'll be me."

Jamie scrunched up his face. "Who?"

But Callum did not answer. He flicked his reins and left his men there on the crest, each one wearing the same gaping expression of astonishment on his face, save for Graham, who snatched Angus's brew out of his large paw. He held it up to the couple descending the ridge, and his lips curled into a grin. "To knights, and the ladies who love them," he toasted, then took a hearty swig of whiskey.

～

"It's Sir Galahad."

"Hmmm?" Callum set his gaze on his home and then on the back of Kate's head. God's teeth, he was so damned happy he was beginning to feel like a fool.

"Sir Galahad, not Galahan," she corrected him, then angled her head to toss him a mischievous smile. "But you'll do, MacGregor."

Behind them, Callum's men heard a sound they all felt quite sure they never heard before. It drifted backward and filled the glen with echoes.

"Did ye hear that?" Brodie slowed his horse, waited a moment, then slammed his fist into Angus's shoulder. "What's in that brew? I'm fearin' 'tis made me daft."

Angus reached out and near broke his cousin's nose—which would have been the third time—with a hefty swing. "Next time ye insult me brew, I'll rid ye of yer teeth, ye bastard MacGregor."

"Yer no' daft, Brodie." Jamie stared on ahead, his huge blue eyes wider than twin seas. "I hear it, too."

Angus jammed his finger in his ear and wiggled it. "I'll be damned, I hear it."

Jamie turned his awe-stricken gaze to Graham. "What does it mean?"

"It means yer laird is laughing, ye bunch of lackwits." Graham kicked his mount's flanks and raced after Callum and Kate, calling over his shoulder. "Have ye never heard the man laugh before?"

Jamie watched his brother ride away, then turned to the others and shrugged his shoulders. "Only before he aimed to kill someone."

Angus tossed him his pouch of brew. "Here, drink up, lad. Things aroond here are aboot to change, I'd wager. Ye're goin' to need all the hair on yer chest ye can gather."

Brodie laughed. "First he'll be needin' some hair on his . . ." He almost swallowed his tongue at the force of Angus's palm striking behind his head.

"Mind yer tongue," the burly warrior warned. And then Jamie took off after his laird, leaving both of his brutish friends on the ground, their fists flying.

Chapter Thirty-Two

CALLUM SAT IN THE GREAT HALL with Graham and had just shoved a slice of bread into his mouth when Brodie dragged a chair across from him and sat. Callum looked up briefly, then set about finishing his meal. After another full moment had passed, Callum lifted his gaze again, quaffed his drink, and then slammed the cup down on the table.

"What the hell are ye starin' at?"

Brodie didn't blink. Instead, he rested his elbows on the table, moved slightly forward, and peered at Callum more intently. Graham snickered and pushed his chair away from his friend's, not wanting to be in the way when Callum started trouncing the poor fool. And by the looks of it, Brodie had been trounced already this day. The bruise around his swollen eye was already turning an interesting shade of purple. Angus most assuredly, Graham decided with another smirk.

"Are ye sufferin' from some ailment we should know aboot?" Brodie asked him quite seriously and went back to studying him.

Callum turned to Graham, seeking some interpretation. When none came, he slid his gaze back to Brodie. "Do I appear ill to ye?"

"Aye." Brodie nodded. "Ye do." The corners of his eyes crinkled from his continued scrutiny. "Yer a bit flushed aroond the ears, and the way ye were howlin' ootside we figgered ye must be ill . . . or goin' daft." He sat back and added a low mumble.

Graham moved farther away in his chair, taking his cup with him. But the reaction he expected never came. Callum did not throw his chair back and yank Brodie to him by the scruff of his neck. He simply sat there, a wry quirk playing at the corners of his mouth. "Brodie, where's yer wife?"

His cousin looked around the great hall, then shrugged. "She's aroond here somewhere."

"Ye should be with her."

"I should?"

Callum nodded, "Aye, ye should."

"Why?"

"Ye love her, dinna ye?"

"Eh? What the hell has that got to do wi' anythin'?" Brodie asked him, sincerely confounded.

Before Callum could answer him, or, heaven forbid it, laugh again, Angus threw himself down into the seat nearest Brodie. "I think I broke me finger on yer face."

Jamie appeared and took his place at Callum's left. "Speakin' of faces." He reached for a hunk of bread on the table. "What happened after ye saved Kate from her attackers?"

Callum scowled at him, then went back to eating, ignoring the lad's eager eyes.

"He recited a saintly prayer over her bonny head and raced her back here, where he would have nae time alone w' her." Brodie shook his head at Jamie. "What the hell do ye think happened after that, ye whiskerless pup?"

Realization finally dawned on the youngest of Callum's warriors, and he blushed a fresh shade of scarlet. "Are ye claimin' her, then?"

Callum downed the rest of his ale, then looked up at them. "Aye, I am."

The smirk Brodie wore on his face vanished suddenly and he dropped his mutton back into his trencher. "That's why ye asked me if I loved Netta. Christ, Callum, ye dinna love the lass d'ye?"

"Should I send fer Faither Lachlan, then?" Jamie asked eagerly.

"Dinna bother," Callum said as he stood from his seat. "Our sacraments are no' recognized by the church. But I dinna need a priest to approve our union. She's mine, and I'll protect her from the law." He swept his gaze over each of them. "Do any of ye take issue with my decision?" His men shook their heads. "Good, then I'll be goin' to bed."

"Bed?" Jamie asked incredulously. "But 'tis still light oot."

Angus threw his head back and bellowed with laughter, but Callum barely heard as he picked up his pace heading for the stairs. When he was sure he was out of his men's vision, he took the stairs three at a time. Kate was in his chambers, and he'd been eager to get there since she left him for a bath. She did not need one, he reasoned. She smelled fine already.

He stopped on the stairs, lifted his arm, and took a sniff. No' too bad, he thought. At least he smelled like a man. Damnation, is this what love did to a man? Was he destined to become a smiling, blithering fool, so concerned with his odor that he would forget how refreshing fighting felt? By the time he reached the second landing his scowl turned into full-blown brooding.

His men had already noticed the change in him. Why, Brodie even thought he looked ill. With that thought souring his mood further, Callum ran his hand over his jaw, feeling for any sign of softness. He cursed under his breath and set his hard gaze on his chamber door. Kate was probably in there neatly arranging pink lilies in delicate little vases. He kicked an empty bucket out of his path. Now that she was his, she'd be staying in his chambers. Hell, he was going to have to get used to having a woman loitering around in his things. He stopped and paled as an even more horrid thought came to him. Mayhap she was polishing his bloodstained swords. God's blood! He picked up his steps and almost sprinted the rest of the way.

The door to his chambers was slightly ajar when he reached it. He was about to plunge inside and stop Kate from whatever she was doing when he heard her voice.

"Umm, does that not feel good?"

Her silky groan of delight pricked his ears and froze his blood. Heart pounding, he splayed his palms on either side of the doorframe and moved closer to the opening.

"It feels like silk. It is so smooth. I can scarcely wait until it grows."

Callum ground his teeth together, thinking of the slowest and most painful way of killing the rogue bastard in there with his woman. With his bare hands, he decided.

"Yer efforts are fer naught."

His stomach twisted when he heard his sister in there, as well, her voice pensive and soft. "It does not seem to be working. He has not tried to kiss me yet."

Kate giggled. "That's because he's afraid of your brother."

And well he should be, Callum thought, plunging into the room. He looked around, ready to remove someone's head. His sister offered him a grin from where she sat while Kate meticulously brushed her hair.

"What's . . . what's goin' on here?" he asked rather weakly, all the wind blowing out of his sails.

Kate offered him a smile that knotted his pitiful guts. "Your sister agreed to let me brush her hair. She is quite bonny, aye?"

Callum's gaze dipped to Maggie. "Aye." It sounded to his ears like a squeak, and hell, he would have scowled if he could stop the damn grin that insisted on curling his lips.

"Callum," his sister inquired. "Are ye ill?"

There. His scowl returned to him full force. He almost sighed with relief, fearing it had abandoned him altogether. Maggie laughed and he melted all over again. Was this his sister sitting here with bows in her hair where crickets had once roamed? She was clean! She was wearing a fresh gown! And all at once, before Callum could stop them, his eyes misted. He blinked a few times as if some flying mote had landed in his eyes, then went to her.

"Ye're a bonny lass." He slipped two fingers under Maggie's chin and lifted her face to his. "Who woulda thought it?"

"Och, go on with ye." Maggie waved him away. "Ye knew I was bonny all along."

He laughed, and his gaze was involuntarily drawn back to Kate. Their eyes met. For a moment Callum lost all thought. His laughter faded into a heart-wrenching smile of intimacy that sent Kate's pulse racing.

Suddenly there was a hand waving before his eyes. Callum wrenched his gaze away from Kate's and looked down at his sister. She grinned up at him, her teeth flashing. "Thank ye fer bringing her back."

Callum kissed his sister's clean head and sent her on her way. He followed her to the door and bolted it when she was gone.

Watching him, Kate was not sure if it was the mere sight of him that made her breath fail, or the smoldering intent in his gaze when he turned back to her. Her eyes glided over his form. There was so much of him, and all of it so wonderfully defined. Beneath his plaid of dyed wool, his shirt stretched across the broad flare of his shoulders. His belt hung low on his lean hips. The tattered edge of his plaid reached just above his knees, revealing a few inches of his bare muscular calves, encased in his hide boots. She searched her mind but couldn't seem to remember any man in her father's or uncle's guard who was as handsome as Callum.

"Ye didna bathe yet." The husky timbre of his voice heated Kate's blood. He stepped forward, unbuckling the belt at his waist.

"I was tending to Maggie and have not had the chance." She didn't know she was holding her breath until Callum reached her and she sighed. Hands that killed with great skill closed around hers.

His powerful fingers feathered over her flesh like a

butterfly's wings, once more astounding her that he could be so gentle.

Somewhere in the back of her thoughts, Kate realized that she should be, at the very least, apprehensive about the pure male power he exuded. She had been a virgin who had never even been kissed up until a few weeks ago. She should be frightened, coy, demure, anxious— something. But she could not pretend. Not when she was standing so close to the man she had waited for all her life. He bent his head to her and she looked up, too weak to stand. What were those breathtaking eyes trying to tell her? Or was it simply the inky darkness of his lashes that made his eyes appear to glimmer like firelight?

He lifted both of her hands to his lips and kissed them, sending currents of heat throughout her body. Without a word, he unfastened the laces of her kirtle. His breath against her cheek thrilled her; the tender touch of his fingers and the intoxicating heat from his body made her ache for him. He tunneled his fingers through the thick curls at her temples, then traced a deliciously sweet path down the sides of her face, all the while his eyes tracing her features, worshipping what he saw. She arched her head back, exposing her throat to his silken touch and then to his hungry mouth. She was barely aware of her skirts and shift falling away from her body, mindful only of the full impact this man had on her.

"Have I told you, Callum MacGregor, how right it feels when you hold me?"

"Ye dinna have to tell me," he whispered to her and carried her to his bed.

Setting her down within his fur blankets, he stepped back and simply reveled in her beauty. And then he shed his garments, and the last stone that made up the wall around his heart.

Kate held her arms out to the glorious man standing over her. She beckoned and he came to her, giving her power she never thought to possess. Though his dominating weight covered her from toe to crown, she experimented liberally, using her lips, her tongue, and her teeth over all the hard planes of his body. She was fascinated to find that she could control every deep groan this warrior uttered.

The power shifted when he grasped her hands and held them over her head. Her surrender was swift. His deft attack of warm, sultry kisses down her neck, between the satiny hollow of her breasts, and then over each milky mound conquered the arrogant victory she so fleetingly possessed. His tongue, more deadly than any sword forged, traced a heathen path over her belly, pausing to allow his lips to kiss the tingling muscles of her abdomen. Her heart went still for just a moment when she realized the destination his tongue sought. But then his face dipped, and, using a beguiling combination of tenderness and mastery, he partook of the passion's nectar she offered him. Her back arched, and violent jolts of sheer pleasure coursed through her and made her quiver to her toes.

Her tormented groans snapped Callum's control. He rose up like a languid god after devouring a bountiful feast. He lowered his hips to hers, and the touch of his rigid manhood between the crux of her thighs was so primal, so arousing, it shuddered Kate to her soul. He surged against her once, almost driving her to the brink of madness, then impaled himself in her as deeply as she could take him.

Pleasure so replete, so raw and ruthlessly erotic,

rushed through Kate's blood like a deluge. Her senses ignited until his ragged breath became her own. The scent of his desire clinging to his skin was as intoxicating as a field of bursting heather blossoms. The feel of his sculpted arms encasing her was more magical than any dream of being held in the arms of a knight could ever be.

He ground his hips against hers, withdrew slowly, then sank deep within her again. She curved her back, tempting him to suckle the ripe nipples stretching toward his hungry mouth. His appetite ripped a fevered moan from the back of her throat. Slipping his hand beneath her, his strong fingers spread over her buttocks, pressing her upward. He angled his hips to stroke the crest of her passion. His gaze fastened on her, taking in the pure beauty of her climax, and the sight of her was his undoing. He tried to wait, for he wanted to watch her like this forever, but the pleasure she took in him, the hot sheath convulsing around him, drove him wild, and finally he closed his eyes, lifted his head, and released the scalding bounty of his seed deep inside her.

Drifting off her body, Callum pulled her close against him and held her, kissing the damp curls at her forehead while she gasped with spent energy.

Later he bathed her, and it was the single most sensuous experience of Kate's life. He reveled in each wonderful inch of her body with his soapy hands and feral gaze. He scrubbed her hair and massaged her scalp with titillating thoroughness, then playfully dunked her and kissed the droplets of water off her mouth and the breath clean out of her body.

Chapter Thirty-Three

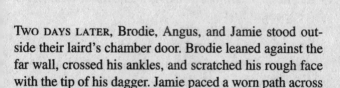

TWO DAYS LATER, Brodie, Angus, and Jamie stood outside their laird's chamber door. Brodie leaned against the far wall, crossed his ankles, and scratched his rough face with the tip of his dagger. Jamie paced a worn path across the threshold.

"Graham said to tell him posthaste."

Angus dragged his rapt attention from the door and cast Jamie a sharp glance. "Then go ahead and knock, lad."

Jamie's pacing paused and he looked up. "I will." He resumed his fretful trek without knocking. "Callum needs to know the MacLeod is comin'."

Angus shrugged his hefty shoulders. "It ain't like MacLeod's at the doors. What's the hurry in tellin' Callum? Yer gonna get yer arse thrashed good."

"Graham said to tell him." Finally, Jamie raised his hand to knock, but a low, sensuous groan drifted through the door. Jamie's fist stopped in midair.

"I wouldna knock just yet, were I ye," Brodie said with a laugh.

"Hell, this could take all day," Jamie mumbled, eyeing the door.

"Pity Brodie isna the laird," Angus quipped. "We wouldna have to wait longer than a dozen breaths before 'twas over."

"And I'd still have ye beat by ten," Brodie returned with a grin.

"I'm knockin'," Jamie said, ignoring them both. "He'll want to know aboot the MacLeod."

Angus grinned harder and folded his arms across his brawny chest. "Ye have much to learn, pup. Nae man wants to be interrupted while he's enjoyin' a woman. As ye're aboot to find oot."

"I'm no'—" They all heard the door open, but it was too late for Jamie. "—afraid of him."

Callum stood there naked but for his plaid wrapped around his waist, his face darkening with murderous intent. He didn't know who to glower at first, so he glowered at all of them. Angus looked down the long hall, wondering how quickly he could get to the stairs and save his arse. Jamie backed up when Callum took a step forward.

"What the hell are all three of ye doin' standin' ootside my door?"

Brodie pushed himself off the wall and looked up and around like a dimwit who'd wandered into the hall and found himself lost.

Jamie cleared his throat. "Graham sent me to give ye the news."

"What news?" When Jamie told him, Callum still wasn't satisfied. "And it took all of ye to tell me this?" The slight smirk on Brodie's face told him the truth of it.

He and Angus had followed hoping to see Jamie get thrashed for disturbing their laird.

The menacing glint in Callum's eyes when he set them back on Jamie froze the lad's blood. "Ye thought the MacLeod's visit was important enough to trouble me with it?"

"Aye, my apologies." Jamie bowed his head. "Angus and Brodie told me I shouldna do it." When he felt a brisk slap on the back, he looked up.

Callum nodded at him. "Ye were right to tell me. Ye're a braw lad. That's why yer brother sent ye, and no' either one of these sorry excuses fer men."

Brodie knew enough to keep his mouth shut. Besides, his blood-rusted sword spoke well enough about his bravery in battle.

"What's that supposed to mean?" Angus bristled. "I was ready to break the bloody door doun to give ye the news."

"Then ye must be sadly disappointed that I opened it, Angus." Callum tossed him a foul grin. "Meet me ootdoors after ye break fast and ye can prove to me that ye can still lift yer sword."

"We've already finished supper, Callum," Brodie informed him without shielding his smirk. "A quick glance oot the window woulda told ye that if ye cared to look."

"Shut up, Brodie," Callum ordered.

Angus sputtered for a good five breaths after Callum strolled down the hall and disappeared inside the garderobe. Brodie whacked him on the back to induce breathing. "Best go practice, cousin." He grinned, winked, and exited the hall with Jamie, leaving Angus there alone to rifle through the folds of his plaid for his pouch of brew.

When Callum left the garderobe, he found yet another

one of his men waiting for him. Graham leaned against the opposite wall with his arms folded across his chest. The cool scent of fresh air drifting off him attested to his recent return to the castle.

" 'Tis good to see ye among the living," the commander said with a casual smile.

" 'Tis good to know I was missed."

"Ye weren't. Kate was."

Callum nodded and then had to smile as he headed back to his chambers. What a pack of miserably ruthless bastards he had saddled himself with. God's blood, he was fortunate, indeed.

"Jamie gave ye the news about the MacLeod?" Graham came up beside him.

"Aye. When is he comin'?"

"He'll be arriving on the morrow. But there's another matter of more urgency to discuss. A band of Campbells was seen in Glengarry."

Callum's steps halted. "How long ago?"

"Two days."

"How many?"

"Forty, mayhap fifty horsemen."

"Send William and a dozen of his best fighters to scout the coast, and I want Rob and twenty others in Glenelg by nightfall. I want to know where the Campbells are. I want to know their every move." When he reached the door to his chamber, Graham held back. "Come," Callum invited him inside. "There is one other thing I wish to discuss with you."

Graham entered the room, lowering his gaze when Kate, still lying in bed, bare as the day she was born, yanked the fur blanket up to her chin. She glared at Callum, but he only winked at her.

Shaking her head at the callous brute, Kate cursed under her breath and sank deeper under the covers. She peeked out at Graham while Callum dressed.

My, but the commander looked especially comely today, she thought, admiring him from her bed. He wore a white wide-sleeved tunic beneath his plaid, and his kidskin boots were scrubbed clean of mud. She particularly liked the way he donned his cap backward, with the brim behind his head rather than on the side of it, his spray of burnished curls peeking out at his nape.

Graham caught her admiration of him and tossed her a smile she was sure felled many hearts.

"Are ye both done?" Callum yanked his plaid off his waist and dashed it to the ground, then reached for a fresh tunic.

Graham and Kate looked at Callum at the same time. The commander cleared his throat and picked an imaginary mote of lint off his plaid.

"Callum, Graham is comely, but surely his buttocks are not as well formed as yours." Kate blinked her long black lashes at Callum so innocently, he swore he saw a halo hovering over her head. That is, after he finished blushing a dark shade of crimson. He snatched up his plaid again and tossed it swiftly over his form.

"Kate, I dinna think 'tis proper to speak that way in front of Graham, especially if ye're to be my wife."

She popped her head out fully from under the blanket. "Your wife?"

"Aye." He turned to Graham. "Send fer Faither Lachlan. Last I heard, he was in Moray."

"Ye have my blessing." Graham was happy to hear such news and smiled at Kate again.

"We're goin' to need it," Callum mumbled. "And quit starin' at her."

"Just a moment, please," Kate said from the bed. "I don't remember being asked."

"Asked?" Callum barely looked up from securing his plaid.

"Aye, asked," Kate repeated stubbornly. It was difficult to challenge him on this issue, especially since she wanted to leap out of the bed and fling herself in his arms. But hell, the man was too arrogant for his own good. "I will not be *told* who I am to marry."

Now he set his eyes on her and scowled for all he was worth. "You were willing to be *told* to marry Lord Mortimer of Newbury."

Mortimer of Newbury! Kate almost slapped her thigh at the recollection of her imaginary betrothed's name. And what was this? Callum knew it all along? The fact that he remembered the name with such clarity warmed her heart for some odd reason.

"Well?"

"Well what?" Kate blinked at him through dreamy eyes.

Callum glanced heavenward, then back to her. His jaw clenched, and beside him, Graham tried hard to conceal his grin. "Will ye be my wife, Kate?"

Graham slipped out of the room as Kate smiled, nodding her head, and Callum near sprang for the bed.

~

Callum did not meet Angus outdoors that eve, and the burly warrior was quite astounded to hear his battle-hardened laird's laughter filling the great hall.

"I'd never be believin' it if I didna see it wi' me own

eyes." Angus pulled his head back from its spying position behind the thick curtain separating him from the hall. He snatched his pouch of brew from Brodie's mouth, spilling a godawful amount on his cousin's plaid and cursing in the process.

Brodie stepped around Angus's bulky form and peered around the curtain while his cousin guzzled a long swig, covered his mouth, then belched.

Pulling back, Brodie offered him a look that said he was the biggest dimwit ever to wield a sword and he deserved to be killed for it. "What the hell are ye coverin' yer mouth fer? He canna hear those swine sounds ye make over all that laughin', ye drunken fool."

Angus bristled, his broad shoulders stretching his plaid across his chest. "I was tryin' to avoid freein' me delicate breath in yer face."

Brodie snorted. "The only thing delicate on ye, Angus, is yer swing."

His neck near broke from the force of Angus's enormous fist meeting his cheekbone. "Would that be what ye were meanin' by delicate, eh, Brodie, ye son of a whore?"

His cousin merely shook the stars away from his eyes and then threw the full weight of his body upon Angus. They toppled over backward, taking the curtain with them when they crashed to the ground, already swinging.

Everyone in the hall craned their necks to see what the fuss was and then went right back to their conversations. Only Kate gaped and rose to her feet.

"Good Lord, they are going to kill each other! Callum, do something!" He looked at her like another head had just sprouted from her shoulder. "Are you simply going to sit there?" she demanded.

"Aye." He nodded. When she folded her arms across her chest and glowered at him, he chuckled. "What would ye have me do, lass? They fight all the time. Dinna they, Graham?"

"Aye, they do," his friend happily agreed.

Kate could not believe her ears. She had seen them tossing punches here and there while they rode to Skye, but this was preposterous! "Well, if you are not going to do anything about it, I will." She hefted her skirts before Callum could grab her and pounded off toward the two men hammering each other into the rushes.

"Stop it this instant!" she shouted at them. When that failed, she bent neatly and slapped Brodie, since he was on top, across the back of the head.

Behind her, a collective gasp rang out from the inhabitants of Camlochlin while Callum, Graham, and Jamie leaped over tables to get to her before she found her own face embedded to the back of her head.

"She's a damn braw lass to put her hands to Brodie!" someone whispered, astonished.

"Aye, I heard she stabbed our own laird in the leg when first they met," said another.

"I heard the laird is takin' her fer a wife."

"A fittin' choice fer a MacGregor, I'd wager."

Before Callum reached her, Kate had Brodie up on his feet, his ear painfully pinched between her thumb and index finger. "That. Is. Enough!" She emphasized each word with another harsh tug. "And you, Angus. Get up immediately so that I can get a hold of you."

The massive MacGregor lifted his head off the floor and turned it toward Callum. His laird's pitiless gaze told him to do as he was ordered.

When Kate held both men firmly by their ears, she stomped her foot. "This fighting will cease. Do you hear me?" She shook both hands while she made her demand, rattling their heads. "If you both enjoy fighting so much, mayhap a bit more training will do you some good." Immediately, Angus's worried eyes darted to Callum. "If I see you hitting each other again, you will have to come outside and wield your swords against me."

Every jaw in the great hall dropped. "Ye?" Angus looked mildly ill.

"I dinna train wi' women," Brodie drawled, then yelped when she tugged his lobe nearly off his head.

"Well, you will with me, Brodie MacGregor. Won't he, Callum?"

"Nae," Callum informed her sternly.

Kate's head snapped around with such force her hair fanned across her face. She regarded Callum with a look he had never seen on her before, and one he would not want to see her wearing while she was wielding a weapon.

"Aye?" he amended.

She nodded coolly and then turned her attention back to his newly tamed cousins.

"Did you both hear that? Your laird has commanded you to fight with me the next time you feel like tossing your fists." She released them, slapped her hands together, and turned crisply on her heel.

The crowd behind her took a unified step back, but each face wore a smile of respect. Kate's heart leapt. If she'd known that slapping a few of their most ruthless warriors around would win her their favor, she would have done the like sooner.

Chapter Thirty-Four

~

KATE LEANED OUT THE WINDOW to steal a glimpse of their guest before actually meeting him. It was the first time in her life she had ever received anyone of import at her home. It was the first time she had received anyone *at all,* for that matter, save for her uncle and his guard. Her heart raced and her cheeks flushed with worry. What if the MacLeod did not like her because she was a Campbell? Would he consider her a Lowlander? She had learned from almost everyone living in the castle that most Campbells were considered Lowlanders. And no Lowlander was deemed worth his weight in spit. Keddy the cook even went so far as to say Lowlanders were as bad as the English. And Rabbie the tanner called them Protestant whoresons. Kate squeaked with apprehension and patted her cheek with her palm. She looked down at the dozen or so men whose horses clopped up right to the doors.

She chewed her bottom lip while she regarded the lead rider, uncertain, by the looks of him, if he was a bear or a man. He wore a thick fur overcoat of sable brown, which matched his long hair. He was not altogether feral, though. For when he saw Graham, his smile was like a ray of light piercing the gloom. Still, Kate gulped when he dismounted and threw his tree-trunk-sized arms around Callum's commander. Whether gentle man or savage, Donald MacLeod was enormous.

Callum came up behind her and slipped his arms around her waist. "What worries ye, lass?"

"Him wanting me dead worries me." She wrung her hands together. "Did you see the size of him, Callum? Why, he's bigger than you! I'd say one—"

Callum leaned down and captured the remainder of her words with a slow, sensual kiss. Her body relaxed in his arms. "He'll no' want ye dead," he promised when he withdrew. "Donald MacLeod is one of the finest lairds I know. He took Maggie and me in when we escaped yer grandfaither's dungeon. He fed us and clothed us, and then he allowed me to build Camlochlin on his land." Callum released her and moved to the window. "D'ye know the risk he took fer me, Katie? He convinced his clan to live with MacGregors, and no' one of them has ever uttered a word that we dwell here. It's his men as well as the MacKinnons who patrol the shores of this isle, aidin' in keepin' us safe." He reached for her again and kissed her brow, speaking there. "Dinna be frightened of him. He and his sons are good men."

Kate nodded, keeping the remainder of her worries silent, and followed Callum out of the room.

She almost hightailed it back up the stairs when, reaching the bottom, the great beast of a man lifted his charcoal gaze, and then the rest of his body from where it bent to Maggie, and bellowed. "When are ye goin' to teach yer sister how to speak like a proper Highlander?"

Kate decided then and there that she could imitate their speech and the MacLeods would be none the wiser. It was clear that she would have to do the like—the man was obviously disturbed by Maggie's Lowland inflection.

The brute's eyes narrowed slightly when Callum chuckled at his query. And then Callum MacGregor, giant of a man that he was, was enveloped in a furry embrace that made him look like a boy of twelve. "Ye remember Alasdair, Rory, and Padraig." The MacLeod turned to his sons, and the three giants standing behind their father swallowed Callum up next. The rest of the men who accompanied the MacLeod were greeted with warm salutations and hefty pats to the back.

When Donald MacLeod's eyes settled on her, Kate straightened her shoulders and forced herself to smile.

"I dinna believe we've met."

"My betrothed." Callum appeared at the man's side. "Katherine Ca—"

"Kate," she cut him off before he had time to say her full name. No reason to have the visiting chieftain hate her so soon.

Her fingers were gently pried off her plaid by the MacLeod and lifted to his lips. "Well met." He kissed her hand, then angled his bent head to Callum. "I'm sorely pained that ye didna send word to me of yer betrothal."

" 'Twas sudden," Callum told him and pounded him on the back. "Come, I've opened my best kegs of whiskey fer yer visit."

They moved on into the great hall, where tankards were dipped into barrels of aged brew and conversations drifted from the coming winter to which clans would be best for raiding in the spring. Some sweet meats and fresh bread were laid out on the tables, but the true feast would come later, after the MacLeods had time to refresh themselves. For now, the men were happy to warm their bellies with good whiskey and their feet by the massive hearth fire.

Kate listened to the clan chief MacLeod's hearty laughter when, after he had taken a seat beside Callum, Maggie plopped Henry the pig into his lap. Kate decided the MacLeod might not be so bad, after all, as long as she did not open her mouth. Now that she thought about it, he had not even mentioned Lowlanders when he spoke about raiding. She began to suspect that living so far from the iron fist of England's rule provided the MacLeods with little chance—or desire—to fight. Why, he seemed not to care at all about anything that went on below Fort William.

"Kate."

Jarred from her thoughtful reverie, Kate blinked her attention to the deep gray gaze fastened on her.

"Tell me," Donald MacLeod said, leaning back in his chair. "D'ye have any sisters of marriageable age? I'm lookin' fer a wife fer m' son, Padraig."

Kate's lip twitched. It was about to happen. She had hoped she could get through the morn without speaking, but she had to answer him now. Her eyes cut to Callum, but Donald's son, Alasdair, was leading him away from the table, back to the barrels of brew.

Kate reminded herself that she had faced far more terrifying men than this one, and cleared her throat before she spoke. "Nae, my laird. I have only a brother."

He arched a speculative brow at her, then sipped his drink. "I see. Where, might I ask, did Callum find ye, lass?"

Kate remembered to breathe. God help her when the man found out she was a Campbell. She inhaled a deep breath. "He saved me from a neighboring clan who were raiding my land."

"In?"

"In Glen Orchy, my laird."

"Och, what in blazes was Callum doin' in Glen Orchy? Was he warrin' wi' the Campbells again?"

Before Kate answered, Callum returned to the table. "Kate, Maggie asks that ye meet her in Netta's chambers."

"Of course." Kate rose from her chair, grateful to be leaving. "I will go right away."

Callum's gaze lingered on her as she raced up the stairs.

"Ye love her," Donald announced, unable to believe what was quite clear to see with is own eyes. When Callum turned to him and nodded, Donald raised his cup to his lips to drink. " 'Tis aboot time is what I say, lad. Mayhap now ye'll find some peace and quit tryin' to kill every damned Campbell who crosses yer path."

"Mayhap," Callum allowed, taking Kate's seat opposite Donald. "Since she's a Campbell, and I dinna want to kill her."

Donald MacLeod sprayed his brew where it belonged after such an announcement—across the room. "What?" he bellowed, wiping his mouth. "Och, saints be wi' me and tell me I heard ye wrong. She's a what?"

"A Campbell."

Donald rolled his head back and shook it at the heavens. When he thought he had gathered enough wits to continue, he returned his stunned gaze to Callum. "Jesus and Mary, a Campbell. Ye fell in love wi' a Campbell."

"Aye, the Duke of Argyll's niece." That sobered the MacLeod well enough. Callum waited patiently while his friend choked out a few unintelligible sounds. When he deemed it safe to continue, he motioned for Lizabeth to bring the laird more whiskey. "I had planned to hold her fer ransom and make Argyll come to me."

"Which is exactly what he's doin'." MacLeod dropped his head in his hands and sighed.

"Aye," Callum agreed. "I expected him to come fer her. But I didna expect her to hold my heart the way she does." Callum downed his brew, then peered at Donald's bent head. "I willna let her go. I wanted this to end with Argyll, but her brother will be her guardian in accordance with English law when their uncle is dead. He may come against me, but I willna let her go."

Lifting his eyes to the lad he had come to love like a son, Donald sighed and then nodded. "Ye willna have to. I know I claimed I'd never get involved wi' yer war, but the MacLeods will stand at yer side if any army comes against ye."

"Nae, Donald. I'll take care of this myself. I promised no' to harm her brother, and if I'm right aboot him, I may no' have to. Just tell me where Argyll is. He is the one I want."

"We dinna know. He reached Glengarry and turned east."

Callum was still taking in that bit of information when Jamie burst into the great hall, his whiskerless face flush with excitement.

"There's a new MacGregor in Camlochlin!" he shouted. He cut a path to a table, snatched a tankard of brew from Alasdair MacLeod's hand, quaffed its entire contents, then swooned on his feet for a moment. He blinked and found Callum standing before him. Feeling a belch of immense proportions rising within his innards, Jamie fought to contain it, not wanting to do the like against his laird's chest. He paled considerably in the process, swooned again, then grinned up into Callum's face. "Brodie has himself a son."

"A son!" Callum turned and called out to everyone in the hall. "May the Lord bless the lad." The hall erupted into cheers of good wishes, and more kegs were opened. "And Netta?" Callum asked Graham's already inebriated brother.

"She does well. Aileen and Murron are with her. 'Tis Brodie who'll need lookin' after. I vow I saw tears in his eyes."

Callum looked around the hall and lifted his cup to Donald MacLeod. "Another MacGregor!" he called out. "And if I have my way, there will be many more to come."

The MacLeod chieftain laughed while Callum turned his attention back to Jamie. "Tell Kate to bring the babe doun so we can have a look at him."

Jamie hiccupped, then blinked to better focus on Callum. "Kate's no' with Netta."

Now Callum turned to face him fully. "Aye, she is. Maggie sent fer her."

Jamie shook his head. "Maggie's no' there, either. She wanted to go to the barn, but I told her to wait doun here fer me."

Callum dashed out of the hall and was outside the castle before anyone had time to follow him. *Please, God, let them be in the barn,* he beseeched. Hell, Maggie knew better than to leave the castle without Jamie. "Kate!" His voice exploded into a roar that echoed off the wall of black rock behind him. He did not wait for an answer but raced toward the barn.

When he reached it, he heard the sound of women's laughter. He thanked God silently before plunging inside. Kate sat with her legs curled beneath her in the hay, with Maggie lying beside her. Both women looked up, and when they saw him, Kate lifted her hand to her mouth, fearing the worst by the looks of him.

"What's wrong?" she asked. "What has happened?"

Callum leaned against the wall, certain that his legs would not hold him up if he didn't. He ran both hands down his ashen face and then, in the time it took Kate to blink, stood towering over them both.

"What the hell are ye doin' in here?" Though he shouted, his voice was laden with emotion. "Ye must tell me when ye wander off." Kate rose to her feet while he turned to his sister. "Maggie, blast ye! How many times must I tell ye to . . ." His words faded into a tight groan when Kate touched her fingertips to his jaw.

She wanted to weep. Not because he shouted, but because he was so frightened for them. For her. "Forgive me, Callum," she said, barely able to resist the urge to throw herself into his arms.

She did not have to. He hauled her against him, crushing her in his embrace until the breath left her body. Neither one of them heard Donald enter the barn, nor his gentle call to Maggie to follow him back out.

"Callum, I cannot breathe," Kate gasped into his chest.

He loosened his hold just a bit and bent his head to her until his gaze was level with hers. He had not wanted to tell her. He did not want her to fret over something neither one of them could stop. But she had to know now. She had to know how dangerous it was to be out of his sight. "Kate, yer uncle was seen near Glengarry a few days past."

Her complexion paled. "And my brother?"

"I dinna know if he accompanies yer uncle. We dinna know where he is. I feared—"

She covered his mouth with her fingers. "Ssh," she whispered. "We will save Robert, and then all will be well." She pressed her lips to his, silencing whatever else he thought to say, until words no longer mattered and the only thing that did were his passionate kisses.

Chapter Thirty-Five

DUNCAN CAMPBELL SPAT on the body at his feet. Godforsaken MacGregors did not talk even under pain of torture. No matter, he would find the rest of them. He was close. He had to be. He was sure he would have found them by now if not for the skirmish with the MacKinnons a pair of days ago. He smacked his leather riding glove against his thigh, and a small cloud of dust rose to his nostrils. Bloody MacKinnons had cost him over twenty of his men before they were questioned and then disposed of.

Squinting against the high afternoon sun, he scanned the misty glens until he found Robert appearing over a small ridge with the rest of his men. Duncan's lips curved into a challenging smile when his nephew scowled at the body crumpled on the ground.

"It is only a MacGregor, nephew. Remember they have abducted your dear sister and have most likely killed her."

Robert held up his hand to halt Duncan's words. "Enough, please. I do not wish to think on such things anymore."

"You *must* think on them," Duncan insisted, moving toward him. "It will take all your fortitude to kill the outlaw." He regarded Robert with a narrowed look. "Or are you going soft already?"

"Nae," Robert ground out between clenched teeth, but his gaze drifted back to the man lying dead a few feet away. In truth, he might be going soft, after all. For he was sickened by his uncle's cruelty, disheartened by the ease with which Duncan killed anyone who refused to aid him.

"I've had much time to think on this. I drank and laughed with Graham Grant many nights. I do not think he will harm Kate." Robert continued despite his uncle's laughter. "I do not believe he would serve a man who would kill a woman."

Duncan's eyes glinted with malice, piercing the mists. "Ah, you mean the clever commander who infiltrated my very own holding in order to find out where our dear Katherine lived."

"They were looking for you," Robert reminded him. "They did not kill any of the women at Kildun."

Duncan shoved his glove over his fingers and reached for his horse. "I do not care. The hunted has become the hunter." When he gained his saddle, he lifted his head and squinted west, toward the giant black mountains in the distance. "I fear we were deceived by the Cameron when he told you those we seek rode east. The only thing we've found so far are wild animals. And I do not mean MacGregors." He eyed the bloody corpse on the ground. "Pity it was not the traitor Grant, aye?" He slid his gaze to Robert, daring him to disagree. "When we find them, I will leave that one for you to kill." He kicked his mount's flanks and disappeared into the thick gray mists like an apparition returning to the churning bowels of the Earth.

~

A lark soared over sheep scampering across the glen. Somewhere close by, children laughed and cattle bells rang while the music of hauntingly beautiful pipes dragged over the distant moors. Lying flat upon a carpet of purple heather, Kate turned her face to smile at Maggie, who was spread out beside her. Tiny blossoms tickled Kate's nose and filled her senses with their wild fragrance. Thoughts of the last few days brought a satisfied sigh to her lips. The MacLeods had left Camlochlin, but not before the chieftain had told her his wistful stories of faeries and romance and heroes long dead yet held forever in the heart. Faither Lachlan had not yet arrived, but Kate did not care. Callum told her that in the Highlands a man need only claim a woman for her to be considered his wife. And he had most definitely claimed her. Angus and Brodie had not thrown a fist in a se'nnight, the latter being too busy carrying his newborn bairn around and wearing an arrogant grin plastered to face to care about fighting, drinking, or anything that did not resemble the downy sprinkle of mink that covered his babe's head. Kate touched her fingers over her own belly, hoping Callum's babe grew there. It was too soon to know. She breathed a perfect sigh again, thinking of how often her beloved worked at planting his seed and the passionate mastery of his endeavors. Even knowing her uncle was close enough to give cause to worry had not stopped Callum from taking her to bed every chance afforded them. Why, he'd even stormed into Maggie's chamber the day before, a thin sheen of sweat from a long day of practice defining the sleek muscles in his arms, and carried her away to his chambers. Kate giggled remembering how angry Maggie had been at her brother for interrupting their session of careful primping. Primping that had begun after Kate had convinced Maggie that a certain young, handsome warrior truly did fancy her.

Kate suspected that Maggie already knew. It was clear to anyone with a decent pair of eyes that Jamie's heart was hopelessly lost to Maggie MacGregor. Maggie's heart was not faring any better, though she was as stubborn when it came to matters of love as was her brother. Still, it had taken only one very appreciative grin from her admirer, aimed at her unstained face and neatly combed hair, to create the meticulous little hellion lying beside Kate now.

And a hellion she was.

Kate had no idea Maggie possessed a temper that could rival Callum's! Despite the lovely day, Maggie's mood was as sour as four-day-old milk. And "'twas all Jamie's fault." According to the wee brooding MacGregor, her would-be suitor had found a new companion. A big, hairy, drunken sot by the name of Angus.

"Do not pout so," Kate said softly and patted her dear friend's hand. "I am sure Jamie would rather be with you."

Maggie angled her head and tossed Kate a sharp look. "Then why are *ye* lyin' here near me instead of him? I have done everything to win his favor, Kate. But he still has not announced his feelings to me. He would rather spend his days with a man who belches more often than he blinks!"

Kate hid her smile behind her fingers.

"I told him this morn that I would prefer it if Graham kept watch over me from this day hence. He had the bollocks to grow angry! But my decision has been made. Graham smiles often, while Jamie looks pained." Maggie paused her tirade for a moment and squinted her large blue eyes on the sky. "Mayhap he *is* pained by having to follow me all over the blasted castle."

She was most definitely in love, Kate decided while Maggie went on to list Jamie's faults. "Aye, you have it right, sweeting," Kate said glumly. "Spare yourself the suffering of his ungracious manner. Jamie is certainly not what any lass, save mayhap for Glenna, would want in a man. More than once have I seen her ogling Jamie with affection dancing in her eyes. Let her—"

"Glenna?" Maggie pushed herself up and tugged on Kate's sleeve. "But I have seen her draped over Graham's arm."

Kate shrugged and closed her eyes, basking in the warm sun. "Mayhap Glenna would be content with either brother. Or both. Now that Jamie is free to . . ." She drew her shoulders up around her ears when Maggie shrieked, and then she said a silent prayer of forgiveness and one of protection for poor Glenna when Maggie stood up and marched toward the castle.

With a satisfied sigh, Kate rose to her feet and wiped a few heather blossoms from her skirts. On her way to the castle, she waved at the women hanging their laundry to dry in the cool breeze outside their cottages. They greeted her in like manner, most coming—she hoped—to accept her as one of their own. Good Lord, but she loved Camlochlin. She loved the MacGregors, and she loved their mighty laird so much it almost made her weep. She prayed that Callum might someday come to love her in return. Dear God, she would give anything just to hear him speak the words. Misty-eyed, she passed the western wall where Callum usually practiced with his men and looked around. He was not there. She turned on her heel to go search him out inside the castle and stepped directly into his crushing embrace.

"Lookin' fer me?" His voice was as deep as an erotic drumbeat against her ear, his breath warm as it fell to her nape.

Aye, she loved him well.

"Kate?" He slipped his arms around her waist and bent to look into her eyes. "Somethin' troubles ye?"

She shook her head. "I was just pondering some things. It is naught to fret over." She blinked back a rush of unwanted tears and stood on the tips of her toes to kiss him on the mouth.

She couldn't help herself and watched the sensual way his lush forest of lashes closed over his eyes. His lips molded beneath hers, firm, yielding, while his fingers splayed over her spine and drew her closer. She wanted to live and die in his arms. She loved him, and it filled her heart to bursting.

"Now tell me what troubles ye, Katie," he coaxed in a low voice when she withdrew from their kiss.

How could she ever begin to tell him the depth of what she felt for him? He would pull away. Tell her it was too dangerous. He cared for her. It was clear, but how could he ever give his heart to the granddaughter of Liam Campbell? Still, when he looked at her . . . She reached out and swept her fingers over his brow. "Your eyes tell me things I do not understand." The words fell from her lips before she could stop them.

"Aye?" His gaze softened with some deep emotion that made her heart thud in her ears. "Is it so difficult to understand that ye mean more to me than anything I am willin' to admit?"

"You are afraid." She nodded, understanding.

"Of many things, but that never stopped me from doin' them."

"Aye, because you are brave and strong. But this is different, Callum." She looked up at him and cursed her quivering lower lip. "This has naught to do with your brawn or your pride."

"What has it to do with, then?" He played with a curl winding down her temple, her trembling lip not escaping his attention.

"Your heart."

"Ah, that."

"Aye." Kate dragged her sleeve across her nose, then broke free of his embrace and stepped back. "Forgive me. It was foolish of me to—"

"I love ye, Kate."

Her lips parted, but only a short gasp fell from them. He smiled, and finally his eyes fully revealed what was there all along.

"I'll love ye until my dyin' day, and if I have any say aboot it, long after that."

She leaped into his arms, quite certain that had he been a smaller man she would have knocked him clean off his feet.

Angus and Jamie watched from a parapet along the castle walls. With a world more experience than Jamie might ever possess, Angus waited with relative ease until Callum carried his wife inside the castle before his belch erupted from his lips.

"I think she was the only one in the whole bloody castle who didna know he loved her. Women are thick-skulled. Dinna ferget that, lad." Angus passed Jamie more brew.

"Aye, thick-skulled," Jamie brooded and almost teetered over the edge of the wall.

Angus caught him easily enough by the scruff of his plaid before the younger man toppled over. "Hell, but ye canna hold yer whiskey."

"Get off me, ye flea-ridden son of a barn rat." Jamie tugged and almost fell over the edge again. His mood was even more sour than Maggie's. But Angus had not been happier since the day he first broke Brodie's nose. He'd thought all hope was lost for any more good, clean sport when Kate demanded that he and Brodie quit brutalizing each other. Doom settled over his heart every time he watched his ruthless cousin tenderly kissing his new babe's head. But now, oh now, a new spark of hope and exhilaration gleamed in Angus's eyes.

"Did ye just insult me, Jamie Grant?" he asked carefully. He would not want to injure the lad in error.

"I did?"

Angus decided to ignore the glassy, bewildered set of big blue eyes staring back at him, so desperate was he for a hearty fight. He nodded and sent his fist into Jamie's guts with a satisfied sigh that rivaled any belch he could produce.

In response, Jamie promptly emptied the contents of his belly onto Angus's boots.

Chapter Thirty-Six

DUNCAN CAMPBELL BLEW DIRT out of his mouth. He waited in the thick brush until he was sure the MacLeod scouts had moved on before scrambling on his belly toward his men.

Cutting his uncle a contemptuous side glance, Robert realized just how much of a serpent the Earl of Argyll really was. For the past three days, they had done naught but kill until the sight of their own blood-soaked plaids churned Robert's stomach. He had met the Devil, looked into those eyes filled with raw contempt. Aye, Callum MacGregor thought naught of killing Campbells, but Duncan was no better. Feuds, for whatever truth lie behind them, were one thing. Cutting the heads from the dead was another entirely. And Duncan Campbell had done the like to a score of men already.

When his uncle reached him, he looked out first amid the thick tangle of bushes that separated him and his men from the rocky cliffs of Elgol, then at Robert.

"Now do you see why I traded the horses? They would

never make it over those crags. We will travel over the cliffs on foot," he whispered. "If we meet up with anyone, we will tell them we are MacLeods. If they try to stop us, we kill them."

Fearing his uncle had finally gone mad—or mayhap he only just now noticed it—Robert was tempted to laugh. But it would have been a joyless sound. He was sorry the poor drunkard they killed the day before had not only admitted that a clan of MacGregors lived on the isle of Skye but had directed them toward the right path. Only sixteen of them remained, and Robert knew it was not enough to take the MacGregor holding, should they truly find it.

"Uncle, hear me," he tried to explain for the hundredth time that morn. "I do not think your plan will succeed. We cannot simply slip into their midst. Think you Mac-Gregor does not know the faces of his people? I want my sister. If I must kill the laird to get her back, I will do so. But I do not intend to murder this Margaret MacGregor, be she the Devil's weakness or not. There is no honor in that."

"Honor?" Duncan sneered. "What do I care of honor? I suffered the greatest humiliation any son should have to endure because of that ill-bred bastard. Callum MacGregor is an outlaw. He defies every decree set forth by England."

"Then arrest him and see him punished in accordance with the law. Why are you so eager to kill or injure everyone but the man you seek? And why did you not seek him before he took my sister?"

"Enough questions," Duncan snapped at him. "Get

up." He rose and hauled his nephew up by the arm. The rest of his men followed.

"Do you fear him, then?" Robert demanded, seeing the evidence of it clearly now on Duncan's face. "Am I to do that which you cannot?"

Chuckling, Duncan began climbing the first of many jagged cliffs. "When the time comes for such a task, I fear your heart will fail you, nephew. But after he cuts the withered organ from your chest, I will prove my worth when I kill his sister."

Prove his worth? Robert wanted to ask him what he meant, but the path was a treacherous one. He needed his wits to make it up the cliff.

As if to confirm his decision to remain silent and concentrate was the right one, a stone came loose beneath Duncan's boot and fell, though not far, since they only just began to climb. Nonetheless, it smashed against the serrated precipice and disappeared into the raging current below. Robert made no move to steady his uncle, shamefully imagining it was Duncan's head instead of the rock that took such a beating on the way down. A short while later, and a bit higher up, Alasdair Drummond followed the rock and plunged to his death. Finally, Duncan stopped the troop and commanded Kevin Menzie to return to Sleat and procure a boat.

"We cannot return this way." He peered over the edge to the water below. "Hire a captain and return here to meet us. Once we are done, we will return to the mainland upon Loch Scavaig. Go, make haste."

Robert's fingers were raw by the time they reached a narrow ledge more than one hundred feet above the thunderous whitecaps. He decided he did not care for this desolate place, and then decided it did not care for them, either, when the skies suddenly blackened and opened up like the mouth of some great beast spitting its torrential vengeance upon them. Duncan pressed onward, losing two more men before he conceded his defeat to the elements.

"Uncle," Robert said while they sat with their backs pressed against the sheer sheet of rock and waited out the storm. "Graham told me that MacGregor and his sister were imprisoned as children. Is this true?"

"Aye."

Robert's stomach balled into a knot. He closed his eyes and leaned his head back. What else of what Graham had told him was true? "Why was this done to them?"

"There were many reasons," Duncan said. "Mainly because they were MacGregors, enemies of the realm. The MacGregors have tried for centuries to convince anyone who would listen that our clan had wronged them. They pitifully sought excuses for their savagery against our kin. The Devil's father was a known rebel who had taken up arms against the Campbells."

"But they were children," Robert said quietly, heartsick.

"It does not matter. Liam Campbell did what he wanted to do. I did not question him."

"Did my father question him?"

Duncan's expression darkened as he stared out over the landscape that was as harsh as the memory of his father's face. "He was given his own holding at Glen Orchy and chose not to hunt the outlaws. When he found out about the children he sent word of his protest. He was naught like our father. But my father forgave him." Duncan swiped the rain from his eyes. "Even when Colin later argued the Devil's reasons for killing so many Campbells, my father forgave him."

Chilled by the seething emotion beneath his uncle's smooth veneer of indifference, Robert turned to look at him while he spoke.

"I think your grandfather was glad MacGregor had brought chaos to Kildun. For it forced his favored son to return."

"So my father was not at Kildun when the Devil escaped," Robert said softly, as facts he had never been told became clear to him now. "When did Callum MacGregor put the sword to him, then? You did say it was The Devil who killed my father, did you not? Why did he do it if, as you say, my father did not fault him entirely for his actions?"

Duncan slid his gaze to Robert's. A trace of unease flittered across his features but lasted only an instant before his cool demeanor returned.

"Nephew, if you insist on knowing the shameful truth, then here it is. Your father was a sympathizer. A fool who received a fool's recompense."

"Nae," Robert argued. "It is not foolish to show mercy to others. Amish and John taught me—"

Duncan's voice dipped low so the others could not hear as he turned to stare at his nephew fully. "Pray they have not made you heir to such weak-minded sentiments. Pray more that your sister does not adhere to the same folly."

"And if she does?"

"Then she will suffer the same justice as they. It is the law of England."

For a terrifying instant Robert thought he would be the

next to fall to his death when he shot to his feet, enraged, stunned, and quite literally dumbstruck. "By whose hand will she suffer, Uncle?"

Duncan's tight shrug was his only answer to that particular query. "Let us hope she fights them even now."

"I tell you if you harm her, I will stand with the MacGregors and see you dead! Christ." Robert tore his fingers through his hair as another grave truth dawned on him. "My father was a sympathizer. He never spoke unkindly of the MacGregors. He never spoke of them at all." His frenzied gaze fastened on Duncan. "Tell me truly who put the sword to him."

Robert would have preferred it if Duncan shouted at him, erupted in indignant fury at what his nephew was suggesting. Instead, all he received was an icy smirk.

"What will it gain you to know of it now, Robert?" Duncan looked up at the heavy pewter clouds overhead. "Rain's stopped." He turned to the others, just ahead of them. "Let us continue."

Robert did not move. He was certain that if he did, it would be to fling his uncle off the side of the cliff. Disbelief and disillusionment nagged at the edge of reason. Surely Amish or John would have told him if Duncan had been the one to cut their laird down. Mayhap they had not known, Robert considered. After all, the fatal wound had been inflicted from behind. Nae, nae, not his father's own brother. Robert leaned over the high crag, fighting to keep the contents of his belly where they belonged.

Besieged by fury he had never known before, Robert leaped after his uncle and caught him by the shoulder. "Why did you do it?" he demanded, spinning Duncan around to face him. Both men teetered on the pebbly ledge. Duncan gripped Robert's arms to steady himself.

"God slay you!" the earl spat angrily. "I swear I will do it myself if you unbalance me again."

Robert's voice rumbled like the distant thunder. "And I swear I will hurl you to the sea if you do not give me a reply."

Duncan looked over his shoulder and gave the command for the others to continue on. Though he was certain they could not hear, he leaned into Robert's shoulder and spoke in a quiet voice. "Very well, I will tell you." When Robert felt the sharp sting of his uncle's blade pressing against his ribs, he ground his jaw. "With a handful of his men," his uncle whispered, "your father set out to find the savage who massacred his comrades. He did not intend to bring him to justice, but rather to deliver him to safety. I followed him. It was night when I found him. He and his men were asleep." Duncan withdrew slightly and tilted his head up to look directly into Robert's eyes, his own gaze mildly remorseful. "In truth, I hated killing him, but there is no place for regret in war.

"My father believed the Devil killed his son," Duncan continued, unfazed by the murderous rage in his nephew's eyes. "I could not tell him the truth, for though he hated sympathizers, he would not have understood."

"Did Amish and John know?" Robert could barely keep his fury under control.

"Nae, but they were sympathizers, as well." Duncan sighed when Robert closed his eyes with the realization of what had become of the two men who helped raised him and his sister. "They outlived their purpose, Robert. You had already left Glen Orchy, and Katherine was to come with me. You've no idea how I have worried over you both through the years."

The sincerity in his voice was almost an extraordinary thing to hear. If Robert was not afraid of screaming until the cliffs around him crumbled, he would have opened his mouth to laugh.

"You worried we would become sympathizers," Robert pointed out tightly.

"Nae, I visited often enough to see that that never happened."

"It is true, I have hated the MacGregors all my life," Robert said, hating even more the honor he cherished as a boy, the glory that had lured him away from his true duty of protecting his sister. "Had I not gone to Kildun, my sister would still be safe in Glen Orchy."

"Soon"—Duncan placed his hand on Robert's shoulder—"she will be safe once again in Inverary. I vow it." When Robert said nothing, he turned and continued on his way along the edge.

Robert followed after him in silence, his features defined with steadfast determination to find his sister and mayhap, with the MacGregor's aid, bring the true devil to justice.

Chapter Thirty-Seven

THE NEXT DAY and three men later, the Earl of Argyll crouched at the summit of a grassy incline and craned his neck to gaze at a castle just as black and impenetrable as the mammoth mountain wall looming over it. He snapped his mouth shut.

"This cannot be the MacGregor holding," he said a moment later when his wonder switched to denial. "The old drunk must have directed us toward the wrong path and we have stumbled upon a MacLeod castle."

The fortress ahead had to belong to the MacLeods, Duncan told himself over and over while he gaped. He refused to believe a rebel outlaw had such a magnificent holding. It was smaller than Kildun, but far too grand for a MacGregor. He let his steely gray gaze drift over the dozens of thatched-roof bothys scattered throughout the vale and felt his blood boil.

"They can see in every direction that matters," Robert said, pointing to the Highlanders patrolling the battlements. He turned to his uncle. "What do you suggest we do now?"

"We wait here until nightfall, then make our way opposite the loch, along those hills where there is more shadow, and slip inside the castle."

Robert snorted, "You're mad. We will be shot down before we reach the front doors. And even if we do breach—"

"You will find the MacGregor and kill him while the rest of us search for Katherine. If you ever want to see her alive again, you will do as I say."

The meager group of men waited atop the crest for night to fall, but darkness never came. Instead, a heavy mist rolled down the mountain wall, chilling their bones.

Duncan insisted they wait until the mist covered the entire vale. It was as good as darkness. Even better.

Robert fully intended to follow his uncle into the castle. He did not, however, intend to kill Callum MacGregor. He prayed Katherine was alive and unharmed. Graham had been truthful with him, and he had been so in defense of his friend. Robert did not believe a man like Graham could be loyal to a heartless beast. He did not believe they had harmed his sister. He would find MacGregor and plead to speak with him. Nae, he decided an instant later, the laird would slay him the moment he discovered Duncan was inside the castle. Robert had to find a way to get inside without Duncan and his burly friends.

They were Menzies, who likely would not give a rat's arse about Duncan's crime against his brother. But would they feel differently if the earl was guilty of killing the earl before him?

Robert turned to him and, in a voice loud enough for the others to hear, said, "Colin was your father's favored son."

Duncan met his gaze. "What?"

"You said earlier that your father's favored son had returned to Kildun, aye?"

Duncan did not flinch, but his eyes sharpened on his nephew. "Aye, Liam favored him."

"You said your father would forgive him anything, even for being a MacGregor sympathizer. You hated Colin for finding favor in your father's eyes when you suffered humiliation in them." He looked over Duncan's shoulder at the Menzies and was pleased to see them listening intently. "Tell me, uncle, did your father suspect you of treachery when his favored son was killed *after* MacGregor escaped? Is that why you killed him?"

Without even an off-pitch breath to betray his intention, Duncan reached for a large rock and smashed it into Robert's temple. When his nephew fell limp to the ground, Duncan pushed back the hair that had fallen over his own brow from the force of his blow, drew his dagger, and turned on the men gaping at him.

~

Duncan Campbell stepped into the mists with a single purpose, to destroy the Devil and regain what had been taken from him.

Chapter Thirty-Eight

KATE OPENED HER EYES and then closed them again at
the glaring beam of sunlight pouring into the chamber
from the window. She really would have to have a word
with Callum about hanging some draperies—very thick
ones. At the thought of him, she smiled and turned over
in the bed, intending to help him welcome the new day
with a few strategically placed kisses.

She squeaked when she saw Maggie sitting in his spot
instead, her legs crisscrossed beneath her and a comb
clutched in her fist.

"I thought ye'd never be waking up."

"Maggie, what are you doing here so early? Where is
your brother?"

"He's around somewhere," Maggie advised her
hastily. There was no time to answer silly queries now.
"Are ye intending to sleep all day? My hair and I are waiting for ye."

Kate could not help the smile Maggie always brought
to her lips. "I'm awake." She hauled herself out of bed

and tried to run her fingers through her own hair. She tugged on a few tangled curls. "My hair is waiting for me, as well."

"Hurry, Kate. He'll be up and about soon." Maggie sprang from the bed and pushed Kate toward the stool where she usually prepared Maggie for the day.

"Who?" Kate tried to conceal her knowing smile, but it pulled at the corners of her mouth.

"Who? Why, Jamie, of course. Who else? Honestly, Kate, sometimes I think ye and Callum are more suited to each other than either of ye realize."

Kate gave her a surprised look and then burst into laughter. "Goodness, poor Jamie hasn't a chance against you."

Maggie cast her an askew look, but then her lips curled into a mischievous smile. "At least not after today, I hope."

"What happens today?" Kate asked her, sobering. "What are you going to do?"

"I am going to tell him what I think of him before we are both too old to care," Maggie said, thrusting her comb into Kate's hand. "And I would prefer to look bonny doing it. So, if ye please?"

Kate nodded, taking the comb. How braw this wee woman was. Even Kate had begun to wonder when Jamie would finally begin their courtship. The poor lad was afraid of Callum, but Kate was certain Callum would be as happy as she was about their union.

"I think a lovely blue snood in your hair will bring out the beauty of your eyes," Kate said gently, offering Maggie the stool to begin.

Kate and Maggie made their way down the stairs, peek-ing left and right in hopes of spotting Jamie and saunter-ing past him. It would take him no time at all to follow. Maggie intended on leading him directly to the barn, where she would finally reveal her heart. She was so dis-appointed when they did not find him, she stomped her foot and muttered an expletive that would have made Brodie proud.

They were about to exit the castle when they walked straight into Callum. "I was just comin' back to bed," he said, pulling Kate into his arms. "Where are ye off to?"

"To the barn," Maggie brooded.

"Give me a moment and I'll come with ye."

"Nae!" both women exclaimed at the same time, which earned them a fierce scowl.

"Send Jamie, Callum." Kate offered him a wink that made his scowl deepen. "Please," she begged with a slight kiss to his chin. "I will come to you soon," she whispered along his jaw.

"Verra well," he conceded, wondering when he had become such a soft pup of a man. "Wait here and I'll find him." He planted a kiss squarely on Kate's mouth and whispered to her before he let her go. "Make haste back to bed."

He met Angus in his search and inquired as to Jamie's whereabouts.

"He's likely off pickin' daffodils fer yer sister. He's been avoidin' me company, and I'm beginnin' to feel slighted by it."

"Check the meadow, and if ye find him send him

here." Callum continued on his way up the stairs without turning. "And be quick aboot it, Angus."

~

Thin beams of sunshine broke through the loose-paneled barn walls, creating a web of dancing, dust-infused light. Henry squealed with delight when Kate and Maggie entered and plodded toward them on his stubby legs. Matilda honked but was too busy nibbling on a string of corn that had fallen from the rafters to greet them properly.

"Bertrid, stop chasing that little mouse." Maggie picked up her cat and nuzzled the feline beneath her chin. "Do ye think Jamie will come?"

"Of course he will," Kate assured her. "But I think we should have remained in the castle. Callum is going to be angry with us." When Maggie shrugged her concerns away, reminding Kate that the castle was but a stone's throw away, Kate sighed and reached for a large bag of feed and began filling each animal's bowl. Ahern pushed her arm with his nose, urging her to feed him first. "As soon as Jamie arrives, I will leave the two of you alone."

When the barn door opened again a few moments later, Henry squealed and took off running. Matilda spread her wings, her corn string forgotten, and honked wildly, waddling toward the door as if someone had sounded a duck battle call.

Casting Maggie a knowing wink, Kate turned to greet the flaxen-haired warrior. The barn door swung closed slowly, but no one stood at its entrance.

"Jamie?" Kate called out. She strained to see into the shadowy corners. Her gaze darted to Maggie clutching Bertrid tightly to her chest. "The wind, mayhap," she said and started for the door to close it. She had taken only a few steps past Maggie when the lass screeched her name.

Kate swung around and then staggered backward.

Her uncle stood behind Callum's sister, stretching her spine straight as one arm looped around her throat and his other hand clutched a dagger pointed at her belly. "Hush, Katherine," he said softly. His gaze narrowed on her across the filtered light. "You have settled in quite nicely here, I see."

Terror gripped Kate's muscles, paralyzing her. She almost retched with the force of stifling a scream. Her skin crawled just looking at him. He was filthy. Dark stains of dried blood crusted his hands and plaid. Dear God, whose blood was it?

"You do not look pleased to see me, niece." He moved his blade upward toward Maggie's throat.

Gathering every ounce of control she possessed, Kate inhaled, flaring her nostrils, and tilted her head belligerently. "What took you so long in finding me, Uncle? I was beginning to think you would never arrive."

That seemed to mollify him, but only for a moment before he snarled at her again. "You look remarkably well, Katherine. Getting along with the savages, are you?"

"Och, come now." She sighed as if he were too daft to understand. "What would you have me do? I stayed alive, as you did." Her scornful smile told him she was remembering the fight in her father's yard with the McColls. "Now, have you come to converse with me, or take me home?"

Maggie shook her head and began to cry. Bertrid slipped from her arms and fled into the shadows. "Do not go away, Kate." Her plea was so stricken with sorrow,

Kate almost ran to her. She stopped herself, swallowing back her fear and guilt. The sooner she convinced her uncle to take her home, the safer everyone would be. She would worry about returning later.

Duncan yanked Maggie's neck to quiet her, and Kate took a step forward. "Uncle." She tried to pull his attention away from her dearest friend.

"Where is the MacGregor?" he suddenly demanded.

Kate shrugged her shoulders and was about to tell him she did not know or care, when the barn door swung open again.

Jamie stood at the entrance, his arms cradling a dense spray of yellow daffodils. His smile faded almost instantly when he saw the Earl of Argyll. He reached for his sword, spilling the flowers around his feet. Before he had time to unsheathe his weapon, Duncan hurled his dagger at him.

Kate cried out, but Maggie only gaped, stricken with horror as her beloved gripped the hilt protruding from his belly and then collapsed to the ground. Duncan moved instantly, kicking the door closed and retrieving his blade from where it was lodged. Without pause, he cut across the barn and gripped Maggie by the hair, yanking her head back.

Kate hurled herself at him, ready to fight him to the death. He swung and sliced open her palm. Blood shot outward, splattering across Maggie's face. Her blue eyes, already glazed with the haunting images from her past, went vacant and she opened her mouth to begin screaming.

Duncan silenced her with a blow to her head, using the hilt of his dagger. Kate went deathly still when he pointed the tip to Maggie's neck, his eyes wild with what he meant to do.

"Uncle, nae!" Kate took a step forward, reaching out to him with her bloody hand. "I beg you. I beg you, nae."

"You plead for the life of a MacGregor?" he accused, craning Maggie's head farther back.

"Aye, I do. I will do whatever you ask of me."

Duncan's eyes shot to the door, then back to her. "Very well. We are leaving. If the guards call out, you will cast your lovely smile on them and convince them you are in no danger. It is clear these people are your friends. Make them believe you, Katherine, or I will cut her throat."

"I will do it," Kate promised. "But you will release her now." When the earl laughed, she continued quickly. "If you do not let her go, I will not move from this spot. Are you prepared to die, Uncle? It is only a matter of time before Callum's men come barreling in here. You stand no chance against them, I assure you." Her muscles spasmed when he inched his blade closer to Maggie's flesh, ready to refuse her demands. "Do it," she challenged him, suppressing the need to scream, the urge to throw herself at his feet and plead for Maggie's life. "And then cut my throat, as well. But know this, you will die this day, also."

She almost staggered with relief when he tossed Maggie aside. When Kate moved to go to her, her uncle snatched her by the back of her neck and dragged her to the door.

"Betray me," he warned silkily against her ear while he covered his face with his plaid, "and I vow I will escape and return to Kildun—and to your brother."

Chapter Thirty-Nine

⌒

ROBERT GROANED and struggled to open his eyes. Searing jolts of fire shot through his head. He brought his hands up to cradle his forehead and felt warm, sticky blood drying over his eyes. He waited a few moments and lifted his lids slowly. A swath of bright noontide sky greeted him. He blinked as the memory of the night before returned to him. His uncle had struck him with something, a tree trunk if his tormented skull had anything to say about it. With a tight moan and a muttered oath, he pushed himself up on his elbows. He looked around, already knowing Duncan was not there with him. The madman was most likely dead. Robert hoped it was so. He dragged himself to his knees, too weak to stand, and began to crawl down the sloping hill toward the castle. He had to find Kate. If MacGregor found him first, so be it. He would worry over it when the time came.

He almost crawled over the dead body of one of the Menzie men. "Och, God." Robert moaned. His gaze glided a little to the left, where he found the others, as dead as the first. Sickened, Robert had no doubt about who had killed them.

He turned his attention to the fortress ahead. Where was his uncle? Was he already inside? Everything was too quiet. If the MacGregors had discovered Duncan and killed him, the entire holding would be alive with commotion. The Earl of Argyll was still alive, lurking somewhere, waiting for an opportunity to kill. Rising to his feet, Robert fought the desire to pass out from the pain exploding through his skull, and he began to run.

When he was just a few yards away from the castle, the heavy doors began to open. He skidded to a halt, his heart crashing against his ribs.

Someone stepped outside, his mop of golden curls glimmering like a halo beneath the sunlight.

Graham Grant!

The commander looked around and then stopped dead when he saw Robert. "Christ!"

Robert lifted his palms to quiet him. "Nae, Graham, wait."

"Guard!" Grant bellowed, dragging his sword from its sheath at the same time.

Robert shouted his name. "My uncle is here somewhere . . ." He looked around at the vast landscape. ". . . hiding."

"Step closer!" Graham commanded.

Robert took a step forward and then swayed. He rubbed his head to help clear it, but it only made the ground spin faster. The MacGregor was being alerted. Soon the chieftain would rush out of the castle and kill him. "Graham . . . damn you, hear me. My uncle is here and he means to kill Margaret Mac—"

Graham began running just as Robert fell flat on his face.

Without pausing at the barn door, Graham kicked it almost off its hinges and braced himself for an attack. "Maggie!" he shouted over the angry honks and squeals of her barn friends. His eyes settled on a body sprawled in the hay. "Nae," Graham choked and then rushed forward. When he reached his brother, he dropped his sword and fell to his knees. "Jamie! Callum!" he screamed toward the door for help.

Men began racing into the barn, blocking the sun from the entrance. Callum led them, his sword drawn. He slowed his pace when he saw Graham leaning over Jamie, but he did not stop. Panic engulfed him, so terrifying it made his legs feel like butter. He shoved heavy bundles of hay aside as if they were as light as leaves. Searching . . .

Brodie found her first. When Callum reached them, he crouched before the trembling form of his sister. He reached out and touched her shoulder and she reeled back, her eyes huge and haunted. But she did not scream.

Callum controlled himself from going mad as he looked at the dried droplets of blood on Maggie's face. She was too far away for it to be Jamie's blood.

"Maggie, where is Kate?"

At the sound of his voice, Maggie suddenly grabbed for him. "He . . . he killt Jamie."

"Nae," Brodie soothed her. "Jamie lives. He was hit too far to the right to cause a fatal wound," he said, more to Callum. "He has lost much blood, though. Graham and Angus have already taken him to his sisters. They will know what to do."

Callum closed his eyes in silent thanks. When he opened them again, he stood up and roared a command of orders that made his sister shrink back. He wanted men searching the castle, the stable, and every bothy in the vale. He wanted others saddled within the instant and ready to cover every inch of his land, in every direction. He wanted Kate found. Now!

As he strode toward the door to leave, Angus returned from the castle with Graham close behind him and Robert Campbell's collar clutched in his fist.

"Mayhap he can tell us where to find her," the beefy Highlander suggested.

Callum took a step forward and lifted his sword. There was no mercy in his gaze, only raw, uncontrolled rage. Robert closed his eyes and turned away. Callum whirled his massive blade over his head, preparing the most lethal blow he could deliver. Angus released his prisoner and leaped backward to avoid being cut in half along with Robert.

"Nae!" Graham leaped forward and landed with the full weight of his body on Callum. Both men tumbled to the ground. The sword flashed beneath a beam of light as it hurled end over end into the shadows. Callum sprang to feet, his fury fully unleashed. He snatched fistfuls of Graham's plaid and lifted him until their eyes were level. Then, as if his commander weighed nothing more than a thought, Callum flung him into the nearest wall.

With determination void of anything save its single purpose, Callum reached Robert and hauled him closer using only his fingers wrapped tightly around Campbell's neck.

But Graham appeared again and valiantly wedged his

body between his friend and his friend's enemy. "I beg ye, do not kill him." His hands shook when he placed them on his friend's shoulders. "Callum, look ye to yer sister, please. Do not make her witness this again, I beg ye."

Callum swallowed so suddenly a slight moan escaped him. He did not want to look at Maggie. "Brodie, get her oot of here. Guard her with yer life."

"Callum." Graham still had not let him go. "Ye cannot kill this man. He is Kate's brother. Ye vowed not to harm him. Hear me, we will find her, I vow it. He had the chance to ambush me outside, but he warned me of Argyll instead."

Slowly, Callum lifted his gaze to Graham. He waited until his sister was safely out of the barn before he spoke. "If she dies, he dies with her."

Graham nodded, finally breathing again, and gave Callum's shoulders a firm pat. "Just let me speak to him, aye?"

Turning to face their captive after Callum nodded, Graham was first struck with pity at the terror in Robert's eyes. He understood it, for he had felt it, as well, a few moments before. "Rest easy. He is a man of his word and will not kill ye."

Robert's eyes darted from Graham's to Callum's, then back again. "Where is my sister?" he asked, ignoring his throbbing skull and the fear that made his mouth dry.

"We were hoping you could tell us," Graham said. "Where is your uncle?"

"I do not know," Robert told him, tunneling his fingers though his hair and then grimacing at the huge knot on his head. "He struck me last eve. I awoke to find him gone. We came here for my sister, but he said he was going to kill—" Robert paused when he looked at the chieftain. "—MacGregor's sister."

Callum moved forward again and Robert took a step back. "When I find Argyll, and I will, his screams will be heard in England."

"I do not mean to stop you," Robert promised him. "It was he who put the blade to my father and my grandfather. We must move quickly. I am confident he is not still here. Your men are wasting time searching the castle."

In one fluid motion, Callum seized Robert's plaid in both hands and hauled him closer. "Then where should we be searchin'?"

His sister had been trapped here with this beast, Robert thought, unable to look anywhere but into the Devil's unholy gaze. "Leave Kate out of this feud," he managed with more courage in his voice than he felt.

Graham closed his eyes, praying that Callum would give him a wee bit more time. He knew Robert feared for Kate at the hands of the outlaw MacGregor. "Robert," he said hastily. "She has come to no harm here. Camlochlin is her home now—by her choice."

Robert shook his head with disbelief. He would have laughed if he was not so terrified.

"Aye, she loves him, I swear it," Graham stunned him further. "And look ye to him. Ye have seen him before—at Kildun—remember? Look at him now and believe that 'tis his love fer her that drives him mad with concern."

Robert looked, but he was not relieved at what he saw. Instead, his eyes darkened with something worse than horror. "My God, what have you done?" When the MacGregor's murderous glare impaled him, he did not flinch.

"He will kill her. Just as he killed our father for being a sympathizer."

"Nae," Callum breathed on a mangled groan, his dark intent fading into complete sorrow he could no longer control. He had done this. He had known Kate's life would be forfeit for loving him, and he allowed her to love him anyway. "Nae!" This time the word came down like a hammer. He released Robert and headed for the door but turned when he reached it. "You are the one who taught Kate about heroes. Tell me where to look fer yer uncle and help me save her, Robert Campbell, if there's any honor in ye."

Robert nodded. He had no other choice but to trust this man. "He has a boat waiting to sail him to the mainland. It is . . ."

Callum was already gone. Robert turned to look at Graham, and then they ran, as well.

Chapter Forty

KATE GRIPPED HER BELLY with one hand and the side of
the boat with the other. It felt as if she had been on the
water for hours. The waves crashed beneath her, rocking
and dipping the vessel until Kate's skin turned pale green.
She felt like she was dying a slow, sickening death, but
she used the time leaning over the edge to try to think of
what she was going to do about the man watching her.
Duncan Campbell looked quite pleased with himself,
smiling at her when she met his gaze.

"Why did Robert not come with you?" she asked him,
straightening.

"I ordered him to stay at Kildun. I knew I would lose
many men coming here, and I was correct." Duncan gave
her a somewhat rueful look. "Many died trying to save
you, Katherine."

She thought of Jamie, and immediately tears clouded
her vision. "How many MacGregors did you murder?"
she asked, sickened by the sight of this man who was her
blood kin.

Duncan's regard on her grew so dark, Kate thought he was going to haul her over the side. She waited, unafraid. She had no weapon but her feet, and she would use them to render his male organ useless for the next fortnight.

"Your concern for them is most alarming, niece," he said, remaining where he was.

"You find so many things alarming, Uncle," she retorted icily. "But I am no coward."

Duncan wanted to strike her for her cheek, but he would wait until she was in his bed. He felt too jubilant at his own cunning to do anything but grin. He'd outfoxed the Devil! He had walked straight onto MacGregor land and taken his niece from under the rebel's nose. Hell, but he was clever . . . and braw! His father would even have to admit it, were he alive . . . the bastard. Aye, he had stepped into the hornet's nest with the courage of a thousand men and walked away unscathed and taken back his pride. He almost laughed at how easy it had been. Colin would never have had the resolve to do such a thing. But then, most sympathizers were afraid of the MacGregors. It was why they aided the outlaws. Liam Campbell despised sympathizers, save one.

Duncan let his eyes graze over Kate's fine curves. He would not be so forgiving.

～

Robert Campbell was so relieved to be off his battered feet and on a horse that every so often he almost forgot he was riding with a troop of the most aggressive outlaws ever to inhabit Scotland. Remembering was simple enough, though. All he had to do was cast his glance left or right, in front or behind him. They were everywhere, and according to Graham, the MacGregors of Rannoch would meet up with them once they left Skye and entered the main Highlands. That they did so on horseback and not by boat was because there simply were none large enough at Camlochlin to bear the weight of the horses, and they would need them when they reached the mainland. Robert did not think they would lose too much time, for they flew across the landscape like a plague on the wind.

At first, the idea of being one Campbell amongst hundreds of his clan's centuries-long enemy chilled Robert's bones to the marrow. But traveling with them was quite different than when he had fought them at Kildun. They were a rowdy bunch, most certainly, and definitely hard as granite around the edges, but they possessed a wildness that appealed to Robert's most basic nature. He almost pitied his uncle and anyone else who came against them. They had suffered years of persecution. But instead of growing weaker, they possessed the power of raw brawn and unmatched belligerence. Who, indeed, could stop them?

"How do ye fare, Robert?" The sudden appearance of Graham Grant at his side almost startled him off his horse. Only his sense of pride kept Robert's exhausted body seated in his saddle. His surprise that Graham would be concerned for his well-being was another matter entirely.

"I fare well. You have my thanks for inquiring."

Then Graham did something else Robert did not expect. He smiled before he kicked his horse's flanks and raced on ahead.

They had to stop and refresh their horses by a flowing stream. The decision to halt was not Callum's, though he knew the animals would never make it through the night at the speed with which he and his men rode them if they did not rest. He also knew Argyll would reach Kildun before him, so he ordered his men to make haste.

His gaze cut to a large boulder where Robert Campbell sat alone. Graham joined Kate's brother a moment later, causing a scowl to mar Callum's brow. Graham had pleaded for the lad's life at Kildun, even going so far as to declare Robert Campbell his friend. He near got himself killed this day by protecting Robert yet again. Callum wondered if Graham harbored some fondness toward Argyll's nephew.

Curiosity got the better of Callum, and he strolled over to where the two men sat together now.

"Robert was just telling me how his small troop arrived at Camlochlin." Graham looked up briefly when Callum reached them.

"And how was that?" Callum asked and sat right beside Robert, who visibly paled at the sheer size of the MacGregor laird so close. Callum caught the apple Graham tossed him, tore his dagger from his boot, and began slicing.

"We . . ." Robert eyed the dagger. "We climbed along the cliffs from Elgol to Camlochlin."

"On foot?" Callum asked, sincerely surprised. "'Tis a wonder ye were no' killed." He cut a wedge of apple and handed it to Robert.

"We lost men." Robert accepted the offering and took a bite.

"'Tis a long way doun," Callum said, then, "Are ye certain 'twas he who killed yer grandfaither? I've wondered who was responsible fer that."

"Aye, he told me." Robert admitted and then grew quiet again.

"Ye were correct about yer sister," Graham said,

sensing the young Campbell's unease and hoping to ease it. "She is quite braw."

Robert smiled before he even realized he did. "Aye, I told you she fears little." He looked up as Callum rose to his feet.

"We've wasted enough time," the laird snapped. "Get back to yer horses." He walked off without another word. When he reached the others, he barked at them to move their arses, then leaped into his saddle with surprising grace for a man his size.

Graham rose to follow, but Robert's voice stopped him. "I considered you my friend. The first I had, if the truth be known. You led me outdoors that night . . ." Kate's brother rose to his feet and set his gaze directly on Graham. "Was it an easy thing to betray me?"

What was there to say? It didn't matter if Graham liked the lad. Their names made them enemies, made them do things they might not have done under another set of circumstances. Finally, Graham shook his head before he turned for his horse. "Nae, 'twas verra difficult, indeed."

⁓

They crossed the narrows a little before dusk and then continued on without stopping again. Robert was bone weary, but he was grateful they did not tarry. And even more that the fearsome Devil MacGregor was going to help him save his sister.

Chapter Forty-One

THEY REACHED INVERARY leaving a trail of whispered rumors that an army of MacGregors was heading south, unharmed and unhindered by a Campbell knight who led them! Callum would have preferred the truth of it be known; they rode unharmed and unhindered thanks to the staggering fear that settled over anyone unfortunate enough to come upon them. They might be an outlawed clan whose heads were used to pardon the most offensive crimes, but they were bloody fierce, and people knew it.

Duncan Campbell knew it, as well, which was why he had wasted no time in gathering his allies to his side on his journey home. Callum and his men found themselves facing an army of Menzies, Drummonds, and Robertsons when they finally arrived at Kildun. True, the men looked less than confident when they saw the feral-looking Highlanders thundering toward them, each warrior taller in the saddle than the next. But Campbell's army outnumbered the MacGregors by at least two to one, and that, according to Callum's way of thinking, was what gave them the courage to draw their swords.

Callum was ready for battle—more than that, he was eager for it. He dragged his blade from its sheath and held it up, ready to plow his way through the wall of soldiers and take back the woman he loved.

Robert thundered past him and tugged his reins to a halt a moment before he, too, would have plundered through Duncan's army. "Put down your weapons!" he called out with all the authority of a king. "Hear me! I am Robert Campbell, grandson of Liam Campbell, Ninth Earl of Argyll. These men have come here at my request to save my sister from the clutches of a madman, Duncan Campbell."

"You speak treason against the earl," one of the men shot back.

"Aye," shouted another. "You ride with MacGregors and would turn your kin over to them. You betray your clan!"

"Nae!" Robert shouted. "It is my uncle who has betrayed his clan by killing his . . ."

One man broke rank and sped toward the MacGregors and Robert. His sword unsheathed for battle, Callum's mouth hooked into a snarl as the rest followed immediately behind, emboldened by their comrade's bravery.

Raising his sword, Callum dug his heels into his mount and charged into the oncoming legion.

For an instant, Robert simply sat atop his steed with a look of disbelief and horror on his face. Indeed, it seemed just an instant had passed while the MacGregor chieftain's heavy claymore fell upon his enemy's head, cutting down to between the soldier's eyes. The bloody blade came up again, and before his first victim's body fell from its horse, another rider's head was cut from his shoulders. Blood splashed across the Devil's face giving credence to his worthy title. A third man only had time to stifle a gasp while looking into the burning vengeance of his executioner's eyes before he was run through to the hilt.

Angus's giant sword found its mark, smashing bones like glass under the strength of his arm. And Brodie's merciless sword left even horses dead.

Fools! That was all the time Robert had to consider his uncle's men before ten of them were upon him. He barely had time to unsheathe his blade and deflect a blow to his chest before another swipe just missed severing his arm. Hell, he hadn't trained his whole life to die after just two battles, and certainly not during one that didn't even need to be fought! Lunging forward, he thrust his sword into the belly of another attacker, yanked it back, and struck at the next man closest to him. His swings were well practiced and almost elegant in their delivery compared to the brutal skill of the MacGregors. But just as efficient. Until one particularly huge soldier brought down his blade hard enough to bend Robert's suddenly meager weapon.

Seeing his opponent's disadvantage, the soldier looped his sword, holding the hilt with both hands, and brought it down just above Robert's skull.

But the fatal blow was blocked in midair. Sparks rained down on Robert as he watched Graham make a quick end of his would-be assassin.

Within minutes, most of the Earl of Argyll's men were cut down, with the same savage proficiency Robert had witnessed the first time he saw the MacGregors fight at Kildun. The rest took off running. No matter what his uncle had lied about, he had been correct about one thing. The MacGregors were to be feared.

With no one left to bar entrance into Kildun, Robert gathered his courage around his shoulders and brought his mount to stand before Callum's. "You may go inside with me to find my sister. Many have died today. I would ask that you spare my uncle's life." Callum shook his head. "I fully intend," Robert continued, "to bring charges against him in Edinburgh. He will be hanged for killing the earl. Reconsider, I pray you. There is no honor in revenge."

When Callum made no move to answer him, Robert started toward the castle. He paused for just a breath when he heard the conversation behind him.

"He's a braw lad. What think ye?" It was Graham's voice, answered a moment later by Callum's.

"I think he is the second Campbell I've met that I didna want to kill."

"Well done, Robert!" Another voice, this one less deadly than the one before, but no less chilling, halted Robert completely. He rounded his mount and reached for his hilt as his uncle stepped out from behind the western wall.

With his sword pointed at her throat, Duncan Campbell held Kate before him like a shield to ward off the enormous MacGregor dismounting a few feet away.

"Nephew, pardon me for not applauding you and your companions' swift execution of my countrymen, but as you can see, my hands are otherwise occupied." Duncan adjusted the sharp edge of his blade beneath Kate's chin. "I want you to know that I blame myself for what you and your sister have become. I should have known Amish and

John would teach you your father's ways, and killed them sooner."

Hearing this, Kate struggled to be free, but his hold on her was firm.

"Release her, Uncle," Robert demanded, "and there will be a chance you will not die this day. You need only look around to know it is your only option."

Callum spotted the flash of panic in Argyll's eyes as they swept the ground and the dead around him. Men did deadly things when they were afraid. "No one else here will lay a hand on ye." Callum did not move as he spoke. "Let her go and we will meet as men."

"Ah, MacGregor." Duncan glared at him and backed away, dragging Kate with him. "You mean as savages, do you not?"

Callum offered him a lethal smile. "If ye like." He spared a glance at Kate. She appeared unharmed. "Come," he spoke softly, calmly. "Ye were braw enough to take a swing at me once, long ago. Ye have no' turned coward since that day, have ye, Argyll?"

"Coward?" Duncan spat, enraged. "I will mount your head in my solar this very night. And if I don't, you will be dead by nightfall. You see, I've sent word to our Lord Protector, giving him the location of your holding. I also informed him that you kidnapped my niece, killed the men I sent to find you, and were on your way here to kill me next." Duncan's grin was a slash of victory. "If I die, he will know it was by your hand. You will bring the law down hard on your people for many more years to come." He turned his cold gray eyes on Robert. "I am not the man with no options. He is."

"Nae!" Kate screamed. She tried to claw her uncle's

arm away, but he dug his blade deeper into her skin. She didn't care. "Callum! Do not kill him!" She caught his gaze and held it. "You are not what he calls you."

Duncan yanked her back by her hair to quiet her and then turned to Callum. "You will not be pardoned but by my mercy, if I am alive to give it."

"It is no surprise"—Robert's voice dripped with revulsion at his uncle—"that your father found you so unworthy. You are worse than a coward." He squared his shoulders and turned to Callum. "I offer you another option. Whether he dies by your hand or the law's, I will be the next earl. Leave him to the law and you and your people will have my mercy."

"This is why we hang sympathizers," Duncan sneered.

Callum looked at him with the fury that had waited nine years for release blazing in his eyes. "Argyll, ye should have waited fer me to kill yer faither. Ye knew I would come back fer him. Ye took what was mine, just as he did, and inherited his crimes as I did fer my faither." He held his hilt in both hands and waved the blade at Duncan. "Stop pissin' in yer hose and come kill me, Campbell."

"Nae! Callum, please!" Kate screamed and was tossed aside as her uncle readied his sword for battle.

Robert leaped from his saddle and ran to her. They both watched Callum whirl his long blade with a simple twist of his wrist. "Come on."

Duncan obliged by springing at him and swinging. Callum avoided the blow with ease and returned with a backward strike that left Duncan's arms trembling. Duncan whirled around and jabbed, barely coming close to his target. Callum brought his arms down for a savage blow that near felled the earl to his knees. Each time Duncan attacked, Callum parried and returned with twice the power. It was clear to all who watched that the mighty laird could kill Duncan Campbell at any time. He chose to humiliate him first.

When Argyll finally did fall to his knees, Callum waited, challenging him to get up. With a final swing, he smacked Duncan's sword from his hands when the earl held it up and then shattered Duncan's nose with his fist. Argyll reeled backward, his eyes glazed above a spray of blood.

Not so long ago, Callum would have been satisfied with nothing less than death to this enemy. But another massive blow that broke Duncan's jaw was as sweet a victory as he would get this day. 'Twould be enough, Callum knew. For he was not a monster.

As Duncan lost consciousness, Callum turned to look at Kate clutched in her brother's arms. Suddenly, a hundred men and their mounts vanished into thin air and only a lass, more bonny and more beloved than all the land in Scotland, existed.

"Come here, Katie."

She did not move but stared at him, her dark eyes furious. "You frightened the hell out of me, MacGregor."

He ached to hold her. "Fergive me," he repented sincerely. "I had nae intentions of killin' him and losin' ye, but I would no' have had the satisfaction of kickin' his arse had I just walked away." He thought of his sister, his future with Kate. One now filled with hope. "It's over. It ends with me."

Kate smiled with him and then ran into his arms. He caught her up in an embrace that near crushed the life out of her. When he finished kissing her senseless, he swept his fingertips over her smile. He had escaped Liam's dungeon, but he had remained a prisoner to his own hatred and guilt. Kate's love had set his heart free to love again, to feel again.

Angus helped Robert carry the unconscious earl back to the castle. When they passed him, Callum stopped them, untied the leather cuffs at his wrists, and tucked them under Duncan's belt. He was alive, and he had Katherine Campbell to thank for it.

spring. Callum had torn the invitation in half, grumbling for a good hour that he'd be damned before he set foot in the "cesspit of the Campbells." Although she desperately wanted to see her brother, Kate had not argued, but merely nodded and left him to rant in the solar. It wasn't long after that he found her, shoved a parchment and quill in her hands, and ordered her to write to her brother and gracefully accept. Kate smiled to herself now, remembering how she had looked up from her writing to find her husband watching her, shaking his head, and mumbling something about how soft he had become.

She wondered if his notion of soft included hanging draperies on his windows and filling their chambers with wild sprigs of heather. Or mayhap when he thought of soft, it meant not smashing his sword over Brodie's head. He had been angry enough to do it after Kate had rushed headlong into the men while they practiced their sword-play and Brodie's blade nearly sliced off her head. Of course, it was not Brodie's fault. She had been chasing Matilda, who had escaped from the barn, and if Kate had not caught her, supper that night would have been roasted duck. She had saved Brodie's life and Matilda's, as well, with naught but a smile and a gentle peck to her husband's mouth—which seemed to melt him to his very core. If that was soft, then aye, mayhap he was soft indeed.

Even after he found out that she had not only accepted Robert's invitation but invited him to Camlochlin to celebrate Jamie and Maggie's marriage, her husband simply glowered at her and moved his lips around a few words Kate was sure would have been quite unpleasant had he uttered them. He finally managed a somewhat tight "Verra well" before he politely excused himself and stormed off to pound poor Angus into the ground. She knew he was angry, but she made it up to him that night and many nights after, proving to him that he was anything but soft.

Good heavens but she loved him. She loved his smoldering eyes that lit when she entered a room, and the sound of his deep, musical laughter, which had become a common occurrence in Camlochlin rather than a rarity. Callum MacGregor was happy, and she was the reason for it. She hoped to make him even happier when she told him of his bairn growing in her womb. Mayhap tomorrow, after the ceremony. He would be in a fine mood, for as she had suspected, he was pleased when Jamie finally asked him for Maggie's hand.

She dipped her hands to her belly and rubbed the soft roundness of it.

She startled, then sighed with joy when two powerfully large hands came around her waist from behind and covered her fingers.

"What are ye doin' up here, love?"

"Thinking about how wonderful you are," she muttered, tilting her cheek to his when Callum buried his face in the folds of her hair. She lifted his hands from her belly and brought them to her lips for a kiss.

"How many times must I tell ye, wife, that I'm a cold-hearted bastard?" She felt him smile against her nape and giggled in response. He wrapped his arms around her chest and looked out over the glen. "Ye're simply blind to my shortcomins."

"I have yet to see them, husband."

He turned her in his arms and pulled her close against his body. He traced the soft contours at her temple down to her jaw with gentle fingertips. "How long will I be blessed to look into yer bonny eyes and see a hero reflected there?"

"Forever," she breathed, her lips curling into a smile he longed to kiss.

"Then I want to live forever, Katie."

Perhaps this was the perfect moment she had been waiting for. She parted her lips to tell him, but he moved his mouth over hers, devouring its softness, and all her thoughts fled save one that made her burn below her belly.

His breath was ragged when he swooped down to lift her in his arms. He wanted to take her to his bed and make love to her like tomorrow might not come. He almost made it to the archway leading down the stairs when one of the tower guards called out, alerting him that a small group of riders was approaching.

He narrowed his eyes, looking toward the hills, then rolled them toward Heaven.

"Robert!" Kate near squealed and leaped from his arms. Callum forced himself to smile when she lifted her beautiful grin to him. But the moment she looked away, he mumbled an oath or two under his breath. Campbells in his castle! He had to be daft, damn him, daft indeed. He scowled in full force when his wife began talking incessantly about how wonderful it was going to be having her dear brother here at Camlochlin. "And will it not be delightful to see Graham again? I've missed him, but I am happy he and Robert have become such good friends."

"Aye, delightful," Callum brooded.

"I'm certain you will come to love my brother as much as I after a few months."

"A few months?"

"Aye." She offered him her softest smile. "I've invited him to remain for the winter."

"Nae, Kate." He scowled darker than Kate had seen in months. "I willna—"

She leaned up on the tips of her toes and whispered something in his ear.

"Yer what?" He stared at her, his face a mask of many emotions, anger not among them.

"With child," Kate repeated softly, then lifted her fingers to her husband's eyes, thinking that what she saw there could not be real. For how could a mere woman bring this strong, proud mountain of a man to tears? He blinked and then snatched her up clean off the ground in a crushing embrace. She thought about telling him she could barely breathe but decided against it. As he had once promised, he held her heart in his hands in much the same way, and it did not hurt. She had known from the moment he saved her from the McColls that it never would. For he was her outlaw knight in the most radiant armor.

Of course, Callum MacGregor would have disagreed. For 'twas she who had done the rescuing.

Author's Note

In gratitude for the MacGregors' support in his struggle to regain the throne, Charles II repealed the laws against the MacGregors in 1661. Their name was restored, but their lands were not. In 1693 the proscription was fully imposed once again by William of Orange. The persecution of Clan MacGregor finally ended in 1774 when the proscription against them was lifted once and for all, 171 years after it was enacted.

About the Author

PAULA QUINN has been married to her childhood sweetheart for seventeen years. They have three children, a dog, and too many reptiles to count. She lives in New York City and is currently at work on her next novel. Write to her at paula@paulaquinn.com.

THE DISH

Where authors give you the inside scoop!

♥ ♥ ♥ ♥ ♥ ♥ ♥ ♥ ♥ ♥ ♥ ♥ ♥ ♥ ♥ ♥

Dear Reader,

While rummaging together through an antique store full of furniture and clothing, we came across two curious books. The first, bound by leather so soft and worn it almost fell apart in my hands, was the journal of Highland laird. The second book was more modern with sketches in the margins written by an ancient vampire bent on revenge.

Paula Quinn

Laird of the Mist

Robin Hogg

Lord of the Night

～～

Dear Reader,

When yer called the Devil, there isna much to prove to the world anymore save that the title is a deservin' one. I am an outlaw, a murderer, and a legend to be feared. I dinna seek fergiveness fer my many sins. My road to perdition has been long and my iniquities too numerous and too savage fer redemption. There is naught in my soul but darkness, and I am driven by one purpose: to kill those who have created this beast no one dares call a man.

I wasna born from my mother's womb as such a detestable creature. I was formed in the dank dungeons of Kildun castle, home of my kin's lifelong enemies the Campbells. Taken as a young lad by the Earl of Argyll, after his men slaughtered everyone in my village, I was shackled to a wall and tortured fer my faither's crimes against the realm. My faither was an outlaw as I am. His crime was refusing to surrender his name during the MacGregor proscription. Mayhap, some would find my faither guilty. But I was sinless as was my sister, who bore his punishment with me and grew to adulthood in the caverns of hell. It took many years, but we did escape. When all that made me human was finally stripped bare, I massacred Kildun's mighty garrison and fled north with my sister to the misty Isle of Skye. But I canna escape what I have become, and my hunger fer revenge against the Campbells is all I have left.

Fer six years now I have ridden forth from the obscure mists to exact payment fer that which was robbed from me and from my clan. I have killed withoot sympathy, fer what does a devil know of mercy? Aye, I am a cold-hearted beast whose name alone strikes terror in the hearts of his enemies. Save fer one.

Kate Campbell is the granddaughter of the man who imprisoned me. A woman I should despise. I took her from her home with the intention to lure her uncle, the current Earl of Argyll, to me. I didna expect her to slice me with her blade or to awaken a part of me I thought long dead with her saucy mouth and tantalizing curves. But most of all, I wasna prepared to find atonement fer my sins in the bonny eyes of a Campbell lass. And now, instead of killing my enemy, I must do all I can to keep her alive.

Callum MacGregor
Clan chieftain of the MacGregors, and Laird of the Mist

～∾～

Dear Reader,

I am neither man nor monster, and yet I am both. Killed by a chupacabra four-hundred years ago, I died and rose again as a vampire.

I killed friends and family before I learned to control the blood-lust. I killed for food, taking lives so that I might live. But no more. Now I kill others of my kind to protect the human residents of Hocksley, England.

I still reside in the Winslow family castle and have watched each generation of my brothers' descendents come into this world. I've watched them grow and trained many to become vampire slayers. Their time upon this earth is far too brief, and when they pass each one takes a part of me with them.

Over the years, I've lived a thousand lives and died a thousand deaths. There are times when I long to meet the sunrise and end it all, but my responsibilities are too great. Should I die, who would protect my family from the scores of vampires not even they know exist? And who would protect my friends from the Winslow slayers?

Yes. I have friends. Michael, Sedrick, and Ty Ellington—my best friends in life—and better friends in death. Killed by the same chupacabra that killed me, we have endured the test of time. Michael runs the local lair and I control the slayers. Together, we rule the night.

This arrangement has worked well for years.

Now things have changed.

Sedrick is dead. I found his body the other night cut down by the blade of a slayer's sword. But not by a Winslow, for all three—Gerard, Jess, and Kacie—are out of town. This is a new player and his actions will not be tolerated. He will pay for his deed—with his life. This I have vowed to Michael, lest he turn his lair of vampires loose on the innocent residents of Hocksley.

I have lost a great friend and the tenuous balance between vampires and humans that I've worked hard to maintain is threatened. I can't imagine how the situation can get any worse.

Then, I run into Kacie Winslow in the streets of Hocksley, her sword still dripping red with the blood, and I know I'm wrong.

Erik Winslow
Earl of Hocksley, Lord of the Night

Dear Reader,

I hope you enjoyed reading *Laird of the Mist* as much as I enjoyed writing it. I loved Callum's friends so much that I've written more about them for my next Forever release, *Surrender in the Mist.* My most notorious rogue yet, Graham Grant, just had to have his own story, and since I totally fell in love with the honorable Robert Campbell he'll be in *Surrender,* as well.

Want to know a little bit more about *Surrender in the Mist?* Check out my Web site at www.PaulaQuinn.com for a sneak peek.

Paula Quinn